Splitting Heirs

ALSO BY ANNE CHADWICK

Pacific in My Soul (2005)

Balancing the World (Graphics — 2006)

Splitting Heirs

A Novel

Anne Chadwick

McCaa Books • Santa Rosa, CA

McCaa Books
684 Benicia Drive #50
Santa Rosa, CA 95409

Splitting Heirs is a work of fiction. References to real people, events, establishments, organizations, and locales are intended only to provide a sense of authenticity and are used fictitiously. All other characters and all incidents and dialogue are drawn from the author's imagination and are not to be construed as real.

First published in 2021 by McCaa Books,
an imprint of McCaa Publications.

Library of Congress Control Number: 2021911874
ISBN 978-1-7363451-7-7

Printed in the United States of America
Set in Minion Pro
Book design by Waights Taylor Jr.
Cover design and illustrations by Anne Chadwick

www.mccaabooks.com

For my family, in all its forms — immediate, extended, and chosen — with deep gratitude

"*The Impartial Friend: Death, the only immortal who treats us all alike, whose pity and whose peace and whose refuge are for all — the soiled and the pure, the rich and the poor, the loved and the unloved.*"

Mark Twain

I. ENIGMA & ENTANGLEMENT

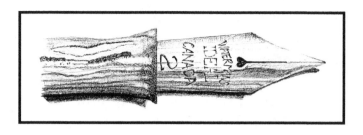

1

Busby: January 15, 1923 — Los Angeles

I WAS SNOOPING AROUND THE CORONER'S OFFICE when a call came in about a death that might have involved foul play. My clues came from eavesdropping on the half of the conversation that the clerk, Jimmy Irwin, tried in vain to keep from me by cupping his mouth to the phone. "Electrocution?" he mumbled. "Was he alone?" After saying something about calling the police, he hung up the phone, and I jumped in with a barrage of questions.

"Wh-who died? Why the police? Is it…? You thinking it's foul play? Murder, even?" I couldn't help myself.

Jimmy shrugged. "Busby, you know I can't tell you nothin'. We been through this a thousand times. You shouldn't even be here." I was fresh out of Columbia University, newly arrived in Los Angeles with every intention of establishing a career on the crime beat. But the *L.A. Times* put me in an entry-level job as a cub reporter covering obituaries. Aiming for a scoop that would elevate me to the level I deserved, I camped out on the bench beside the clerk's desk at the County Coroner's office, which beat the heck out of my basement office in the *Times* building.

"Okay, p-please just tell me where the guy died," I begged. "And if his name happens to slip out, you just may find a box of those chocolates you like on your desk in the morning." I gave him my best angelic smile.

"Alright, but you're not hearin' this from me, bub. The deceased is a Mister Marcel Morel, and he died in his room at the Imperial Hotel on South Spring. You know, it's that flea-bag 'residence hotel' where the riff-raff hang out."

I jotted down the information, grabbed my suit jacket, over-coat, and hat, and bounded out the door. When I caught my reflection in the window, I realized there was an ink stain in the pocket of my white shirt. Most of my shirts had similar stains because my lucky pen also happened to be a leaky pen. I put on my jacket and buttoned it up to hide the mess.

"No nuts in my chocolates, kid!" Jimmy shouted at my backside.

PERPETUALLY SHORT ON CASH, I ignored a line of taxi cabs and jogged to the Imperial Hotel, just a few blocks away. Two police-men walked into the lobby just as I arrived, and I was pleased to find no other reporters on the scene. This could be my big break — a chance to show the *Times* what I could do. I tailed the officers to the front desk and made no effort to hide my eavesdropping. They were focused on their job and paid no attention to me.

The receptionist said that Morel — he called him "Monsieur" — had lived in the hotel for many years, but kept to himself and rarely chatted with staff or other residents. Escorting the two policemen to the fifth floor, the fellow said that Monsieur's apart-ment included a small kitchen, but the man took most of his meals at a diner around the corner. He said Morel seemed absent-minded. "The man's socks, if he even bothered to wear them, usually didn't match. I'm pretty sure he never dragged a comb through his crazy hair. A comb could get lost up there for months," he said. Morel wore the same coat every day: a gray tweed with elbow patches that needed patches. I used my most confident stride to keep up with the officers as they entered room 515.

Morel's lifeless body bent over the kitchen stove, arms reach-ing toward the wall where two electrical wires seemed to hold him in place. His gaunt body, wild hair, hollow cheeks, and dark circles under his wide-open eyes made him look ancient, but I knew that lifestyle and experience could age a man beyond his years. I'd seen it in my grandfather, and knew better than to guess at a dead man's age. The body was still taut from the shock that must have traveled up the wire, through the poor guy's hands, up his arms, and into his heart. The hands appeared strong and muscular. One of the officers opened his death grip and remarked that the fingertips on his left hand seemed white, calloused. His palms were slightly singed.

Morel's leather shoes, worn without socks like the receptionist said, were scuffed and battered. His pants, frayed at the cuffs, appeared thin through the seat. The sleeves of his white shirt were rolled up to his elbows, and a brown tie hung loosely around his leathery neck. A tweed jacket with marginal elbow patches hung on the back of the door, along with a well-worn fedora and a tattered straw hat. I'm six-foot-two and skinny as a razor, and the jacket looked like it might almost fit my shoulders, but the sleeves would be way too short.

Stacks of newspapers accumulated on a shabby couch, and books — some in French, others in English — mounded on the floor nearby. Breakfast dishes, stained yellow with egg yolks, sat on a small table pressed against the wall to the left of the stove, with a single chair at a solitary place setting. A cold cup of coffee rested beside a tattered volume of Victor Hugo's *L'Année Terrible*, propped open to page forty-five.

An unmade single bed occupied the far corner of the dingy room. Pajamas puddled on the floor, their pant legs rumpled exactly where they'd hit the ground. I noticed that the walls were bare except for a yellowed map of France, and the tiny closet sported only a few threadbare shirts and one pair of dungarees. A violin nestled in an open case near the bed. Sheets of music amassed on the floor on either side of the instrument.

I edged over to a small desk under the room's sole window, searching for clues about Morel's personal life, hoping to find something the cops might miss. Mountains of papers leaned precariously on both sides of a blotter that doubled as a calendar, and I noticed a bank statement from Farmers and Merchants National Bank of Los Angeles and a thick, hand-written ledger with several columns of numbers. A pair of reading glasses lay beside several sharp pencils and a fountain pen. The calendar, showing a month at a time, had only two notations, which I jotted in my notebook: "F&M — 2p" on January 16, and "R.H. @ Diner — 8a" on the 22nd. A tattered wallet perched on the desk's front corner.

It seemed odd that there were no pictures on the walls or desk, and I looked in vain for any personal letters or a diary. I scribbled a few words to capture my impressions of the man and his castle: *parsimonious, frugal, shabby, disheveled, simple, meager.* And this was from a starving Columbia grad who lived in a messy little apartment on the cheap side of town.

"Hey, kid, don't touch anything," the older officer shouted in my direction. "And, by the way, who the heck are you, anyway?"

"Um, Brick Busby, sir. I'm a, er…I'm an investigative reporter for the *Times.*" I reached in my pockets pretending to look for a business card.

"Officer Ridley, LAPD." He extended his hand. "Not much to tell here. Looks like the guy fried some eggs and then fried himself trying to fiddle with the stove."

"C-can I…? Would you at least tell me his full name, date of birth, that sort of thing?" I nodded toward the wallet on the desk, not daring to touch it. "You know, the boy on the obit desk will want to know."

The wallet contained two identity cards — one issued in Los Angeles, the other in the *Département de Vaucluse*, in France. Both indicated the victim was born on the 13th of April, 1859, making him just shy of sixty-four years old. One card included a grainy photograph of the man, the other just text. The image showed a very thin face, long and narrow, with a nose like a collie, and eyes too close together. He stared out from under thick eyebrows and a shock of wild dark hair with a stunned expression.

The wallet also held a small, slightly damaged photograph of a woman, probably in her thirties. Motion blur made it hard to pick out her features, other than dark hair and piecing eyes set into an angular face. On the back, in tidy script, was written "Estelle/ Goult/1865."

"Look, kid, I don't think there's much of a story here. Let's let the coroner deal with the body, and we'll shut down the apartment," Ridley said, escorting me to the door. "You can check with me at the station in a day or two to see if the story gets any more interesting than this."

"But wait," I protested. "What about foul play?"

"Who would want anything in this sorry excuse for an apartment?"

"Whaddya…who..wha…?" The door clicked shut and I found myself in the hallway. I looked down at my size-thirteen shoes and my mother's voice popped into my head. She'd always told me I was a leader, an innovator, and survivor. How did she know? Well, she had an answer for that: my second toe juts beyond my big toe, just like hers, and she was certain that indicated strong drive and superior intelligence. Besides, she said, the toe was the only way she knew I was her baby, because in every other way I'm the spitting image of my father: tall, thin, and angular, with eyebrows constantly arched, mouth slightly agape, as if in a perpetual state of surprise, according to her. She used to tousle my hair, which she described as "mousy brown." I never relished my resemblance to a rodent.

Trying to live up to my mother's confidence in my second-toe characteristics, I headed down the hallway and knocked on the first door. No answer. Next door, same story. At the third apartment, a tiny older woman cracked the door open.

I introduced myself as the investigative journalist I aspired to be, and she cracked the door open a few inches wider. I gently broke the news of her neighbor's death, to which she showed surprise but no sadness.

"I knew him only in passing, really," she said.

"Did he…? Did you ever speak to him?" My mother had tried to break me of the habit of changing my mind mid-sentence, which she said made me stutter. But my attention jumped so quickly from one thought to the next, my mouth just couldn't keep up with the pinball bouncing through my brain.

"Once or twice," the woman replied. "He didn't seem to have much to say to anybody. Kept to himself, don't you know."

"What can you tell me about him, his habits, friends?"

"I don't think he had any visitors, but he did seem to take care of a few things around here," she said. "Sometimes I'd see him washing the windows at the ends of the hallways. But mostly he stayed in. You could hear him playing violin well into the night."

"Did he play well?" I just wanted to keep the conversation going.

"Not bad, from what I could hear through the walls."

"Anything else?"

"One time, I saw him fix a squeaky door in the oddest way. He used a pat of butter — something he probably lifted from the diner around the corner — and he rubbed it on the hinge until it stopped squeaking. It was right there, across the hall." She offered nothing more, so I thanked her and headed for the next apartment.

At the far end of the hallway, a man approached. I introduced myself, using my most confident voice. "Brick Busby, investigative reporter. Just wanted to ask you a couple of questions about the gentleman down the hall, Monsieur Morel. You know him?"

"Yes, I did." Past tense, so he already knew of the death.

"And you are?"

"John McIntyre, manager of this hotel."

"And, how, er…? What can you tell me about your tenant?"

"Tenant, yes," replied McIntyre. "And owner."

"You mean, uh, he was a renter, right? You can't own a room in a place like this, can you?"

"No, young man, I mean he owned the *entire* building. I managed it for him."

"But, c'mon, we must be talking about a different person," I said. "I'm talking about Marcel Morel, the old gentleman in room 515."

"That's right. Didn't look like he could rub two dimes together, but a reporter like yourself knows better than to judge a book by its cover, right?" McIntyre excused himself, said the police were expecting him.

"Are you positive you've got this right, kid?" My editor grilled me.

I fidgeted in a chair at the edge of the boss's cluttered desk. "The hotel manager told me that Morel owned the building." I tapped my notepad with a jittery index finger. "And the old lady down the hall, er, I…. She said he did maintenance, like fixing doors and cleaning windows."

"But the dead man looked like a hobo, lived like a hobo, and everybody thought he was a hobo? What gives?"

I admitted the story smelled fishy, and that's why I wanted to spend more time investigating and not just bury it in the obituaries. I'd convinced myself that this would be the story to lift me out of the basement, off the obit page, and into the investigative pool. My editor wasn't so sure.

"Run it as an obit, and if you have time, you can look into the rest of the story," he said. "But don't waste a bunch of energy on it, and for God's sake, don't get your hopes up."

I wrote an obituary worthy of a Columbia grad, embellishing it with all the flair I could muster in three column-inches. I mentioned Morel's reputation as a recluse, even a hobo, with no known relatives. Unable to verify Morel's ownership of the Imperial Hotel before deadline, I wrote it as a question, throwing in enough mystery to make any reader long for more. The rest of the account, I hoped, would be printed by week's end, and not on the obit page.

1/15/1923
Morel dies

5/3/1923
Trial Begins

8/2/1923
Verdict

2

Busby: May 3 — Los Angeles

THE COURTROOM WAS STANDING-ROOM ONLY when Judge Fergus Murphy began proceedings in Superior Court of Los Angeles on May 3 in the case referred to simply as "the Matter of Morel." I sat in the press box, having finally convinced my boss that I would be too busy for obituaries in the coming months, and that this trial deserved my full attention. Lucky for me, Morel owned a lot more than the Imperial Hotel, so the story grabbed headlines. Turns out, his real estate holdings and oil rights added up to more than five million dollars, and there was no shortage of fortune-hunters out to get a piece of the inheritance. The first thing Judge Murphy had done was issue an order under Section 1080 of the Probate Code directing the entry of a default against all persons who, by May 1, had not appeared or filed petitions to determine heirship, a deadline he'd publicized several times. I guess it was his attempt to stanch the flow of fortune hunters — legitimate or otherwise — that had already swelled to more than 450.

A murmur grew in the back of the room as some lawyers whispered to their clients that they'd missed the deadline. No doubt, some were already planning ahead for the possibility of appeal. Other lawyers shot their clients a smug look, as if to say they'd cleared the first hurdle.

"With hundreds of claims before us," Judge Murphy said, "it is essential that we limit the length of preliminary statements and exercise some degree of restraint. I would ask that attorneys eliminate unnecessary and legally inadmissible material so that we might get through the legitimate statements in a reasonable time." Each preliminary statement, he said, would be read and considered, and he anticipated empaneling a jury in the coming weeks to consider the viable claims that remained after this first exercise.

Reid Foster, the attorney representing two claimants from France, led a long list of attorneys presenting opening remarks. His sidekick, Lyle "Witty" Whitman — a self-described "forensic genealogist" — sat a few rows back. He gave me a nod, as if to thank me for introducing him to Reid in the days following the discovery of Morel's body.

"We will establish very clearly the rightful heirs to the estate of Marcel Morel." Reid sounded confident, citing the petition he'd filed claiming heirship, and said he looked forward to presenting his full case to a jury in the coming weeks and months. His tall, athletic frame and deep-set, intelligent eyes added authority to his sanguine presentation. He gave just enough information to tantalize the packed courtroom, which was silent but for the sound of pens scribbling frantic notes. All of us reporters knew this story had the makings of a great saga that could generate headlines and sell papers. The lawyers in the room wanted to document every detail that their most credible rival had to offer. And wishful gold diggers grasped for ideas that might strengthen their own tales when, and if, they had the opportunity to testify.

19

Claims to the fortune emerged from all over the United States, Canada, France, England, Ireland, Algeria, and even Australia. Several lawyers said they represented first cousins, while others alleged their clients were nieces, nephews, or grandchildren. Reid and Witty took detailed notes, even though their rivals most often lacked serious evidence or credible stories. As various lawyers presented preliminary statements, Reid and Witty considered it a good sign when Judge Murphy, normally poker-faced, betrayed his skepticism with a roll of the eyes or a shake of the head.

During a short recess, I elbowed my way to the front of the press corps as we clamored to get statements from Reid. He kept his remarks very short and absolutely on point, saying only that he looked forward to demonstrating that his two clients were the rightful heirs, and that justice would be served. One reporter tried to bait him into elaborating on the "sex scandal" that he had unearthed in Provence, involving the millionaire's brother, but he refused to bite. He stuck to his talking points: he had found the rightful heirs and he looked forward to a just and expedient outcome.

My byline made the front page of the *Los Angeles Times* the next morning. Headline: "First Depositions Read in Fight Over $5,000,000 Morel Estate." Reid found me in the courtroom before the proceedings resumed and asked about the number in the subhead: "Lawyers Start Task of Separating Wheat From Chaff in Field of 180 Claimants to Fortune."

"Well, it was…it's just…I got it last night from the clerk," I said.

"Which clerk?" Reid asked. "The judge's clerk?"

"No, the desk clerk at the Superior Court. Friend of mine. He said that the judge's first order — you know, the one to get rid of anyone who hadn't filed a petition by Tuesday — knocked out a ton of contenders right then and there."

"Are you sure?"

"He's in the know," I said. "He's the guy who has to handle all that paperwork, and he said it was down to 180."

"But I thought there were closer to 450 claimants already."

"I guess a lot of them just said they thought they might be related, or maybe they showed up with a letter or a picture or some phony ID. My pal said more than half of them didn't even know what a petition to determine heirship was."

"Or they couldn't afford a lawyer to take them through the process," Reid speculated.

"That's right. Most of them were desperate for the money, but how do you get the money to flow when you don't have a little coin to prime the pump?"

"Amazing," Reid said. "Any idea how many lawyers are lined up, ready to go?"

"From the looks of it, there may be forty or fifty. That's just my guess from looking around the courtroom yesterday. But that would mean I could tell a lawyer just by looking at him," I gave Reid a playful head-to-toe scan. "I could…I'll ask my buddy whether he has the official count when it comes to actual lawyers."

"Let me know." Reid turned to take his seat for the day's marathon of testimony.

THE READING OF PRELIMINARY STATEMENTS took two weeks, and their length and quality ran the gamut. If the trial were a horse race, the entrants ranged from Shetland Ponies to Clydesdales, and Reid clearly was a thoroughbred. He'd directed his legal assistant, May Wu, to close their office in the afternoons so she could attend court and add another set of eyes and ears to their team. She might pick up some nuances that he and Witty missed, and she could lend a hand researching some of the more credible claims.

One such claim, though a bit far-fetched, might gain traction. A San Francisco woman named Audrey Fife declared that she had been married to Marcel Morel and that her 19-year-old daughter, who went by the name of Betsy Fife, was their child. She said they used the name Fife, her maiden name, because the marriage had fallen apart after a short time. But technically — being Catholic — they remained legally married. Although Audrey allegedly had tried to establish a life with Marcel in Los Angeles, she soon chose to move back to San Francisco, where she raised her child alone. The lawyer representing the Fife family said that the marriage had taken place in San Francisco in a Catholic church on March 28, 1903, and that the daughter was born on December 30 of that same year. Unfortunately, he said, the records of their marriage and the birth had been destroyed in the 1906 fire in the aftermath of the great San Francisco earthquake.

"What do you think of the Fife claim?" I asked Reid during a recess.

"We'll have to discredit this woman once we get in front of a jury," Reid said. "They have no evidence, but we have to make sure the jurors recognize her story as pure fiction."

He said Witty was planning a quick trip to San Francisco to dig into the details. "He'll try to verify that marriage and birth records from 1903 were destroyed in the fire. Check with the Catholic Diocese regarding their records. Dig around in the hospitals. Look for any family connections to Audrey Fife. Witty will try to confirm that she was there, and more critically, that Morel was in San Francisco at that time."

May Wu, meanwhile would look for something to prove that Morel was in Los Angeles at that time, around the alleged wedding date of March 28, 1903. She'd check with Farmers and Merchants Bank, the county recorder — anywhere he might have signed and dated something, or any witnesses who could establish his whereabouts.

Another claim that had teeth alleged a young woman named Mildred Dodge was the illegitimate daughter of Marcel Morel. Her attorney said he would provide proof that her mother, a showgirl with a traveling dance troupe, had a brief affair with Monsieur Morel in the summer of 1895, and that Mildred was

22

born the following spring in Los Angeles. The evidence, the lawyer said, would include photographs of the mother in Los Angeles with Morel and subsequent pictures of her, still performing with the dance company, "great with child." He said witnesses would provide irrefutable proof that the affair had taken place, and that Mildred, now age twenty-seven, was their love child and therefore rightful heir to the fortune.

I'd brought this claim to Reid's attention back in early February, before he and Witty sailed to France. My telegram to them on the east coast had said she might be a serious threat. I mean, she actually had a lawyer and a game plan — more than I could say for most of the fortune-hunters.

3

Busby: January 17 — Los Angeles

I ARRIVED LATE TO MY TINY BASEMENT OFFICE at the *L.A. Times* on Wednesday morning. I'd been at a mortuary, where I'd talked the mortician into letting me lie in a coffin. Turned out to be a pretty creepy form of research, but well worth it to get a sense of the dead. I'd do whatever it took to add authenticity to my obituary writing, if it helped convince the editors of my talent. Having seen Morel's dead body two days earlier had made me realize my utter lack of understanding when it came to death and dying, which — for now — was the main subject of my writing career. Approaching my office, I noticed a gentleman sitting beside my desk, and I jerked to a halt and glanced over each shoulder for a quick reality check. This was a first.

"You, uh, you looking for somebody, sir?" I asked, looking around the room. I tucked my wandering shirt tail into my pants. I never could find shirts long enough for my tall frame.

24

A fleshy gentleman jumped up, extended his ample hand, and nodded slightly. "Allow me to introduce myself, Mister Busby. I am Lyle Whitman of Boston, Massachusetts."

My head swiveled over my shoulder again as I took another glimpse around the office. "And you're looking for me, you say? What's this... how can I be of help?"

"Well, young man, I'm in Los Angeles on legal business, and during my morning coffee I took a gander at the obituaries in your esteemed newspaper. You see, I have a habit of reading the obituaries because my vocation involves the fortunes of the unfortunate — those who have departed this life as we know it," Whitman said. "I understand that you are the eloquent author of the Morel obituary, which I found most interesting. Most interesting, indeed." His light hair, combed straight back, showed more blond than gray, and the combination of his sparkling eyes, upturned nose, and pudgy face gave him a boyish countenance. I placed him in his mid-forties, and did a double-take when I noticed the man's eyes didn't match. One was pure blue, almost impossibly blue, like backlit sapphires. The other eye appeared mostly blue with slices of green and brown, like an Australian Shepherd's.

Whitman said that the obituary had piqued his curiosity, which I took as a compliment. "It makes me wonder," Whitman continued, "what other assets this Morel character might have had, besides the hotel, and whether he was really such a loner. We don't have the complete picture yet, do we, my friend?"

I felt my pulse rise with the thought of chasing the details of this mystery. I had a feeling I could make this story sing. I pictured my byline on the front page, right where my mother would see it with her first sip of morning coffee. But a sense of doubt nagged me back to the reality of my dank basement office.

"Wh-what's in it for you, sir?" I asked. "I mean — if you don't mind me asking — how did you track me down, and why?"

"Oh, I admire your curiosity, my boy," Whitman said, reaching up to place a hand on my bony shoulder. "Indeed, I share your curiosity. That's what got me where I am today." Whitman explained that he served in naval intelligence during the Great War, where he developed a nose for the story behind the story. After the war, he began to pursue a life-long interest in genealogy, a hobby his mother had introduced him to as a boy. "The hobby grew into a business, and now I'm a forensic genealogist."

"What's that you say?" I interjected. "Sounded like you said you were a forensic genealogist."

"That's right. I track down the rightful heirs to folks who have died intestate," Whitman said. "They have no will, no heirs in evidence, and without intervention, the state will jump right in and take the money. Of course, the state loves to grab money from the deceased. It's called escheatment."

"No kidding." It was a new term for me, with the ring of cheating. "And what's in it for you, sir?"

"Oh, I do appreciate your inquisitive, if blunt nature," Whitman said. "I take a commission in return for delivering the estate to its rightful owners. And believe me, they're always so grateful for my work that the commission is never in question."

Whitman asked a lot of questions, and I figured he was hoping to find a local guy to do some of the legwork — tracking down county records, scanning the news media, and just keeping an ear to the ground. I'm guessing he pegged me as earnest, reasonably bright, and underemployed. Pretty accurate assessment.

"Say, maybe you'd like to help me do some research about this Morel character," Whitman said. "With any luck, we can find some living relatives — siblings, uncles, cousins, or even second or third cousins — and turn them into clients." He explained the chain of inheritance. The first question was always whether the decedent was married and whether the spouse was living; if not, did he have any children or grandchildren, also known as "issue." If not, were there surviving parents? How about issue of parents — the decedent's siblings or their children. No? Then they'd look for living grandparents (unlikely for a man of sixty-three), and next consider issue of grandparents — aunts, uncles, cousins, second cousins, cousins once removed, and so on.

"So, uh — Where do we start?" I asked. The thought of doing something — anything — other than obituaries outweighed any hesitation I might have had about working with a complete stranger.

"You can begin by telling me everything you know about this character."

I went through my notes and related the details of my visit to the Imperial Hotel. I covered Morel's age, apparent French ties, the identity cards and photographs in his wallet, bank statements on his desk, violin by the bed, hand-written financial ledgers everywhere, witnesses' impressions of him (or lack thereof), his affinity for the diner, the claim that Morel owned the hotel, and his reputation as a reclusive hobo.

"I had the impression that the only reason his body was discovered quickly — before it started to smell — was that the hotel's main circuit blew when Morel was electrocuted. If it weren't for the power outage, his body may not have been discovered for days, even weeks." An electrician investigating the power outage was the one who discovered the old man slumped over his kitchen stove, gnarled hands still grasping the bare wires he'd been trying to connect. "From what I can tell, no relatives would have noticed his absence, no friends, no associates. I've been asking around. Maybe staff at the diner would miss him, but they might just assume he was away."

"Remarkable. You're off to a good start," Whitman said. "Want to dig deeper?"

My eyes lit up.

"Why don't you start with county records," he said. "Try to verify his ownership of the hotel. Find out whether he owned any other property in the county. See if he co-owns anything with a wife, a child, or anyone else. Did he inherit anything from a relative? Just tap into that curiosity of yours, and you'll be off to the races. Yes sir, off to the races."

"And you?" He had a slick way about him. I didn't want him to think I'd do all the work while he polished his nails.

"You say the bank statements on his desk were from Farmers and Merchants Bank. I'll see whether I can talk to anyone there," Whitman said. "Do you have any ins at the bank?"

"No, sir."

"And I'll need a good estate lawyer. Any connections in that arena?"

I thought for a minute, and remembered a recent article in the *Times* about a movie star who died on Christmas day, just a couple of weeks ago, and there was some to-do about his will. I pawed through a pile of papers and found the issue dated December 27, 1922.

The *Times* reported the unexpected and premature passing of screen cowboy hero Blake Simpson, who shocked his wife by leaving her only his "undying love and affection" while bequeathing his fortune to his 3-year-old son and aging mother. Simpson, a Hollywood star, former world-class athlete, and soldier in the Great War, had died late Christmas night of uremic poisoning following an operation for gallstones.

"After a lovely Christmas at home with his wife and three young daughters, Reid Foster, Esq. was called to Simpson's bedside at the Queen of Angels hospital," the article said. There, they spent a few private moments finalizing the will before Simpson died in the arms of his wife. According to the *Times*, Simpson's last words were, "Alice, I love you so."

I read the highlights to Whitman. "Simpson's will was executed from his cot at the hospital on Christmas night. Relative to the bequest to his wife, he wrote in his will, 'I leave nothing to my wife, Alice Marion Simpson, save my love and affection.' By the terms of the document, Mrs. Simpson is made guardian of their young son and his estate, which amounted to one-half of the actor's fortune. The other half was willed to Simpson's mother, Mrs. Clara Simpson."

I summarized the rest of the article. Although in film circles Simpson was a reputed millionaire, the lawyer Foster told the press only that the estate was valued in excess of $25,000. It was his way of telling reporters that his client was worth a lot, but the extent of it was none of their business. Shortly after her husband's death, Mrs. Simpson was taken to their Beverly Hills home and remained "prostrated with grief and under the care of a physician." The article went on to provide a little background on the beloved movie star, his athletic prowess, his military career, and the story of how he met his wife. The actress Mary Pickford had introduced the couple, according to the article. "Pickford, the silent film star, was visiting wounded soldiers at Camp Kearney, near San Diego, while Simpson recuperated there from a broken leg injured not in military training but in a football competition. Miss Pickford had brought along a friend, Miss Marion, who immediately took a liking to Mister Simpson." The rest was history.

"It was a huge story here at the *Times*," I explained. "I wanted to cover it, but they gave it to the Hollywood beat. You know, gossip and glamor and all that."

"Have you met this lawyer, Reid Foster?"

"No, but his office is just over in the Bradbury building, not far from here."

"Right, then," Whitman said. "You'll hit the county records and I'll see what I learn from the bank. And perhaps this Mister Foster can be of some use to us."

"Thank you so much for this opportunity, Mister Whitman. I won't disappoint you."

"Oh, and why don't you call me 'Witty.' No need for formalities, my friend."

I TUGGED ON THE SLEEVES OF MY SUIT COAT as I entered the musty office of the County Clerk. I wished I could find a suit with sleeves long enough for my gangly reach. I certainly couldn't afford a tailor. *Maybe someday*, I thought. *But first I have to get off the obit beat.*

The clerk gave me full run of the records, seeing as how I claimed to be an investigative reporter from the *Los Angeles Times*. The first thing I did was verify Morel's ownership of the Imperial Hotel. It appeared that he'd owned it since 1913, and had taken out a loan from Farmers and Merchants Bank at the time. Digging deeper, it was easy to see that Monsieur Morel owned at least thirty houses scattered around the county, purchased at various times from 1900 to 1920. None appeared to have a fancy address, like Beverly Hills, and purchase prices were modest — no mansions or big estates. A few undeveloped lots appeared in the records under the ownership of Marcel Morel, including three parcels in Santa Fe Springs purchased in 1917 and 1918. I made a thorough list, thanked the clerk, and headed to the diner where the decedent was said to have taken most of his meals.

Meanwhile, Witty scoped out the banking scene. Here's what I pieced together about his morning, which he described to me in great detail. Witty parked his champagne-yellow Packard on Fourth Street and walked to the entrance of Farmers and Merchants Bank at the southwest corner of Fourth and Main. I knew the building well: not tall, but imposing. Enormous columns framed an arched entrance, and the bright Southern California sun streamed in through gigantic windows. Witty scanned the faces behind various desks, seeking the most likely to blab. The young clerks might be most eager to please, but they likely lacked the history he was looking for. He approached an awkward-looking, middle-aged gentleman who fiddled with an ink well on his tidy desk.

"May I steal a minute of your time, sir?" Witty approached the desk.

"Why, yes, I'm available at the moment," the balding, bespectacled gentleman replied. "What can I do for you today?"

"Well, I'm very sorry to say that I'm here because of the passing of a fellow in this community," Witty said. "Perhaps you were acquainted with Monsieur Marcel Morel?"

"Why, yes, I was. In fact, he missed an appointment yesterday," he said. "Not like him. So sorry to hear of your loss."

"Thank you." And the two proceeded with introductions.

The banker, Ned Harmon, had been with Farmers and Merchants since 1898. He had known Monsieur Morel for a long time, as a matter of fact, but didn't feel that he knew him well. "Always a bit of mystery, that man," Harmon said. "But he was a solid customer, and my boss Mister Hellman certainly appreciated him. Picked him out as a VIP, and made sure we treated him as such." Harmon pointed out that they had to educate the tellers and security staff about Monsieur Morel's status as a top client, because his appearance might otherwise get him kicked out of the bank, or at least treated with great suspicion. "Poor guy dressed like a hobo," Harmon recalled. "And he wasn't much on bathing and grooming, either."

But Morel was a sharp investor, according to Harmon. Back in the early 1880s, he had some kind of job with the railroad, and he saved enough to buy a vacant lot at the edge of what was then the pueblo of Los Angeles. He scraped together enough, through savings and a modest mortgage from Farmers and Merchants, to build a house and rent it out. That proved successful, so he came back to the bank and declared his ambition to build one house for every day of the week and rent all of them. After many months, and many mortgages, he accomplished his goal.

"By the time I came on board, Morel was saying, 'I'll build one house for each day of the month.' And he did, which provided him a hefty income. Over the years, he bought and sold many properties, making substantial profits along the way. He bought the Imperial Hotel in 1913, just before the Great War. The war didn't deter him from buying and selling, and eventually he decided to buy eighty acres of farmland in the Santa Fe Springs area. Perhaps you know what came of that."

"You don't mean the Santa Fe oil fields, do you?" Witty asked.

"That's right! And Bob's your uncle!"

COLE'S PACIFIC ELECTRIC BUFFET, better known as Cole's Diner, was tucked into the ground floor of the gigantic Pacific Electric building at Sixth and Main, a ten-story brick edifice widely recognized as the largest building west of the Mississippi. Feeling lucky, I spent a penny to ride the Red Car train to the diner's front door, rather than hoof it as I normally did around town. The diner's warm, humid air smelled of fried potatoes and bacon. It made my mouth water. The only sound in the place came from the kitchen, where cooks chatted and cleaned up during the lull between breakfast and lunch. I slid across the dark brown leather of a booth near the back.

I caught the eye of a waitress, a petite blonde with her hair pulled back into an austere bun. I placed her in her early thirties, although a little makeup and lipstick could be deceiving. Even with her uniform, it was not hard to tell that she had the figure of a movie star, and I reminded myself to keep my eyes on hers, and not let them wander to points beyond.

"Breakfast or lunch, hon?"

"W-well, maybe you could tell me," I said with concentrated eye contact. "Have you worked here long? I mean, do you...might you have a recommendation?"

"Ten years, and we're known for our Frnch dip," she replied.

"Is that right. Well, I guess I'd better try it out." A frog croaked in my throat. "Say, do you have a few minutes to help a guy out?"

"Depends," she said with a cautious smile.

"I-I'm working on a story for the *L.A. Times*, and I think you might know something about the main character, Marcel Morel. They say he came here often."

"Why sure, I know him a little bit," she said. "He eats here just about every day. Come to think of it, I guess I haven't seen him for a couple days."

I delicately explained the demise of Monsieur Morel and asked if the waitress could take a little break to share a cup of coffee with me. My red ears heard her say yes, and then I remembered to breathe.

Violet Olson had worked in the diner since 1913, five years after its opening. She said Monsieur Morel normally arrived around one in the afternoon for a hot lunch, and he always brought something to read. He rarely said much, never sat with anybody else, and he ate slowly. On occasion he'd stretch a meal to an hour or more, and he preferred his salad after the main course. He never had coffee during the meal, but always wanted some afterward. He could make a cup of coffee last twenty or thirty minutes, according to Violet.

"You'd think he was lingering here just to stay warm, or to have a place to sit. I wasn't sure he could afford a place to live, but he always paid full fare and he tipped well."

"So, er…Not exactly a candidate for the Jonathan Club, then," I said, referring to the tony gentlemen's organization on the building's top floor.

"Not a chance. His look said 'church mouse,' not 'business-man.'"

"Turns out he had plenty of money, or at least that's how it's looking," I said. "He just didn't show it." I asked if she knew anything about his background, family, friends, what he was reading. She'd noticed his French accent and learned that he grew up in the southern part of France — not by the coast, but inland a ways. He'd lived in Los Angeles since he was a young man, and he never spoke of any relatives. His reading included the *Times*, the occasional racing form, and sometimes a novel.

"Must've been in French because I couldn't make out the words," Violet said. The carver motioned to her that the sandwich was ready, and he nodded at the clock. "I'd better get back to work," Violet said.

"One more thing. It looks like Morel was expecting to meet somebody here for breakfast on the twenty-second. Initials R.H."

"I've got nothing." She shook her head. "Look, the owner comes in at lunch, and he'd be steamed to find me sitting with a customer. Sorry I couldn't be more helpful."

"Oh, no, you were quite helpful," I said. "D-do you think anyone else here would have more information about Monsieur Morel?"

Violet said the carver had been there from the beginning and might know a thing or two, so she excused herself and went to find him.

"Morel, the French guy?" the carver said, standing over my booth and wiping his hands on his grease-stained apron. "He oughta be famous!"

"Why's that?"

"Well, he's the guy who complained that the hard crust on the bread was too much for his dental work. You see, he had some work done and it didn't take so good. It was givin' him fits. After a few weeks of eating soups and stews, he said he wanted a roast beef sandwich, which was one of his favorites. But he asked if we could do something about the darn crust, 'cause it was hurtin' his dental work."

"So what did you do?"

"Well, you see that sandwich you're eatin' there," the carver said, pointing to the French dip, "it all started with Monsieur Morel. That day he wanted a sandwich, but he wanted it soft, so he asked me to bring out a bowl of broth to dip the crust in. Something he said his mother used to do in France. Anyhow, he couldn't get enough of it! Every day for a month he ate that sandwich. The other customers saw him dippin' into the sauce — Morel called it *jus* — and they wanted to try it, too."

"So you called it the French dip, put it on the menu, and the rest is history," I said.

"Pretty much," the carver nodded. "The French guy over on Alameda, Philippe Mathieu, he'll tell you that he invented it, but we were doin' it before Philippe's even opened their doors. We were the only joint in town."

"Is that right." I put down my sandwich and picked up my notepad.

4

Witty: January 19 — Los Angeles

A BEAD OF SWEAT STUNG MY EYE as I rounded the fourth-floor landing of the Bradbury Building's elaborate wrought-iron and marble stairway. The winter sun beat down on me through a skylight that capped the ornate building.

I swabbed my forehead with a silk handkerchief, reluctant to soil its delicate fabric with perspiration. Who knew that the building's elaborate open-cage elevators would be out of service that day? I double-checked the room number — 523 — and plodded up the final flight.

I opened the office's heavy oak door to find a slender Oriental girl seated behind a roll-top desk. A name plate identified her as May Wu.

"My dear, my name is Lyle Whitman and I've come to see Mister Foster." My chest still heaved from the march to the top, and I promised myself I would cut back on the clotted cream, starting next week.

"Do you have an appointment, sir?" May Wu eyed me with what I thought was distrust. Maybe I shouldn't have called her my dear.

"Well, the fact is I just arrived in town — drove out from the east coast, you know — and today I intend to bring Mister Foster up to speed on a matter of utmost urgency." I ran the silk handkerchief over my forehead and around my neck. I wished I hadn't knotted my necktie so firmly. "Utmost urgency."

"So you don't have an appointment," she confirmed, gently closing her roll-top desk. "May I ask the nature of this urgent matter?"

"Why certainly, although I wouldn't want to trouble such a lovely lady with all the complex details and whatnot." I placed both hands on the desk and leaned forward with my most charming smile. "Let's just stay I need a good estate lawyer, and anyone who reads the *Los Angeles Times* knows that the Blake Simpson affair proved Mister Foster tops in the field."

I thought I caught May Wu rolling her pale gray eyes skyward as she swiveled her chair around and asked me to wait while she discussed my request with Mister Foster.

WHEN I ENTERED HIS OFFICE, Reid Foster squeezed around the edge of his burled walnut desk to shake my hand, which was damp with sweat after scaling five flights of stairs. "What brings you to Los Angeles, Mister Whitman?"

"Please, call me Lyle, or if you're really feeling friendly, try 'Witty.' That's what my buddies back in Boston call me." Another bead of sweat rolled down my forehead. "This is some building you're in. I became intimately familiar with its stunning staircase because the lifts are on the fritz today."

"Yes, it's quite a building," Reid said. His six-foot-three frame loomed over me, and I looked up to admire his deep-set eyes and dark wavy hair. Sporting a tan in winter, he fit the stereotype of Hollywood actor, without the swagger. "Have you heard about its history?"

"Do tell, my good man," I said. "Do tell."

Reid explained that in the early 1890s, Lewis Bradbury, a mining and real estate millionaire, commissioned an architect by the name of Sumner Hunt to design a spectacular office building. Hunt completed the design work, but after some sort of falling out, which was still a subject of debate in Los Angeles circles, Bradbury hired one of Hunt's draftsmen by the name of George Wyman to take over the project and supervise construction. The building almost died before its foundation was even finished, Reid said. During construction, an active spring under the foundation nearly stopped the builders in their tracks, but Bradbury had enough money to import massive steel rails from Europe for a foundation to continue construction on the less-than-ideal site at Third and Broadway.

"Did you notice the wrought-iron railings on that stairway you climbed? They came from France and were displayed at the Chicago World's Fair before installation here," Reid said. "The marble was imported from Belgium, and the floors are Mexican tile."

"Sounds like Bradbury spared no expense in constructing a monument to himself."

"Sadly, he died before the building opened in 1893," Reid continued. "The initial estimate for the project was under two-hundred thousand dollars, but when all was said and done it cost upwards of half a million. And that was thirty years ago!"

"Poor old fellow never got to see his masterpiece put into play," I remarked. "I bet you would've liked to have had a crack at that estate. But from the looks of you, you're way too young to have had a piece of that action."

Reid eased into a chair and encouraged me to do the same. I felt a rivulet of sweat make its way down my back, and I silently cursed the heavy wool suit I'd donned that morning. Being from Boston, I couldn't imagine being overdressed in mid-January, but this was sunny Southern California where the navel orange harvest was in full swing. Crazy. Looking around the office, I wondered whether Reid was quite as prominent an estate lawyer as the press made him out to be. Maybe the young attorney was just impecunious. The room felt not much bigger than a closet, with no space for a conference table or even a settee. Clients had to make do with two shaker-style wooden chairs, whose straight backs and lack of padding hardly invited lengthy conversations. On the other hand, the Oriental carpet covering the stark room's hardwood floor may well have been an authentic masterpiece worth a small fortune. It was hard to tell. The bookshelves on the north wall held the obligatory leather-bound legal tomes and a few biographies. Two magnificent pink jade pieces, intricately carved in the form of lions' heads, punctuated the law volumes. An elegant porcelain vase, white with a blue floral pattern, held a single string of orchids under the east-facing window. Chinese paintings on silk scrolls graced the walls on each side of the window. They featured dramatic landscapes of trees clinging impossibly to steep cliffs poking through ethereal clouds. Two one-inch blocks of ivory carved with Chinese script weighted the bottom rail of each scroll.

"How can I help you today?" Reid asked, twisting his fountain pen between his fingers.

"My good man, you've no doubt heard the bromide in your line of work, 'Where there's a will there's a lawsuit.' Typically that's where you come in, right? Well, I'm here to tell you that where there's no will, that's when I get involved." I leaned forward in my uncomfortable chair. "That, my friend, is where the opportunity lies."

I went on to describe myself as a forensic genealogist. My longtime hobby of researching people's family histories had grown from a passion to a profession, and my current line of work used my sleuthing skills to track down rightful heirs of those who departed this world without the benefit of a last will and testament. I worked on commission, taking a percentage of each estate I settled. "In my most recent case I unearthed the lineage of a 93-year-old spinster in Maine, Lillian O'Dea, who died at home in the company of twenty-three cats. It took the neighbors a few days to discover her body, and when they did, nobody knew a thing about her family history. Nor did they have any inkling that her estate, mostly real estate and hoards of cash, was worth nearly three-quarters of a million dollars." I had turned up two nieces and five grandnieces and grandnephews in County Clare, Ireland. They had no idea she existed. "Let's just say the newfound relatives were thrilled to make Lillian's posthumous acquaintance."

"And now you're in Los Angeles to investigate another intestate?"

"Intestate, indeed," I replied. "Can I take you into my confidence, young man? Of course, my profession depends on the utmost discretion, perfect confidentiality, and swift response."

"I'll consider this conversation strictly confidential, Mister Whitman," Reid said. "Perhaps you're familiar with scripture's passage, *The law is good, if man use it lawfully.*"

"Ah, well, the gentleman in question went by the name of Marcel Morel," I began, looking over each shoulder as if there were room for an eavesdropper in the tiny office. "He was found in his Los Angeles apartment, actually a room in the residence hotel at 919 South Spring, having electrocuted himself in the course of repairing some shoddy wiring in the kitchen. I guess he wasn't expecting to meet an untimely death, and at the age of sixty-three, he hadn't bothered to prepare a will. Funny thing is, the neighbors thought he was a pauper because he wore shabby clothes, led an austere life, looked terribly unkempt, and kept to himself. From what I can tell, his real estate alone is worth over four million, perhaps closer to five. We're still finding his assets."

Reid dropped the fountain pen and straightened a stack of papers on his desk. "How did he make his fortune?"

"Well, my friend, let me tell you what I know. I found a talkative loan officer at Farmers and Merchants Bank, and with the help of an eager young reporter at the *Times*, we've got a good start on the Frenchman's background. What I know so far is that our

Monsieur Morel came to Los Angeles about forty years ago, in the early eighties, from somewhere in southern France.

"Through a series of escalating real estate investments, he built up a small fortune and parlayed it into a larger one." I went on to describe the rental houses, hotels, and the eighty acres of farmland in Santa Fe Springs. "Does that ring a bell, Reid?"

"You mean the Santa Fe oil field?" Reid nodded his head. "He discovered black gold."

"Black gold, indeed." I felt the hook setting and prepared to reel the young attorney into my quest. "Funny thing is, *notre ami* Marcel barely spent a dime of it. The neighbors thought he was penniless, but in truth he was just eccentric. He rarely popped for a haircut, not to mention fresh clothes or new shoes. They said he didn't even wear socks half the time, and when he did, they didn't match."

I leaned against the stiff back of the wooden chair and filled in details I'd unearthed since the death earlier in the week. Morel never married, had no children, and left no known surviving parents, brothers, or sisters. So far, county records, nosy neighbors, and the chatty chap at Farmers and Merchants Bank had proved to be my best sources. What I needed now was a good estate lawyer to start probate proceedings, screen potential claimants, gather testimony, and weed out fraudulent declarations of heirship. With such an enormous sum on the line, there would be plenty of questionable claims.

"We'll have to do some detective work," I said. "I'll research family records, births, deaths, cemeteries, family Bibles, journals, letters, county records, and whatnot. Your job will be to sniff out the phony fortune hunters and knock down their false claims. A trip to France will be required, and we should start as soon as possible after you open probate here in Los Angeles. And in case you were wondering, we take our expenses off the top, and then we're looking at five percent of the total estate. Each."

Reid folded his hands in his lap and turned his gaze to his thumbs. His eyes darted back and forth, and I imagined he was racing through conflicting thoughts. The excitement of a trip to Paris and Southern France. The pain of being away from home, maybe a young family. A purse of two hundred thousand dollars or more. Would his practice suffer in his absence? Could May Wu hold down the fort while he traveled abroad?

"I appreciate this opportunity, but of course I'll have to see whether I can add to my current client load," Reid said, clearing his throat. "If you're staying in town, perhaps you could join my family for dinner at our home this weekend. I'll have to check with my wife, of course, but maybe Saturday evening could work. We live in Eagle Rock, a few miles northeast of here."

"Saturday — tomorrow. Saturday would be delightful." It would be an audition of sorts. I stood and reached for the door. "Very kind invitation. But don't wait too long to make up your mind, my friend. I don't like to let word of these situations hit the streets before we lay claim to the case. Of course, if you're not interested, there are plenty other estate lawyers in Los Angeles who'd be happy to jump on board. It's entirely up to you, my young friend, entirely up to you."

Reid bade me farewell and then asked May Wu to come into his office. I sensed they didn't know what to make of me. Could I be trusted? Was I for real? No doubt they would give me a thorough vetting and decide whether to take the leap.

5

Reid: March 3 — Paris to Avignon

I HAD KNOWN WITTY FOR ALMOST TWO MONTHS — driven across America with him, made the Atlantic crossing, and explored Paris — and yet I still didn't know what to make of him. He seemed to have a good heart and plenty of brainpower, but he somehow put me on edge. So little self-control, especially around food, alcohol, and women. Had he no moral compass? Nevertheless, our week in Paris had unearthed some encouraging leads, and we were off to Provence — Avignon and the Vaucluse region — in pursuit of rightful heirs to Marcel Morel's fortune. I could see that Witty knew how to follow the trail of inheritance.

In Paris, we'd found a Gilbert Morel, a 43-year-old night watchman at the Louvre, whose mother was from Goult. Was he a son? A nephew? A cousin? The connection wasn't yet clear. We saw a physical resemblance between the younger man and Marcel, and possibly to Estelle — the one in the photograph from Morel's wallet — but maybe it was just wishful thinking.

I sent a telegram to May Wu, who seemed to be handling my law practice just fine without me. Based on a few tantalizing leads, I asked her to let Judge Murphy know our team was making progress. Another month or six weeks would be needed to pursue leads and bring evidence back to Los Angeles. "OBJECTIVE — BUY MAX TIME — STOP"

I know I worry a lot, but this time it felt justified. Busby was reporting that the number of claimants had risen to almost two hundred. The courts wouldn't wait forever while we traipsed around Paris and Provence looking for heirs. I tried to trust Witty, but my gut wasn't so sure. I wanted concrete evidence.

On the train from Paris to Avignon, I felt a change of seasons as we chugged south. The farmers' fields seemed more verdant the farther we got from Paris, and trees were beginning to leaf out. A few bright patches, fields of tulips or daffodils, caught my eye as the train rolled toward the Mediterranean.

During the trip south, Witty and I compared notes on our progress, thought about next moves in the Vaucluse, and then worked on a series of telegrams to send from Avignon. My mind kept coming back to my conversations with Nicole, a delightful young woman I'd met on the ocean liner from New York to Cherbourg, France, who ended up tagging along for some of the sleuthing in Paris. We'd struck up a nice friendship on the ocean passage, and her accomplished French — polished during a degree in European History at Smith College — came in handy when I conducted interviews in Paris with potential heirs.

"Nicole thought the story of Gilbert's natural talent for music, even as a young boy, was the most revealing," I told Witty over the noise of the train. "She found that more compelling than physical traits or geography."

"She thought that, did she," Witty arched an eyebrow.

"Well, yes, she did. And I'm somewhat persuaded."

"Oh, you were persuaded by her, alright."

"What's that supposed to mean?"

"Never mind, my friend. Never you mind," Witty chortled. "With any luck, we'll discover more soon, when we get to Goult."

"Really, Witty, do you have something else to say?"

"I dare not tread on your heartstrings, my friend."

"Are you insinuating that something romantic was developing between Nicole and me?" I asked. "You know I'm a happily married man."

"Of course you are, my friend. Grace is a delightful woman."

Witty had a way of getting on my nerves like nobody else.

We drafted a telegram to Judge Murphy, which I kept very short and simple. Witty wanted to elaborate, but I insisted that we not overstate our progress, which seemed minuscule to me. All we needed was a glimmer of progress to buy us more time.

I also composed a cable to Grace. Normally I was content to send letters, but a telegram seemed more appropriate. I had to admit, Witty's ribbing about Nicole landed hard. My feelings for the young lady back in Paris were stronger than I wanted to admit, so it was time to turn my focus to Grace and our girls back home.

THE LIGHT GREW DIM BY THE TIME we rolled into the Avignon station. We found a modest hotel in the heart of the old walled city and headed out for a walk toward the *Palais des Papes*.

"Let's duck into *La Mirande*," Witty said with a nod to a restaurant sign. "I have a feeling Avignon is our last chance for an elegant meal before we head to the hinterlands." No doubt he was interested in a full bar, live music, a little dancing, and maybe more. "This place has a great reputation. Indulge me."

La Mirande's imposing stone façade featured intricate carvings that ranged from contorted faces of mythological creatures to chubby, smiling cherubs. Back when these places were built, people must have had a lot of time on their hands. We entered through heavy, carved wooden doors and made our way to the bar, which was already lively with well-lubricated revelers. Every barstool was occupied, and Witty set his sights on a conspicuous blonde and sidled up to the bar next to her. I edged in for a glass of water but gave him room to maneuver.

"You can leave me out of this conversation," I said.

"Pardon me," he said to the woman, brushing up against her calf-length, white sequined dress. She wore a head band adorned with flowers and feathers, and she puffed on a cigarette through a long holder. "What do you recommend?"

It appeared that she bought her dresses a size too small, so that every strategic bulge achieved maximum effect.

"*Pardon?*" the leggy blonde said. Witty would have to use his marginal French with her.

"*A boir.* To drink," he said. "Sorry my French is limited, but it gets better after a drink or two. Do you have a favorite at this bar?"

"Oh, I always get the martini. Dry. Gerard, the bartender, makes a tasty one." She giggled and put her hand over her bright red lips. She smelled of cigarettes, vermouth, and a sweet perfume reminiscent of roses mixed with molasses.

"Outstanding." He gave her the head-to-toe inspection. "Just magnificent."

He introduced himself and explained that he was just in from Paris, not familiar with these parts. I was happy to be left out of the introductions.

"Ooh, lucky you! Paris is just so fabulous." She took a sip of her drink and caught the bartender's eye. "One for my friend…"

"Whitman. Lyle Whitman. You can call me Witty."

"One for my new friend, Witty."

"And you are?" Witty couldn't take his eyes off her.

"Oh, my name is Babette Reville. *Enchantée.*"

"*Enchanté, Mademoiselle,*" Witty said, planting a gentle kiss on the back of her hand. She giggled again.

Miss Reville shared a bit about herself. I listened to the conversation the way one watches a train wreck, with reluctant but inevitable attention. She considered herself a local now, but she'd recently lived in Paris on the Left Bank. Life there with her paramour, Pierre, was idyllic, full of adventure, luxury, and excitement. But then Pierre's wife put an abrupt end to it, and that was that.

"He took good care of me. I thought I was all set," she said. "But then his wife, you know — poof!"

"So here you are," Witty said.

"Yes, here I am. Couldn't afford to stay in Paris on my own, by any stretch of the imagination." She put a hand on his arm. "But enough about me. Tell me all about yourself."

"That, my dear, will take some time. May I suggest, if I'm not being too forward, that we find a seat in the courtyard and discuss it over dinner." She tittered and nodded her head. At this point I had to go from eavesdropper to an active, if reserved part of the conversation. We did the usual introductions and followed the waiter to a small table in the courtyard.

The evening air held just enough warmth to allow for a pleasant dinner in the garden, with the Popes' Palace looming over the back wall. Witty ordered a bottle of champagne to kick off what might well be his last evening of luxury before our foray into the tiny towns of the Vaucluse.

"*Je suis desolé. Mon Français n'est pas bon,*" I said, too tired to use my marginal language skills over dinner. "I'm sorry. My French is not good."

"We can try English," Babette replied with a passable accent.

"And how do you know English? Was your father American, by any chance?"

"No, he was French. But I learned very much — including some English — from a very nice American man."

"A benefactor, then."

"Yes," she shot me a coy grin. "That's a good word."

Witty shared his story with Babette, beginning with broad generalizations, but drilling down into more detail as her persistent questions and the champagne encouraged him toward more specifics. Before long, he was elaborating on the case that brought us to France, discussing the details of Marcel Morel's life and death, his surprising fortune, and the task of finding the rightful heirs. He talked about the scant leads we'd unearthed to date, and our hopes of finding more specifics in the little towns east of Avignon.

"It sounds like you're heating the trail." Witty smiled at her slightly bungled idiom. Babette lifted the last of the champagne to her lips. "Funny how such a cool drink can have such a warming effect." She held up her empty glass. "None for you?"

"No, I don't drink alcohol," I said.

"*Garçon*," Witty ordered a bottle of a local red wine to go with the chateaubriand that he and Babette would share. I opted for a fillet of sole. A light salad followed, then a fruit tart and finally a plate of local cheeses. After dinner, we strolled down the street until we heard music drifting out of a little establishment on a side street.

"How do you feel about dancing?" Witty asked Babette.

"It's one of my passions," she said. "What about you, Reid?

"Not for me. I'll leave you to it. It was a pleasure to meet you."

As I walked away, I heard Babette fawning over Witty.

"Oh, Witty!" She planted a kiss on his cheek. "I just don't want this night to end."

"Who said it had to, my lovely?" He took her cheeks in his hands, gazed into her brown eyes, and kissed her deeply. "Who said anything about it ending?"

THE NEXT MORNING, I PACED THE LOBBY of the hotel, wondering when my traveling companion might emerge. I had no idea how, where, or with whom Witty had spent the night, nor did I want to know, but I itched to get underway. We had work to do. The hotel clerk told me that a bus went east each day at noon and, depending on the stops along the way, the trip to Goult could take from one to two hours. Another alternative was to hire a private car and driver, which the hotel could arrange on short notice, the clerk said. Lots of young men were out of work after the war, and one thing they could do was drive.

Finally, I marched upstairs to knock on Witty's door. It took some pounding before I got any response, and when Witty finally answered, it was clear he'd barely slept. Witty's round frame filled the doorway, and he shot the occasional circumspect glance back into the room and urged me to give him a little time.

"*Woe unto them that rise up early in the morning, that they may follow strong drink*," Witty muttered.

"*Woe unto them that call evil good and good evil*," I replied.

"*Touché.*"

"Lyle, I thought we agreed yesterday that one thing we're running out of is time."

"You sound annoyed. You called my Lyle."

"Oh, good heavens, Witty, at least let me know whether you want to take the bus or hire a driver, so I can do something, while you dilly dally here in the room," I pleaded.

"Alright, buddy, alright. Let's go with the car and driver. It'll be much more efficient, and maybe he can be of service if we have to traipse through the valley to some of the outlying towns."

"Fine, I'll plan our departure for two o'clock."

"Be sure it's a large car." Witty started to close the door behind him. "We'll have another passenger."

"Oh, for Pete's sake!" It was as close to swearing as I ever came. "What have you done now?"

"Just let me get ready, and I'll explain when we're on the road," Witty said with a wink. "Trust me, you'll like her once you get to know her."

THE JOURNEY FROM AVIGNON TO GOULT was not the direct route I'd hoped it would be. The first stop was Babette's apartment, or more accurately the room in a friend's house where she'd been storing her belongings, and she needed a few minutes to pull together some "traveling clothes." While she went inside to pack,

I implored Witty to think long and hard about bringing a floozy like her along. Our trip should be strictly business, and the more efficient the better.

"We're under the gun here, Lyle," I said. "You won't have time to work your charms on her. She'll just get in the way."

"Oh, relax, my good man. We'll be fine. She'll grow on you. You'll see."

"Grow on me? I don't want her to grow on me, or anything that she carries, for that matter."

"Now, now," Witty said. "Settle down. She's just along for the ride. I'll keep my eye on the prize. We're getting close, my friend. I can feel it in my gut."

"Well, just make sure your brain is engaged, and keep your gut and the rest of the body out of it."

"Besides, she may be helpful with translation if our combined sixth-grade French becomes a hindrance." Witty nodded over my hunched shoulder. "Look, there's the lovely Babette now. Everybody ready for the next adventure? Let's load up." He opened the back door for his new companion and slid in beside her. I wondered whether her enormous black and white polka-dot hat would fit into the back seat. It looked to me like her tight dress might burst at the seams as she scooted across the leather. The smell of her perfume invaded the Duesenberg, and the driver lowered his window to neutralize the atmosphere. He made his way to the main road east, which would take us to the Luberon Valley in the heart of the *Département de Vaucluse*.

6

Reid: January 20 — Los Angeles

FROM THE VERY START, I was leery of Witty. People tell me I'm too cautious, too reserved, but his bravado and bluster were a bit much for my taste. I wanted Grace to meet him and give me her take. Her ability to judge character was one of her many great qualities.

We lived in a modest bungalow at 3845 Ridgeview Avenue in Eagle Rock, just a few blocks from Occidental College where Grace and I had met as undergraduates. In the summer of 1916, after earning our degrees in world history, we married with little fanfare in the small Presbyterian church at the corner of Addison Way and Eagle Rock Boulevard. That fall, I entered law school at USC and found a job clerking for Judge Hastings in Los Angeles, while Grace worked for the Eagle Rock Water Company to help make ends meet.

Our bungalow, although not a work of the area's most popular architects, Greene and Greene, included many of the features favored by the designing brothers. Heavy eaves, propped up by thick tapered columns of whitewashed wood, swept over a generous front porch. I liked the simple lines that defined clean cedar surfaces both inside and out. Our master bedroom shared the ground floor with a small office, an ample living room with a stone fireplace, and a good-sized kitchen. A rosewood staircase led up to two small bedrooms, each with its own gabled window, and a utilitarian bathroom. Maureen, age four, shared one bedroom with 3-year-old Margaret, and Dorothy, just ten months, occupied the other room.

I inhaled the smells of eucalyptus and sumac, acrid and sweet, as I hopped up three broad steps to the porch. In the kitchen, Grace rubbed a small roasting chicken with rosemary that she'd picked fresh from the backyard garden. Maureen and Margaret played with pots and pans on the kitchen floor, and Dorothy slept in the nursery upstairs.

Word of a potential new client came as welcome news to Grace, who did a good job hiding her doubts about my decision to set up my own practice. She would have liked to see me take up with one of the larger L.A. firms, but I just couldn't imagine working that hard to line somebody else's pockets. My independent streak led me to solo practice, which had been paying the bills for three years. Barely.

"This new case wouldn't pay anything up front," I explained. "The money only flows if we find some rightful heirs and manage to get the inheritance to them, and then they pay us a percentage."

"Does this fellow have a track record? What do you know about him?"

"That's where I need your help, Grace. Mister Whitman, who calls himself Witty, has done this before, but I'm not so sure about his character. You're a much better judge of people. Will you meet him?"

"Okay, let's have Mister Whitman to dinner on Saturday," Grace offered. "May Wu, too. She's a great judge of character. Knows your business better than anyone. Besides, the girls have been begging to see her."

"Are you sure you don't mind cooking for a crowd?" I asked, easing my arms around her waist. "It's awfully short notice." I looked into her wise eyes and worried about her habit of taking on too much. Between keeping track of three small children, volunteering at the Twentieth Century Women's Club, working on the Eagle Rock float for Pasadena's annual Tournament of Roses Parade, and managing the household finances, she had no idle time. But Grace brought a calm air to everything she did, whether presiding over a women's group or acting as referee in a tussle over Maureen and Margaret's toys. She never ceased to amaze me.

"Let's start at five," Grace said. "Maybe we can catch one of our caramel sunsets from the patio before supper. Will he be walking from the trolley?"

"No, no. He has an automobile. Packard, I believe. He can drive right to the house."

THE WINTER SUN, DEEP IN THE SOUTHWESTERN SKY, snuck under a low cover of clouds and turned their undersides every color of red, orange, and pink imaginable. Sideways light threw deep shadows into the steep canyons of the San Gabriel Mountains to the north, their ridges glistening green with January grasses and live oaks. Witty's yellow Packard rolled to the curb at quarter past five. He looked up to see two small faces peering out the bungalow's large picture window, but they disappeared as he approached the front steps.

When I answered the door, I felt like I loomed over Witty's round, short body.

"If it weren't for those fine, unscarred hands," Witty said to me, "I'd have pegged you for an athlete. With your build, you'd have made a good basketballer or footballer, but I take it you're a man of letters, not a letterman."

"You're right about that," I said.

Maureen and Margaret each grabbed at my pant legs and took refuge behind me.

"Well, who have we here?" Witty said with a toothy grin.

"Girls, I'd like you to meet Mister Whitman," I said, pressing the girls forward from their hiding places. "Mister Whitman, this is Maureen, and here we have Margaret."

"Pleased to meetcha," they chirped in unison, grabbing their skirts and dipping slightly, as Grace had taught them.

"Maureen and Margaret!" Witty hooted. "Or is it Moe and the Magpie? Tell you what, ladies, why don't you call me Witty?" He reached into a leather bag hanging from his shoulder, handed each girl a swirled glass marble, and advised them to save them for after dinner. "I've got games for you later!"

May Wu descended the stairs carrying little Dorothy on her hip. As usual, Dorothy was bursting with smiles and curls. Witty didn't recognize May Wu at first, with her straight silky hair hanging nearly to her waist. In the office, she kept her long hair in a tidy bun, but I expect her extraordinary pale gray eyes gave her away. There was no mistaking those quicksilver eyes, which now fixed on Dorothy's.

"You met May Wu at the office, and here is our youngest, Dorothy." I slid my index finger into her eager fist.

"Dorothy. Dodo! Could you be any cuter?" Witty reached out to the baby, who nearly jumped into his arms and gave him an irresistible smile. I couldn't remember when she'd taken so easily to a stranger, especially a man. Witty let her settle onto his left hip while his right hand reached for his leather bag, still full of treasures. "I brought something for you and your lovely wife, whom I have not yet had the pleasure of meeting. Where's the lady of the house?" He handed Dorothy back to May Wu and followed his nose toward the kitchen. As he pushed through a swinging door, he pulled out an unlabeled bottle of wine.

Grace wiped her hands on her apron, greeted the guest, and gingerly placed the bottle in the far corner of the counter. When the pleasantries were finished, she peeked through the swinging door and asked me to go check on the girls. I did, but I overheard their conversation.

"I should tell you," she said, "I mean…you had no way of knowing. My husband will not have any alcohol in his house. None. And it's not just since Prohibition. Of course you don't know his background. Let's just say he's a prominent leader in the Presbyterian Church. Civic leader, too. And then there's his mother."

"Oh dear," Witty said. "What about his mother?"

"Priscilla Foster. Have you heard of her? Quite famous in these parts. She was just elected president of the Women's Christian Temperance Union. Local branch. Headquartered right here in Eagle Rock. She's in charge of the entire western region."

"Ah yes, the beloved WCTU. How does their motto go… 'Moderation in all things healthful; total abstinence from all things harmful.' And a fine motto it is. What about his father?"

"Missionary doctor. Spent much of the last thirty years in China."

"Well, one cannot deny one's heritage, can one?" Witty reached for the bottle and placed it back in his bag. "Please forgive my indiscretion. It won't happen again. And thank you, my dear, for your exquisite candor."

THE CANDLES BURNED SHORT as dinner wound down. Witty's second slice of lemon meringue pie, which Grace had made that afternoon from Meyers picked in the back yard, forced him to reach into his lap and loosen his belt a notch. Evidently, it was a maneuver he performed with skill and subtlety, having practiced it over many years.

"I'm going to cut back on desserts, starting Monday," he said. "But that was too good to pass up, my dear. Too good."

Maureen fingered the marble in her pocket and kept her wide eyes on our guest. It wasn't until she placed her blue and red agate on the table that Witty remembered his promise to play with the little ones after dinner. Dorothy banged a spoon on her tray until her mother reached for her hand.

"Who'd like to join me in a rousing game of marbles?" Witty said. The girls led him into the living room where he plopped down on the oriental rug and explained the gist of the game. Grace and I cleared the table, set about doing the dishes, and put the kettle on for tea. May Wu perched on the sofa to oversee the game of marbles, cuddling Dorothy, who could not seem to take her eyes off the newcomer. Dorothy grew restless and slid down from the couch, crawled across the floor to Witty, and climbed into his lap. She pointed at the largest agate.

"Pretty, isn't it, Dodo?" Witty said. "Not something you get to put in your mouth, though, which no doubt is your number-one goal." He rolled onto his back and lifted Dorothy to the sky, which elicited a high squeal of delight. I glanced out from the kitchen, and next thing I knew, Maureen and Margaret were taking turns getting launched from Witty's bare feet across the rug, tumbling into piles of laughter.

"Honey, he's got our little girls doing circus acts in the sitting room," I said. "Do you think we should stop him? Those dresses you made them are going to get dirty."

"Well, they don't have play clothes. It'll be okay, Reid. It looks like he's being very gentle. Five minutes. Then it's bedtime."

When bedtime arrived, Grace sat in the sitting room with the girls for a few minutes while they told her all about the marvelous games they'd learned. Once they calmed down a bit, she told the children to say goodnight to May Wu and Mister Whitman.

"Goodnight Auntie May. Goodnight Witty. Goodnight Father." They gave each grownup a hug and scooted up the stairs to get ready for bed.

"What was it like, growing up in Boston?" I asked Witty, pouring a cup of tea.

"Fabulous place, Beantown," Witty began. "If you live in the right neighborhood, anyway. I was lucky enough to live in the Beacon Hill section in a grand old home, built around 1850. Just think of it: half the world was coming to California in the middle of the century in search of all the riches your great state had to offer, but my folks had the idea to build bigger and better in the Northeast."

May Wu jumped in with a question about his parents, but his answer sounded anything but direct. She'd been trying to unearth details about Mister Whitman, and she had a pretty good network — mostly other Chinese immigrants around the country — who were able to find a few bits and pieces. One connection pegged him as the son of a housekeeper who worked for the Carlisle family. If her lead was correct, it was the Carlisle family, not the Whitmans, who decided to stay in the Northeast and build bigger and better. The Carlisles's history in New England dated back to whaling days on Nantucket. She suspected Mister Whitman chose to tout their lineage as his own.

"Are your parents still living?" she probed.

"My father is gone, bless his soul. But Mother still lives on Beacon Hill, though she's ailing. To tell you the truth, she's not doing well at all since her episodes began. I look in on her every chance I get, but it's difficult when I'm traveling on a case like the one we've got ahead of us." He patted my shoulder. "Isn't that right, old boy?"

I twisted my gold wedding band around my finger. "How long do you figure we'll spend in France, if we go?"

Witty explained that it all depended on how many alleged heirs came out of the woodwork. With a fortune like Morel's, there would no doubt be a long line of long-lost cousins. Typically he posted notices in the local newspapers and let the claimants come to him. The true heirs, though, tended to emerge through more active research, like tracing birth records, church registries, county records, or even word of mouth. In this case, he would start with the L.A. news media and see who surfaced. In Paris, we would contact government and church officials. And the search would likely take us farther afield, into the provinces.

Grace returned to the living room and reported that the girls were off to sleep. "They included all of you in their prayers before bed," she said. "But don't let me interrupt your shop talk. Do you enjoy the work, Mister Whitman?"

"My heavens do I. You see, my dear, it's the perfect combination of detective work — without the sordid crimes and dead bodies and whatnot — and charitable endeavor. I get to play sleuth, nosing about in various corners of the world, and then I get to change someone's life by granting them an inheritance they knew nothing about. Fabulous feeling!"

Grace asked for specifics, aiming to draw him out. Witty outlined his first case, the one that got him started in his rather unusual line of work. It had come to him through an acquaintance of his mother, named Mister Harold Carlisle. Old Mister Carlisle owned several properties in Boston and on Cape Cod, along with a cottage on Nantucket. In the summer of 1913, an unfortunate thing happened in one of the Cape Cod rentals. The tenant, renting for the season, passed away on the sleeping porch. "Just woke up dead," the caretaker who found him had said. There was no sign of foul play, but they had a heck of a time figuring out what to do with the poor fellow. Nobody knew much about the gentleman, whose wallet contained the identification card of a Fredrik Voss of Bedford, New York.

"Mister Carlisle was telling my mother this story, and somehow she volunteered my services," Witty said. "She knew that I had a passion for genealogy — you know, tracking people's family trees." Carlisle hired Witty to spend a few days in Bedford Village, where he chatted up townspeople, interviewed the minister, listened to gossip at the general store, and bent the ear of the banker. What he pieced together about the village loner was that he had little money in the bank, didn't have a steady job, and may have been headed for the almshouse. Locals said they often saw Mister Voss collecting old produce tossed out of back doors by grocers and chefs. They would see him walking great distances, into the countryside, carrying bags of rejected produce in each hand. They assumed he would throw the old vegetables into a pot of stew that sustained him in a small shack in the woods.

"But they got it all wrong," Witty said. "What the villagers didn't know was that Voss loved horses, and he took culled carrots, collard greens, and apples to the stables. In fact, as a younger man, Voss had inherited enough money to buy a slightly lame stallion that didn't quite measure up to the standards of top breeders."

Over the years, Voss visited the stallion every day and encouraged a young trainer to show him how to exercise the big creature on a lead, ice the bad leg, and soak his sore tendons and wrap them in a eucalyptus paste. Eventually the horse came around, and Voss convinced the trainer to breed him to a couple of his mares.

"Voss vastly preferred horses to people, so he kept a low profile among the equestrian elite. But to make a long story short, let me just tell you that by the time of his death, he owned a good number of top-notch show horses, some worth several thousand dollars," Witty said. "I counted about thirty-five thousand dollars' worth of horse flesh there, and I figured I was onto something. Trouble was, the horses weren't mine to sell, so I had to find an heir before I could get a piece of that action. That's where my genealogy hobby came in handy."

Witty's best source turned out to be the local minister of thirty years, who held services in Bedford's steepled white church on the commons, where Voss attended services only occasionally. He was one of those parishioners likely to overcrowd the church on Easter and Christmas Eve, but you wouldn't see him on a sunny Sunday in May. The only other time Voss came to church was when his relatives from Austria were in town. The minister recalled they were from the Innsbruck area.

"So Mister Carlisle, who thought nothing of spending a few dollars to solve a good mystery, sent me off to Innsbruck. Within a couple of weeks, just by talking to people and checking local records, I found two first cousins of the departed Fredrik Voss. Franz Voss made his living as a baker — actually a pastry chef who made the most amazing concoctions. What that man could do with butter, flour, and marzipan! I recall buying new trousers at the end of the visit, just to accommodate the inches he singlehandedly added to my waistline." Witty tugged on his recently loosened belt. "The other cousin, Hanne, was married to a dairy farmer just outside the village. The husband wasn't much to write home about, if you ask me. Anyhow, the cousins directed me to sell the horses, send them the proceeds, and keep ten percent for myself. They even reimbursed Mister Carlisle for his expenses, and they still couldn't believe their good fortune. We remain friendly to this day, ten years on. Delightful people, Franz and Hanne."

"That's quite a story, Mister Whitman," Grace said. "And all this because your mother recognized you had a talent for tracking people's origins."

"It's true. Mother always saw my potential, always had faith. She's so tickled to hear my stories when I return from one of these adventures. Wants to know every detail, bless her heart. I always make it a point to bring her a few mementos from the places I visit," Witty said. "Truth is, without her, I don't think I'd have amounted to much."

The grandfather clock chimed ten o'clock and I stretched my arms toward the ceiling. Grace and May Wu gathered teacups and carried them to the kitchen. A chill had come over the room since the fire died down.

"What a delightful evening," Witty said. "I'm afraid I went on a bit too long with my stories. Please forgive me."

60

"Not at all," I said. "We enjoyed your company. In fact, if you'd like to join us for services in the morning, we'll be just down the street. First Presbyterian, nine o'clock sharp."

Witty said he'd give it some thought, thanked the ladies for a lovely evening, and drove away into the cool evening.

7

Reid: January 21 — Los Angeles

A N UNSTEADY BREEZE BLEW through sycamores outside Eagle Rock First Presbyterian that Sunday morning. Leaving the church after an inspirational sermon — thoughts on carrying forward the charitable spirit of Christmas throughout the year — I pulled my felt hat down over my unruly hair and tilted the brim into the wind. Grace buttoned the girls' coats around their necks and adjusted the blanket in Dorothy's stroller for the walk home.

I always enjoyed our Sunday morning walk south on Eagle Rock Boulevard past brick storefronts and red awnings, gazing into windows of closed stores. A streetcar rolled past, nearly empty on a weekend morning. During the week, Red Cars ran every ten to twenty minutes, and passengers packed the trolleys for their thirty-minute ride to downtown L.A.

"Can we go to the merry-go-round, Father?" Maureen said when she saw a northbound trolley. The train headed for the circular pavilion built two years earlier at the intersection of Colorado and Eagle Rock Boulevard to shelter streetcar travelers.

"Not today, dear," I said. "Wrong direction." I took her little hand in mine. I asked Grace whether she'd heard the outcome of the Rose Parade competition. It had been almost ten years since Eagle Rock's float won the Silver Cup, and Grace had worked hard on this year's entry.

"They're not due to announce the results for a few weeks. Don't know why they wait so long. The ladies are pretty anxious. I have my doubts."

Margaret waddled down the street like a penguin, her short legs and flat feet better suited to ice floes than Southern California's cement sidewalks. She picked up the seedpod of a liquidambar tree, a spiked brown ball, and started to put it into her coat pocket. She giggled as it stuck to the wool fabric and hung suspended above the pocket itself. Then she reached in and pulled out the marble that Witty had given her the night before. "When is Witty coming back to play with us?"

"We'll see, dear," Grace said. "Mister Whitman is a very busy man." We turned left on Ridgeview and began the half-mile walk up a gentle hill toward home.

"What was your impression of our guest?" I asked Gracie. The girls ran ahead to chase a family of quail into some azalea bushes.

"You know, I think he's alright," she began. "He's a little loquacious for our taste, of course. But I think he really cares about the people. What did you think?"

"If the girls are any judge of character, he's just fine. I've never seen Dorothy take to any man the way she did him," I said. "But I don't know. Something about him puts me on edge."

"If you believe his stories, which I think I do, he seems sincere and competent. He likes his work. He really wants to help the right people. And like you said, the girls adored him. Plus, best of all, he seems to appreciate his mother."

"See, you pick up nuances, like a man's affection for his mother. This is just the sort of thing that escapes me. I mean, my feeling is that he's not being honest with us. This Carlisle character, for example. He wasn't just a friend of the family who sent Witty on a little adventure. I have a feeling that Witty grew up in a big house on Beacon Hill because his mother was Carlisle's servant. And I'm not at all sure that he even knew his own father. Did you hear how he dodged the subject last night? According to May Wu's sources, it may have been just the two of them — the live-in housekeeper and her son."

"That may be true, Reid. But I wonder if it matters now. Witty took an opportunity, pursued his passion, built a career. In a way, I think it's admirable. Don't you?"

"I suppose you could look at it that way." I took her hand in mine.

Maureen ran back to the stroller and handed Dorothy a pine-cone she'd picked up in Mister Hooper's yard. Margaret toodled ahead and peeked through the fence at Pepper, a black Labrador who always greeted them with wags and snuffles. As we neared home, Grace gently reminded me that I might actually earn five percent of a fortune measured in millions. A couple hundred thousand dollars would bring us financial security beyond the reach of most people. "And you're not even thirty years old," she pointed out.

"I may be well into my thirties by the time this case is settled," I predicted. "I'll get May Wu's take on it tomorrow at the office. We can't wait too long, though, Witty's pressing me for a decision."

COMMUTERS PACKED THE RED CAR to downtown L. A. on Monday morning. I always enjoyed the ride, even if I had to stand. We businessmen, all in dark suits and fedoras, gave up our seats to the few ladies who boarded on their way to secretarial or restaurant jobs. That morning I scored a seat on one of the wooden benches, which gave me a chance to catch up on the *L.A. Times*. By the time we arrived downtown, its ink smudges had turned my hands nearly black.

I jogged up five flights of Bradbury Building stairs to my office and spent a few minutes going over an Automobile Club file. The executive director had asked me to attend a hearing that morning at the Department of Water and Power regarding a plan for Los Angeles to annex the city of Eagle Rock, the goal being expansion of L.A.'s water and sewage capacity. I personally opposed the scheme — only in part because I lived in the idyllic community — and I was pleased that my client agreed that the city should take a larger view of its expansion needs. Rather than gobble up small communities on the periphery, Los Angeles had to start developing a master plan for major growth. Although the hearing was about water and sewage, the Auto Club saw it as an opportunity to focus on the big picture, which included its intention to prepare a web of parkways covering the entire basin. We saw it as an opportunity to advocate for Angelenos to look to the Colorado River rather than letting basin cities compete among themselves over the local water supply — a small pie, as it were. Tapping into the enormous waterway was the only way to increase the size of the pie. Why not draw on this tremendous source and build dams, reservoirs, and canals that would quench our thirsty city well into the future? Certainly such a massive undertaking would require a great deal of investment, but the rapid growth of Los Angeles demanded foresight and planning. I argued that this was no time for shortcuts on infrastructure.

AFTER THE HEARING, I RETURNED TO MY OFFICE and asked May Wu to come in for a chat. I always respected her opinion and enjoyed brainstorming with her about clients and cases.

"What's your intuition about Witty by now?" I asked her.

"Well, I have to tell you, I don't give him high marks for honesty or integrity."

"Why not?"

"Did you know that he showed up at your house on Saturday night with hootch? Some kind of bootleg wine he'd drummed up since arriving in California."

"Grace tried to hide it, but I did notice," I said. "So you think he's a bounder?"

"Let's just say I have my reservations about his history in Boston, like whether he truly lived in Beacon Hill. For all we know, he grew up in South Boston. Maybe in his mind the Carlisle house was his, but I think his mother was the cleaning lady. They may have been live-in servants at best. My sources found no record of the Whitmans owning a house."

I shifted in my chair and fingered the fountain pen on my desk.

"On the other hand, I think his heart may be in the right place," May Wu continued. "He does seem interested in his work, and I do think he likes helping people. Being such an extrovert probably serves him well as he traipses around the globe in search of other people's fortunes."

"Doesn't sound too noble, the way you put it."

"But if it helps people and he happens to make a living at it, what's the harm?"

"There could be a lot of money to be made," I said, "not that I consider greed to be an admirable quality of the human race."

"Yes, lots of money, adventure, and intrigue. And you may have a tremendous effect on some poor people who never knew they were entitled to an inheritance," May Wu said. "But I'd be very wary of this Mister Whitman. He'll have to earn your trust, and we both know that's not easy."

"I'll know more after lunch today. We're meeting at the Broiler at noon."

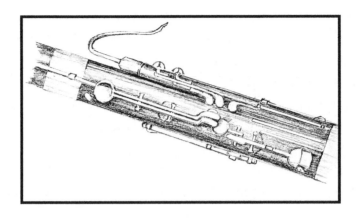

8

Reid: January 22 — Los Angeles

I CHECKED MY WATCH FOR THE THIRD TIME since arriving at The Broiler. I wondered whether this "Witty" character had forgotten our plan to meet for lunch at noon. It was ten past. I took a sip of tea and thought about which side dish to order with my filet mignon.

"Reid, old chap, there you are," Witty bellowed across the room, too loudly for my taste. "Sorry I'm a tad late. Got a little confused driving the Packard down one-way streets, dodging trolleys and even a few horses. So much going on in Los Angeles, one might mistake it for an East-Coast metropolis." Witty bumped his head on the lamp hanging above the table as he slid across the booth's burgundy leather.

"How do you like the City of Angels by now?" I asked. "Treating you well?"

"Fabulous. Just fabulous. Growing like mad in every direction, from what I can see. Soon you'll have your own Waldorf Astoria." He was referring to the Biltmore Hotel, due to open by April just a few blocks from my office. It would be the largest hotel west of

Chicago, built by Schultze and Weaver, the firm responsible for New York's elegant Waldorf Astoria. The Olive Street façade, visible through high scaffolding, promised to infuse Los Angeles with Beaux Arts style and a touch of Renaissance Revival. "I hope you're invested in real estate, my friend. Grab it now before it's too late."

"Yes, real estate," I handed Witty a menu. "I recommend the beef. Any cut. It's always good."

"Excellent. I could use a good slab of prime rib from the western prairie." Witty tugged at his necktie, as if a boa constrictor were beginning to clamp down on him.

Over lunch, I probed for details about the case. I definitely had my doubts about taking it on. How would we establish ourselves as the legitimate hunters of Monsieur Morel's heirs? To what extent would we publicize the quest? Too much publicity would bring every kind of fortune hunter to the fore, but insufficient outreach could mean legitimate heirs might be overlooked. How would we discredit false claimants? What would be the likely timetable?

Witty's answers were few in number and light in detail. I thought he was a bit cavalier about particulars, given the enormous sum of money allegedly at stake. Yet I had to allow for some degree of vagueness. There was no way of knowing how many claimants would emerge or how far afield the search would take us.

"This isn't something they taught you how to do at USC law school, my boy." Witty swabbed his plate with a piece of French bread. "It'll be an adventure that unfolds before our very eyes. We'll see where it takes us. Follow the leads. Pursue the possibilities. Are you in?"

Witty's dessert arrived: steaming fudge over three scoops of vanilla ice cream. No wonder he was always loosening his belt. I asked for another pot of hot water to stretch my tea bag to one more cup.

"Yes, Mister Whitman, you can count on me," I heard myself say. I hoped I wouldn't regret it.

"Outstanding!" Witty reached for his belt. "Forgive me. I'm planning to cut out the desserts starting next week. Anyhow, we should get a move on. You can do your legal thing to get the ball rolling here in Los Angeles, and then we'll drive across the country. The ocean liners out of New York take about ten days to get to northern France."

"Yes, I'll get things going here. May Wu can hold down the fort while we're gone. How long do you think? A month, maybe two?"

"No telling, my friend. Be prepared for a couple of months, I'd say."

"Say, do you think we could make a quick stop in Coachella on our way east?"

"I beg your pardon?" Witty asked in a voice thick with fudge.

"Coachella. The desert. It's a ways east of here, before we get to the Colorado River and the Arizona border. I'd like to visit my father there, just for a day or two."

"How far is it?"

"I normally take the train — a half-day journey."

"Tell you what, pal. It'll be our first stop, and we'll spend as much time as you like with the old man." Witty wiped chocolate from the corners of his mouth, scrunched his napkin into a wad and tossed it onto the table. "You don't mind if I do a little shopping first, do you, for what we on the east coast call a summer suit? These wool togs will be the death of me in California's crazy climate." Witty gave me a hearty slap on the shoulder, and I nearly choked on my tea.

When I thought about it, I wasn't sure I wanted to be cooped up in a car with Witty for a drive across the country. Boy, could he prattle on. On the other hand, it might be a good trial run to see whether we could survive a trip to Europe together. And maybe my father could offer another opinion of Witty's character. I always admired his ability to judge people. But first, I had to complete a preliminary legal filing on the Morel case and contact the news media about our search. We had our work cut out for us.

69

THAT WEDNESDAY, GRACE AND I had Witty to dinner again. A warm rain fell on the sycamores and eucalyptus lining our street. I loved their acrid smell, mixed with wet stones. The girls hopped with excitement when they saw Witty's yellow Packard, and before he could reach the doorbell, our heavy wooden door swung open and two cherubic faces appeared at knee and hip level.

"Moe! Magpie!" Witty shouted, kneeling down to their level. "Where's DoDo?"

"Sleeping," Maureen replied. "She has a smidge of temperature."

"Just a smidge?"

"That's what Mother says," Margaret pitched in. "What did you bring us?"

"Time will tell, my little Magpie. Patience will be rewarded." The girl wriggled with anything but patience. "Okay, let's start with this." He pulled out a box of dominoes and suggested they set up a chain for toppling later.

Grace welcomed Witty into the kitchen and offered him a glass of grape juice. The smell of apples, cinnamon, and pastry caught the big man's attention and he said something about skipping desserts, starting next week.

"I'm quite looking forward to this adventure with your husband, Gracie." Witty swirled his grape juice as if it were the wine he wished were accompanying the exquisite beef dinner to come. "No telling what we'll discover."

"I suppose that's part of the excitement," she said, "solving the mystery. Do you have any hunches?"

"Well, I did track down a good map of France and found a town called Goult in the *Département de Vaucluse*," Witty said. "Monsieur carried a photo of a woman, and on the back it said something about Estelle, Goult, and a date from some time ago. Could be something there. It's in Provence. What do you think, Reid?"

"I'm new to this game," I replied. "But we could be in for a wild chase. I mean, people move around so much these days, it's hard to tell. We might find relatives in Paris, or Normandy, or even another country. Feels a bit like the proverbial needle in the haystack at this stage, doesn't it."

"How long do you think you'll be gone, Witty?" Grace said.

"Well, if you figure a visit to your father-in-law for a couple days, a quick drive across the country, a brief visit with my mother in Boston…that's ten days or two weeks before we get on the steamship," he said. "Ten days to cross the Atlantic, and then we're off to the races." He stole a bite of carrot off the chopping block. "Yes, my dear, off to the races."

I continued the scenario in my head. Three weeks to get to Paris, several weeks traipsing around the city and the Vaucluse region, and then who knows what. I wasn't sure how I felt about being away from Grace and the girls for two or three months. It was a mixed blessing that my mother was nearby. Priscilla could help with the children, but she had a way of being more trouble than she was worth.

"Did you hear, old boy, that Busby's article in the *Times* stirred up quite a fuss?" Witty asked. "He said he might have to shift his so-called annex from the coroner's office to the courthouse because people are starting to sniff around about filing claims."

"My concern is that Busby's decision to publish the estate's value will bring all sorts of false claimants out of the woodwork," I said. "Five million bucks will bring out the crazies."

"Wasn't his decision." Witty filched a hunk of celery from the cutting board. "The kid said his editor made him specify the number. Journalistic principles and whatnot."

"The good news is, it looks like Fergus Murphy is going to be the judge on the case, and I trust he'll keep the nut-jobs at bay while we do our research," I said.

"Friend of yours, is he?" Witty asked.

"He's a good man," I replied.

AFTER DINNER, HAVING BEEN EXCUSED from the table, Maureen tugged on Witty's sleeve and asked what was in the leather bag — a question that no doubt had been on her mind since the moment he walked in the door more than two hours ago. With a subtle tilt of his head and sideways glance, he motioned for her to follow him into the sitting room. Margaret slid off her chair and scurried in behind her sister. Witty reached into the leather pouch and extracted a long rectangular black leather case, its corners raw and beaten, its handle worn from extensive clutching. Inside the case sat four cylinders of wood with shiny silver buttons and levers running their length.

"What is it, Witty?" The girls squirmed.

He pieced together the sections to form a long woodwind instrument. "It's a bassoon," he said. "And this is called a reed." He placed the reed in his mouth to dampen it before attaching it to the silver tube rising from the instrument's core.

"A reed," Margaret said, "like Daddy?"

"I suppose you could say they share the same name, with a slight variation in spelling. Homophones, if you will."

To the utter enchantment of both girls, Witty then did the most amazing thing they'd ever seen. He lit a cigar, inhaled deeply, and blew a note on the bassoon. Smoke billowed out the end of the cylinder just as its sound pierced the room. Screams of delight followed, not exactly in harmony with Witty's melody. A puff of smoke rose from the instrument each time he blew a note.

"Daddy, look what Witty did! The bassoon is smoking!"

"Marvelous," I rolled my eyes. "Mister Whitman is full of surprises, isn't he? One more song, and then it's off to bed for you two."

Witty broke into a rousing rendition of "Felix Kept on Walking." They got up to dance. "An excellent tune by which to march up the stairs to bed, just like Felix the Cat," Grace chimed in.

9

Witty: April 18 — Los Angeles

BABETTE AND I ROLLED INTO LOS ANGELES on the afternoon of Wednesday, April 18, happy but exhausted by our return trip from France and a leisurely drive across the country. With Babette's copious luggage in tow, we checked into a single room in the new Biltmore Hotel, not far from the courthouse, and I suggested that she use my last name for the sake of appearances. I saw no point in spending money on a separate room for her. But I also made it clear that the use of my surname was just a practical matter, not in any way a movement toward marriage and whatnot. She seemed to take it in stride. If she was disappointed, she did a good job of hiding it.

After checking in, we strolled through the hotel's enormous gallery and ballroom, admiring its frescoes and murals, marble fountains, crystal chandeliers, and exquisite tapestries.

"Look up," I heard a voice say when we entered the Crystal Ballroom. In the corner, a young man in the hotel's burgundy uniform pointed to the ceiling. "This mural was hand-painted by Giovanni Smeraldi, an Italian artist better known for his work in the Vatican and the White House. It took him seven months. Finished just in time for the grand opening." I looked past enormous Austrian chandeliers, twelve feet in diameter, to admire the fresco's figures of Greek and Roman gods, angels, cherubs, and mythological figures. "They're serving afternoon tea in the Rendezvous Court," the young man said. "Have a look at the ceiling in there, too. It's got 24-carat-gold accents, along with a couple of chandeliers just in from Italy. And don't miss the astrological clock."

I loosened my belt to make room for cookies and cakes that came with the hotel's luxurious afternoon tea. Frankly, I was beginning to wonder what to do with Babette in the coming months. The trial threatened to be very consuming, with all the claimants and their hungry lawyers swarming around the proceedings.

"You know, my dear, I won't be available to show you around the city once the trial starts," I said. "I hope you won't be disappointed."

"Would it be okay if I came to the courtroom?" she asked. "Just to watch you work."

"It may bore you to death, my darling," I said. "But you're welcome to observe." I was a little surprised and even flattered by her interest.

Before we retired to our room for the evening, I placed a call to Reid at home. We agreed to meet at his office in the morning and prepare for the May 3 court proceeding.

"Opening day will be here before we know it, so we may be putting in some long hours," Reid said.

"I'm all yours, my good man. All yours. We should file the petition this week or early next, so we'll have no doubt about getting in under the May 1 deadline," I said.

"Well, enjoy the rest of your evening. It may be our last chance to relax for some time. What will Babette do while you're working? Are you just going to let her loose in L.A?" Reid's tone seemed uneasy. His judgmental side was showing again.

"You sound concerned."

"She's just a bit of a…" he hesitated. "Well, frankly, I'm just not that comfortable with her."

"Look, man. Just say it. Do you mistrust her?"

"Witty, forgive me, but do you ever feel like she's latched onto you for your money?"

"Oh please. For one thing, give me a little credit for my charm with the ladies. And for another, well, I'm not that wealthy. "

"Not yet, but if we prevail in this trial you'll be more than comfortable. *The lips of a strange woman drop as honeycomb, and her mouth is smoother than oil, but her end is bitter as wormwood, sharp as a two-edged sword.*"

"Look, I'm no dummy. Why do you always have to be so cautious?"

"Never mind."

BY EARLY MAY, ONCE THE TRIAL GOT UNDERWAY and preliminary statements were presented, it became pretty clear that we would have to do more sleuthing into the Fife family. Audrey Fife claimed her brief marriage to Marcel Morel had resulted in their daughter Betsy, who could be a competing heir. The story warranted a good defense. Since Audrey asserted she had married Marcel in San Francisco in 1903, we decided I should make a trip north to see what I could dig up.

I could hardly wait to tell Babette about my plan for a road trip from Los Angeles to San Francisco. We could pick up our travels where we'd left off. Sure, I'd have to work during the week, but I'd have evenings free to spend with her.

"What about our things?" she said, looking around our hotel suite at her trunks of clothes and treasures.

"Our things?" I tilted my head. "I suppose we can just keep this suite and leave our belongings here while we travel. It should just be a week or so. In fact, I have to be back before jury selection begins May 18."

"That's a long time," she said.

"What's your concern?"

"Oh, it's just that I'm a little tired. Perhaps you could go without me. I'd still be here when you got back, honey."

"Are you feeling okay?" I worried that she might be getting ill, or worse yet — with child. "Tell me there's nothing wrong."

"No, no, I'm fine. Too much travel is all. I just don't think I'm interested in another road trip on such short notice." She assured me she'd be fine without me, and that I should feel no qualms about going to San Francisco to do my research. The conversation troubled me, but I had little time to waste. I told her I'd get an early start in the morning, hoping to drive at least halfway on the first day.

10

Witty: May 13 — San Francisco

MY BEAUTIFUL PACKARD GLOWED in the fading light as I pulled into San Francisco that Sunday afternoon. I felt weary from the drive but thrilled with the beauty of the city. I found a room at the St. Francis Hotel on Union Square. Based on the map that May Wu had provided from the Automobile Club, I figured I could walk or take cable cars to most of my appointments from there.

I craved a stiff drink, but that would be hard to come by back in the good old U S of A, with Prohibition and whatnot. Dry, I set out to explore the Calvary graveyard, which covered forty-eight acres bordered by Geary, Turk, Saint Joseph's, and Masonic streets. It was one of the few Catholic graveyards still in use in the city, where property values had pressed people to relocate their dead in favor of high-rise buildings. In fact, the city had considered closing the cemetery in 1914, but voters rejected the notion. Another ballot measure was being discussed for the 1924 docket, with the high price of real estate expected to weigh heavily against the desire to let the deceased rest in peace.

I wandered through the graveyard, feeling the last rays of sun on my back as the air took on a chill that reminded me I wasn't in Los Angeles. May Wu's research was terrific: Established in 1860, the cemetery had become the most popular resting place for Catholics in San Francisco. By 1923, it contained close to 30,000 dead, and headstones stood like corn in a field, almost too close to walk through. I found a directory and scanned it for Morel, just in case, and Fife. It contained no listings for Morel, but I did find a few for Fife, dating back to the end of the nineteenth century.

I made my way to the tombstone of a William Henry Fife. "William Henry Fife, 1870-1915, Husband of Audrey Banes Fife, Father of Betsy Jane Fife. Died in the name of freedom." Yet another victim of the so-called Great War, I thought. Not far away I noticed other Banes family tombstones, maybe Audrey's parents, and I wondered if they might be rolling over in their graves at the thought of their daughter claiming to have married Marcel when she was married to poor William. A heavy fog rolled in and darkness settled quickly, making my walk back to the street a bit of a challenge.

On Monday morning, my first stop was at the Archdiocese of San Francisco. Again, May Wu's notes, which I had reviewed over a cup of coffee in the vast lobby of the St. Francis before setting out, provided good background. The current Archbishop, Edward Hanna, had been in the position since 1915 and was highly respected among civic and labor leaders, as well as various religious denominations. He was the third Archbishop of San Francisco since Pope Pius IX established the Archdiocese in 1853, covering a tremendous territory from the Oregon border south to Monterey, and all the way east into Colorado.

I met with a deacon who said their records had survived the 1906 earthquake and its resulting fires. In fact, the deacon shared a dramatic photo showing much of San Francisco engulfed in flames, with St. Mary's cathedral safe in the foreground. "The fires burned in the city for days following the quake," the deacon said. "Patrick

Riordan was Archbishop at the time, and he visited people living in temporary camps all over the city. He led an open-air Mass, and he worked nonstop to visit thousands of individuals. His message was all about working to make San Francisco an even better place. He gave them hope that they could rebuild this great city."

"Remarkable," I said. "And the church was spared. Chalk it up to clean living?"

"Actually, four churches crumbled in the quake, and twelve churches burned. Their parishes were virtually wiped off the map. We lost schools, hospitals, and St. Ignatius, the Jesuit college. It was devastating."

"But some of the records survived?"

"Yes, many of the records were here with us," the deacon said.

We scoured the files for any mention of Marcel Morel and found none. A search for Fife, on the other hand, turned up a key piece of evidence. Audrey Banes had been truthful about one thing. She did get married in San Francisco on Saturday, March 28, 1903. It just wasn't to Marcel Morel. Instead, it was to William Henry Fife, the man whose tombstone I'd found the previous night.

"Might you have the christening record of their daughter, Betsy Jane?" I asked. "I believe she was born at the end of the same year."

The deacon combed the files, but found no such record. He suggested that I visit the local parishes, but thought it best to narrow my search because there were now so many in the city. "Do you know where they lived?"

"Not yet," I said. "Maybe I'll stop by the municipal offices first, to see whether I can find them. Do you think the child might have been born in a Catholic hospital?"

"It's possible, but again, you'd want to narrow your search. St. Mary's Hospital on Rincon Hill was completely destroyed in the fire, so I'm sure you wouldn't find any records there. The amazing thing is, no patients were lost. They were able to ferry all the people and even some of the equipment across the bay to Providence Hospital."

"One can only imagine the chaos." I got a copy of the marriage record and thanked the deacon. "You've been most helpful."

My visit to the municipal offices yielded nothing. Their records had been destroyed in the 1906 fire, so anything from 1903 would have been lost. They had no subsequent record of property ownership by William or Audrey Fife, and the clerk said many people rented apartments, rather than owning, anyhow.

A visit to the *San Francisco Chronicle* also proved to be a dead end. I found nothing about Morel or Fife, though I didn't really know what to look for. Perhaps an obituary on William Fife would have stated that he was survived by his wife and daughter, but during the war years there were so many deaths, it may have gone unreported.

Taking another blind stab, I stopped by Sacred Heart Cathedral Prep School in the Cathedral Hill neighborhood. It was the city's oldest Catholic school, founded in 1852, and the first co-ed high school. A helpful young clerk helped me find a record of Betsy Fife, who graduated in 1921. She dug up a photograph of the graduating class, but the faces were so small they stood little chance of proving useful in court. Nonetheless, I got a copy of both the photograph and the graduation record. If nothing else, it would prove that the girl lived in San Francisco.

That evening, I made a couple of phone calls. I gave Reid a quick rundown of my findings and told him I was unlikely to discover much more. "As you said, when it comes to finding Morel in San Francisco, I could spend a lifetime trying to prove the negative. As far as I know, he wasn't here, but who's to say?"

"No luck with a birth certificate or christening record for the girl?"

"You know, tomorrow, I'll go to the parish in the Cathedral Hill district and try my luck there," I said. "That's where she went to school, so maybe it was their neighborhood."

"What else can you do?"

"Not much, really," I said. "I think I might as well head home tomorrow afternoon. I was thinking that, as a last resort, we could call the girl as a witness and have her testify about her father. Chances are she grew up with William as her father, and for all we know she never even heard of Marcel Morel until he appeared in the *Times*."

"I hate to put a child on the witness stand," Reid said.

"She's almost twenty years old now, my friend. It's not exactly child abuse," I said. "Call it what you will — fabrication or fantasy — I just don't think Audrey's story has any relationship to truth."

"I see your point. We'll keep the girl's testimony in the quiver."

My second call was to the Biltmore Hotel, where I left a message for Babette in room 329. "I miss you, darling, home soon." I have to admit, my heart sank when they had no messages for me. I hoped Babette was feeling all right. Her unwillingness to come to San Francisco continued to baffle me.

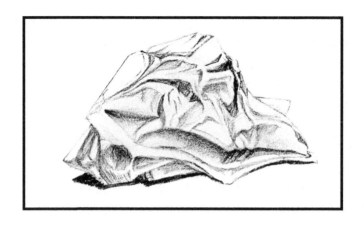

11

Witty: May 16 — Los Angeles

THE LOS ANGELES AIR FELT WARM AND DRY compared to San Francisco. I rolled into the basin with the Packard's windows open to the breeze. I went straight to the hotel, eager to reunite with Babette. But when I opened the door, I found the suite nearly empty. Her elegant Parisian clothes were missing from the closet. Her bags of toiletries and makeup no longer cluttered the marble counters of the bathroom. Her jewelry box had disappeared. Her trunks were gone. All my things remained right where I'd left them, but the only sign of Babette was the lingering scent of her Chanel Number Five.

Stunned, I sat on the edge of the bed and tried to think of where she could have gone. If she'd taken ill, she might be in a hospital somewhere, but then she wouldn't have packed up all of her belongings. No, she had left. But why? And where? I noticed an envelope on the coffee table of the suite's sitting room. It contained a note, in her handwriting, on hotel stationery.

"My deer, I appologise in advance for what I am going to do. Thank you for all you have done. You are a fine man which I like very much. But I know you wouldnt' marrie me. The carrots are cooked. Please dont' worrie about me." She had kissed the paper with her blood red lipstick, and signed her name just below the image.

I read the note again and again. I turned it over to see if the back side could reveal more, but each time I looked, it remained blank. I was completely mystified. What had gone wrong? We never fought, not even a little kerfuffle. I treated her like a princess. She seemed so content. What possibly could have gone wrong?

I crumpled the paper in my fist and threw it across the room. I dug down to the bottom of my traveling trunk, where I unearthed a bottle of Cognac that I'd smuggled from France. I opened it and poured myself a glass. The amber liquid burned on its first run down my throat, and then its warmth spread into my chest, around my ears and right to the top of my head. The second sip felt smooth, comforting me like an old friend. What could she have meant, apologizing for what she was about to do? I'd always thought I could read people pretty well. What had I missed? I poured another glass.

A PERSISTENT KNOCK ON THE DOOR WOKE ME. Light streamed in through the window like daggers into the narrow slits of my eyes. I realized I was still dressed, folded uncomfortably on the sofa where I'd fallen asleep who knew how long ago. I pulled myself up, straightened my hair, and opened the door. It was not Babette, as I hoped, but the hotel maid offering to clean the suite. I asked her to come back later, and made my way to the shower.

I arrived at Reid's office just before ten o'clock where May Wu and Reid were strategizing about questions for jury selection. I described the scene at my hotel, bewildered by Babette's disappearance. I recited the contents of her note, which I'd memorized.

"Did you keep it?" Reid asked. I gave him a blank stare. "The note. Do you have it?"

"No, I tossed it."

"That's too bad. You might need it."

"What on earth for?"

"It did sound a bit ominous," May Wu said. "Like she's planning to do something terrible, saying she's sorry in advance. Did she seem depressed, like she might hurt herself?"

"No, no, not at all." I thought back through the haze of my hangover.

"What did she mean about the carrots?"

"Oh, it's probably one of her strange idioms." I rubbed my head. "You know, the note may be right where I left it. I mean, I threw it across the room. Next thing I remember was getting thoroughly spiffed on Cognac."

"Call the hotel right now." Reid picked up the phone. "Tell them not to enter the room. No cleaning, no towels, no service."

"Did she take anything with her?" May Wu asked.

"She took everything. Well, everything that was hers, including all the dresses, jewelry, hats, perfumes, and baubles that I'd bought her." I was still stunned. "But I don't think she took anything of mine. I mean, I left her quite a bit of cash so she'd be comfortable while I was in San Francisco. But I don't think she stole from me, if that's what you mean."

"I'm so sorry, Witty. You must be very upset."

"Perplexed is the word that comes to mind at the moment," I said. "Baffled. Bamboozled."

We resumed our discussion of jury selection, and then caught up on the potential claims. We agreed that my research in San Francisco would all but eliminate the threat that Audrey Fife might get her hands on the money. May Wu had found a property deed, recorded at the county clerk's office, that Marcel Morel signed and dated on March 27, 1903. "If he were in Los Angeles signing papers on a Friday, there's no way he could be at a church wedding in San Francisco on Saturday," she said.

"Especially a Catholic wedding," Reid added. He felt we had plenty of ways to poke holes in Mrs. Fife's fanciful story. "It's not Fife who keeps me awake at night. The one who gives me nightmares is Mildred Dodge. Let's review what we know of her claim."

We went over her story and decided to reconnect with Brick Busby at the *Times*, since he'd written an article about her while we were in Europe.

We met Busby for lunch at Cole's Diner. His choice.

"I eat here v-virtually every day now, sort of a s-standing date with Violet, even though the midday shift usually keeps her too busy for more than a flash of her beautiful smile now and then," Busby beamed.

"Terrific. What can you tell us about Mildred Dodge?" Reid was all about business.

"Miss Dodge is claiming to be the illegitimate daughter of Marcel Morel," Busby said. "She says her mother was a showgirl who had an affair with Morel, and she's the daughter who is now entitled to the whole fortune."

"Does she have any credible proof?" Reid asked.

"She's not entirely...what I mean...well, Miss Dodge has some photographs, but frankly they could be pics of any baby in any carriage anywhere, as far as I can tell. Not that I know anything about babies."

"And the girl asserts that she was sent to a convent in Texas, if I recall," Reid said.

"That's right. A Catholic convent in Fort Worth, where her mother...if you...the showgirl, dropped her off when she realized she was in no position to raise a child."

"Did she sound convincing?" I asked. "Offer any proof beyond the generic baby pics?"

"Not really, but I was just trying to get a story, you know. I'm not the judge or jury here." He waved a French fry in the air. "I brought copies of the photographs, which we kept at the *Times*."

One photograph showed three people at a beach: a man with his back to the camera, a woman whose face was visible in profile, as she looked at him, and an infant that the woman held in her arms. It looked like the beach could have been in Southern California, although it was hard to tell.

The second photograph showed the mother and infant on a blanket on a lawn, palm trees in the background. Again, it could have been in Southern California, but there were no distinguishing buildings or landmarks. Reid noticed a name on the front of the photograph, in the bottom left corner.

"Harvey Macklin," he said. "Is that the photographer?"

"That's right," Busby said. "He's still in business. He does some work for the *Times*, although I think his main beat is portraits and weddings."

I offered to track him down. "May I borrow these prints?"

"Just be sure to bring them back. I'm not supposed to take files out of the office." He took a bite of his French dip.

12

Busby: May 25 — Los Angeles

I FOUND IT HARD TO SIT STILL IN THE PRESS BOX, where my knees butted up against the seat in front of me. The reporter ahead of me, a white-haired gentleman from the Riverside paper, occasionally turned around with a dirty look aiming to get me to stop bouncing my leg, which made his chair shake. According to my mom, I'd always been a fidgety kid.

Jury selection had taken a full week. The first task was to weed out folks who knew any of the hundred and eighty claimants or their myriad attorneys. Nobody in the jury pool knew Marcel Morel or had any knowledge of his family, apart from what they'd read in the newspapers — mostly my reports. It made me nervous to think I might have a key role in "justice at work." All the candidates admitted to being overwhelmed by the size of the fortune and the complexity of the case before them. Anyone with small children, health issues, or pressing employment demands was excused, as this promised to be a long, drawn-out process.

The jury ended up being seven women and five men ranging in age from thirty to sixty-seven. Each dressed professionally in suits or conservative dresses. All the ladies wore modest hats and simple gloves. Each gentleman wore a tie and had a coordinated handkerchief visible in the left breast pocket of his suit jacket. One woman taught English at a Catholic prep school, which had just finished its academic year, so she would have nearly three months free. The 67-year-old gentleman was a retired Baptist minister from Oklahoma who had recently moved to California to be closer to his family. All of the jurors were Caucasian, reasonably well-educated, and financially comfortable but not particularly wealthy.

Heirship proceedings began Monday, May 28, 1923, Judge Fergus Murphy presiding. Claimants, attorneys, reporters, and onlookers filled the courtroom for what they knew would be a marathon. And then it got complicated. On the following Friday, June 1, Judge Murphy received an anonymous letter that read:

I am writing you in regard to Marcel Morel which died this year. I was his very deer American friend. We were like brothers. M. Morel had a daughter somewhere which he hadnt' seen since she was a baby. He had reason to believe she was in Los Angeles or France. About six months before he died, he told me that her name was Babette Reville. He wanted me to find her. I looked for her for months but had no chance so I stopped looking. He gave me some money as a fee for my services but the money is all gone and I am in very bad health. I am very sorrie that I couldnt' find M. Morel his daughter which I promised him. I thought you might like to know these things. Please dont' worrie about me, although in reality I am severely deprimed. This letter will be mailed to you after I am dead.

Judge Murphy called a conference with all of the attorneys to inform them of the letter, but he said it would not affect the case because it was received well after the deadline of May 1. He let them know that the conference was simply to keep them informed of the development, and that no further action would be required.

Saturday morning's headline in the *Los Angeles Times* read "Court Learns Morel Daughter Somewhere In Los Angeles: Anonymous Letter Throws Wrench In Battle For Estate of Millionaire Believed To Be Bachelor." I didn't write the article. In fact, it came as a total surprise to me. Somehow, the editor of the society column got his mitts on a copy of the hand-written letter, and got the green light to run the story. The *Times* printed the letter verbatim, including the misspellings and improper use of apostrophes.

"What do you make of this?" I asked Reid when I caught up with him during a break.

"It appears that Babette has spoken — from somewhere in the great beyond." He looked pained to say it, like he had just swallowed a handful of spiders. "Had I mentioned that I didn't trust that woman?"

"Are you sure she's behind the letter?"

"Let's call it a strong hunch. It shouldn't affect the case, but you never know."

"Is there any way she could wiggle her way into the trial?"

"Doubtful, but it's worth keeping an eye on. I have a feeling she's a lot more clever than she lets on."

THE LOS ANGELES WEATHER WARMED into the nineties during the first week of the jury trial. Normally at that time of year, the basin's heat is moderated by what the Southern California coastal dwellers called "June Gloom," when a thick marine layer covers the beach and creeps well inland. But this felt like late June, when intense sun had a way of winning out over fog. The courtroom sweltered by mid-afternoon. The bailiff set up electric fans, but the heat became oppressive. I was so relieved when the judge suggested that all participants simply agree to accept casual attire when the temperature surpassed eighty degrees. The men gladly removed their coats and loosened their ties, and most of the ladies removed their hats. I snuck in without socks.

Several of the claimants presented such weak arguments, accompanied by a total lack of credible evidence, that Reid moved for their dismissal. Some of his motions were successful, and the courtroom became slightly less congested with fortune hunters, their attorneys, and curious onlookers. The dwindling crowd did little to ease the stifling heat.

On Monday, June 4, Miss Mildred Dodge took the stand. A smartly dressed lawyer guided her through her claim of being the illegitimate daughter of Marcel Morel.

"I chose to tell my story now because it's about my legacy," Dodge said. "I'm worthy. I matter. I have a right to say who I am, and to be proud of it. It's not about the money." Witty, sitting a few rows back, barely disguised his audible laugh as a cough.

She testified that she was twenty-seven years old and that her mother had abandoned her as an infant, leaving her to be raised in a Catholic convent in Fort Worth, Texas. She presented little evidence, although the attorney did submit the photographs that Mildred had shared with me for my article back in February. Could have been any baby anywhere, as far as I could tell. When his turn came to challenge the Dodge story, Reid stood and approached the jury with a confident smile.

Watch this, I thought. *Like stealing acorns from a blind pig.*

"I'd like to call to the stand a Mister Harvey Macklin," Reid said. I grinned. I'd helped track down the photographer, who'd done business in Los Angeles for some thirty-two years. Macklin's full head of gray hair framed his round face, cascading down his forehead toward small circular glasses. They looked like something President Teddy Roosevelt would have worn. His wide smile appeared only occasionally, and he came across as having a calm and self-assured demeanor. Age fifty-nine, he'd been photographing people professionally since he was twenty-seven, mostly at weddings, christenings, graduations, and in his studio. Occasionally, he ventured out to photograph families outdoors — at the beach, at Mt. Lowe, in the park, and so on. He had dabbled in landscape photography, but portraiture was his strong suit.

"Would it be fair to say that you've seen a lot of faces, and in fact captured images of many faces, over the years?" Reid asked the witness.

"One could say that," Macklin said.

"And, in your opinion, do you have a strong ability to recall those faces?"

"They say I never forget a face, if that's what you mean."

"Yes, thank you." Reid walked to his table and picked up a photograph of Marcel Morel. "Have you ever seen this face?"

"Of course I've seen that photograph in the newspapers," Macklin said. "Can't miss it these days."

"Indeed. And have you ever seen this man in person?"

"No, never."

"Take your time, Mister Macklin. Is it possible that you did a photo shoot with this gentleman back in the late nineties? He would have looked considerably younger back then."

"I'm quite confident that I never met him."

Reid then produced the photographs that Mildred Dodge was using to claim her relation to the millionaire. Macklin confirmed that he had taken the photographs in question, and he identified their location as the vicinity of Hermosa Beach. He recalled that the couple and their infant daughter were visiting relatives in California, although he couldn't remember exactly how they were related. His connection was that he'd been the photographer at the California couple's wedding a few years earlier.

"I don't know the name of this family from Texas, in the photos, but there are two things I can tell you. The gentleman looked nothing like the photographs I've seen of Marcel Morel, and the man in the photograph spoke with a strong Texas accent. In fact, the wife did, too."

"Wife?" Reid said. "Do you have reason to believe they were married?"

"Oh yes, they seemed to be a normal young married couple with their little daughter in tow. They were introduced as mister and missus so-and-so, and I had no reason to think they were bending the truth." He looked closely at the photograph that showed mother and child, and pointed out that she was wearing a wedding ring.

The next move that Reid made seemed a bit risky. Attorneys like to know the answers to all the questions they asked on the stand — don't like surprises — but he seemed to have a strong hunch about Mildred Dodge. He recalled her to the witness stand and began his cross-examination.

"You say that your mother turned you over to a Roman Catholic convent in Fort Worth, where you were raised by whom?"

"I was raised by Catholic nuns," she said. "They were very strict."

"I see." He looked at the jury and then returned his attention to the witness. "Would you please recite the Lord's Prayer for us, Miss Dodge."

"Objection!" her attorney rose. "This is not a church."

"Mister Foster," Judge Murphy said, "we do recognize the separation of church and state in this courtroom. I trust your request will serve a valid purpose."

"Yes, your honor," Reid said. "I ask that we allow Miss Dodge to recite the Lord's Prayer. It will just take a minute."

"Objection overruled," the judge said.

Mildred Dodge proceeded to recite the prayer:

"Our father, who art in Heaven,
Hallowed be thy name;
Thy kingdom come,
Thy will be done.
On earth, as it is in Heaven.
Give us this day our daily bread;
And forgive us our debts
As we have forgiven our debtors;
And lead us not into temptation,

But deliver us from evil.
For thine is the kingdom,
And the power,
And the glory,
Forever."

"Thank you, Miss Dodge," Reid said. "You were finished, weren't you?

"Yes, sir." She hesitated, and then added, "Amen."

Reid caught the eye of the Catholic schoolteacher in the jury, who shook her head, her face betraying a slight smirk. The retired Baptist minister, seated just behind her and to the left, had a knowing smile on his face. He made eye contact with Reid as if to convey that he understood the point. Miss Dodge had just recited the traditional English version of the Lord's Prayer, favored by Protestants. The Roman Catholic version did not use the terms "debt" and "debtors," but said "forgive us our trespasses as we forgive those who trespass against us." It ended at "deliver us from evil," and did not go on to say "for thine is the kingdom, and the power, and the glory, forever."

Based on the looks from the jury, Reid felt confident he had discredited Miss Dodge, creating enough doubt for them to reject her flimsy claim to the fortune.

WHEN COURT CONVENED ON TUESDAY, Judge Murphy announced he had received a motion from attorney Jake Tresan on behalf of a Miss Babette Reville, who was claiming to be the daughter of Marcel Morel. A murmur went through the pool of attorneys. I glanced at Witty, who looked like he'd taken a pitchfork to the chest. He and Reid exchanged glances. Witty shook his head and gave a shrug, as if to say that he was just as puzzled as anyone by this development. I noticed Babette standing at the back of the courtroom. I'd only met her once when she was out with Witty, but a dame like that makes an impression on a fella like me pretty quickly.

"With due respect, Your Honor," Reid piped up, "my under-standing is that no new claims are being considered, as we are well past the May 1 deadline to submit petitions for heirship."

"Point taken, Mister Foster. Would you like to pursue that thought in the form of a motion to dismiss?"

"Yes, Your Honor," Reid stood up from the table and paced across the room, giving himself a little time to gather his thoughts. "On behalf of the Morel claimants, I move to dismiss the claim of Babette Reville on the grounds that it is in violation of the court's order, under Section 1080 of the Probate Code, directing the entry of a default against all persons who, by May 1, had not appeared or filed petitions to determine heirship."

"Thank you, Mister Foster. I will take your motion under consideration," Judge Murphy said. "Let me also inform all of the claimants that Miss Reville's attorney, Jake Tresan, has indicated he is prepared to appeal any ruling that would deny his client standing in this case."

"On what grounds?" one of the attorneys asked.

"I'll leave that up to Mister Tresan," Murphy said. "But be prepared for a delay, because we'll have to go through due process, as you know." The judge threw an apologetic look to the jury and then called for a brief recess. I did not relish extra hours sitting in the cramped press box.

During the next break, Witty approached Reid at the table and put a hand on his shoulder. I stayed to eavesdrop.

"I can't believe this is happening," Witty said. "You know, I really thought there was something between us. And then she pulls this stunt."

"Sorry, Witty."

"She can't possibly think she has a shot at the money."

"She found a bulldog of a lawyer in Jake Tresan," Reid said. "He has a reputation in this town."

"But they're too late," Witty said. "Please tell me they're too late."

94

"They are, but in this business we never assume we're safe until the jury announces its verdict. Even then, the possibility of appeal is very real."

"Unbelievable. I can't believe she would do this. I really cared for her."

If Reid were tempted to say "I told you so," he sidestepped it. No need to make Witty feel any worse. Not only was their case becoming complicated, but I figured the poor man's heart may have been bruised, if not broken.

That afternoon the judge granted the motion to dismiss the claim, and he announced that the trial would move forward regardless of any concurrent appeal. He said there was so much evidence to hear that it was critical they continue considering existing claims. They would deal with the Reville issue if and when the appellate court ruled in her favor. His tone indicated that he found it unlikely that they would ever hear from her again, but he maintained his judicial veneer of respect.

II. ENDANGERMENT & ENDEARMENT

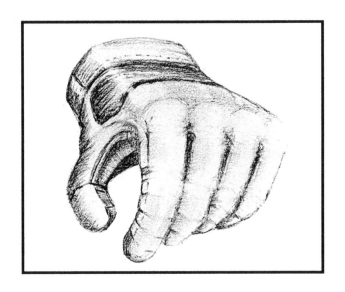

13

Busby: January 22 — Los Angeles

Back when I was playing detective in Morel's apartment the day he died, I'd noted that he had an appointment on his calendar for January 22nd: "R.H. @ Diner — 8a." He couldn't keep the appointment, being six feet under, but I certainly intended to be there.

I arrived at Cole's Diner at ten minutes before eight and grabbed a seat by the front window, hoping to catch a glimpse of R.H., whoever that was. It was all I could do to keep my eyes on the door, instead of the cute waitress I'd met when I first came in to ask about Morel. She brought me a cup of coffee and offered a breakfast menu.

"No, I…how are…I'm just here for a quick cup of coffee." I wondered whether Violet noticed my face turning into a tomato.

According to a large clock on the wall, it was two minutes after eight when a short, disheveled man with red hair, thick mustache, and ruddy face walked in and scanned the tables. It looked to me like he'd had a nose job, courtesy of somebody's fist. He wore a glove on his left hand but not his right. Even from a distance, I picked up the smell of stale cigar smoke and petroleum fumes.

"You seen Morel?" he asked Violet. "You know, the weird French guy."

"He won't be coming in, sir."

"He sure as shit better." Violet took a step away from the man. "We made this goddamn appointment weeks ago." His angry eyes didn't point the same direction and one eyelid drooped while the other widened with rage. A jagged scar ran from his left ear across his jaw, stopping just short of his Adam's apple. "How do you know he ain't comin'?"

"Sir, I hate to tell you this…" she took another step back from his twisted face and gave me a quick glance. I nodded, as if to say I had her covered. "Monsieur Morel passed away."

"Died? He fucking died?" He stomped an oily boot on the black and white tile floor, leaving a dirty print.

"I'm sorry," Violet said.

"Goddammit!"

"I'm going to have to ask you to leave, sir."

"Glad to. Fucking waste of time." He stormed out.

The coffee pot shook in Violet's hand when she tried to refill my cup.

"You okay? What an awful man," I said. "Ever seen him before?"

"Heavens no! I'd remember."

"I gotta…what was his beef? Did Morel ever mention anybody like that?"

"Oh, I don't know. He did seem worried about some guy giving him a hard time, but I didn't pay much attention. Just made sure to keep his coffee cup full and hot. He liked it hot."

"Did you get a name?"

"No. Monsieur didn't share much. He seemed worried about oil-business stuff like leases and licenses and taxes. Called it the Wild West. Said the politicians ought to hurry up and lay down some laws."

I put my coffee cup beside my notebook. "Did he mention anything illegal, like bribes? Threats?"

"Mister H. That's what he called him. You know, when he fretted about the guy who was hassling him."

"Blackmail?"

"What are you thinking? You don't think somebody was out to get Monsieur, do you?"

The cook bellowed from the kitchen. Orders were backing up. "Gotta run."

THE NEXT MORNING, I WAS HALF ASLEEP on the bench at the coroner's office when the ring of the telephone woke me. The clerk, Jimmy Irwin, removed a cigarette from his mouth and picked up the phone.

"Brick Busby? Yeah, he's here in his office *annex*," Jimmy said. "Hold on, lemme get him."

My eyebrows shot up. Who could be calling me here? I apologized to Jimmy. "I don't fancy bein' your personal secretary, Bub," Jimmy said. I put the receiver to my ear and heard the voice of Witty, who had looked for me in the *Times* building and was directed to the coroner's office. Witty proposed meeting for a cup of coffee because he had a proposition for me. Reid Foster would be joining us.

"S-Sure, let's meet at Cole's Diner at the corner of Sixth and Main," I proposed. "It was Morel's favorite lunch spot, and I wouldn't mind seeing the waitress again."

"Oh, to be young again," Witty said into the phone. "See you there in twenty minutes."

I gathered my notebook, coat, and hat.

"What's with the name 'Brick,' anyways?" Jimmy asked. "Is that for real?"

"Well, I suppose it depends on what you mean by 'real.' I mean, it's the name I use everywhere, even for publication. But if you...so, really, it's not on my birth certificate, if that's what you're asking."

"So what's the scoop?"

"Oh, my parents named me Richard, intending to call me 'Rick.' And then they had six more boys, the first named Brian, the second Brooks, and on down the line. Every one of my brothers has a name that starts with the letters b and r — unless you get technical with Randall, who goes by Brandy. You know, had to fit in with Brady, Bruce, and Bradley."

"If you have a kid, you can name him Russell and call him Sprout." It took me a minute.

COLE'S DINER WAS QUIET AGAIN, in the lull between breakfast and lunch. I was the first to arrive, and I tipped my hat toward Violet. She seemed pleased to see me.

"Well, I'd...Table for three, Violet," I said.

"Weren't you just here, Mister Busby?"

"Brick, please. Er, please call me Brick, m'lady," I said, extending my hand in an overly formal, playful gesture with a slight bow. "I wanted to make sure you were alright after that creep from yesterday. He didn't come back, did he?"

"No, he's long gone."

"Good riddance."

Witty and Reid arrived, found me in the corner booth, and went through proper introductions. Reid was about my height, but much broader in an athletic sort of way. He was younger than I expected, not even thirty, but carried himself like he knew what he was doing. He was even more handsome than he looked in the newspapers. Dark, wavy hair tumbled down his forehead toward deep-set, thoughtful eyes.

They told me about their plans to open probate proceedings, even though they hadn't located any heirs yet. They hoped to get a friendly judge who would let them file on behalf of "the issue of the parents or grandparents of Marcel Morel," or something to that effect.

"And then we'll leave for France," Witty said. "Steamship to Cherbourg, train to Paris, and we'll see where we go from there."

"Seems like you should explore this *Département de Vaucluse*," I said. "It was on his identity card, you know."

"Yes, the Vaucluse is a good start," Witty replied.

Reid jumped in to explain the role they envisioned for me. He wanted me to write an article about the filing of the case here in Los Angeles. The purpose, he said, would be to notify potential heirs that Monsieur Morel had died intestate, and that assets of a substantial value were left behind.

"Well, sir, if you don't mind me saying," I said, "a good journalist tries to be very specific about the facts. Don't you think I should give the value of the estate, as we know it to date? We're looking at more than four million dollars, right?"

"Based on the bank records and property deeds — which you confirmed with the county, if I'm not mistaken — four million may be the low end," Witty said. "It's looking like at least five."

Reid squirmed in the leather booth at the mention of such an enormous sum. "I prefer to leave it at 'substantial,' for a couple of reasons," he said. "I'd like to spark interest — you know, create a buzz — but not instigate a riot." He feared a feeding frenzy of false claimants if the true value were known and, besides, it wasn't his style to talk about money. I said I'd do my best, and reminded the gentlemen that I'd have to get this through an editor or two, and there were no guarantees that I could get it published as they wished. Hell, I wondered if they'd keep letting me write anything other than obits.

"We know you'll put your best effort into it, my boy," Witty said. "Best effort, no doubt." He went on to propose that I continue to follow developments in Los Angeles while he and Reid were traveling. "There may be court filings and various public statements from fortune hunters — legitimate and otherwise," Witty predicted. "You'd be most helpful as our eyes and ears here on the ground, using your best investigative skills, of course."

I lit up at the idea, and suggested letters and cablegrams to report any developments.

"Excellent idea," Witty said. "Can we give you a stipend for your troubles?"

"Heavens, no!" Reid said, nearly spewing his tea across the table. "We couldn't possibly provide compensation to a reporter, Mister Whitman." He went all formal on us. "We have to avoid any conflict of interest if we face even the slightest chance of a trial when we get back from France."

"Right you are, my man," Witty said. "So right." The men got up to leave.

"What do you...Have you ever...What if it was foul play?" I blurted. Reid and Witty shot me a confused look. "Let me back up." I told them about the two entries in Morel's desk calendar. Witty confirmed that the first, F&M, was an appointment at Farmers' and Merchants Bank, which Morel of course missed. The second was yesterday's encounter.

"I'm pretty sure R.H. is some kind of shady character from the oil fields, maybe a wildcatter," I said.

"What makes you think that?" Reid sounded skeptical. I described the man who showed up at the diner, his awful smell, his horrible language, rough treatment of Violet, and the way he stormed out when he learned Morel was dead.

"What are you getting at, Brick?" Witty asked.

"I'm just...have you ever thought...well, what if Morel was murdered?"

"Oh, come now, my young friend."

"No, really. A man with that much money, in today's oil business...no friends...low profile. Why not?"

"I think you have a lively imagination."

"But he's a perfect target. Rich, lonely, nobody looking out for him."

"But he electrocuted himself with bad wiring in his own kitchen," Reid said. "How do you stage that?"

"And if this R.H. character was the murderer, why did he show up at the diner and throw such a fit?" Witty added.

"I haven't figured out that part just yet." I put on my hat. "I'm working on it."

14

Witty: January 26 — Los Angeles

FROM THE VERY START OF OUR JOURNEY, I wasn't sure Reid and I would be able to work together. He was so cautious and skeptical, I wondered how he even got out of bed in the morning. But he was bright, precise, and no doubt dependable. Maybe he'd loosen up when he got away from his office and family.

Reid looked a little pale when I rolled up in the Packard ready to start our cross-country journey. "One day at a time," I reassured him. "We're just going to Coachella today." He kissed each of his children, who were too young to anticipate how their father's long absence would feel. Grace fought back tears as she gave her husband a final embrace.

"*Weeping may endure for a night, but joy cometh in the morning, my love,*" Reid said. He picked up his bags and started down the front steps. "Hurry up, May Wu. Let's not keep Mister Whitman waiting."

"Are you sure it's okay?" May Wu asked, hesitating at the top of the steps. She wore a dark blue A-line skirt, white blouse buttoned to the top with a navy ribbon tied at the collar, and she carried a charcoal gray overcoat. Her hat matched the coat, and she'd worn low navy heels for traveling. Very practical. Her left hand gripped a small overnight bag.

"Absolutely. We have plenty of room, and Father will be so pleased to see you."

I raised my eyebrows but said nothing when I realized that the young Chinese beauty was coming with us. I simply opened the Packard's trunk and helped Reid load his luggage.

"Just one bag?" I asked May Wu. Reid explained that she was just going as far as Coachella, and would return by rail on her own. He motioned for her to ride in the front seat.

At the back of the car, I pushed an elbow into Reid's ribs and said, "You're just full of surprises, old boy." I winked. "Full of surprises."

As the Packard pulled away, Reid looked over his shoulder to see his daughters waving madly, their blond curls bouncing with each little hop of excitement. Grace hid her face in a handkerchief.

May Wu proved to be an excellent navigator, using maps from their Automobile Club client. She directed me out the Arroyo Parkway to Pasadena, and then along the foothills of the San Gabriel Mountains eastward toward San Bernardino. Despite mild temperatures in the basin, the peaks to our left were dusted with snow, rising like mythic gods from the valley floor. I wondered out loud how in the world we could be driving through groves of citrus and palm trees within sight of snow-capped mountains.

"Who's hungry?" About three hours into the drive, I was starving. "You must know a good place for lunch in these parts, Reid. My treat."

We decided on the Mission Inn, a stunning adobe that was a favorite of movie stars and honeymooners. The dining room, simple but elegant with its arched doorways and intricate tile work, featured a good array of luncheon choices. May Wu settled on a

Waldorf salad, Reid chose a chicken salad sandwich, and I ordered the French dip, in honor of Monsieur Morel.

"How about switching drivers after lunch, my friends," I suggested.

May Wu glanced sideways at Reid and chuckled. "He doesn't drive, Witty."

"Good Lord! How can you represent the Automobile Club and not drive a car?"

"He prefers trains, bicycles, feet, or even horses to the horse-less carriage," May Wu said. "You know, he hasn't made the leap from horses to horsepower." It was clear that the juxtaposition of Reid's disdain for the automobile and his representation of the Automobile Club had come up before.

"Oh, horsefeathers! We'll have to fix that," I said. "I have no intention of being your chauffeur for our three-thousand-mile journey across the country."

Reid explained that he didn't even have a driver's license, so he would not be taking the wheel of the Packard. Cautious, as usual. But I promised to have him driving by the time we crossed the Colorado River. "By then," I said, "There'll be no law enforcement to check on your legal status as a driver." May Wu laughed into her napkin.

DOCTOR DAVID FOSTER'S WINTER HOME was a simple two-bed-room bungalow on half an acre. The garden, with every kind of cactus, palm, ornamental grass, and wildflower imaginable, felt like a magical oasis in the desert. Enormous date palms towered over the small home, and jacaranda trees framed the front yard alongside two small orange trees. The house was sparsely fur-nished, almost Spartan, but David didn't seem to mind because he spent most of his time outdoors. He slept on the porch when nights were warm, and usually did his reading in a rocking chair adjacent to a birdbath in the garden. That's where he sat reading a tome on botany when we arrived.

David wore sunshades over thick glasses and held the book close to his face for reading. His hands shook a little, and he was slow to pull himself out of his comfortable chair to greet us. But the sight of May Wu quickened his step.

"My dear, what a thrill to see you!" He gave her a warm hug. He whispered something in Chinese into her ear as he held her close. He shook his son's hand and gripped his shoulder.

"Father, please meet Mister Lyle Whitman, my colleague and traveling companion for the foreseeable future," Reid said.

"Pleasure to meet you, Doctor Foster." I held out my hand. "Pleasure, indeed." The man smelled like a farmer, an agreeable combination of soil, sweat, and citrus.

We sat on the porch overlooking the magnificent garden and sipped fresh orange juice that David had squeezed from fruit he'd picked that morning.

"I always thought the pictures of orange trees and palms with snowy mountains in the background were just propaganda to lure east-coasters like myself to California," I said, raising my glass. "Now I'm beginning to get the picture in earnest. It feels like you could reach out and touch that peak."

"That's Mount San Jacinto," David said as we looked west into the afternoon sun. "I believe it's over 10,000 feet at the top."

"Extraordinary."

"Brings to mind a passage in Psalms: *the mountains skipped like rams, and the little hills like lambs*," David said.

I asked about the plants in the garden, and David's response was long and detailed — that of a passionate botanist. A soft-spoken man, he seemed fairly stingy with words, but he could carry on at length given the right topic. David said he had not always been a botanist, although it had been an interest and hobby for many years. As a younger man, he'd worked as an ophthalmologist, first in New York and then in China. He and his wife Priscilla had gone to China as Presbyterian missionaries in 1892, where he'd set up a medical clinic in the village of Shan Tung. Although he was an eye specialist, he found himself dealing with the most basic issues of health and hygiene, teaching people to use soap and drink only safe water.

Word of David's healing powers traveled quickly around Shan Tung, and he earned a great reputation throughout the region. Those patients strong enough to come to his clinic traveled for days to see the doctor. Occasionally he would pack his supplies on a donkey and walk from village to village helping weaker patients who could not travel. As his reputation grew, the wealthier members of society sought out his services, as well. They would send for him to perform surgery in city hospitals. He even treated the Empress Dowager, whose cataracts had nearly caused blindness by the time David was able to perform a delicate operation to restore her eyesight. The successful operation lifted him to a status near miracle worker.

David and Priscilla didn't let the demands of life in China discourage them from starting a family. Reid was born in Shan Tung in 1894, and two younger brothers came along during the next several years. With the uprising of the Boxer Rebellion and its murderous rage against foreigners, the entire family fled in 1900 with just a donkey and whatever belongings they could fit in its cart. They escaped to the coast and managed to secure passage to California, where they settled in Eagle Rock.

David soon missed the satisfaction of helping the Chinese villagers, so he took his two oldest sons and returned to China in 1902 after the turmoil subsided. He hired a French governess, the daughter of fellow missionaries, to help with the boys' education, not to mention care and feeding. Reid stayed in China until 1908, when his mother insisted he return to the United States to complete high school. David and his second son remained in Shan Tung for two more years, during which time the doctor contracted malaria. The disease ravaged his body and made it nearly impossible for him to tend to his son or minister to the villagers. They returned to Los Angeles in 1910, and with them came May Wu, whose mother had died from complications of malaria earlier that year. May Wu was only eleven when she arrived in America. I could only imagine that she would have been overwhelmed, and so lucky to have a stable family that would take her in. Knowing this, I could see why she and Reid were close, but I could swear there was more to their relationship than childhood ties.

David gradually recovered much of his strength, but malaria cost him his career. His eyes were damaged, and his hands became too unsteady to practice ophthalmology. In 1915, he began coming to the desert to work with a group of botanists who, like him, had lived overseas — some as missionaries, other as explorers — and had brought back seeds and cuttings from around the world. Together, these men pursued their love of plants and developed botanical gardens and research facilities. One of David's passions, the date palm, was becoming a commercial success in the desert.

"And what's your newest research, Doctor?" I asked, mopping my brow. Even my new, lightweight summer suit felt oppressive in this climate.

"I fear it may appear a bit self-serving, but I'm looking into medicinal plants for the treatment of malaria," David said. "We have several botanists and doctors returning from posts in tropical climates, and we may be onto something."

"I'd love to learn more about it," I said. "You see, my mother contracted malaria, probably on a trip to Louisiana some years ago, and her symptoms are getting worse every year." We talked in depth about his research on treatment, and perhaps even prevention of the disease using extracts from the bark of the cinchona tree. David nursed three of the trees, native to tropical South America, in his yard. They looked like tall shrubs, with flat, waxy leaves and small pink flowers. The bark, he explained, contained various alkaloids, including the anti-malarial compound quinine. He was experimenting with ways to dry and powder the bark, and incorporate the powder into pills or solutions.

"Use of cinchona bark has been in the works since the sixteenth or seventeenth century," David explained. "It's been traded throughout Europe and Asia for hundreds of years. Legend has it that the first European ever to be cured of malaria was the wife of the Spanish Viceroy of Peru, the countess of Chinchon. In 1638, European doctors tried and failed to relieve the countess of her symptoms, until they administered some medicine obtained from local Indians. Its source was the bark of this tree, which Carl Linnaeus later named cinchona after the countess." David had used the medicine with some success on patients in China, but wanted to improve the formula and delivery. In the end, David offered samples for me to share with my mother when we reached Boston. He recommended that we visit Doctor McDonald, a fellow Presbyterian missionary doctor whom David had known in China. McDonald had returned to his Boston roots within the last year or two.

While David and I talked, May Wu and Reid stretched their legs on a walk through the neighboring fruit orchards and vegetable fields. With a wide underground aquifer, the area had become a key growing area for oranges, mandarins, peppers, grapes, and lettuce. A fledgling movement toward wine grapes died with the advent of Prohibition. But most of all, the Coachella Valley was known as the ideal climate for growing dates, which liked their feet wet and their heads in the sun. Since the late 1800s, botanists had been importing date-palm cuttings from Iraq, Egypt, Israel, and Algeria. The U.S. Department of Agriculture even dedicated a full-time horticulturist to working on date breeding in the area. The tall date groves made for a pleasant stroll, providing shade on a warm afternoon.

I don't know what they talked about, but I saw May Wu slip her arm through his, and they seemed in no hurry to get back to the house.

On Sunday morning, I rolled over on the lumpy couch to see that David was an early riser. He recited his prayers and performed a little Tai Chi in the garden, facing the rising sun. By eight o'clock he'd made a scrumptious stack of buckwheat pancakes for all of us, and by nine o'clock we were all at Coachella Presbyterian for services. I had wanted to avoid the religious routine, but couldn't come up with an excuse, so I went along. After the sermon, lots of members of the congregation approached David, exchanging small talk about the weather and local news. I couldn't remember being surrounded by so many Scots, and realized that must be the origin of a slight accent I'd noticed in David's speech.

MY BACK ACHED FROM THE SOFA when I woke on Monday morning, and the prospect of sitting in the Packard for the next week or ten days didn't appeal. But I knew it was time to move on and leave the pleasant conversation and climate behind. The place struck me as beautiful and serene, but I wondered how a person could live in such isolation and not go absolutely nutty. A few days in the desert confirmed that I'm a city boy, through and through.

"It was my sincere pleasure getting to know you, Witty," David said as we loaded the Packard. "To both of you: *Be strong and of good courage; be not afraid, neither be thou dismayed, for the Lord thy God is with thee whithersoever thou goest.*"

"The pleasure was mine, my friend," I said, "all mine."

May Wu wished us well and reminded us to write with updates at least twice a week. She promised to wire news of the Morel case to Boston in time for our arrival. And then she let out a curious chuckle.

"What's that about?" I asked.

"I'm just picturing the two of you — as odd a pair as could exist — driving across the country, not to mention sharing close quarters for the next two months. Good luck."

15

Reid: January 29 — Cross-Country Drive

WHEN WE CROSSED THE COLORADO RIVER into Arizona, Witty pulled the car to the side of the road, gave me a head-to-toe-and-back-again look, and said, "This is it, old boy. You're going to drive for a while."

"Malarkey!"

"Come now, I know you can do it."

No amount of protest could disabuse Witty of this notion. He was not, under any circumstances, willing to pilot the vehicle for every mile from here to Boston. So I settled in behind the wheel, adjusted myself to get as comfortable as possible, studied all the controls, and followed Witty's command to let the clutch out slowly. The car lurched forward and the engine sputtered to a halt.

"Oh dear me," Witty said, "This is going to be a long ride."

I tried again. On the third try, the vehicle hiccuped into motion, and it kept moving just above a crawl.

"Okay, Alice, now you have to get up some speed and get out of first gear. Jesus Christ, we'll never get there at this rate!"

"No need to take the Lord's name in vain. I'll get the hang of it." I realized my grip on the steering wheel was exceptionally tight.

I managed to shift gears without stalling or driving off the road, thanks to Witty yelling at me to watch the road, not the shifter. I gained comfort with the beast once we got up to speed on the open road. I just dreaded the moment when I would have to stop and start again. I spent the first hour looking over my shoulder for law enforcement. As an attorney and a religious man, I was loathe to put myself in a situation that contradicted the law. If stopped, I would not lie to an officer, but simply explain our journey and our dilemma. It would be important to keep Witty out of the conversation, because he was likely to embellish far beyond what was appropriate.

About two hours into the drive, I glanced over at Witty. The man's head was tilted back, his eyes closed, mouth open wide, and spittle began to trail down his chin. Each time we hit a bump, Witty's head would snap forward and he'd give a little snort. I didn't mind the silence, using the time to get comfortable with this new skill of driving an automobile.

Another hour passed, and I managed to change my focus from the mechanics of driving to other things, like the Morel case. I thought about the kind of evidence we would need to convince a judge, and maybe a jury — *if* we were lucky enough to find the rightful heirs to the fortune. With any luck, we might find official records from a county seat, although I didn't know quite how the French provincial system operated. If the Morel family were religious, there might be a family Bible showing births and deaths. Church records could be helpful, but again, I would have to learn how the French handled these things. Of course, a leap of faith was required to assume that Morel came from France, and particularly from the *Département de Vaucluse*. Even that information could be a red herring, for all I knew.

I also wondered how in the world I would defend against false claimants. At this stage, speculation served no purpose, but I couldn't keep my mind off the challenge.

The car jolted as the right front wheel dipped into a hole the size of a laundry tub, and Witty woke with a start.

"Good God! What's that?" he shouted. "What happened?"

"Sorry, Witty, I didn't realize the size of the hole."

"Pull over, man. Let's see if there's any damage."

I steered the car to the side of the road, stepped on the brake, but forgot to depress the clutch. The car coughed to a stop as the engine stalled. We walked around the yellow beast, and Witty checked the wheels and axles for soundness. Everything appeared in good order.

"Keep driving, my friend," Witty said. "Carry on. You're doing fine."

Witty grabbed a bag from the back of the car and placed it at his feet in front of the passenger seat. I managed to get the car rolling again, with minimal fits and starts, and kept an eye out for more pits and potholes. A mile or two down the road, Witty pulled a pewter flask out of his bag and removed the top.

"Want a sip?"

"Sure, I'm a little thirsty." I put the flask to my lips, took a swig, and promptly spit it out the window. "What in the world is this?!"

"Why, it's perfectly good whiskey, as far as I know," Witty answered. "Let me taste it."

"Good Lord, Witty, don't you know I don't drink alcohol?"

"I thought that was just in front of the dames."

"Oh, for Heaven's sake!" I handed back the flask as if it were a fouled diaper. Witty took a long pull, replaced the cap, and put the flask back in his bag. He fumbled through the satchel for a minute and then pulled out his bassoon, which was in its carrying case. "You don't mind if I practice while you drive, do you?" He assembled the instrument, took a deep breath, and blew a few sour notes. "Takes me a while to get warmed up, so bear with me here."

"Witty, perhaps you could open the window and point your noise, er, music, in a southerly direction."

Rolling down the window was a good suggestion because it not only alleviated the noise a tiny bit, but it also redirected the smell of alcohol blowing through the noise-maker. "The drive would go faster for both of us if you took a few sips of whiskey now and then, old chap," Witty offered. But I just shook my head and kept my eyes on the road.

The drive proceeded smoothly over the next several days. I insisted that Witty drive in the morning, when his attention was more likely to stay on the road, and I took over after lunch. Then Witty could have his whiskey, play his bassoon, and take his nap. I have to admit, I actually started to enjoy being behind the wheel. It felt relaxing and meditative — that was, until my passenger blew a foul note or insisted on smoking another of his nasty cigars. When we crossed into the Midwestern states, temperatures dropped and I often agonized between the grim options of an open window sucking bitter cold into the cab or a closed window trapping cigar smoke, bassoon music, and the smell of whiskey. I developed the habit of wearing my heaviest overcoat after lunch.

"How fast will this thing go, Witty?"

"A few years back some fellow set a land speed record in the twelve-cylinder model. Close to a hundred and fifty miles per hour, if memory serves."

"And this model?"

"This is the twin six, man. Not likely to break any records, but you're welcome to try," Witty said. "Are you in a hurry to get somewhere?" He reached over and slapped my knee, causing a slight jerk on the accelerator. "Easy, now. We don't want you getting pulled over for reckless driving, what without a license and whatnot."

I rolled my eyes and the corners of my mouth lifted just a tad.

The chances of getting pulled over for much of anything were slim in the middle of the country. Law enforcement officials rarely patrolled the roads and stuck close to their own jurisdictions.

Several states, including California and New York, had laws against drunk driving, but everybody knew that inebriation was nearly impossible to prove, or even define.

We stopped for lunch in a restaurant or diner just about every day, enjoying the chance to shake off the dust and stretch our legs. I carried a large bag of apples and ate one each day. Not wanting to waste anything, I ate every bit of the apple — core, seeds, and all. Always had.

"Reid, I hope you're giving your ears a good cleaning every night."

"What in the world are you talking about?"

"My good friend, you're in great danger that apple trees will start growing out of them, what with all the seeds you swallow."

16

Reid: February 5 — Boston

WHEN WITTY PULLED INTO A LONG DRIVEWAY at 823 Myrtle Street in Boston, falling snow made mesmerizing patterns in the glare of the Packard's headlights. We pried ourselves from the seats where we'd spent most of our waking hours for what seemed like an interminable journey. Witty led the way to a side door, where he knocked and waited, shifting his weight from one snowy foot to the other. Witty's mother welcomed her son with hugs and kisses. She had a soft handshake for me, and warm cookies for both of us.

Mrs. Whitman glowed with warmth, her abundant cheeks radiant under sparkling azure eyes that she couldn't take off her son. She wore her gray hair in braids that edged each side of her face and then met in a bun at the back of her head. She smelled of fresh laundry and hot biscuits. Her hands were rough, the skin almost raw over swollen joints that looked like they'd be painful to flex. With a stature on the short and round side, she struggled to crane her neck upward to meet my gaze. We all took a seat at the kitchen table, a long wooden plank that looked like it had been hauled in from a farm.

"We'll just eat in the kitchen tonight, sugar," Mrs. Whitman said. "I made your favorite beef stew and pluckin' rolls."

"Oh, Mama, I've been thinking about your cooking since somewhere in Texas," Witty replied. "Reid, you're in for a treat. A real treat."

That evening Witty dove into the stew as if he were hoping to find a gold ring at the bottom. He lunged into the pluckin' rolls — a sticky concoction of bread, butter, cinnamon, and more butter — with both hands. I ate my portion with knife and fork, and hoped I didn't offend my hostess when I declined her repeated offers of a second serving.

We finished the meal with apple cobbler and a cup of tea, and conversation turned toward memories of the old days in Boston. I figured this would be a good time to excuse myself and let mother and son catch up. Mrs. Whitman showed me to my room, which was through the kitchen, down a hallway, up a stairway, and down another hallway. The spacious bedroom had its own bathroom, with lush towels and lavender soaps — pure luxury compared to the motor inns we'd experienced across the country.

"I almost forgot," Mrs. Whitman said. "This arrived for you." She pulled a telegram from the pocket of her apron. It was from Busby in Los Angeles. In the week since we'd left California, word had gotten out about the Morel fortune, and the loonies were showing up in droves to grab for it. "EIGHTEEN CLAIMANTS TO DATE STOP TWO OR THREE SERIOUS STOP CALL ME AT WORK STOP" I wondered if this was just the beginning of the onslaught.

WHEN I WOKE EARLY THE NEXT MORNING, it took me a minute to remember where I was. Reluctant to leave the comfort and warmth of my bed, but curious to explore the surroundings, I got up and dressed for the day. The sun had not yet risen, so I walked quietly down the hall and pushed through a large door, only to realize it was not the one I'd passed through the night before. This door opened to a two-story atrium, granite-gray light reaching through skylights high above. I found myself standing on a walkway that continued around the atrium's perimeter, giving access to several other doors. Directly across from me, an open door led to what appeared to be a library.

I peered over the second-floor balustrade to admire the mosaic work on the first floor. It had an exotic flair, possibly Middle-Eastern or North African. I could see now that the home featured a magnificent entry way with enormous mahogany doors and intricate leaded windows on each side. I entered the library and inhaled the scent of leather and old paper. Books lined the walls from floor to ceiling, and a library ladder leaned against the far wall's top rail. A quick glance at the collection revealed eclectic taste, including scholarly works, poetry, classic plays, modern novels, technical volumes, and several selections in German and Greek.

"Good morning!" The deep voice startled me. I turned to see an elderly gentleman standing in the doorway, wearing a robe and slippers.

"Forgive me," I said. "You've caught me snooping."

"I'm Harold Carlisle, and I'm more than happy to welcome you into my home."

"Reid Foster, from California. Traveling with Lyle Whitman. Thank you so much, sir."

Carlisle stood nearly as tall as I, very lean, and he moved with an athletic grace that hinted at his former stature. A full head of white hair set off strong blue eyes that lit up when he smiled. "You've found my favorite room in the house," he said. "My wife, God rest her soul, loved the finery of the dining room and the parlor, and she always kept fresh flowers in the sitting room. But this has always been my sanctuary, my retreat."

"So sorry to invade."

"No, no, not at all. Are you a lover of books?"

"Let's say a man of letters. So much of my time is spent reading legal tomes and writing even more, I rarely take the time to sit and read for pleasure any more." I reflected on what a pleasure it would be.

"Well, please make yourself at home here. Mrs. Whitman hardly feels like a housekeeper any more — more like family now — and any guest of hers is a guest of mine."

Carlisle turned to leave the library and again urged me to help myself to any books or writing papers. I took a seat at a lovely little writing desk and gazed out the window. The rising sun's saffron rays danced across the tops of snow-covered trees. I found paper and pen, and began a letter to Grace. I made a habit of writing to her every other day, just to let her know I was thinking of her. It helped clear my head, but wasn't the same as the long chats we normally enjoyed each evening after the girls were tucked into bed. I missed them all, and could only hope I'd made the right decision to go heir hunting in Europe. In the back of my mind, I harbored doubts that the search would turn up legitimate heirs, and I still wondered how in the world we'd present the legal case even if it did. Was this quest for heirs, and the sacrifice of my limited clientele, simply hubris? Should I have followed Gracie's advice and joined an established law firm in Los Angeles?

Mrs. Whitman cooked up an enormous breakfast of eggs, bacon, hot cakes, and Vermont maple syrup. We ate at the kitchen table, and I realized that the Whitmans lived in this wing of the house, the servants' quarters. May Wu had been right about Witty, who'd been honest about being raised in Beacon Hill, yet careful to avoid the detail that he was the housekeeper's son. The pedigree didn't matter much, but the lack of openness concerned me.

Later that day, Mrs. Whitman found me back in the library. "Mister Foster, you have mail and a telegram. Hope it's good news." Two letters were from Grace, and one from May Wu. The Carlisle house had a telephone, and we managed to call Busby at the *Times* before closing time in Los Angeles. He updated us on the number of claimants to the Morel fortune, now at twenty-five. Most of them sounded flimsy, like the young woman who said her mother — a trapeze artist with a traveling circus — met Morel when the circus came to the west coast.

"Sh-she told me in an interview that the two fell in love, had a s-steamy affair, and that she was their l-love child," Busby said. "The gal offered a few details to beef up her story, like Morel's mother disapproving of the circus entertainer on m-moral grounds, forbidding them to marry. But it was all talk, and I doubted she had any hard evidence to go with her vivid imagination. Besides, I couldn't imagine a loner like Morel carrying on with a flying trapeze artist."

"Do any of the claims seem to have merit?" I asked.

"Well, I c-came across a young lady named Mildred Dodge, who might be for real." Busby said she promised proof — letters and photographs — to show that her father was Marcel Morel. She said her mother, a showgirl with a traveling dance troupe, had a brief affair with Monsieur Morel in the summer of 1895. Mildred was born the following spring in Los Angeles, was sent as a very young girl to a convent in Fort Worth, Texas, and was now twenty-seven years old.

"I-it's that…you see…at first, she claimed that Morel had married her mother," he said over a scratchy telephone connection. "But when I asked her about a marriage certificate, she switched horses faster than a trick rider…said maybe it was an illegitimate affair. She says she has some letters, like one from her mother to this Catholic convent in Fort Worth. Sh-she wanted them to raise her daughter." He hadn't seen any letters or photographs, but Miss Dodge seemed confident and specific about her facts, apart from whether or not her parents had ever married. "Miss Dodge left a lot of g-gaps to fill in, but at least she has some notion that she'll need hard evidence," he said. "I'm hoping to interview her for an article next week."

We discussed a couple of other fortune hunters, but so far the links sounded very weak. Most folks just said they'd fallen on hard times and could really use the money. He said they didn't understand the legal system, had no lawyers, and failed to grasp the concept of evidence.

I SAVORED THE TWO LETTERS FROM GRACE. She was giddy that the Eagle Rock float had won top prize in the Rose Parade. She'd put in so many long hours organizing volunteers, working with designers, overseeing construction, and finally helping to apply each petal, twig, and seed to create a magnificent entry. She'd been volunteering for several years, and this marked their first victory under her watch. Finally.

The girls, she said, were doing fine, although they missed me. Maureen had been in bed with a cold for two days, but seemed to be on the mend. Margaret spent hours playing with the marbles Witty had given them. And Dorothy was growing like a bean stalk, pulling herself up and scooting back and forth along the couch. She seemed almost ready to walk, but it hadn't happened yet. Grace relayed best wishes from my mother, who had come by often to sit with the girls and share a meal. Priscilla's big project involved lining up support for a Women's Christian Temperance Union building in Eagle Rock, and it seemed to occupy most of her waking hours. And probably her dreams, for that matter, Grace added.

Grace closed each letter with a sentence or two about how much she and the girls missed me. But she took great care to avoid whining, and added a some final words of encouragement and support.

I folded each letter with care and placed them back in their envelopes. I lifted them to my nose and inhaled. Was it my imagination, or could I smell a hint of Grace? For just a moment, I let warm thoughts of family and home push aside worries about work, travel, and money.

MRS. WHITMAN LOVED HAVING HER SON HOME. She made all his favorite foods, soaked up the colorful tales of his latest adventures, and skirted complaints of her own aches and pains. Privately, she told me the fever and chills of malaria came and went, and each bout seemed to leave her joints and muscles a little less functional, incrementally more achy. Most days she felt a dull fatigue, and the pain in her back rarely subsided. The doctors chased symptoms around her body, expressing concern for her spleen, liver, and even her mind in the long run. But there wasn't much they could do for her.

Witty seemed eager to help. "I can tell it's getting harder, Mama. Reid's father knows a doctor in town, McDonald, and I think we should see him."

"Oh honey, I'll be fine."

"Mama…"

"Why throw good money after the flimsy hope of a cure?"

He told her about the new remedies my father was exploring, and insisted she try the cinchona-bark extract from the desert. "If it works," he said, "he can send more. And he said McDonald is on the cutting edge right here in town."

We agreed to extend our Boston visit for a week, mainly for the sake of Mrs. Whitman, and booked passage from New York to Cherbourg on the *Berengaria* for February 16. While Witty tended to his mother, I enjoyed daily walks, despite the bitter cold. I used the electric railway to venture into downtown Boston and explore the colorful waterfront, government square, and historic markets that dated back to the seventeenth century. Haymarket Square bustled on Friday and Saturday, despite February weather, and vendors showed up to sell root vegetables, woven baskets, and a variety of crafts. I escaped the cold in Faneuil Hall, where

I explored its enclosed arcades to find a wonderful array of shops and restaurants, and found comfortable spaces to sit and compose letters to Grace and May Wu. Each day I spent a couple of hours in the public library, which had a respectable legal collection. I read up on inheritance law, taking copious notes to study further on the Atlantic crossing.

We stayed in touch with Busby by telephone during the week. "I managed to get a sh-short article published about Miss Dodge and her claim of being Morel's daughter," Busby said, "but my editor cut me short, so I had to leave out some details."

"Still, you got it published. Congratulations!"

"We didn't run any photographs or letters she planned to submit as evidence. But my little blurb, well, I think it had a big impact," he beamed over the dodgy phone line. "In just three days, the number of claims shot from twenty-five to fifty-three."

"Great," I said with a pinch of sarcasm.

"I'll have to sort through them to see if any have merit, of course. But my editor, you know, he isn't thrilled about having me spend more time at the courthouse than the morgue."

"Still wants to keep you on obituaries, does he?" Witty said. "Well, we appreciate any information you can share. I have a feeling the Morel affair is going to prove to be more interesting than the demise of the average septuagenarian from Pasadena."

"For me, it's already a whole lot more interesting," Busby said. "Some of these claims are pretty imaginative, like the young man from Algeria who says Marcel Morel was his adoptive father. Something about Morel having commercial ties to the colony, and stumbling into an orphanage while on business there, and adopting this baby."

"Any merit to this one?" I asked.

"I doubt it, but I don't suppose you can just count him out. Like I said, most of these people have no concept of legal evidence, but they sure want the money."

"Five million big ones are nothing to sneeze at," Witty said. "Nothing to sneeze at."

We agreed to talk again before the Atlantic crossing, and he promised to send a package of newspaper clippings and notes to us in Paris.

I decided to place one more phone call before heading to Europe, this one to May Wu in the office. She answered in her usual professional tone, but when she heard me on the line her pitch rose and a tremor invaded her voice.

"The most awful man came into the office this morning," she began. "Stunk to high heaven."

"What did he want?"

"Reeked of oil and alcohol. Foulest mouth I've ever heard."

"Why was he there?"

"He marched in and demanded to speak with whoever's in charge of Morel's money. I guess the *L.A. Times* story clued him in that we're managing the estate. Anyway, I think he's a creditor."

"Predator?" I said. "What makes you think that?"

"Creditor, with a c. He says Morel owed him money."

"Bad connection. Sorry. What's his claim?"

"Now that you mention it, he felt like a predator. Said he should get a cut of what comes off two of the rigs in the Santa Fe Springs field, but when I asked about paperwork I thought he was going to haul off and punch me. Says it was all done on a handshake."

"A handshake with a dead man. Sounds like a wildcatter. They're nothing but gamblers." The static on the line did nothing to filter my disdain. "He didn't hit you, did he?"

"No. I'm pretty sure it would've been a right hook, since his left arm didn't seem to work. He wore a glove on his left hand," May Wu said. "Anyhow, when I suggested he'd get further if he had proper paperwork, he stomped out of the office. I still have all the windows open trying to get rid of that smell."

"Sorry you had to go through that, May Wu. Look, keep the door locked while you're alone there."

"Done."

"Why don't you call Busby, from the *Times*, and compare notes. I think he's seen this guy before. Crooked face?"

"Droopy eye, big scar. He looks like a walrus. He's got big dopey eyes, puffy cheeks, a bristly mustache — everything but the tusks. His eyes don't point the same direction, so it's hard to read him. You've never sure where to look when he's talking to you. He didn't even take off his hat when he came into the office."

"Did you get a name?"

"Randy Hardaway. I won't forget him anytime soon."

17

Witty: February 16 — Atlantic Crossing

I'D RESERVED A SUITE OF ROOMS for the Atlantic crossing, first class, with two bedrooms and a drawing room. I had to remind tightwad Reid that we could afford it because we were on an expense account, or at least we would be if we found the rightful heirs.

"Sure, *if* we find the rightful heirs *and* convince them to pursue the legal steps *and* they agree to our commission *and* the expenses get deducted from the inheritance *and* the judge and jury buy our case *and....*"

"My, my," I interrupted. "A little tense, are we?"

"Well, what do we need a sitting room for, anyhow?"

"We'll need it for entertaining and whatnot."

"And just whom do you intend to entertain?" Reid asked with a mix of apprehension and disbelief.

"There's no telling who we'll meet on our journey, my young friend. No telling."

129

I was no stranger to the *RMS Berengaria,* although my previous passage on the ship took place under entirely different circumstances. I was an intelligence officer in the U.S. Navy when I'd made the voyage from Brest to New York on the huge vessel four years earlier. Built in 1912 in Germany for the Hamburg America Line, the ocean liner was originally named the *SS Imperator.* On paper, she was fabulous: the largest ship of her time, at 906 feet long, 98 feet abeam, three funnels, and more than 50,000 tons. But the *Imperator* had an inauspicious start. She struggled with engine fires, instability, stranding, and economic disaster. Her terrible listing earned her the nickname *Limperator.* What a debacle. Engineers discovered that her center of gravity was too high, so they removed all the marble bathroom suites in first class, replaced heavy furniture with lightweight wicker, and poured two thousand tons of cement into the ship's double bottom.

By the time she was reworked and ready to sail in 1914, the world was at war. Horrible times. The ship was laid up at Hamburg and remained inactive for four years, rusting and stuck in the mud on the Elbe until the 1918 Armistice. At that point, she was allocated to the United States for temporary use as transport bringing military personnel home from France. The gigantic ocean liner made three voyages from Brest to New York, returning more than 25,000 troops, nurses, and civilians to America.

Needless to say, I was anxious to get home at the end of the war. Europe was at peace, but it was no place to be. So badly torn apart. A sad scene on so many fronts. After several false starts, I finally got passage aboard the *Imperator* in June of 1919. Little did I know, after its service to the U.S. Military, the ship would be transferred to the British as reparation for the *Lusitania,* and become the new flagship of the Cunard Line. Rechristened the *Berengaria,* she became one of the most elegant and popular liners of her time.

Boarding the massive ship, I rubbed my hands together, eager to compare today's luxury liner to the utilitarian bathtub I remembered. I'd last seen the ship in its dilapidated state, and the dingy room I'd shared with three other men had been the antithesis of first class. Fortunately, in the post-war euphoria, class differences fell away and I was able to mix with civilians, nurses, and fellow military personnel on every level. Each evening, a make-shift band struck up the latest ragtime tunes and occasionally ventured into cutting-edge jazz, which I adored. I often stayed until the wee hours, blowing my bassoon when most passengers had stumbled back to their sleeping quarters.

The new *Berengaria* was a different story altogether. It reeked of elegance. Natural light poured into a spacious first-class lounge through a domed glass ceiling and enormous arched windows. The grand room showcased Italian landscape paintings, elegant wall sconces, and fine wool carpeting with intricate floral designs. I loved this stuff! Crown moldings featured exquisite carvings, and a lush display of palm trees, ivy, and flowers adorned one side of the room. Topping the adjacent ballroom was a smaller, oval-shaped glass ceiling. It looked to me like the towering mahogany columns would be a hazard on the massive parquet dance floor.

My mouth watered as I looked at the ship's options for dining, including the formal Dining Salon, the Ritz Restaurant, a less elegant Garden Restaurant, and an even more casual Palm Court. I scooted past the gymnasium and massive Pompeian swimming pool, and then stuck my head into the first-class Ladies Lounge. I scoped out the smoking room, which had a rustic feel, with a faux brick floor, exposed timbers, and a large fireplace. The stench of stale cigarettes and pipe smoke turned me away, but I figured the best defense would be a strong offense, so I'd come back with my finest cigars in good time. All in good time.

When I popped my head back into our suite, Reid was flaked out in his sleeping quarters, which adjoined a sitting room that attached to my bedroom. He'd already unpacked his bags and settled in for the journey. So neat and tidy. The man liked order, that's for sure. He'd placed a stack of books on the bedside table, Bible on top, and laid out his writing pads and fountain pens on the room's small desk. His suits hung neatly in the closet and no doubt he'd folded sweaters and undergarments into drawers under the bed.

I returned to the upper deck when the ship's whistle blew, so I could take in the sights of the magnificent New York harbor and see landmarks slip away as the huge ship entered open ocean. Though I knew none of the well-wishers on shore, I waved back at a tangle of arms until they were mere dots on the horizon.

I'M AFRAID MY STRAINS OF "FELIX KEPT ON WALKING" on the bassoon pierced Reid's reverie. So much for his afternoon nap. He pulled himself out of bed, ran a comb through his hair, straightened his trousers and shirt, and poked his sleepy head into the sitting room. He looked a bit shocked to see me dancing around the room, bassoon tethered around my neck, serenading a young dame seated on the settee with a bottle of champagne in one hand and a half-empty flute in the other.

"Reid Foster, old boy, meet Sally Wolfe," I said. "She's one of our more lovely traveling companions. I checked."

"Miss Wolfe," Reid said as his initial shock subsided. "Delighted to meet you."

"Delighted, I'm sure." She offered him a glass of champagne in place of a handshake. "Witty bought the whole bottle!" Her flimsy dress hung off her shoulders as if it were still on a coat hanger, giving her the androgynous look that was all the rage.

Reid declined her offer of champagne and suggested that I dress for dinner, then excused himself to do likewise.

"What'll it be tonight, Reid," I said. "I was thinking white dress shirt, white tie, and tuxedo, no tails.

"I wouldn't have a clue."

"Let's do that. No need for gloves or a hat, and we can always return for them if we've made the wrong choice."

We found our way to the first-class dining salon. The elegant room's main floor was nearly full, with tables for two, three, or four filling quickly. The room extended two stories to a graceful domed ceiling, and additional seating was available on a second floor that wrapped around the edges of the room, two tables deep. It left a grand opening in the middle, where the captain and his special guests would dine each evening. My kind of place. The steward asked if we wouldn't mind sitting upstairs, as we appeared more able-bodied than some of the elderly passengers, and the stairway could be a bit of a challenge when the ship was underway. He seated us at a table at the edge of a balcony overlooking the main room, which pleased me to no end because the people-watching was fabulous.

"Such pulchritude!" I said, gazing over the balcony.

"The architecture is stunning, isn't it," Reid said.

"Not that, old boy. The girls! You must have noticed." Two youthful ladies sat with an older couple — perhaps sisters and their parents — marveling at the menu. At another table, two gals who looked to be in their early thirties chatted like teenagers discussing their secret crushes. While older women wore longer skirts of multiple layers, most of the younger set sported mid-calf dresses with dropped waists and straight lines from shoulder to knee, showing off their slender hips. All wore some form of hat adorned with feathers, beadwork, or fabric flowers. Younger ladies seemed to prefer one or two long strands of pearls or beads, and the older crowd stuck with a shorter necklace that rested above the bosom. My eyes feasted on all of it.

A waiter who introduced himself as Thomas explained the menu. He said that he would be our waiter in the Dining Salon throughout the passage, and that we should let him know of special dietary needs or preferences. "Early and often" were mine. Tonight's meal would begin, he said, with an *amuse-bouche* of cantaloupe wrapped with prosciutto, followed by tomato bisque. "Serving sizes are modest, but you can always request a second round," Thomas said in my direction. "You'll be able to choose from three main courses each evening, and again, while we normally serve one choice, the well-fed gentleman may prefer to sample two or three." He had my number! The evening's selections were Sole Frite with tartar sauce, Lobster Newburg, and roast beef with horseradish. "Tonight's dessert is the chef's fabulous Crepe Suzette, a French creation with a hot sauce of caramelized sugar, orange juice, lightly grated orange peel, and citrus liqueur."

I opted for lobster and roast beef, while Reid selected sole. I ordered a bottle of burgundy wine, which posed no legal problem since being at sea excused us from the ridiculous rules of Prohibition. Reid drank water and told Thomas he looked forward to hot tea at the conclusion of the feast. To each his own.

AFTER DINNER, I TOOK REID ASIDE TO ASK if he would mind if the young lady, Miss Wolfe, came back to our sitting room for a nightcap.

"She's a flapper, for Pete's sake!" Reid said.

"What gave her away?" I asked, not even trying to tone down my sarcasm.

Sally's bobbed hair and short, fringed dress were all the rage for young women with a slightly rebellious edge. It worked for me. The dress, which didn't even cover her arms, revealed powdered knees above turned-down hose. She wore makeup on her face, including candy-apple lipstick. A long string of beads hung down to her slim waist and another necklace choked her neck.

"How do you know her, anyway?" Reid said.

"Know her? I just met her. She looked like she'd be a lot of fun on this dreary crossing, so I asked her to the hop."

"The hop?"

"Yes, my friend. You should find yourself a date. Their dance cards fill up fast."

"What are your intentions with Sally?"

"Who are you, her father?" I said. "Lighten up, man, I just want to have a little fun on the voyage. Is that so bad?"

"She's what, half your age?"

"And how!" I knocked back the last of my wine and recited a Dorothy Parker ode to the flapper:

The Playful flapper here we see,
The fairest of the fair.
She's not what Grandma used to be —
You might say, au contraire.
Her girlish ways may make a stir,
Her manners cause a scene,
But there is no more harm in her
Than in a submarine.
She nightly knocks for many a goal
The usual dancing men.
Her speed is great, but her control
Is something else again.
All spotlights focus on her pranks.
All tongues her prowess herald.
For which she well may render thanks
To God and Scott Fitzgerald.
Her golden rule is plain enough —
Just get them young and treat them
rough.

I chuckled and threw Reid a playful punch to the shoulder.

"Do as you wish, Lyle," Reid said. "I've no business telling you how to conduct yourself on this voyage, or anywhere else, for that matter. It's just…"

"It's just what, man? Perhaps you could let it go for ten days, whatever your mother would think, or your God would think. Live a little. Have fun with me."

Reid shook his head and accompanied me back to our quarters.

"It certainly was interesting getting to know your father just a bit in Coachella." I thought the subject might lighten him up. "Fascinating chap. Quite a life."

"Yes, he's never been one to shy from adventure," Reid reflected. "Usually helps people out in some way while he's at it."

"And I'm so pleased that May Wu joined us for the jaunt to the desert." I raised one eyebrow. "Seems to me that you have a very close relationship with her."

Reid looked at the back of his hands.

"Am I right, old boy? I mean, there's more to her than a secretary, if I'm not mistaken. Not that I've been around long enough to put all the pieces together, but if you don't mind me asking…"

"I do mind," Reid interrupted. "May Wu is not a subject I care to discuss with you or anybody else."

"I beg your pardon, my friend. Enough said. Forgive my impertinence."

18

Busby: February 21 — Los Angeles

THE MOREL CASE CONTINUED TO HEAT UP. The number of claimants climbed to well over a hundred. May Wu had told me a couple of weeks earlier about how Randy Hardaway had barged into her office and scared her to pieces, and I just had to follow up. She was terrified. I had no firm evidence tying Hardaway to Morel's death, but I was pretty sure the oil man wasn't in the running for citizen of the year.

Against my editor's wishes, I spent a fair amount of time tracking down Hardaway after the creep scared May Wu, not to mention Violet back at the diner. I did all the research for a great article, but never did get it published. Anyway, sniffing around in the oil fields of Santa Fe Springs and Signal Hill, I figured out that Hardaway was a wildcatter who had drilled wells on speculation all across the country. Originally from Pennsylvania, the guy had been on the move since his early twenties, following oil booms through

West Virginia, Louisiana, Ohio, Illinois, Florida, and even Mexico and Colombia.

Rumor had it that Hardaway had little education, having left school as a boy to work in a Pittsburgh flour mill. The job required long hours for low wages, typically just $16 a month. His mill-working career ended when his left sleeve got caught in a grinding mill's massive gears, badly mangling his arm and nearly pulling his head into the machine. He spent more than a year in the hospital, unsure at age twenty whether he would ever see blue sky again. When he gained enough strength, he left Pittsburgh and got his first job building derricks in the oil fields of West Virginia, despite limited use of his left arm.

Hardaway learned the drilling trade quickly but found himself unable to stick with a crew because he kept getting into fights and sure didn't want to take orders from an oil company boss. So he developed an itinerant lifestyle, pulling together enough men to drill a well or two in the most promising new fields. Superstition played a big role in determining where to drill, and he succeeded just often enough to barely get by. His crews never stayed together long, and he'd been on the move his entire life.

By the time he arrived in Los Angeles in 1922, at age fifty-four, Hardaway feared he'd missed the boat. Signal Hill was dubbed "Porcupine Hill" for its prickly appearance, covered with hundreds of wooden oil derricks. By 1923, the Los Angeles basin accounted for 20 percent of world oil production and the automobile's rise pushed prices from sixty-four cents a barrel in 1916 to more than three dollars in 1920. With few regulations on well spacing and leases, the industry developed a Wild West atmosphere.

Hardaway had a reputation for slanting his drill bores underneath neighboring properties, draining oil from adjacent leases. The practice was unethical at best, and probably illegal, but hard to prove. Of course, he never stayed in one place long enough to find out. I was pretty sure Hardaway must be tied to Morel's death, but for the life of me I could not connect the dots. If only I could break the case, I'd graduate from obits for good.

I put as much of this as I could into a letter to the guys and mailed it to the U.S. Embassy in Paris. Seemed like they should know about this scoundrel.

19

Reid: March 4 — Goult

I NEVER UNDERSTOOD THE ALLURE OF BABETTE REVILLE and her
power to draw Witty into her web. Sure, she had curves in all
the right places and she dressed like a movie star, but I'd always
figured those types couldn't be trusted. She didn't evoke any sense
of depth, but apparently that's not what Witty was after. Somehow,
somewhere in the *Département de Vaucluse*, she must have put her
spell on the poor man. Maybe the allure of Provence enhanced her
charm, at least in Witty's eyes.

When the Duesenberg pulled into Goult, a tiny village in the
Luberon Valley, I got out to inquire at a café about possible rooms
to rent. The town of Goult perched on a hill, as did every village in
the Luberon. The settlements dated back to medieval times when
hilltops provided security against marauders from neighboring
towns. With the advent of the automobile, each outcropping felt
close to the next — only ten or fifteen minutes away — but back
in the day of travel on foot and horseback, the hilltops signified

greater distance. Some of the towns showed remains of stone walls, ramparts, and cannon bays, and each community had its own church and cemetery.

The Café de la Poste, marked by a windowed arch above its double wooden doors, looked out on the town square and appeared to be the center of activity in the tiny village. Three cars were parked in front, one being a small Citroën painted red and white to match the establishment's prominent sign. Several patrons sat at the bar drinking pastis or absinthe, which I found disturbing, particularly for a Sunday afternoon.

The barman walked me out the front door, pointed up a narrow street, and indicated that in the third house on the right, Madame Henri might have rooms available. She had turned her home into a guest house after losing her husband and two of her three sons in the Great War. Goult wasn't exactly a tourist destination, the barman said, but the widow patched together a living from the trickle of people passing through on their way here and there.

Madame Henri was a stout woman with graying hair and tender eyes. She reminded me of Witty's mother in Boston — younger, but worn down by a difficult life.

"Might you have room for the three of us?" Witty inquired.

"How long are you staying?"

"Not quite sure. Let's say a week."

"How many rooms? Are you married to this lady? Is he?" she gestured toward me, and I withdrew a step.

"No, my good lady. We're here to do some research," Witty said. "Strictly business. Three rooms, if you have them."

"Let me show you what I have. The third room is a bit small, in the attic, but we can set up a bed and make it work if you're staying just a week," she said. "My middle son used to live up there, and he found it comfortable enough."

I could only imagine the tragedy this poor woman had endured, like so many others in Europe during the Great War. Most families had lost one or more men to the terrible fighting, and it seemed that the continent had sacrificed nearly a whole generation to the conflict. Of course many Americans put their lives on the line as well, including Witty and two of my cousins, but upon meeting Madame Henri I realized that these families lost not one or two members, but often more. And for what?

"Reid, my good man, you're young and fit," Witty said. "Perhaps you'd volunteer for the attic just this once."

"Of course," I said. "I'd be honored to sleep in your son's room, Madame."

Apart from the fact that I had to duck under its low ceiling, the tiny room suited me just fine: private, cozy, with a little desk by a window that opened eastward to capture the morning sun. I set my books and letters on the desk. I placed my Bible by the bed, and put sheets on a mattress we'd hauled up narrow stairs from a storage space below. Other than a little dust and a musty smell, it seemed comfortable enough. I opened the window and reached to push open a wooden shutter, which proved quite a reach because the stone walls of the massive old building were so thick. A warm breeze pushed in fresh air, and I peeked out across the tile roofs of the village.

Once we were settled into the guest house, the three of us set out to explore the small town before afternoon light faded. We climbed up a narrow street, which rose to the south until it took a sharp turn to avoid a steep cliff that dropped off to a spectacu-lar view of the Luberon Valley. Remnants of old city walls were still visible.

"Just think how difficult it would be to attack from this side," Witty mused, "especially if soldiers were sending cannonballs and vats of hot oil down on their enemies, as they tended to do in the not-so-good-old medieval times."

The valley below was a patchwork of farms. I guessed apples, pears, and cherries, based on the climate. The trees, nearing the end of their spring bloom, held on to a few pink and white blos-soms and a delicate display of emerging leaves. Other fields were varying shades of green, probably alfalfa in the dark hues, wheat or barley the lighter. A few homes dotted the landscape, along with the occasional barn, but it appeared that most houses nestled in hilltop towns, leaving the fertile valley floor for farming. Good planning.

We worked our way along the cliff top and picked up a ridge-top road curving back to the north. Soon we arrived at the base of the town's lone windmill, an odd feature in this part of the world. "I thought those only worked in Holland," Babette said, craning her neck to see the full height of the structure. "It's not even turning."

"Not enough wind today," Witty said.

"Oh, I see now what is a windmill. Serve me some humility pie." Still learning our idioms.

"No shame in asking, my lamb. Today there's just not enough wind, which is fine with me. The weather couldn't be more delightful." Witty noted the sharp contrast to the frigid air we'd left behind in Paris.

A cat ran across the road and scooted through a garden, up a fence, and into an open window, pushing aside a lace curtain that provided a thin veil of privacy. Down the next hill, houses were built into native stone in a way that made it difficult to tell where earth ended and masonry began. It was a short stroll back to the center of town, a modest square bordered by the Café de la Poste to the west, a row of stores — butcher, bakery, and green grocer — to the south, homes to the east, and a small church to the north.

In the center of the square stood a stone monument, a simple, four-sided column, twenty feet high, carved with the names of local men who had perished in the Great War. Sunlight slanted across engraved lettering, giving it a depth that seemed appropriate. On one side was written *"Aux Enfants de Goult, Morts Pour La Patrie, 1914-1918."* Around the top of the column were the words *Patrie, Honneur, Justice, and Gloire.* The names of those who had sacrificed their lives for country were divided by year, with the casualties highest in 1917.

We spotted the surname Henri in several places and could only assume that the lives lost were loved ones of our hostess. Other names included:

BOURNOT Louis
BONNOT Emile
VERGER Joseph
BRANCHE Louis
DOCHE Louis
IMBERT Albert
BOURDON Leon
GREGOIRE Leon
BOST Jean
CHAVIN Clovis
CHABAUD Celestin
LAUGIER Marcel

The list went on, names carved in stone, lives cut short in battle.

"Look!" shouted Witty. "Come and see this."

I walked to Witty's side and followed his finger to the name "MOREL Emmanuel." Witty did a little hop. "This is what I live for. The treasure hunt is on, my friend. We're on the trail now."

"Yes, but, how do we know…"

"It's an unusual family name, my good man," Witty said. "In Goult, a town of what, a hundred, two hundred at the most?"

"But who was Emmanuel? We don't even know his age."

"That's why we're here." Witty turned with open arms to the little town square. "The monument, the church, the graveyard, even the café. This is how it's done. We've picked up the scent."

"Okay, what's next?"

THE NEXT DAY, WE SPLIT UP AND tried chatting up the locals.

"Why don't Babsie and I visit the café. Seems to be a popular spot." Witty took Babette's arm.

"I was thinking of a visit to the church," I said. "Maybe they'll have some records that'll start to fill in the blanks."

"Outstanding. It's a plan. And tomorrow we can stroll through the cemetery,"

The church on the north side of the town square appeared stark and simple, the opposite of the vast cathedrals of Paris. The church dated to the seventeenth century, built of local stone to form a straightforward rectangle. No arches, no flying buttresses, no intricate carvings. A square clocktower loomed over the structure. Its small bell, suspended atop the tower by a tangle of iron work, rang on the half hour and hour. A weather vane in the shape of a rooster perched over the structure. The building's roof, like many in the village, featured rounded tiles stacked intricately toward a peaking ridgeline. A few tall, narrow windows, sharply arched at the top, let light in through clear glass — a far cry from the elaborate rose windows of Sainte Chapelle and Notre Dame de Paris.

I entered through a small door that was cut into a larger wooden door. I stepped inside, cherishing the quiet, cool atmosphere and paused a moment to feel the presence of the Lord. While I admired the workmanship of grand cathedrals, I somehow felt closer to God in a simple little church like this. Who was I to judge what God's preference might be, but I've always favored simplicity over ostentation. I saw nobody inside, so I made my way to the altar, where two large bouquets of fresh flowers suggested recent activity. I knelt to offer a prayer of gratitude and hope. With nobody to interview, and not wanting to snoop, I decided to return to my attic sanctuary.

When I returned to the guest house, I saw Madame Henri coming out of the cellar with her apron pulled up to carry a lapfull of root vegetables. "Allow me to get the door for you, Madame," I said in my most polite French. Not sure it was correct, but it was worth a try. "May I help you carry those?"

"No, thank you, young man." She scooted up the stairs. "But do join me in the kitchen if you would like. I can open some table wine."

"Thank you, but I don't drink alcohol."

"Good, then join me for a cup of tea and I'll get started chopping vegetables for my stew." The kitchen already smelled heavenly, as she'd braised a rabbit with some onions and set it aside for stew. She told me it would cook slowly all night and be ready for tomorrow's lunch. "What brings you to our little village? We don't get many Americans through here since the end of the war."

I explained, briefly, the death of Marcel Morel in Los Angeles, his lack of close connections, and the mystery of his ancestry. I told her about the photo of Estelle and the identification card from *Département de Vaucluse* indicating he might be from this area.

"I think my mother knew an Estelle here in Goult who had two or three children, but they didn't stay. I don't remember exactly what happened to the family. Some tragedy, I think, and they vanished from town." She waved her knife in the air as if trying to stab at some elusive memory. "There was a dark story behind their departure, but it escapes me now. I just know that by the time I was in school, there were no Morel children among us."

"Forgive me if I sound impertinent, Madame, but what years were you in school here?"

"Let me think." She traced numbers in the air with her knife. "I'm fifty-one now, born in 1872, so let's say I started at age five. That would be 1877, no?"

"Excellent. And you did not know any Morel children?

"No, I'm almost certain." She took a sip of tea and thought for a moment. "I have a brother who is four years older. Maybe he'd know something. When do you think this Marcel was born?"

"We believe 1859. We're not exactly sure when he arrived in America, but it may have been the early eighties."

Madame Henri went back to chopping her vegetables with the skill of a surgeon. "You should find my brother, Bernard. He's likely to be at the bar down the street at this hour. You know, Café de la Poste. He goes there most days when he's done in the apple orchard. His last name is Chabaud."

"Café de la Poste," I said. "Is that the only pub in town, then?"

"Yes. It's the place for coffee and croissants in the morning, a decent meal at midday, and the pub in the evening," she said. "A few of our villagers mix up their hours, so don't be surprised if you see some stray drinkers at the bar in the morning. I never know if they're getting an early start on the day or a late finish on the night. In any case, the Café is pretty much the center of town. It also has a telegraph and, rumor has it, a telephone, though I've never had occasion to use one."

I finished my tea and excused myself to go upstairs.

20

Witty: March 4 — Goult

IT DIDN'T TAKE BABETTE AND ME LONG TO FIGURE OUT that the Café de la Poste served as café, business center, pub, and meeting place. We noticed that the other hub of activity was a bakery, where locals popped in to get their afternoon baguette or the occasional *tarte*. It was standing room only all afternoon. In fact, if one hesitated to contemplate the virtues of *baguette simple* versus *baguette a l'ancien*, one might create a line out the door of the tiny *boulangerie*.

Clientele at the bar consisted of men who looked like they were ready to wind down after a hard day of labor. Several wore the blue coveralls of farmers, and others may have been masons, carpenters, drivers, or workers in nearby fruit packing houses. Conversations covered weather, the price of cheese, the local soccer team, and more about weather. I asked the bartender for a recommendation on a local white, and he redirected me to red if I really wanted local. The barman gestured to a table and suggested we take it there. I got the hint the bar was no place for a lady. Or were we being singled out because I was American? Either way, it could be difficult to chat up the locals about the Morel family.

"My darling, you look so lovely this evening in your red dress and black hat. How did you find a shade of lipstick that goes so well with your outfit?" I gushed, pouring the wine. It looked heavy as I swirled it in the glass. "Good legs, just like you."

"Oh, you're sweet like the honey!" Charming syntax. So sexy.

"Now, if you don't mind, I'm going to venture over to the bar and chat up a couple of gentlemen who might know something about our Monsieur Morel," I said. "You don't mind sitting by yourself for a few minutes, do you?"

"Of course not. You have important work. I understand."

"And if you do visit with anyone, it might be a good idea not to mention too much about the case. You know, funny things can happen when people find out there's a load of money on the table."

Reid entered the Café de la Poste and noticed Babette sitting alone at a table nursing a glass of wine. He didn't see me, and I just waited to see what he would do. He approached Babette. She seemed perfectly content by herself, staring at nothing in particular.

"May I join you?" he asked, taking off his hat.

"The pleasure would be for me," she said. "Let's get you a glass, er, a cup of tea. Witty tells me you don't consume alcohol."

"Not a problem. I've just come from the guest house where I had a cup of tea with Madame Henri."

The pleasantries continued, and Reid sat down and filled her in on his conversation with Madame Henri.

"Do you think you're making tracks, Reid?" Babette said. "Any progress?"

"I must say, I'm beginning to feel more optimistic," he replied. "We may finally be on to something here. Right now I'm looking for a farmer named Bernard Chabaud, about fifty-five years old. He might be here in the bar."

"That's nice." She lifted the red wine to her lips. "I was wondering, Reid, how the legal part works."

"What do you mean?"

"Well, let's say that Marcel Morel had a child, you know, even though he wasn't married. I mean, let's just pretend that he did. Would that child get his five million dollars?"

"I can see that our friend Witty has shared some of the details of the case with you," Reid said.

She giggled. "Well, how does it work, I mean a relative by blood who's not, you know, a 'legitimate' child?"

"In fact, inheritance laws honor blood lines," Reed said. "Why do you ask?"

"Just curious like the cat," she said. She took another sip of wine.

Reid finally noticed me at the bar and excused himself, leaving Babette with her wine. He scooted in between the patrons and placed a hand on my shoulder. In our fancy garb, we had no chance of looking inconspicuous among working men at the bar. I took Reid's arrival as an opportunity for formal introductions all around. I was determined to get the name of everyone we met, and in truth would have appreciated their mothers' maiden names.

Reid lit up when one of the men introduced himself as Bernard Chabaud, an apple grower in the valley. The other gentleman, François Cortasse, grew pears on the neighboring ranch. Reid gave me a look that indicated these men were worth further investigation, and we promptly invited them to move to our table. François said he had to get home to his wife, but Bernard gladly accepted the invitation.

Bernard Chabaud was a stocky man, his weathered face reflecting every one of his fifty-some years of hard work in the orchards. His attentive eyes were the color of wild irises. His broad grin gave the appearance that he had more than the conventional number of teeth.

After proper introductions, Reid jumped right into his line of questioning.

"Is it true, sir, that you are the brother of Madame Henri who runs the guest house just up the street?"

"Why yes, how did you know?" Bernard seemed a bit startled.

"We were just discussing your history," Reid said. I kicked him under the table and gestured for him to calm down. No need to make our sole lead feel like he was under interrogation. Reid took the hint. Too lawyerly. Reid explained that the three of us had just rolled into town and had been lucky enough to find rooms in his sister's guest house.

"Lovely place," I added.

"And your sister is a real gem," Babette piped in.

Eventually Reid returned to his line of questioning, but with a less officious tone this time. Bernard said he attended school at the same time as the youngest of the three Morel children. He didn't know her — just knew of her — because she was four or five years ahead of him in school.

"You know how it is," he said. "Four of five years is a lifetime when you're that age. But you know the older kids' names, even if they have no idea that you exist. In fact, there was this one girl, Nathalie, three years older, who had no clue who I was, but I was pretty sure I was in love with her." He chuckled at the memory.

"What do you know of the Morel family now?" I asked. I would've loved to have heard about past crushes, but we had to stay on task.

"I don't really know," Bernard said. A somber look came over his face. "It's been decades since I thought of them. You know, one of those tragic stories you try to forget."

We ordered some food and asked him to share anything and everything he could remember.

Bernard recalled that the Morel family, like so many in Goult, had worked in the apple and pear business. They got by, just barely supporting themselves and their three children. They were always playing music. Estelle, the mother, played piano and sang, and the kids seemed to be able to pick up any instrument and play it at first sight. Marcel and his brother Paul played violin, and Marie gravitated to piano and organ. Even as a young girl, she played the church organ on some occasions.

"What about the father?" I asked.

"Don't know much about the father. I think his name was Jean-Louis or Jean-Mari. Jean-something, for sure. He kept to himself. No music there, not even much conversation. He was a bit strange, from what little I knew. I'll tell you in a minute what happened to him, but first let me get to the real story." Reid took out his note-book to jot down details.

"It was toward the end of the school year, late spring, and I don't know whether Marie was due to graduate or still had one year to go. As I said, she had four or five years on me, but I know she was still in school. Her brothers had graduated. Marcel was the eldest, let's say nineteen or twenty, with Paul right behind him. They worked in the pear orchard and, like any teenagers with too much time on their hands, they were a bit rowdy."

"Boys are like that," Babette chimed in. I put my hand on hers and motioned for Bernard to continue.

"I'm not sure anybody really knew all the details, and of course it was more than forty years ago, but my understanding was that the boys took off one weekend, without permission, and made their way to the source of the Sorgue River. It's the strangest place, about twenty kilometers west of here. You can visit it these days no problem, but it seemed far at the time. Anyhow, the river comes surging up out of a hole in the ground in a volume that you just cannot believe. You just have to see it for yourself to understand what I'm talking about. At this time of year there will be a bit of water, but later in the spring, it's beyond your wildest imagination." He went on to describe a huge pool of unknown depth that welled up from the base of tremendous cliffs, perhaps 250 meters high. From the pool, the water tumbled over a lip and roared into a gorge, racing through enormous boulders and waterfalls toward the town below, where it took a sharp left and flattened out into the Sorgue River.

"I noticed the signs for Isle-sur-la-Sorgue when we drove in from Avignon," Reid said. "I assume it's a town on the same river."

"Yes, and it's well worth a visit, too. The river divides into several channels that run through town, and each branch has water wheels dating back to the twelfth century." The town, he explained, had been the chief city of the Comtat, known for its silk, wool, and paper.

"Fascinating," I interjected. "Simply fascinating. And what of our boys, Marcel and Paul?"

"Right. The boys." A somber look returned to Bernard's animated face. He lit a cigarette and took a deep drag, blowing it out toward the ceiling. "The story is that the boys — probably fueled by a bit too much to drink, and maybe on a dare from their pals — stole a boat from a house in town. You'll see if you visit — which you really should — that people leave their boats tied up right outside their homes on either side of the river, once it flattens out. So it would be easy to take one." He put down his cigarette and took a sip of wine. "That's what they did. They stole a boat and hauled it up to the huge pool at the source. Who knows whether they meant to plunge over the lip, or if the dare was to come as close as possible without going over. But over they went, and of course it shattered the little wooden boat."

Babette gasped.

"And it shattered the boys. It's just that, well, Marcel lived and Paul did not." He took another swig. "I still remember the mood in town in the weeks following the accident. Nobody could talk about it, but it was the only thing on people's minds. Of course, as kids, we whispered about it among ourselves, but the adults sort of shut down for what seemed like a very long time."

"Did they hold a funeral for the boy?" Reid asked.

"Yes, and the entire town spent the day memorializing him and trying to console the parents."

"And the parents were Estelle and...?" I asked.

153

"The father, Jean-something…I'm not sure," he hesitated. "It'll come back to me, or we can ask someone who remembers. But the father, he's the real tragedy."

"You mean Paul's death wasn't tragic enough?" Babette asked.

"Well, yes, of course it was. But the father was absolutely devastated. He never recovered from the grief, and some say the anger. About a month after the funeral the father took his own life. Hung himself from the rafters of their pear shed."

"*Mon dieu!*" Babette whispered under her breath.

Bernard speculated that Marcel may have been able to live with the death of his younger brother, which many said was just a dreadful accident. One of the many perils of restless youth. But the loss of his father weighed heavily on him. The combination proved too much for him to endure. He disappeared that summer. "Some thought he may have also taken his own life, but there was no body, and he did take some belongings with him," he said. "A few clothes, books, his violin, you know — they say he didn't have much. I don't think he was ever heard from again, at least not that anybody mentioned." Reid scribbled in his notebook, trying to capture every detail. My mind always latched onto details like Chabaud's mention of the violin. It's what fascinated me about my work. Reid no doubt was thinking about the kind of evidence he would need to convince judge and jury that we had the right man.

"Had you ever heard that he went to America?" I asked. "Did he write to his family?"

"No. I suppose that, even if he wrote letters to his mother, she wouldn't have wanted to share his news with the townspeople," Chabaud speculated. "We may never know."

With apologies, Bernard Chabaud excused himself to find his way home. His wife would be wondering where he was, as it was well past dark and they had chatted right through the dinner hour.

"Of course, my good man," I said. "Please offer our collective apology to your lovely wife. You've been most helpful."

"Do you think we could find time tomorrow to continue the story?" Reid asked. "You've been extremely helpful so far. You might have more thoughts tonight about the history. We'd like to know more about what happened to the mother and sister. And maybe you'll think of further details about Marcel and Paul."

"I'll be at work by sunrise tomorrow if you'd care to come by the ranch in the morning. My tractor's been acting up, so chances are I'll be in the shed," Bernard said. "Take the road south out of town, turn right at the river, and mine's the second barn on the right. You'll see the sign, *Chabaud et Fils*, on the barn."

21

Reid: March 5 — Goult

An orange glow through my attic window told me the time had come to dress, wake Witty, and find our way to Bernard Chabaud's barn. I had arranged the night before to rent the little Citroën from the café's owner for at least a day, maybe two or three.

I ventured outside toward the town square, rubbed my hands and hunched my shoulders against the frosty dawn. I would enjoy a little time alone before Witty was ready to head out. I smelled stale wood smoke from fires that had died in the night. The rising sun reflected off the bottom of cumulus clouds to the east, bringing a radiant glow to the valley that dropped away from the hilltop town. A few brilliant rays streamed under clouds and made their way to the church clock tower, lighting the bell suspended in silence above. At the Great War monument, I pressed my finger over letters engraved into chilly stone, cold as the dead whose names I read. I walked around each face of the pillar, reading the words "Country, Honor, Justice, and Glory." I thought of my girls, playful and innocent in the idyllic world of Southern California, and prayed they would never know the horrors of war. I prayed for all the children of this world that this horrendous conflict truly would be the war to end all wars, as the politicians liked to say.

Witty emerged from the guest house looking like a man dragged from his bed too soon, eyes bleary, hair protruding at angles that defied gravity. He squinted at the day, although the early light was still gentle, and we made our way to Café de la Poste. The barman had to run up the street to the bakery to retrieve a couple of croissants for us, and he boiled water for a pot of tea.

At the barn, we found Bernard hunched over a tractor, muttering French words that weren't taught in American schools or uttered by polite society. Witty told me he recognized a few choice phrases from his days in the Navy. Bernard said he needed a certain wrench, which his neighbor might have, and asked if we would walk with him through the orchard to find Monsieur Cortasse.

The last of the blossoms still clung to their trees like delicate white pearls reflecting the morning sun. Bernard wore rubber boots and blue coveralls, as seemed standard for every French farmer, while Witty and I picked our way through the field in our street shoes and dress pants. Within three minutes, my socks and trousers were soaked through as dew from the morning grass found its way deep into each fiber below knee level. Fecund soil, the color of chocolate cake, worked its way into my shoes and squished between my toes.

"Last night my wife and I went over and over this story," Bernard said, setting off through rows of trees at a pace we found impossible to match. "It's been years since we gave it much thought, but a few things came up. They might interest you."

"Do tell, my good man, do tell." Witty huffed to keep up. The rich ground smelled faintly of mushrooms.

"Another part of the story, which I had forgotten, just adds to the tragedy of it all." His breath was visible in the chill. "It had to do with Paul's girlfriend, Annette." He said that Paul and Annette had planned to marry that summer, although they were just out of school and only eighteen years old. They'd been sweethearts through high school, and never had any doubt that they would marry and start a family. In fact, in the months after Paul's death, it became evident that they had jumped the gun. Annette was pregnant with Paul's child.

"Of course, she couldn't stay in town," Bernard continued. "It was just too scandalous. Even with Paul's death, there was no support for this poor girl having a child, you know, without a husband. Her parents sent her away to have the baby — my wife thinks to Paris — and we don't believe she ever came back."

"Do you know the child's name, or where they ended up?" Witty asked.

"Not a thing," Bernard said. "Annette vanished from our lives and, as far as we know, she never returned."

Bernard found his neighbor and they went off in search of the wrench.

"Fascinating stuff," Witty said. "What do you make of it?" I ran the numbers in my head. Annette, if she were still alive would now be sixty-two, and her child, born in 1880, would be forty-three years old. The ages aligned with what we knew about Gilbert Morel, the night watchman at the Louvre. I knew from my brief meeting with Gilbert in Paris that he was forty-three, played the viola, had natural musical talent, and knew little to nothing about his father.

"Looks like we need to find out a lot more about Gilbert," Witty said. "We can revisit him on our way back through Paris, but it looks for all the world like he's Marcel Morel's nephew." When Bernard returned from his chat with Monsieur Cortasse, we slogged back to the barn. We quizzed Bernard about Marcel's sister, Marie, who was still in school when tragedy struck the Morel family.

"You know, I think Estelle, the mother, decided it was just too painful to stay in Goult. In a town this size — even today — everybody knows everything about everybody, and there's just no escaping your past. No chance to reinvent yourself. I imagine they wanted to get away from the constant pity. I know I would."

"Where did they go?" I asked.

"Roussillon." He gestured northeast. "It's not far. You can see it from the windmill in Goult. But it's a world away, if you know what I mean."

"Yes, yes, of course," Witty nodded. "Far enough to start fresh in a new community. Just what the doctor ordered, I'm sure."

"My wife thinks Marie married into the ochre business there, but I really don't know. Once a person leaves Goult, we tend to lose track of them."

Witty and I thanked Bernard profusely. I asked if I could write up a document for him to sign, which we could submit in court in lieu of a personal appearance. "It'll save you a trip to California to testify at the trial."

"Then I'm all for it," Bernard said, with a look that indicated he would never make it as far as Avignon, not to mention Paris or the United States. "You can find me at Café de la Poste most afternoons, or here every morning except Sunday."

THE VILLAGE OF ROUSSILLON WAS INDEED VISIBLE from the windmill in Goult. Looking across the valley to the northeast, the next hilltop town appeared colorful, with varying shades of red rock glowing even from a distance. We piled into the tiny Citroën, with my lanky frame folded in the minimalist backseat to make room for Babette up front, and made our way to Roussillon. The town, a little bigger than Goult, perched on a far more dramatic cliff.

Roussillon had grown up around the ochre trade. Since the 1700s, workers had mined the colorful mineral from cliffs that varied in hue from bright yellow to deep red. Years of mining and erosion left the area looking as if a giant bear had clawed its canyon walls. The rich pigment had been sent to all corners of the world to color everything from artists' palettes to textiles.

The buildings of Roussillon — including its houses, shops, and restaurants that stair-stepped up a steep hill to a church at the summit — took on tones of the surrounding cliffs. All the building materials were harvested from nearby soils and stone, which made the town glow with oranges, reds, pinks, and yellows visible for miles around. The Citroën groaned under the weight of three passengers as it climbed to the saddle of a ridge where the town rose to the west and tombstones dotted a hill to the east.

"Reid, my good man, you must fill me in on how depositions work," Witty said with a glance into the rear-view mirror. "Sorry to talk business, Babette, but we're on a mission here." She giggled.

"What do you need to know?" I tried shifting in the tiny seat, but found nowhere to go.

"Well, does the court consider depositions with the same weight as live testimony? Are they binding? How are they presented? When are they used?"

"Okay. If a witness is unavailable for trial, the court will accept a deposition in lieu of live testimony. In the past I've used them when a witness is seriously ill — even posthumously — but in this case we'll use them because the witnesses are out of the district and more than one hundred miles away."

"Only a hundred miles? That's nothing these days!"

"Not everyone has access to the automobile, Witty."

"No, but we have trains and buses and whatnot."

"You're right," I admitted. "The rules of discovery are under debate back home. Some believe the deposition is on its way out, but others feel it provides equal access for witnesses of all means, physical states, and locations. It's a question of equal access to due process. The idea is to preserve potential testimony and prevent delay of justice."

"And we can just take this testimony, with no opposing counsel, or whatever you call it?"

"That's right. If you really want details, since 1842, the Federal Equity Rules have allowed a party or the party's counsel to conduct questioning during examination. We can pose follow-up questions, conduct a thorough interview, and submit it basically as an examiner's report."

"Now you sound like a lawyer." He put a hand on Babette's knee, offering silent apology for the business chatter. "So our witnesses just have to sign it."

"Yes. I expect when we get back home this trial will have days' or weeks' worth of depositions for presentation to a jury."

Witty parked at the edge of the town square, which nestled into a sort of topographic saddle, defined on its northern side by a vertiginous red cliff that dropped away to the valley floor far below. The morning market was just finishing in the town square, and farmers were busy packing what remained of their produce.

"Do you hold the market here every day?" I asked one of the vendors, who hefted a basket of turnips onto a cart behind a sturdy-looking horse.

"No, just Monday. Tomorrow we go to Isle-Sur-La-Sorgue, Wednesday to Goult, Thursday Gordes, and so on." He offered me a turnip, but I politely declined, having no need to cook.

"Let's stroll through the cemetery first," Witty said. "Maybe it'll tell us something about the town's prominent families."

On a hillside just east of the town square, tombstones echoed the colorful geology of Roussillon. Near the cemetery's entrance, a large crypt with crimson walls and an arched roof bore the name of *la famille DeFrasne*. The crypt resembled a miniature cathedral. An elaborate cross loomed over an arched doorway that featured ornate wrought iron gates hanging from sturdy columns of stone. Other monuments to the departed were slightly less imposing, but intricate nonetheless. One column, about eight feet tall, featured sophisticated carvings with a family crest and religious icons. It bore the family name of Lazare. Toward the center of the cemetery, a monument reminiscent of the one in Goult honored the men who had perished in the Great War.

The cemetery afforded an extraordinary view of Roussillon to the west, the valley to the south, and russet cliffs to the north and east. In the distance, far north, a mountain loomed above the valley, its white peak emerging above the clouds. From this viewpoint, it would be easy to mistake the peak's topping for snow, but I'd read that Mont Ventoux appeared white because of limestone deposits at its 6,000-foot peak.

Fresh flowers adorned several gravesites, and a stooped old man with thick hands and a weathered face tended a little garden at the entrance of a small crypt. I shot him a sympathetic look and wondered who lay there: wife? children? even grandsons? The war had ravaged an entire generation of young men, probably the age of this man's grandchildren.

After a good survey of the grounds, I doubled back to Witty and Babette, who'd made their way up and down about half the rows.

"Noticing any patterns?" Witty asked.

"Yes. The Mathieu family certainly is prominent in this town," I said. "Has been for several generations, from the looks of it."

"Good observation." Witty took Babette's hand. "I'm always amazed by how much you learn about a community from a visit to its cemetery. The name Mathieu does appear often."

"And I've seen a few other families, like Madon and Donat."

"I noticed a few with a couple of family names together," Babette said, "Like Henri and Donat, or this one, Jacqueline Bessalem — née DeFrasne. How would my name sound, Babette Whitman, née Reville."

"Now, now," Witty said. "Let's not get ahead of ourselves."

"Did you say you came upon one with the name Henri?" I asked, coming to his rescue.

"Yes, back there, toward the end of that row."

I walked over to it, wondering if the deceased were a relative of our hostess at the guest house. "What we're really looking for, of course, is Morel. Has anyone seen Morel?"

Nobody had, so we made the rounds one more time to make sure we hadn't missed anything. I took out my notepad and jotted down the names of the prominent families, Mathieu being far and away the most frequent.

Afternoon sun brought pleasant warmth to the hillside cemetery and added a rich glow to varying shades of red and yellow stone throughout the graveyard.

"Is anyone thirsty?" Witty asked.

"I'd love a drink, honey."

"Let's see what we can find in the big town of Roussillon, Babsie," he said, taking her arm and motioning for me to come along.

"Why don't you two go ahead," I said. "I'd like to take a walk into the ochre canyons." We agreed to meet back at the Citroën at dark, if we hadn't found each other in town before then.

I noticed a trail that led uphill to the east and followed a ridge through sparse pines, interspersed with oaks, before it curved north and dropped into a series of dramatic cliffs. The ground smelled of cool earth and wet stones.

Up ahead, a sheer precipice dropped at least one-hundred feet, exposing a range of colors and textures along the way. One enormous tree root reached down at least fifteen feet over the edge of the cliff, passing from the top layer of rosy soil down into a bright yellow band of rock, then a profound vermillion layer, and back into golden colors that stretched most of the way down to the base. I continued along the trail, which wound steeply downward and then leveled off at the bottom of more cliffs.

The clay formations looming above my head reminded me of a descent into Bryce Canyon, which I'd visited with Father several years earlier. The columns of red and yellow, remarkable striations, and "hoodoos" left from years of erosion could have been in Utah, not southern France, though Bryce dwarfed Roussillon for scale. I heard the rumble of a truck on the ridge above and followed a trail branch that climbed in that direction.

163

By the time I reached a road at the top of the next ridge, I'd taken off my jacket and tie and rolled up my sleeves. Runnels of sweat streamed down my back and I brushed the hair off my damp forehead. A truck rolled to a stop. The driver seemed startled to see me and asked if I needed help.

"I would appreciate a ride back toward town, if you're going that direction," I said. I would have been happy to walk, and even may have preferred the solitude of a hike through the forest, but I also wanted to see what I might learn from the driver.

"What in the name of Mary and Joseph are you doing out here?" the driver said.

"Research on some family history." I climbed into the seat. "Are you from this area?"

The driver, covered with a fine layer of orange dust, appeared to be in his late thirties or early forties. A *Gauloise* hung from his lower lip, and he wore a blue cap that did little to contain his curly brown hair, which escaped around his ears and down his neck. His crinkly brown eyes sparkled from under the brim of his cap, and his broad smile revealed a couple of missing teeth. "I grew up in Roussillon, but now I drive as far as Marseille," he explained. "We haul ochre to the port twice a week."

"Really. I didn't know it was an international business."

"Oh yeah. They say it goes to all the places our country colonized over the years. The stuff reminds the French settlers of home or something. I guess there aren't a lot of sources like the one we're on here. Been going for hundreds of years."

"Fascinating." I took out my notebook but found it impossible to write with the truck bouncing over the rough road. "Do you happen to know anyone from the Morel family? Might originally be from Goult?"

The truck jostled over a washboard section of the road, which took a slight turn to the right, prescribed by a sheer cliff to the left. I feared the driver was taking it too fast, but told myself the man had lived this long without an American in a suit telling him

164

how to handle his truck, so I kept quiet and tried to remember to breathe. The driver showed no fear, although he did finally bother to take the cigarette from his mouth after the shimmying shook its dangling ashes all over his lap.

"Sorry, this section's a bit rough. I wish they'd fix the road."

"Yes, I can understand that," I said. "Does the name Morel mean anything to you?"

"Oh, sorry," he said. "No, no, doesn't sound familiar. You know, the big name around here is Mathieu. They've run the ochre business all these years, and now they seem to run most of the other businesses in town. Restaurants, markets, movie theater — you name it."

I scribbled "Mathieu" despite the bumps, and knew it was just legible enough to jog my memory later.

"Hey, I doubt you want a ride all the way to Marseilles. Do you want me to drop you at the office? It's not a bad walk into town from there."

"Perfect." I thanked him, jotted down his name, Dominique Bernard, and descended from the cab.

The afternoon had slipped away and the sun was disappearing over the horizon. In fact, I could just see it scoot behind the bell in a church tower that perched above the colorful village. I headed that direction, hoping to explore for a few minutes before meeting Witty and his lady friend back at the car.

22

Reid: June 6 — Los Angeles

Babette's motion for standing in the Morel case had us in shock. I couldn't believe she had found Jake Tresan to represent her, let alone that she had the gumption to go after the money. Witty was still reeling from being jilted, so he wasn't much help in thinking through what her strategy might be. Lord knows what he had shared with her in Provence, Paris, and on their return trip across the states. She must have had something up her sleeve, because the State Supreme Court agreed to hear her appeal for standing. Heaven help us.

Grace and I hosted dinner that night at our Eagle Rock home with May Wu and Witty. The children bounced and bubbled upon seeing Witty again, and he set aside his melancholy just long enough to play a rousing game of marbles with them until their mother took them off to bed. And then the strategy session began. May Wu volunteered to monitor the ongoing proceedings in Superior Court, and I said I'd have to turn my attention to the Supreme Court and Babette's appeal for standing, for as long as it took. Witty offered to join me in focusing on the appeal, and to be ready to track down any leads on evidence she might have been able to fabricate.

"If by some miracle she gets standing, we may have to call you as a witness, Witty," I said. "I hate to do that to you, but you've known her since Avignon, and you can testify that she'd never heard of Morel until we appeared on the scene."

"You want me to say that I was duped," Witty said. "Admit that she pumped me for information, learned all about the case, and even the workings of American law..."

"You're shining a pretty harsh light on it," I said. "We can cross that bridge when we get to it."

"Will that fly in court? I mean, I'm the researcher for the Morel claimants. I can't imagine Murphy would allow me to be your chief witness."

"He's right," May Wu offered. "I think you'd need to have some independent witnesses. Witty's too close to the case."

"As I said, we'll cross that bridge later," I said. "One thing we should do though, is make copies of that note Babette left you when she fled the Biltmore. We might need to enter it as evidence if she does wheedle her way into the trial. Meanwhile, let's step back and think about the strength of our case. Have we done all we can for our clients?"

We spent the rest of the evening, until almost midnight, discussing the strengths and weaknesses of our own case as well as the others presented to date. After the guests went home, I stayed up until two o'clock composing telegrams to the Morel heirs in Paris and Provence, suggesting they come to Los Angeles. People often accused me of worrying too much. This time, my concerns felt justified.

III. CONNECTION & COMPLICATION

23

Reid: June 7 — Los Angeles

"THIS IS AN APPLICATION FOR A WRIT of mandate to compel the California Supreme Court to permit the petitioner to participate in a proceeding to determine heirship pending in that court in the matter of the estate of Marcel Morel," Jake Tresan announced at the opening of Babette's appeal. I knew quite a bit about Tresan, who was in his late thirties, a stocky man with a full head of brown hair slicked back from his high forehead. He'd been a football star at UCLA and then switched to USC for law school, and he still carried the Big-Man-on-Campus swagger.

Tresan continued his convoluted statement. "On May 1, 1923, the Superior Court of Los Angeles County, in response to a motion by counsel for a certain group of the numerous claimants to the Morel estate, made its order directing the entry of a default against all persons who had not at that date appeared or filed petitions to determine heirship. Since the making of that order, the court has been engaged in reviewing the numerous depositions and documentary evidence on behalf of various claimants before a jury, as

171

demanded." He was the kind of lawyer who gave us all a bad name. He read the clunky statement with little flair, like he had a gun to his head. Maybe he thought a bland tone would add credence to his verbose legal ramblings. "On June 5, 1923, the petitioner, Babette Reville, herein served and filed a notice of motion that she would move said court for an order permitting the filing of her appearance and statement of claim of interest in the estate. This motion was accompanied by an affidavit of merits setting forth the reasons for the petitioner's delay in presenting her claim as the daughter of the deceased Marcel Morel."

Witty and I took careful notes, both wondering what possible reasons she'd invented to justify her delay.

"According to her account of various controlling factors entering into her personal background and family history, supported by a genealogical chart and appropriate letters corroborating her recital of material events, the petitioner first learned of the death of Marcel Morel and the contest over his estate on June 1, 1923, when her attention was directed to a current newspaper article referring to the heirship proceeding and the alleged existence of a daughter of the deceased. Upon her discovery of the pendency of this proceeding, Miss Reville consulted me as to her rights in the matter and, pursuant to my advice, presented her motion for leave to file her claim, as above mentioned."

I glanced at Witty and rolled my eyes. Tresan was exceeding expectations for verbosity. "He's all potatoes and no meat," Witty whispered to me.

"Affidavits in opposition to Miss Reville's motion were filed on behalf of other claimants to the estate, and presiding Judge Fergus Murphy denied her motion on the grounds that it was in defiance of the general default order of May 1, 1923, and further, that it was a sham, a fraud, and a contempt of court. That's a direct quote."

Tresan's presentation continued in this vein for almost an hour. The justices asked a few questions about the technical procedures of the Superior Court in the case, but none about the merits of

Babette's evidence. Their job, after all, was to determine whether the court had followed proper process, not to do the jury's job of deciding the merits of fortune hunters' claims.

When the justices broke for a midday recess, Witty said he wanted a quick word with Babette.

"Be careful. She's the opposition now," I warned.

"I know. Just give me a few minutes," Witty said. He intercepted Babette and her attorney on the courthouse steps. I stayed just close enough to hear their conversation.

"Miss Reville," Witty said, "might I have a moment of your time."

"Sure, sugar," she said with a vacuous smile. "Give us a minute, Jake."

"You've taken me completely by surprise," Witty said. "I was worried that something had happened to you, the way you just disappeared."

"Yes, well, something came up."

"How long have you been planning this scheme?"

"I don't think I should be having this conversation with you. I don't mean to sound crumpy."

"I think you mean grumpy. Anyhow, how long do you think you can pursue this run for the riches?"

"Really, Witty, I am truly sorry that you're in the middle of this," she said, putting her hand on his arm. She was tightly packed into an outfit they'd bought together in Paris. The pearl necklace he'd given her for the Atlantic crossing rested smoothly on her ample chest. "But from now on, Jake says he should do all the talking for me."

"You could have had it all, Babette, if you'd just stayed with me." She smelled of the Chanel Number Five that he'd given her.

"That's not true. It's all — what's your word? Horsefeathers? You said you were not interested in marriage. What was I supposed to think? I'd still be in Paris with Pierre if I wanted to settle for being the mistress."

"I know you're disappointed, but please don't jump into the legal battle."

"It's a doggie-dog world, as you Americans are so fond of saying."

"That's dog *eat* dog."

"*Bauf!* That's disgusting!"

"Look, I really thought you cared for me," Witty said.

"That's beside the point." She turned and walked down the steps to join Tresan, who whisked her into a waiting cab.

At the Broiler, Witty was the most subdued I'd ever seen him. Witty's rock-hard confidence just crumbled under the blow of Babette's betrayal. The depth of his melancholy came as a surprise. I'd always thought of Witty as a *bon vivant* who simply enjoyed the pleasures of life, not one to be susceptible to the vicissitudes of feminine wiles. And while my impression of Babette had gone from mindless floozy to cunning gold digger, I could scarcely imagine Witty having serious feelings for her. But there was no accounting for taste. At lunch, I tried to keep our focus on strategy, but soon realized that Witty just needed time to be miserable.

THE SUPREME COURT ISSUED ITS DECISION the following Monday, June 11. The majority opinion read, "Every consideration of justice and sound policy requires that the estates of decedents be distributed to persons rightfully entitled thereto, and that every concern and endeavor of a probate court should be directed to the accomplishment of that objective.… We find that the petitioner's statement of heirship was legally sufficient, and we order that the petitioner be permitted to file her claim, in disregard of the general default order of May 1, 1923."

On the motion opposing Babette's standing based on the allegation that the petition was a "sham, fraud, and a contempt of court," the justices punted, saying that those charges should be addressed by the jury that had been empaneled to determine the proper distribution of the Morel fortune. "Section 1081 of the

Probate code, relating to the conduct of the hearing in an heirship proceeding, provides that a trial of the facts must be by jury, unless a jury is waived," the ruling read. "Since the very nature of this litigation fixes the determination of the alleged existence of a relationship borne by the claimant to the deceased to be the controlling factor, Section 1081 must be construed as giving to this claimant, whether upon initiating a petition or statement of heirship presented after the commencement of the proceeding, the right to have all evidence affecting the disposition of this single, ultimate issue submitted to the jury for its consideration. Consistent with this requirement of Section 1081 and the empanelment of a jury for the trial of the facts in the Morel heirship proceeding, it is manifest that the respondent court, in passing upon the merits of the petitioner's claim incidental to its order dismissing her from the proceeding, usurped the functions of the jury."

That night, as had been the case far too often since the trial began, I could not sleep. Grace worried that I was taking the trial too personally, and now that Babette was a factor, the problem seemed ten times worse.

"Do you want to talk about it?" she asked, checking the bedside clock. Half past one in the morning.

"I'm sorry, Grace. Did I wake you?"

"I can just tell that you're not sleeping. It's not healthy, Reid."

"Go back to sleep. I'll go to the study."

"No, let's talk it through. We're both awake now." Grace had a way of being a salve on my emotional sunburn.

We talked about Babette's case, her obnoxious lawyer, her duping of Witty, and her possible next moves. I also confessed that, for the first time since the trial began, I thought we actually might lose the case. The fear of wasting all the time and money we'd spent in France, not to mention neglecting my existing practice, gnawed deep in my gut. I also felt a duty to the Morel heirs. What would I tell them if Babette ended up with all the money?

I was convinced that she had no viable case, and therefore no credible evidence, but I could see from the Supreme Court's ruling that we'd have to consider her a real threat. So far, it seemed that her claim would rely on letters, a bogus genealogical chart, and whatever story she dreamt up for the witness stand.

"Does she have any real evidence?" Grace rubbed sleep from her eyes. "Witnesses?"

"I can't imagine she could produce a witness, unless she grabbed a bum off the street and paid him off."

"Have you seen the letter that the judge received? The one that started this ball rolling?" Grace asked.

"Well, of course, I read it in the *Times* like everybody else."

"No, I mean the actual letter," she said. "What kind of stationery is it on? How about the ink? What does the handwriting look like?"

"I see where you're going," I said. "Chances are, Babette wrote the letter herself, or maybe she persuaded ole Jake-the-Snake Tresan to write it for her."

"How would you disprove the authenticity of a letter like that? What about the other letters she calls evidence?"

"Let's think about it. I suppose there are handwriting experts, and maybe we could find one that would have some credibility with the jury," I said. "It's not exactly hard science, but it might be worth a try."

"And you could hire a linguist to look for patterns in the spelling or syntax."

"Right. And I wonder if there's a difference in papers. You know, whether a scientist could tell the age of a paper, or whether it was commonly used in France versus California."

"We may be on to something, dear. Now would you let it go for tonight and give me a back rub?"

176

24

Witty: March 5 — Roussillon

SOMETIMES A MAN, DESPITE HIS BEST INTENTIONS, can be blinded by love. Lust might do the trick, too, I suppose. Anyhow, Babette and I spent the better part of the afternoon strolling through the picturesque town of Roussillon, enjoying colorful walls that mirrored the varied hues found in surrounding bluffs. Stunning scenery. From the top of the hill, where the church sat, we thought we could make out Goult's little windmill across the valley to the southwest. We strolled through the church garden, flush with daffodils well past their prime and irises still approaching theirs.

"Witty, tell me how this works," Babette cooed, taking my arm.

"How what works, my lovely?"

"The family thing," she said. I stopped and turned to look at her, hoping that by *the family thing* she did not mean marriage or procreation, although I certainly was enjoying her company. "You know, the inheritance thing," she clarified. I breathed a sigh of relief and bent to pick an iris for her. "I mean, what if you find out that Marcel Morel had a cousin, and that cousin had children, and even grandchildren by now. Would they get the money? Or do you just give it to his children and maybe nieces and nephews."

"Well, the papers we filed with the court back in Los Angeles, which were really just a placeholder, stated that we're off to find the *issue* of Marcel or of his parents."

"You'll have to explain that one," she burbled, covering her scarlet lips.

"Issue just means offspring, blood relatives, who descended from the party in question," I said. She still looked confused. "So if we found out that Marcel had children, they'd be first in line. If they were deceased — dead — we'd look for grandchildren. That seems unlikely. I think our man was a bit of a hermit. Who knows whether he ever even enjoyed the company of a woman."

Babette sniggled again and squeezed my arm.

"So then we look for the issue of his parents, which means his siblings — brothers and sisters — and again, if they're deceased, we try to find the next generation. That would be Marcel's nieces and nephews." I explained that, since we believed we had located at least one heir — a nephew — we would not broaden the search to include second or third cousins.

"I see," she said. "This is all just so fascinating."

We descended a narrow road from the church that passed through an archway barely wide enough for a Citroën. "You know, my dear, my Packard would be too long and wide to navigate these streets. I once heard that the narrow streets of these medieval towns were built to be wide enough for a horse and cart to pass, long before anyone envisioned a horseless carriage."

About halfway down the hill, we found a small art gallery that featured sculptures made from colorful local stones, as well as a few Impressionist paintings. A smartly dressed woman welcomed us to the gallery, offered a cup of coffee, and volunteered to answer any questions. We admired the artwork and then I went into research mode. I did the usual introductions and explained my quest. The kind lady introduced herself as Lise DuPont. Her delicate features and fine dress contrasted with her strong, almost masculine hands. Her fingernails, though scrubbed clean on top, harbored red clay underneath, betraying her pursuit of sculpture or pottery.

"Have you lived in Roussillon your entire life?" I asked.

"Yes, except two years to study art in Paris." She looked wistful when she mentioned the great city.

"And now you run the gallery," I said. "I'm guessing you're an artist, yourself." She smiled and pointed out two of her own sculptures.

"I suppose you could call me an artist. I enjoy trying, anyhow."

"We're looking for information regarding the Morel family. Does that name mean anything to you?"

"Oh, yes." Lise's face lit up. "Isn't Marie Mathieu a Morel? I think that's her maiden name."

"You may be right," I said. "What can you tell us about her?" I didn't want to lead her on, so I kept my questions open-ended.

"Marie is a quiet person, but such a talented musician. She's our church organist — always volunteering with the choir, helping children who have any hint of talent, and organizing events around the holidays."

"What do you know about her background?"

"Well, you know, she's a woman of a certain age, I'm guessing close to sixty, and I don't know when she came to Roussillon," Lise said. "Come to think of it, I don't know much about her family. I think she's from the Luberon Valley, but you know she married into the Mathieu family, and they're so strong here in town." She noted that the Mathieu family had run the ochre business for decades, if not centuries, and now controlled most of the other viable businesses in town. "If you're not one of the Mathieu brothers, or a cousin, it's not easy to make much of a mark here," she said. "I'm lucky to be in the art business, which doesn't compete with their more practical enterprises, if you know what I mean. But most of the paints and pigments that my artists use come from their plant, so I suppose even my little gallery is linked to their empire."

"Is Marie still alive?" Babette asked. I reached over and put my hand on hers. I wanted to run the interview solo.

"Oh yes, very much so," Lise said. "In fact, you can probably catch her tonight at the picture show. She plays piano for the movies. It's a hoot!"

"And her husband?" I asked.

"Fernande was killed in the war. He wasn't even in combat — too old for that — but he was running transport to the troops. You know, they have all those trucks for their business, so that was a way he could support the war effort. They think he was on a bridge over the Rhone when an airplane bombed it."

"Tragic." I put down my coffee. "Just tragic."

"Their only son, Marc, also lost his life in the Great War. So many of our young men did," she said. "He was a lovely guy, maybe twenty-five when he died, right toward the beginning of fighting."

"Married? Children?"

"No. Lots of women would have been happy to settle down with Marc, but he hadn't cooperated. I think he was leaving his options open."

I wondered whether Lise might have had her eyes on Marc, but thought better of posing impertinent questions.

Lise noted that the light was fading, so she excused herself to close up shop and get home for supper before the show. "Will we see you at the pictures tonight?"

"Quite likely, yes," I said. "And might we find you here tomorrow? My colleague will want to meet you, and perhaps put some of your insights down on paper. Lawyers, you know."

"I don't open until ten and close from one to two, but for the most part, I should be here. I'd be pleased to help." She offered her hand. "Hope to see you at the picture show. It starts at eight."

25

Witty: March 5 — Roussillon

THE SUN HAD SET BEHIND THE Roussillon church when Babette and I met Reid back at the Citroën. We agreed to find a quick meal and then go to the movie. I, for one, was thrilled to have a little entertainment, and of course we wanted to meet Marie Morel Mathieu.

"It looks to me like we're on the trail of Marcel's sister." I filled Reid in on our conversation with Lise at her gallery. "What do you think, old boy?"

"Sounds promising." But mister skeptic reeled off oodles of evidence he'd need before buying in: photographs, letters, family treasures, records of birth, christening, and death, and of course her own testimony. "Gut instinct doesn't hold up in court. We should line up a photographer to come and document our findings."

"Excellent idea. We'll put out the word for a photographer," I said. "Must be somebody around here who's looking for a little

181

work. It looks to me like in this town you either work for Mathieu or you wish you did."

We found a little restaurant called the Café de la Paix, not far from Lise's art gallery. I ordered steak, which came with heavenly *pommes frites*, and Babette chose *coq au vin*. Reid opted for rabbit stew, something he said he'd been craving ever since watching Madame Henri prepare hers back at the guest house in Goult.

As dinner wound down, we noticed an increasing flow of people walking uphill past the café — a young couple holding hands, parents with their teenage children, a group of ladies — no doubt bound for the picture show. A cluster of children scooted by, probably ten to twelve years old. One boy had the reddest hair I'd ever seen, with wild blue eyes.

"I think the ochre got into his bloodstream," Reid said. "It almost looks like somebody grabbed him by the ankles, held him upside down, and ran that hair through the dust as if he were a swab. You wouldn't believe the colors I saw on today's hike."

"That's what makes this town so extraordinary," Babette said. "To think that all of these colorful buildings came right out of the ground around here. I mean, Avignon is beautiful and all, but it's all the same creamy color, if you know what I mean."

We followed the crowd to a small theater that used to be one of the church buildings. The simplest of rectangles, the structure had a few small windows and a heavy-looking stone roof. We bought tickets for one franc each and entered through large wooden doors to a dank, cool space that we could only hope would get warmer with the crowd filing in. The building smelled of damp stone and warm bodies.

At the front of the chamber, a woman worked the keys of an upright piano with the intensity of a concert luminary. Babette went to secure three seats together while Reid and I made our way to the front for a glimpse of the woman we hoped was the sister of Marcel Morel.

The theater's dim light made it difficult to see much, but I took Marie to be an older woman, gray hair pulled up neatly under a simple hat. Sitting at the piano, she appeared to have a thick middle and a slight stoop in her spine. She seemed completely absorbed in the music, oblivious to townspeople filling seats behind her.

"It looks like the entire town turned out for the show," I said, turning to look at the audience. I spotted eager faces of wide-eyed children and weathered visages of aging grandparents. Most men wore neckties, and all the ladies wore skirts and some sort of hat, ranging from simple to elaborate. I hoped Babette had found seats behind some of the lower-profile hats.

The movie, *Robin Hood*, starred Douglas Fairbanks and Wallace Beery. I'd seen the film in Boston, where it received solid reviews and drew attention as the first production to cost more than $1,000,000. Reid had never been to a moving picture, as he considered it a frivolous waste of time and money. He only agreed to darken the door of a movie theater now because his work required him to do so. The intertitles were in English, and I wondered how the French audience would track the plot, although I knew the action would be easy to follow.

After the movie, we worked our way to the front of the theater — an uphill battle against the crowd streaming out — and gathered around the piano just as Marie packed up the last of her sheet music.

"Madame Mathieu, allow me to make a quick introduction," I began, using the most polite French I could muster. She looked startled and a bit afraid of this intrusion by strangers, like a mole peeking out into sunlight. I explained that we were doing some research and had come across information that led to her.

"What type of research?" she asked in a wary tone.

"Genealogical," I said. "Family ties, you might say."

"I have nothing to offer," she said, picking up her bag and heading toward the side door. She was not going to make this easy.

"I understand that it's late, and you must be eager to get home," Reid piped up in a mixture of French and English that she seemed to understand, "and I wonder if we might arrange to meet with you tomorrow."

"I don't see the point," she said. She clearly had no interest in sharing her history with strangers.

"Please, Madame, it's important," I said. "We have information that will be of great interest to you. Trust us. It's good news."

"Ten o'clock at the Café de la Paix," she declared. And off she went into the night.

RAIN ARRIVED IN SHEETS OVERNIGHT. Lightning skittered through massive clouds and thunder rattled the glass in every window. At daybreak, people shot across Goult's central square like marbles, scooting from one awning to the next on their morning rounds. Reid and I turned the Café de la Poste into our own little business center, taking over a corner table to discuss strategy, write up notes, create to-do lists, and compose telegrams. Reid sent word to May Wu directing her to let the judge know that we were gathering evidence from two living heirs to the Morel fortune: a nephew, Gilbert, in Paris and a sister, Marie, in Roussillon, in the *Département de Vaucluse.* "FURTHER CONFIRMATION FORTHWITH — STOP" We hoped we weren't getting ahead of ourselves, but we had to offer the court something.

We sent Busby a telegram with similar information and he responded with an update on the latest claims. The pace of new claims had tapered off, and a few hopefuls had withdrawn when they realized a court would require actual evidence. What a concept.

I tracked down a photographer, Pierre LaRusse, who happened to be the brother-in-law of the café owner. He would meet us in the café at 9:30 and, for a fee, could make himself available for the next few days to help document any evidence gathered.

"How much is this going to cost us?" Reid asked me.

184

"The photographer is five francs a day, plus expenses," I replied. "Are you still worried about money, my good man?"

"A little," he said. "And while we're on the subject of expenses, let me just clarify that I don't think it's proper to include anything beyond the daily necessities in our books."

"First, let me remind you that we're about to pin down at least two very legitimate heirs to a fortune that's worth five million dollars," I said. I tried to sound kind but firm. "Second, let me jog your memory: we are entitled to ten percent of that fortune, provided we complete the job that we're well on our way to sewing up. And third, well, third, just what expenses — beyond our daily necessities — are you worried about?"

"You know what I'm saying, don't you?"

"You'll have to be explicit."

"Let's call it the care and feeding of your companion." Reid inspected the tops of his leather shoes. "The extra room in the guest house, the additional meals, all that alcohol you drink."

"Would you be happier if Babette and I shared a room? Would that be less offensive to your puritanical senses?"

"I just think her expenses should be kept separate, for the sake of the heirs, and that our costs should be kept to a minimum." Reid picked up a spoon and began polishing it with his napkin. "I'm sorry, it's just the way I operate."

"Yes, yes, and in some ways I admire you for it," I said. "But your life is about to change almost as much as our friend the night watchman. Think of what two hundred and fifty thousand dollars will mean to your family. You'll be in clover, man."

"That's if we're successful, which is not a certainty by any means." The next clap of thunder came almost in synch with a lightning flash.

I conceded we had a long way to go, not just gathering evidence in France, but also in convincing a judge and jury that we'd found the only legitimate heirs. I agreed to keep track of expenses separately and decide later how much would be reimbursed from the fortune. Money had never worried me much, even when I didn't have it. I found the whole conversation quite trivial and merely wanted to keep the peace.

The photographer entered the café, greeted his brother-in-law behind the bar, and introduced himself to us. He shook water off a tarp that he'd draped over his head and shoulders to cover a tripod, two cameras, and two bags of paraphernalia. His gait wasn't quite right, and I guessed by his age that he may have wounded a leg in the war. But he looked perfectly capable of keeping up with us for the next couple of days. The main challenge, apart from navigating the hilly cemetery and streets of Roussillon, might be getting some photographs on the Sorgue River where Marcel's brother, Paul, had lost his life on a dare some forty-five years earlier.

We piled into the Citroën, Reid again squeezing his long limbs into the tiny back seat so LaRusse and his equipment could fill the front passenger seat. The little car chugged up to Roussillon and we arrived at the Café de la Paix a few minutes before the appointed hour. We warned LaRusse that Marie had seemed reticent the previous night, and advised that he make himself scarce for an hour or so while we conducted an interview. If she were willing, he could take her photograph after we chatted.

"Perfect," LaRusse said, gathering his cameras, bags, and tripod. "I'll just explore the village a bit then, if you don't mind. The weather is letting up, and I might be able to record a few photographs if something looks promising. You say the family names you're after are Morel and Mathieu?"

"Right you are," I said. "But don't take a picture every time you see the name Mathieu. You'll run out of film in no time."

By the time Marie arrived, a clock perched above one of the city's medieval ramparts read 10:15. Reid had started to make alternate plans for the day, worried that she wouldn't show, but I insisted we stay. "Your nervous energy won't help things," I said as I saw her walking toward the café, "so just take a deep breath and try to relax."

After a few introductions, pleasantries, and a request for coffee all around, I explained our search for the Morel family. We conducted most of the conversation in French, but Marie revealed an adequate understanding of English that came from reading bits of American literature ranging from Shakespeare to Hemingway. Without revealing the sum at stake, I gently informed Marie that Marcel had passed away in Los Angeles, and that we would like to learn more about his surviving relatives. She barely reacted to the news of her brother's death, but seemed distraught when we asked about the last time she saw him.

"It was 1879. A horrible time for our family," she said. "We had lost poor Paul. Such a beautiful boy."

"We heard about the boating accident. So sorry," I said. "What was Paul like?"

"You know, at the time I thought my big brother was a man. But what did I know at sixteen? Now I realize that, as a boy of eighteen, he was still a child. He was just beginning life." She took a sip of coffee and stared out the window. "Sun's coming out."

"What do you remember about Marcel?"

"Wasn't much for people. For him, it was music and books." Thunder rumbled in the distance, where the storm was headed. "He preferred to be by himself," she said.

"Were you close?" I prompted her, for fear she would shut down the interview.

"Never. He was always distant. When attention turned to him, after the accident, he withdrew even more."

"And your father?"

"You see, he had the same gentle, warm soul as Paul." She returned her gaze to her coffee cup. "Not outgoing, but kind. He — both of them — always left you wanting more." Her eyes grew softer when she spoke of them. "I suppose they were soul mates, if there is such a thing. Or they shared a special bond. They had the same subtle sense of humor."

"And when Paul died…?" I was almost afraid to ask.

187

"You may have heard, my father took his own life," she hesitated, her brows pinched in pain. "I suppose he did not want to be in this world without his soul mate."

Reid took meticulous notes, knowing that he would ask her to sign them and allow them to be used as evidence back home. "If you don't mind me asking, where is he buried?"

"He's in the cemetery in Goult," she said. "Next to Paul."

We'd already made plans to visit the cemetery that afternoon, with the photographer.

"Can you tell us any more about Marcel?" I asked.

"Not really. He didn't even come to our father's funeral. He took his violin, some books, a few clothes, and disappeared. Didn't even leave a note. We knew it wasn't suicide, since he did take a few of his things, but we had no idea where he went." She picked up her coffee cup and cradled it in both hands. "I never knew he'd gone to California," she said, "until today."

I continued the questioning at a slow pace. I could only imagine what she was going through. Learning that her brother had fled to America. That he recently died. Reliving the tragedy of her youth. Simply awful.

"And your mother?" I felt like I was picking scabs off a wound.

Marie sank back in her chair. "My mother, Estelle, decided it would be best for the two of us to move away from Goult. I wanted to finish school there, but she insisted that I do my last year here in Roussillon. I can understand now that she needed to get away from the pity and the gossip. They even talked about Paul's girlfriend being with child, but Mother would have none of it."

I shot Reid a look that said to skip it for now.

"Mother found enough work as an organist — at the church, teaching music to children, organizing choirs — to just get by. And she got some money from selling the pear orchard, which helped us through those first few years." Marie brightened a tiny bit when she spoke of meeting Fernande Mathieu during that last year of high school. She joked about her perfect timing, since he'd grown tired of the local girls, whom he'd known since *la crèche*. She showed up as the new girl, just different enough to catch his eye. "I was lucky to land the town's most eligible bachelor, I suppose. I always thought so, anyhow."

I figured that Marie's marriage into the Mathieu family would have alleviated any financial concerns that the widow Estelle faced. "Did your mother stay here in Roussillon?"

"Oh yes," Marie said. "She had no interest in going backward. Goult seemed a continent away, or even a lifetime away, once she settled into a comfortable life here."

"I'm assuming she is no longer with us," Reid said.

"No, she passed away in 1905." Marie thought for a moment. "She would have been eighty-eight this year, but she died peacefully at home one afternoon when she was just seventy. She never complained. It seemed that her heart just stopped beating during her regular afternoon nap. At the time, seventy seemed like a long life, but now that I'm approaching that age, it sounds way too young."

"Too young, indeed," I said. "I'm sorry for your loss."

"That was a long time ago. But one never grows immune. To the loss, I mean. I expect you've heard that my husband and my son both died in the war."

"Oh my heavens, dear lady. So sorry. How old was your son?"

"Marc was born in 1889 and he died at the beginning of the war, in 1914. He was only twenty-five, sweet boy. Sometimes I would see him out of the corner of my eye and mistake him for my brother Paul. He took after his uncle. Similar looks and personality."

"Tragic," I said. "Just too tragic."

We spent the rest of the morning filling in various details, probing to see whether there might be any other living relatives in the immediate family, and eventually explaining what was at stake.

"We noticed an Emmanuel Morel listed on the war memorial in Goult," Reid said. "Was he any relation?"

"He was my cousin's son. A year younger than my son."

"And your cousins, where are they?"

"Moved to Paris after the war. We're not in touch."

We kept the value of the estate a bit vague for the time being, in order to temper expectations and hedge against the possibility that more false heirs would surface. But we did let her know that the fortune was in the millions.

If she felt a rush of excitement about the prospect of inheriting millions, she hid it well, in keeping with her subdued demeanor. For one thing, she wasn't wanting for money, having married into the most successful enterprise in the region. Moreover, she just didn't seem like the type of person who equated money with happiness. She'd suffered so much loss throughout her sixty years, no amount of riches could obliterate the pain of losing all those loved ones.

"You may be expecting me to jump for joy," she said. "Maybe it will come to me. Right now, I'm just thinking how all that money might help the church, and the children I teach, and some of the war widows." Her voice trailed off.

"You'll have plenty of time to think about it," Reid said in his softest tone. "It could be a long legal battle, and there's no guarantee that we'll prevail. But with your cooperation, Madame, we have a better chance of assuring that the money ends up where it belongs." He explained the type of evidence they would need, including photographs, letters, birth and death records, and mementos. She invited us to come to her home, where she might have a few things that we could use, provided we promised to return them.

"Would you like a little time to yourself before we descend upon your home?" I stood and moved around to pull out her chair. "I know this process can be disturbing."

"No, let's do it now and be done with it." She rose, putting on her coat. "It will be on my mind now, so we might as well deal with it."

When we emerged from the café, LaRusse stood just down the street taking a photograph. At least I assumed LaRusse was the figure lurking under the black cloth draped over man and tripod, a lens poking out toward a weathered door with a handle in the shape of a delicate human hand.

He took a few minutes to complete his shot, and then packed up to join us at Marie's house. Reid offered to carry one of his bags and we headed up a narrow street.

"Goodness, man, what do you have in this bag?" Reid said. "Bricks? And you carry all this whenever you go out to shoot?"

"More or less."

26

Busby: July 2 — Los Angeles

BABETTE REVILLE, THE NEWLY SELF-PROCLAIMED illegitimate daughter of Marcel Morel, wore her most conservative dress and smallest hat the morning her attorney, Jake Tresan began presenting her case to the jury. I could smell her perfume from the press box. It had been three long weeks since she'd gained standing in the case, and her big moment finally had arrived. Tresan, with that Big-Man-On-Campus strut, promised to submit an exchange of letters, affidavits, and an eye witness to establish that his client was the millionaire's daughter and rightful heir.

"Marcel Morel met Babette's mother, Colette Reville, in Los Angeles in 1888 when she was touring with a theater group," Tresan said. "The beautiful actress Colette fell deeply in love with Marcel and a tumultuous romance ensued. The outcome was that little Babette was born in March of 1889." He said "little Babette" as if he were cuddling a toddler. I thought I noticed an eye roll from Reid. "Marcel had wanted to marry Colette, but she would agree to marry him only if he committed to returning to France." Tresan promised the jury a riveting series of letters exchanged between Marcel and Colette after she lost her job with the theater company, unable to stay on because she was with child. "You will see that poor Colette, heartbroken and out of work, had returned to Avignon for good, and she longed for the father of her child to join her there."

I glanced at Witty, who looked as if he might lose his breakfast right there in the courtroom.

"In addition to the exchange of letters and supporting affidavits," Tresan said, "we will present an eye witness. Mister Randy Hardaway will recall details of the 1888 Los Angeles liaison between Marcel Morel and Colette Reville. The witness will provide insight into the rise and fall of their relationship."

I nearly jumped out of my seat at the mention of Randy Hardaway. I caught Reid's eye and shot him a look that said *we have to talk.*

During a brief morning recess, I found Reid and Witty in a hallway outside the courtroom. "C-can you believe they're gonna use Randy Hardaway as a witness? Where did...how could...do you think Tresan knows him?"

"All good questions." Reid checked around for eavesdroppers. "Can you come to my office at lunch and tell us what you know about this character?"

"Sure. I did a ton of research for a story that never ran. You know, my editor still thinks I belong in obituaries."

"Let's get May Wu in on this, too," Reid said. "She had a terrifying encounter with him in the office while we were away."

When the trial resumed, Tresan discussed the exchange of letters allegedly sent between Colette in Avignon and Marcel in Los Angeles following their affair. In the first letter, dated January 3, 1889, Colette pleaded with Marcel to come to Avignon, where they could build a life together and raise their child. It described her dream of living in a small hilltop house with a view over the river. She envisioned their child — and perhaps more to come — playing in the fields and so on. She disparaged the pueblo of Los Angeles and begged him to return to civilization. The entire letter was written in French, signed, *"Bisous, Colette."*

The second letter, dated January 27, allegedly was Marcel's tortured response. It was a terse, negative reply to Colette's plea. It used an odd mixture of French and English, as if Marcel were somehow torn between his native France and adopted country of America. He wrote that, when he left France after the tragedy in his family, he vowed he would never return. His letter averred his love for Colette, but said he could not give up his life in Los Angeles.

A third letter, dated February 20, from Colette, seemed more desperate. She was close to giving birth, she said, and the baby would need its father. In this letter she appealed to his moral sense and Catholic values.

Marcel's final response, dated March 23, simply said that Colette would be on her own. "I am sorrie," it said. "I did love you, but I must stay in California."

These letters, along with two affidavits claiming witness to Marcel and Colette's relationship in Los Angeles, were the primary pieces of evidence. One affidavit came in the form of a telegram from Avignon, allegedly from a 57-year-old woman, a contemporary of Colette Reville, who had been in the theater company with her.

"Colette and Marcel met in Los Angeles in 1888. They fell in love. Marcel refused to return to France. Babette was born 1889 in Avignon," the telegram read.

A second affidavit, allegedly from a male actor in the theater company, also from Avignon, greatly resembled the first. After the two were entered into the record, Judge Murphy announced a break for lunch.

"How the hell did Tresan get hold of Hardaway?" I asked, standing beside Reid's tiny desk. May Wu and Witty wedged themselves into the two uncomfortable chairs in his cramped office.

"I wonder if Babette found *him*," May Wu said.

"How would she know anything about Hardaway? I never got to run my article."

Witty stood and took a step to the window. "I may have mentioned him in passing." All eyes were on him. "She mentioned running into an awful man on the first day of trial, and I wondered out loud if it was Hardaway. We had a very brief conversation about him, but I thought nothing of it." He ran his hand through his hair. "You know, we talked about him during the trip, too, Reid."

"That's right," Reid said. "We were worried he might hurt you, May Wu."

After a long silence, May Wu said, "Regardless of how they found Hardaway, he's now their primary witness. What are we going to do about it?"

I was surprised that the team discussed strategy with me in the room, and I offered to step out, but they said they had some questions for me about this guy. Reid wanted to discredit him as a wildcatter by showing that he was nothing but an itinerant gambler and that he would do anything for a quick buck, including bearing false witness. But there was little chance they could prove his testimony was paid. Most likely, only cash would change hands, and Hardaway would have no qualms lying about it under oath. Certainly he had motive: May Wu blanched when she recalled his invasion of her office to demand money from the Morel estate.

"Th-the guy's a drifter," I said. "C-can't stay in one place, probably because he gets chased out of every town he's ever stayed in more than a year."

"You're right." The color returned to May Wu's face. "I doubt he would last long in Los Angeles."

"You may be onto something." Reid pushed his chair back from his desk. "Let's think about the timeline, where he's been. Busby, what can you tell us."

I relayed what I knew about the man, starting with the fact that he was born and raised in Pittsburgh, left school early to work in a flour mill, suffered a terrible accident that mangled his arm, and then he started working in the oil business as soon as he recovered. His work took him all over the country and into Mexico and Colombia. I couldn't say for sure whether his arrival in Los Angeles last year marked his first time in California. It wasn't something I thought to ask when I interviewed him.

"Back up a minute," May Wu said. "Do you know what year he was born?"

"Yeah. 1868."

"How old was he when his sleeve got caught in the mill?"

"He told me it was two days before his twentieth birthday. He didn't get out of the hospital until he was twenty-one."

"Do you know his exact birthday?" Witty jumped in.

"Nope. Sorry." But I could see where this was going. If he spent his twenty-first year in a hospital in Pittsburgh, that means he wasn't in Los Angeles in 1888.

May Wu offered to do some research in hopes of verifying the man's date of birth and, with any luck, his hospital stay.

"Tresan said this morning that Babette was born in March of 1889, so he's alleging that the affair took place in the summer of 1888," Reid said. It was fun to see the wheels turn, but then they asked me to leave the room while they went deeper into strategy.

WHEN THE TRIAL RESUMED AFTER LUNCH, Jake Tresan added to the record a copy of the so-called anonymous letter that had been sent to Judge Murphy. His next move was to call Babette to the stand. Through questioning, he established that she was born in Avignon to Colette Reville on March 9, 1889. She had no birth certificate or record of christening and speculated that her mother did not keep such records because the baby was illegitimate. Babette went on to say that her mother had told her, when she was old enough, that her father was a man named Marcel, who lived in Los Angeles but originally was from France.

Babette was able to provide significant details about Marcel, of course, having been on the research trip with Witty and Reid in the Luberon Valley. She relayed details about Marcel's family, the boating tragedy that killed his brother, his father's suicide, and Marcel's disappearance to California. Tresan submitted a family tree showing Marcel and his siblings, Marcel's alleged coupling with Colette, and a line leading to Babette as his sole descendant. Babette testified that her mother had passed away in 1919, in Avignon, of consumption.

"She always loved Marcel," Babette said. "I think he broke her heart. She never married." Tresan took the handkerchief from his breast pocket and handed it to his client, who dabbed invisible tears from the corners of her eyes. Nice touch.

I heard Witty and Reid talking after court recessed for the evening.

"If her mother really was a beautiful actress, she didn't fall far from the tree," Witty said.

"*Her words are softer than oil, yet they are drawn swords,*" Reid said. "Psalms, you know."

27

Reid: February 17 — Atlantic Crossing

OUR FIRST MORNING AT SEA, I AWOKE to find a menu that the stealthy cabin steward had left in the sitting room during the night. The Cunard Line offered innumerable breakfast choices, but a walk around the decks seemed the better option. Kippered herring in bed just didn't appeal. Having heard not a peep from Witty, I wandered upstairs on my own. Inky clouds folded over the horizon. My morning constitutional — multiple laps on the Promenade Deck — had me swaying from side to side, occasionally grabbing a handrail to steady myself against the ship's movement.

"They say we're headed for high winds by this evening, sir," a young deckhand offered from above. "Could be in for a mean swell."

The smell of the ocean, vibration of the ship's engines, and tug of the swell reminded me of my Pacific crossings. Just six years old when our family fled China's Boxer Rebellion, I barely remembered that first passage in 1900. But my return to China with Father and my younger brother two years later was a voyage I recalled with great fondness. The three of us had played parlor games, invented outdoor games on the deck with rings and nets, and read from the Bible each day. I played with other children who also were heading to the missionary life with devoted parents and young siblings. Having been born and raised in China, my brother and I gained celebrity status among the kids who were going to Asia for the first time. We taught them phrases in Mandarin, shared games we'd learned there, and described different foods they would encounter. We were lucky to be immune to any malaise from being at sea.

My next journey, as a young teenager responding to Mother's insistence that I enter high school in California, had filled me with conflicting emotions. I was leaving China, the land of my birth, where I'd spent all but two of my fourteen years. I had struggled to say farewell to friends, teachers, preachers, my French governess, mentors, and landscapes that had shaped my identity. Ahead, in California, were my mother, youngest brother, new friends, new schools, and a new church. Too many unknowns to contemplate.

I decided on the Palm Court for breakfast. It seemed the least ostentatious setting. Out of the corner of my eye, I spotted Sally Wolfe entering just after I'd been seated. I was relieved when the spidery waif joined an acquaintance at the far side of the room. With her hat pulled down to shade her eyes, Sally looked a little rough around the edges, and considerably more pale in the face than the previous night. I couldn't tell whether it was the late hours she kept, the morning's lack of makeup, or the growing sway of the ship that cast such pallor on her narrow features.

AFTER A LEISURELY MORNING OF EXPLORING the ship and settling in for a little reading, I came across Witty in the dining salon.

"Join us, my young friend," he bellowed across the room. "I slept right through breakfast, so we're diving straight into lunch."

"Is that so?"

"Yes, indeed. I would've slept longer, but there are people to meet, food to eat, cigars to smoke, booze to drink, and so on and so forth. Such a big day ahead!" From the smell of him, he'd already stopped in the smoking lounge for a cigar and a visit to the grog tray. I simply could not imagine. "Look, there's Sally Wolfe now." He beckoned her to join us.

"Greetings, friends!" Sally had a friend in tow. "Have you all met? Nicole, meet Mister Whitman — Witty — and his colleague Reid Foster. Nicole's heading to Paris, where she'll visit cousins and do a little research about her family history."

"Are you a genealogist, then?" Witty asked the petite redhead.

"I'm no pro, but let's just say the curiosity is there, if not the expertise." Nicole adjusted her hat so she could see him a little better. "Are you interested in people's lineages?"

"Why, yes, as a matter of fact I'm a forensic genealogist. That's what brings me across the Atlantic this time." He launched into a brief description of the Morel case, but didn't let it get in the way of ordering his noon meal of lobster bisque, endive salad, and calf's liver, with a side of deviled beef bones. He asked the steward to bring out the Bordeaux he had opened last night. The ladies ordered Waldorf salads and Crab Louie, and Sally talked them into a bottle of champagne. I settled on Chinese-style vegetables with rice and a cup of tea.

"My family in New York goes by Culbert, but my Paris cousins' last name is Colbert, and we think our lineage may go back to the court of Louis the Fourteenth," Nicole told us. "There was a Jean-Baptiste Colbert, controller of finances in the mid-seventeenth century during the reign of Louis Quatorze, and we're going to try to connect the dots. Apparently he was a brilliant economist, but he had trouble balancing the budget because of the King's exorbitant spending on the military. You know, all those wars and so on."

"History does tend to repeat itself, doesn't it?" Witty said. He suggested that she join us for dinner to discuss it further. "Maybe we can even make plans to meet up in Paris. Perhaps I can lend some expertise to your search." Sally sidled closer to Witty and looped her arm into his, lest he forget that she connected with him first. He deftly patted her hand while at the same time throwing a wink at Nicole. The man had no shame.

THAT AFTERNOON I HAD NO TROUBLE SECURING a window table in the Writing Room. I felt a bit distracted by the constant rise and fall of the horizon, where metallic sea met menacing sky. I wrote to Grace, describing how being at sea stirred memories of my Pacific crossings as a boy. There wasn't much else to share yet, so I asked about her volunteer work, the goings on at church, and the girls' latest antics. My next letter, to May Wu, started with inquiries about the business, although I knew she could manage whatever tasks our short list of clients requested. And then my letter drifted to more reflection on our time together in China, the transition to California, and an appreciation for what she must have experienced. I wasn't sure I'd ever truly told her, but I was in awe of her courage, resourcefulness, and ability to adapt.

In one more letter, this one to Father, I just wanted to let him know how much I appreciated him. We don't say it often enough. "In your wisdom," I wrote, "I'm sure you've already realized what I'm just discovering: that travel generates new perspectives on one's life, bringing a fresh appreciation for the places we call home. So as I travel east toward the great unknowns of Europe, I reflect on the spots I've been lucky enough to call home. Thanks to you, they offer rich contrasts in history, culture, climate, and experience. Your dedication to The Lord, sharing your faith, healing the sick, and nurturing the needy have helped countless people over the years, but none so much as our family."

A few other passengers wandered in and out of the Writing Room, some staying to compose a letter or read a book, but no one spoke. The only sound was that of the engines straining against the growing swell. Their vibrations seemed to increase over the course of the afternoon, and the rocking grew stronger. A steward came through to secure shelves and pick up any glasses that might tumble.

I collected my papers and books, then made my way outside where I could inhale the sea air and check the eastern sky. Sea spray spritzed my face and I tasted its salt on my lips.

"Dark skies ahead, sir," a voice came from the wind. I looked around to find a young man doing something with a winch in the middle of the aft deck.

"What do you make of it?" I asked.

"Could be in for a rough night. Maybe even coupla days, they're saying." His voice carried a strong English accent through blustery air.

I returned to my cozy quarters, picked up my copy of F. Scott Fitzgerald's *The Beautiful and the Damned,* and made myself comfortable on the bed. I'd noticed several other passengers also reading Fitzgerald's new novel, which was especially popular because the author described an Atlantic crossing on the *Berengaria* in some detail. I found myself nodding off after just a few pages, surprised at how sleepy I'd become on this minimally taxing day. Perhaps I spent more energy than I realized by simply reacting to the ship's constant movement. And no doubt the chilly ocean air had taken something out of me.

28

Reid: February 18 — Atlantic Crossing

As THE DAY CAME TO A CLOSE, storm clouds loomed like a dark bruise on the horizon. I found Witty in our suite, sipping champagne with his new constant companion, Sally Wolfe.

"Fabulous news, Kiddo," Witty said, slopping booze into their glasses. "So many passengers have begged off dinner — something about rough seas — we've been invited to the Captain's Table tonight."

"I'd better start dressing, if you gentlemen will excuse me," Sally said. Witty stood and gave her a soft peck on the cheek as she stepped out into the hallway. He promised to call on her at ten 'til seven, in plenty of time to walk to the Dining Salon.

"They say they're dropping like flies around here," Witty said. "We got you a date."

"I beg your pardon?"

"Nicole Culbert. You'll love her." Witty reminded me that she was the young redhead we'd met earlier, the one on a quest to track

203

her heritage back to Colbert from the reign of Louis XIV. "You should get to know her. Delightful young thing. Student of French history. Seems to know her stuff. We've made a plan to meet up in Paris."

With a roll of my eyes, I asked about attire for the evening.

"I thought it would be a good night for black tie and tails," Witty suggested. "If not tonight with our captain, then when?"

The elegant table was set for Captain Trevor Ferris and his seven guests of honor, with place cards indicating where each distinguished diner should sit. On the captain's right would be Senator Reed Smoot, and on his left Mister George Johnson and his wife Emily, a diplomatic couple I'd met briefly over breakfast. The less distinguished guests, myself included, sat farther away, which was fine with me. But I did feel a bit apprehensive about sitting next to Senator Smoot, the Mormon gentleman from Utah.

The steward apologized that old-fashioned glasses would have to take the place of less stable wine glasses for the turbulent evening ahead. The evening's menu choices were rack of lamb cooked with rosemary and garlic, and halibut with *beurre blanc*. Side dishes included *pommes de terre au gratin, salsifis*, and *haricots verts*.

I must say I was pleasantly surprised by the grace and wit of Miss Culbert, seated to my right. With a degree from Smith College in European history, she offered a bit of insight into French culture and history, subjects I wanted to study up on before arriving in Paris. Her enormous green eyes lit up when she talked about her research, and she waved her delicate hands through the air with unbridled enthusiasm for all things French. I found her animated smile infectious as I peppered her with questions about the revolution.

Unfortunately, our conversation was incessantly interrupted by Senator Smoot, who was under the mistaken impression that all dinner guests would be fascinated by his endless chatter about himself.

"When I was first elected in 1903," he began — not that anybody had asked — "there was some question as to whether I would be allowed to fill my seat. You see, I am an apostle in the Church of Latter Day Saints, and just a few years earlier, my friend B.H. Roberts had been barred from filling a seat he won in the U.S. House of Representatives. Let me tell you, he was duly elected by the good people of the fine state of Utah, but the poor fellow wasn't allowed to serve because of some objection to his plural marriage, of all things. As if his personal life should affect his service to the nation."

I shifted in my seat, wishing I could gracefully resume my conversation with Miss Culbert to my right. But the man on my left continued as if he were responding to an intrigued, invisible interviewer. "We fought about my right to serve — must have been four years before they gave it up — and I've been there twenty years now. Good thing, too, because I'm one of the few men with enough spine to speak out against U.S. involvement overseas. The good news is, I just became chair of the Senate Finance Committee, so now we can take this country in the right direction." He went on to advocate isolationism, including tariffs high enough to choke a giraffe. He also championed barriers to immigration, especially of what he referred to as the lesser races.

"Tell me about your family, Senator," I interrupted. I hoped my inquiry would redirect the senator off his isolationist rant, and I confess reluctant curiosity about the senator's stance on plural marriage.

"My wife, Alpha, is a lovely woman. She's at home with our children."

"How many kids do you have?" the captain asked.

"Seven. So far, that is. Three boys and four girls. Alpha's a busy lady, she is."

Smoot droned on about himself, oblivious to the lack of interest from either side of him. After a while, I tuned him out and concentrated on the delicious rack of lamb. Smoot's banter eventually became like the distant barking of a dog, annoying but not demanding any response. But then Smoot posed a question, which startled me out of my culinary reverie.

"Enough about me," Smoot said. "Tell me something about yourself. What did *you* think of my book?" I fumbled for an answer, unaware that the senator had authored a book. I wondered if this "special captain's dinner" would ever end.

When Nicole suggested that we adjourn to the ballroom for a little dancing, I jumped at the chance. It wasn't like me to embrace the notion of dancing, not without Grace there to ease my awkward steps, but I would have agreed to walk the plank if it provided relief from Senator Smoot's narcissistic ranting.

Few passengers gathered in the Grand Ballroom, and those who did timed their strides across the dance floor to coincide with the ship's pull from side to side. The band, a small orchestra with an eclectic repertoire ranging from Strauss to Joplin, tried to time its rhythms with the swell.

"I'm afraid I'm not much of a dancer," I said to Nicole as we entered the magnificent hall.

"That makes two of us," she said. "We had a few dances at Smith with the boys from other colleges, but it was pretty slim pickin's at an all-girls' school. We tried practicing the latest dances with each other, but now I never know whether to lead or follow."

"If your toes are feeling brave, I'd be honored to try the next waltz with you. That, or the foxtrot. That's about the extent of my ability to trip the light fantastic."

We joined Witty and Sally at a small table, where brandy sloshed in snifters the size of their heads. Witty offered us drinks, as well, and both of us opted for a cup of tea while we waited for a waltz. The four of us compared notes about our dinner conversations, Witty being quite pleased to have met the diplomat and his wife, who were both so engaging and current on world affairs.

"I think Senator Smoot would benefit from the wisdom of Apocrypha: *Let thy speech be short, comprehending much in few words,*" I offered. "*The discourse of fools is irksome.*"

"*Let another man praise thee, and not thine own mouth,*" Nicole added. I smiled and nodded, just a bit surprised that she would quote Proverbs.

"*Whosoever shall exalt himself shall be abased; and he that shall humble himself shall be exalted.*"

"There's our waltz," Nicole said, adjusting her hat as if she expected that the brisk pace of our dancing might dislodge it. Witty and Sally left their snifters behind and jumped right into the three-beat rhythm. Thank goodness most passengers had retreated from the storm; it gave me more room to try my awkward steps, but I still worried about backing poor Nicole into a pillar or potted plant.

"Sorry we're so mismatched," I said, looking down into her smiling eyes. She smelled faintly of gardenias.

"Why do you say that? I think we're doing just fine."

"I'm so tall, I hardly know where my feet are," I said. "And you're just so…" Words escaped me. I wanted to say "perfect," but stopped short. I couldn't help but notice her petite features, her perfect proportions, her tiny waist, and her confident posture. Nicole's delicate hand and small wrist felt so precious in mine, like a flawless lily in spring. Yet her energy shouted confidence and curiosity, countering any inkling that her slight build and delicate features made her an untouchable porcelain doll.

After a couple of dances, the band turned to the Charleston and I suggested we retreat to our table, apologizing that the new dances were far beyond my capabilities. Our conversation easily transitioned to Paris, genealogical research, and French society.

THAT NIGHT I FELL INTO A DEEP SLEEP, dreaming of dolphins. By daybreak, my body had fully embraced the movements of the sea. While other passengers bemoaned the continued pitching of the boat, I approached my morning constitutional on the Promenade Deck with new vigor.

I returned to the suite after a refreshing walk, but found no sign of Witty. No telling how late the man had stayed out carousing, but presumably Witty had made it into bed and was still ensconced. Careful to be quiet, I gathered my reading and writing materials and headed up to breakfast in the Palm Court. From there, I was hoping for another serene day in the Writing Room. I would reread Gracie's wonderful letters and write a few pages to send from the dock in Cherbourg. No use looking for Witty, who had talked of a visit to the barber, the masseuse, and even the manicurist. I just couldn't imagine a journey grand enough to adopt the film star's lifestyle. Why it had that effect on so many passengers was beyond me.

The days passed quietly, as most passengers remained sequestered in their rooms during the storm. I quite enjoyed the solitude, enveloped in the tempest, taking advantage of the time to read, write, and reflect. Nicole tolerated the rough seas, as well, and on several afternoons we felt as if we had the ship to ourselves. We found blankets and huddled up on our pick of recliners in the lounge, gazing at the endless horizon and sharing stories hour after hour.

The storm brought rivers of ominous clouds that spilled like black mud over the sea, with winds whipping the surface to a froth. Nicole and I read sonnets to each other and worked on a massive jigsaw puzzle. On some afternoons, hours passed without words, the silence between us as comfortable as if we'd known each other a lifetime.

On several mornings, Witty turned a bit green as the sea continued to roil, but — not being one to miss many meals — he usually managed to appear for dinner and rally for a late night with whatever pretty young things had stamina. Gin and tonics seemed to settle his stomach, so he made sure to have one at the ready during most of his waking hours. By midnight he was smoking cigars and playing bassoon, with or without the band.

I AWOKE ON THE TENTH MORNING of the journey well before dawn. I noticed a strange light shining into my room and realized I was catching a glimpse of the moon through clear skies. A finger of silver stretched across my chamber and tickled the mirror. I felt uneasy, sensing that something had changed. The sky had cleared, yes, but the odd thing was a total lack of movement or sound from the ship — no rocking with the swell, no surging through waves, not even vibration from the ship's powerful engines. I feared that something had gone terribly wrong.

I dressed quickly and surfaced on the Promenade Deck. The water was glass, not a whisper of wind, and the engines were dead silent. The quiet almost hurt my ears, and I could not recall a time when I'd felt the world stand so still. The first light of dawn thawed the eastern sky. The still water took on a tangerine glow.

"Top of the morning to you, Mister Foster," a voice said from above. I looked up a ladder to see an engineer standing on a small platform above. "Come up and have a look," he said in an excited whisper.

"What in the world is going on?" I said, my voice hushed to match the stillness.

"Storm's over. We're a bit ahead of schedule and we'll have to wait for our berth at Cherbourg," the engineer said. "A little bit ago, Captain Ferris realized we'd stumbled into a pod of sperm whales. So he cut the engines to give us all a rest."

"How far are we from Cherbourg?"

"We're less than two hundred miles from the west coast of France, sir, and then it takes us a while to scoot around the north and navigate into port. It's always slow going at the end. Still, we've got plenty of time, seeing as how the winds and currents shot us right across the Atlantic."

"That was quite a storm."

"Yes, sir, it was," the young man replied. "Right nice of the captain to let us all enjoy a little peace and quiet this morning."

"Remarkable." I looked out at the water and, as my eyes adjusted to the growing light, I began to see dozens of objects on the surface. They looked like logs floating in a river, long, cylindrical, and dark. Only when some of them moved, ever so slightly, and took gentle breaths, did I realize they were individual sperm whales resting at the surface. They rubbed up against each other, rolled on the calm water, and blew quiet breaths.

"Can you see why they call this behavior 'logrolling,' sir?" the sailor asked.

"Exactly. But what are they doing?"

"Not entirely sure, but it's like they're just floating. Relaxing. It almost seems like they're cuddling, if you can imagine a whale being cuddly."

"This is unbelievable!" The dark shapes rolled on the caramel surface, barely making a ripple.

"Listen carefully for a few minutes. Don't make a sound. You can actually hear them calling to each other."

We listened. If I held my breath, I could hear a faint, high pitch coming from the water. The songs seemed mournful and sweet at the same time.

"Sublime," I whispered. I felt a prickle rise from my throat up into my nose and then out to the tips of my ears. My eyes began to water. Never in my wildest dreams — even my fabulous dolphin dreams — could I have conjured this moment.

The passage of time held no meaning for me that morning, but I eventually realized that my chilled limbs had grown stiff, and I'd lost the feeling in my feet. As the sun climbed into the freshly washed sky, it warmed my face and reached deep down into my soul. I closed my eyes, leaned into the new day, and said a silent prayer of gratitude. I tacked on a little apology to the whales for this ship disturbing their peace.

I retreated to the Promenade Deck and slowly made my way around the perimeter, spotting whales in every direction. When I rounded the corner and glanced in the window of the lounge, I spotted Nicole curled up on a recliner with a book on her lap. I tapped on the window and beckoned her to come outside.

"You have to see this," I whispered when I met her at the door. She stood draped in a blanket, taking on an air of royalty.

"What's going on? It's so quiet."

I pointed out the whales and we made our way to the bow, where the view was best. "Listen," I said. Their blows pierced the silence and the faint sound of their song penetrated the morning air. Nicole said nothing. She opened her blanket and reached her arms around my waist. I looked down to see tears streaming down her cheeks, glistening on her creamy skin. I returned her embrace. There were no words.

29

Witty: February 26 — Cherbourg

IT WAS A TREAT TO SEE LAND, SOLID GROUND glistening under scattered clouds after ten days of endless sea and sky. The square walls of an old fort stood at the top of a rocky promontory that dominated the landscape. Sailboats danced between freighters, and barges maneuvered through deep channels outside the harbor walls. I thought I noticed Nicole cozying up to Reid on the Promenade Deck as the *Berengaria* crept into the vast port of Cherbourg.

"We're seeing the north tip of the Cotentin Peninsula," Nicole said. "It's been occupied by Romans, Vikings, British, French, and fought over by Protestants and Catholics. All drawn in by this huge natural port. The British took control for a short time during the Seven Years' War, I think in 1758."

"Wow, I knew you'd studied French history, but…" Reid said.

"Too much?"

"Not at all." Reid was enthralled.

"The Brits tried again to take it during the Napoleonic Wars, but by then the French had built up the harbor for better defense. The harbor kept growing, long after Napoleon's death, and of course now it's one of the main ports for trans-Atlantic passages. You know, it was the Titanic's first stop out of Southampton."

"What would you recommend I see, if I were to spend just a day in town?" Reid asked.

"How's your French? Will you be able to get around comfortably?"

"It used to be pretty good, since we had a French governess in China, but I expect it'll feel rusty. Should be fine for sightseeing, but I'm a little anxious about it for legal work when we get to Paris."

"Up on the hill there, about a two-mile walk from the town center, is a magnificent fort, and I think you'll find ruins dating back to Roman times. In any event, it has a fabulous view of the port and city," she said. "And in town you'll see a park — botanical garden, really — and fabulous churches from the twelfth and thirteenth centuries. Just strolling the crooked streets and alleys may be all the entertainment you need. You'll see."

Passengers crowded the railings, some scanning the throngs on shore for loved ones waiting with flowers, kisses, and open arms. Others gathered to say their goodbyes to fellow voyagers. Nicole kissed her girlfriends goodbye and hailed a cab to take her to the train station. She promised to connect with us next week in Paris.

"We're looking forward to it, aren't we, Reid?" I said.

His ears turned red and he let out a barely audible "Yes."

Two telegrams from Busby awaited us at the Cunard offices in Cherbourg. Reid also got two letters from Grace and posted three letters to her. "Those might all arrive at once, old boy."

"I know, Witty," he smiled. "I assume they'll be welcome, anyway."

"Let's grab a cup of tea." I spotted a sidewalk café across the street.

"Does it feel to you like the ground is rocking?" Reid asked.

"They say the better you adjusted to the ship's movement, the worse you'll feel on solid ground," I said. "You could be in for a few days of staggering around like the drunkard I am!" Reid chuckled, squared his shoulders, and tried his best to walk a straight line across the street.

Busby's first cable reported that the number of claimants had risen to 112. He hadn't had a chance to sort through them all, but promised to provide a more complete report in a few days. "How could there be so many?" Reid shook his head in disbelief.

"As I said, where there's no will there's a lawsuit," I said. "People have a way of surfacing when the stakes are in the millions of dollars."

Busby's other telegram warned of trouble back home. "STATE ATTORNEY NOW INVOLVED — STOP — GUV KEEN ON CLAIMING MOREL FORTUNE TO FUND INFRASTRUCTURE PROJECTS — STOP"

"Do you think the state's involvement will help or hurt?" I asked Reid.

"Well, they'll be our ally in disproving false claimants, so I supposed they can be useful in sorting through the hundred-plus fortune hunters."

"That number's growing as we speak, I expect."

"*Wealth maketh many friends.*" Reid blew cool air over the surface of his steaming tea. "Of course, if we find an heir or heirs, the state will be our adversary. They'll be against all claims, right or wrong."

"Justice at work," I mused. "Good old Justice at work."

We drank the last of our tea and agreed to find a hotel for one night before catching a train to Paris. We followed signs to the *Place Centrale*, where the sun shone on a lovely fountain surrounded by park benches. A few daffodils and tulips poked their heads up to brave the last days of winter. Bare trees were skeletons reaching over brown grasses battered by winter's cold, short days. Strolling north a few blocks, we stumbled upon the *Basilique de la Trinité*, a magnificent structure with a square clock tower at the north end and a prominent nave in the middle.

"Do you mind if I have a look inside?" Reid asked.

"I'll join you, kiddo, if you don't mind."

The church, which appeared rather stark and cold from the outside, came to life once we entered. Sun streaked through stained-glass windows that depicted multiple scenes from scriptures. The light-filled walls soared to celestial heights, cradling the Bible written in light. The windows' deep blues, bright reds, vibrant yellows, and subtle greens combined to bring warmth and light to the cold stone edifice that dated back to the fifteenth century. Looking up at the ribbed vault of a ceiling, I wondered out loud how the people of that time, with so little machinery and technology, could have erected such an imposing structure.

"It took generations," Reid replied. "And hundreds, if not thousands of laborers. Many gave their lives in the process, no doubt."

We stood in awed silence, admiring the massive stone interior and relishing the artistry of windows, woodwork, and masonry. I inhaled cool, damp air, which carried scents of generations of masons, carpenters, painters, and worshipers. The smell of the basilica took me back to my days in France during the Great War, when I sometimes found refuge in churches and abbeys. They'd offered peace amid the chaos.

Leaving the church, we squinted into bright sunlight and turned left to the Rue de la Marine. A small hotel had room for us, and we sent for our bags at the dock. I ventured down to the train station to book our passage to Paris for the next day. Reid settled into sunny park bench, no doubt to savor each of the letters from home.

I slept soundly and woke to a stream of sunlight across my bed. Our train wouldn't leave until late morning, and I figured I had time for a stroll around town and a little breakfast. My legs still didn't want to carry me in a straight line, forever compensating for the roll of the ocean, but fresh air would do me good. Reid headed for the *Fort du Roule*, where defenders — be they Roman, Norman, British, or modern French — had perched over the years.

The village came to life as the sun warmed its narrow streets. Vendors pushed wagons delivering milk, bread, and vegetables. A young goat herder moved his flock through town, stopping occasionally to sell cheese or milk to women who flagged him down.

I wandered through botanical gardens named for Emmanuel Liais, an astronomer born in Cherbourg in 1826, who worked at the Paris Observatory, traveled to Brazil for a solar eclipse, studied botany, and had something to do with the planet Mars. Another big thinker. I imagined how much more impressive the gray garden would be in spring and summer.

Back at the hotel, I was tickled to find two fetching young ladies waiting to be seated for breakfast. I chatted them up and finagled an invitation to join them. Delightful young things.

When Reid returned from his hike up the hill, I beckoned him to join us. "Meet the Woodward sisters from Vermont, Emma and Lola."

"How do you do?" Reid overcame his reticence and pulled up a chair.

"You *must* have the croissant," Emma chimed in. "They say it's fresh this morning from the *boulangerie* across the street."

"How they get so much butter into one pastry is beyond me," Lola said. "Try it, and you'll never be the same again."

He ordered a plain croissant, not wanting to disappoint the ladies, and a cup of tea.

"It's better with *chocolat a l'ancien*," Emma said. "Hot chocolate to die for."

"I'll stick with tea, thanks," Reid said, no doubt imagining the ruinous combination of butter and sugar on his constitution. How could a person get through life with such self-restraint? But judging from the look on his face when he took the first bite of his first real French croissant, he had never experienced anything so light, rich, delicious, and satisfying. Flakes fell to the plate and stuck to his fingertips. The pastry's texture in one's mouth defied logic. "You may be right," he admitted. "I may never be the same after this." He took another bite.

"Train to Paris leaves at eleven-thirty," I said. "You'll have plenty of time to pack, and I've arranged for a cab to come for us at ten forty-five."

30

Witty: February 27 — Paris

PARIS SMELLED OF WOOD FIRES, COAL SMOKE, horses, and rain.
After arriving from Cherbourg, we made our way to the Hotel
des Marronniers on the Left Bank, in Saint-Germain-des-Prés. At
21 Rue Jacob, the hotel's façade appeared a bit plain for my taste,
with six stories of unadorned windows peering out through yellow stone. At the reception, a lovely young lady welcomed us to
our week-long stay. I understood most of her rapid-fire French
as she explained that breakfast would be served in the courtyard
on mornings when weather permitted, and in the lounge during
inclement times. Our rooms, she said, would look out over the
courtyard, unless we preferred a street view.

In the courtyard, sounds of the city evaporated and gave way
to the chirping of birds that hopped among branches of still-bare
trees arching over tulips, camellias, and daffodils. Upstairs, our
rooms were small but elegant, with gold wallpaper and cranberry
colored quilts, pillows, and chairs. Reid and I agreed to meet in

an hour to explore the neighborhood and seek out a suitable place for dinner.

"There will be no shortage of choices in this *arrondissement,* buddy," I assured Reid. Even during the war, the left bank had a reputation for elegance. I could imagine what it had become during peacetime.

After a cursory shower, I wandered downstairs to see if the cute receptionist's offer of an aperitif still stood. With any luck, I could chat her up for some local gossip about the best salons, finest restaurants, and developments on the art scene. Reid, no doubt, would stay in his room, obsessively organizing his books — Bible on top — writing papers, and pens and pencils. I could just picture him making sure everything was lined up by size, every corner square, and each writing utensil parallel.

That evening we strolled west on Rue Jacob to Rue Bonaparte and turned left into a small, open square. The Abbey of Saint-Germain-des-Prés, with its square clock tower, loomed over the plaza. Opposite the abbey, wrapping itself around the corner of Rue Bonaparte and the Boulevard St. Germain, was the Café Deux Magots, where I suggested we find a bite to eat.

"The sweet young receptionist at the hotel, Magrite, suggested that we eat here or at Café Flore, just across the street," I said. "She says these two cafés are all the rage at the moment with the bohemian crowd. Writers like Hemingway, Sartre, and Beauvoir practically call this place home, according to Magrite. And that young artist who's causing such a fuss, Picasso, shows up when he can get somebody to pay for a meal and some drinks."

"Is it expensive?" Reid asked.

"Don't forget, the dollar goes a long way here in the City of Light, my good friend." I grabbed his shoulder. "And besides, this will seem a pittance once we find our fortune."

"I've been meaning to talk to you about that…."

"Great. Let's discuss it over an aperitif inside Deux Magots."

219

We scooted under a large green awning, entering massive wooden doors that marked the building's corner. The fabulous structure reached four stories high, with intricate wrought-iron railings guarding picture windows set into boldly carved stone. Reid had to turn his broad shoulders sideways to inch between animated patrons, whose average age made him seem ancient at twenty-nine. The host peered through cigarette smoke to find a table for two, tucked away in a far corner.

I started with *tartare de boeuf,* while Reid opted for carrot soup with lobster.

"About this fortune," Reid began.

"Yes, yes. I suggest we spend a bit of our time here in Paris snooping around whatever public records we can find. Perhaps our man Morel served in the military. Might have had a criminal record, for all we know. Maybe he had a job cleaning toilets in the Senate building. Or he was a poet whose work sits in the national library. We know so little! But let's see if we can find him through the national government while we're here in Paris."

"And then?"

"If we're lucky enough to find him, we might gather some history on him: a home address, or a reference to next of kin. You just never know, but you have to start somewhere."

"And if he doesn't show up in the national records?"

"The main thing is to keep our eyes and ears open. Talk to as many people as we can, and see where it takes us," I said. "If we don't find something here in this first week, we can head to Goult and begin a more localized search."

For the main course, I chose the Dorado filet, and Reid tried the *entrecote de Salers.* We shared two sides of vegetables and *pommes frites,* which the waiter deftly served from a silver tray with a fork and spoon pinched in one hand.

Reid used his knife and fork to separate each side dish into its own space on his plate, so they would not touch the *entrecôte.*

"Bugs the hell out of you, doesn't it?" I said.

"What?"

"The way the waiter piles your food up on the plate, everything touching everything else."

"Is it that obvious?" If only one could harvest Reid's nervous energy, there'd be no need for the oil industry.

"Absolutely! What's the story?"

"Ever since I was a little kid, I've kept my plate divided, you know, so things don't get mixed up. My mother taught us to eat the things we don't like first, and save the best for last."

"And you never outgrew it." I could tell he was saving his fries for last, like dessert. "You don't eat much, my boy. You're getting so thin that if you stand up straight and stick out your tongue, people might mistake you for a zipper." I chuckled. "I, on the other hand, may have to get a bigger suit. But I swear I'm going to give up desserts. After Paris."

Service and food were both outstanding. The noise level grew as the evening wore on, with a young, lively crowd arriving for dinner around nine.

"This search all seems so…" Reid searched for a word, "unlikely. Random."

"It always does at the beginning. And there are no guarantees. But I have a good feeling about this one, my friend. Bear with me."

"What can I do? I feel so useless."

"Just keep those keen eyes and ears of yours open," I said. "And try to enjoy yourself. Why don't we contact Nicole and see how her search is going? I think her cousin lives here in the sixth." Reid flushed at the mention of Nicole's name.

Reid sent Busby a telegram at the *Los Angeles Times* asking if he had any news, and requesting all messages go to Hotel des Marronniers for the next week until our departure to Provence. Busby responded with a cable saying the California Attorney General's office was putting pressure on Judge Murphy to bring the Morel case before the courts sooner than later. If the state had its way, the matter would be tried and done before we had a chance to do our research.

"We need to take action," Reid said over breakfast of *pain au chocolat* and sliced blood oranges.

"How can we buy some time here? The state would like nothing better than to add a few million to its coffers."

"I'll get hold of May Wu and have her update the judge on our progress. What sort of highlights can we send in a cable to her?"

"Not much to report, apart from our arrival in the most beautiful city in the world." I took a bite of my pastry, and chocolate oozed out the side of my mouth.

"C'mon. We need *something*. More intentions than progress, since we're only getting started."

"Ah yes, we do have noble intentions." The chocolate dissolved into my next swig of coffee, giving it a delightful taste. "Noble intentions, indeed."

Reid began composing the cable in his head. "May Wu can let the judge know that we have reason to believe we will find the rightful heirs in the Luberon Valley of Provence, based on evidence collected at the scene of Morel's death."

"Will that be enough to buy us some time?"

"I don't know. Do you have any more specifics?" Reid seemed ready to grasp at whatever straws I could offer.

"Not really. This process often seems like a wild goose chase at first, and then — with any luck — things start to fall into place. I mean, you could mention that we're in Paris scouring government records and whatnot. If you think it would do any good."

"Worth a try. But I'll insist that she stick to the facts. She's not a fiction writer." Why did I get the feeling he didn't trust me?

We split up for the morning, with Reid visiting the administrative offices of the Senate while I headed to the national employment office. We agreed to meet for lunch at one o'clock at a *brasserie* on Place St. Michel in the Latin Quarter. It wasn't my idea of *haute cuisine*, but it would be easy for Reid to find, even as a newcomer to Paris. I sent a messenger to the home of Guillaume Colbert, Nicole's cousin, in hopes that she would be there to receive my invitation to join us for lunch. If not then, I suggested, she rendezvous with us at the hotel for drinks at day's end.

THE SUN SHONE ON SIDEWALK TABLES at the Brasserie du Pont, making it just warm enough to sit outside and watch young people come and go from the famous Fontaine St. Michel, with its water-spewing dragons and pink marble columns. The people-watching was fabulous.

"Any luck this morning?" Reid asked. His soup arrived, its hearty smell rising to compete with the omnipresent scent of *Gauloise* cigarettes.

"It took most of the morning just to find somebody who could direct me to past employment records. Their main focus right now is placing people in jobs. Lots of war veterans there, you know. Some are missing an arm or a leg, others seem to be lacking their mental faculties. Very sad." I sliced into my beef, very rare, just the way I like it.

"Truly sad." We had already noticed several wounded young men in the city, their vacant stares indicating wounds less visible, but perhaps more debilitating, than missing limbs.

"And you?" I asked. "How did you fare?"

"Actually, I did find a little something. I talked to a secretary in the office of Senator Bretand, who represents the Vaucluse district where Goult is located. She's worked there for twenty-five years and seems to have a great handle on the comings and goings of the district. She recalled a young man by the name of Morel — thought maybe Michel was his first name — who interned in the office between high school and university. He stayed for a couple of years, on and off, until the war. And that was the end of him. Lost his life during the first six months of fighting, she said."

"Did she have any information about his family?"

"She didn't know. Said he was a quiet boy, kept to himself." Reid broke off another hunk of baguette and used it to soak up his salad dressing. "She did think that at one time the Morel family had a substantial presence in the Vaucluse, but they somehow dispersed or died off. She suggested we check the cemeteries."

"Good work. You see, this is the kind of intelligence that just might lead to something down the line. You're getting the hang of it, my good lad. And now you can tell May Wu to let the judge know we may be on to something."

"I won't ask her to lie, you know."

"Heavens, no. Just a little teaser to give us some time." I finished my glass of wine and signaled to the waiter for another one.

Reid's watchful eyes searched the sidewalk several times, probably hoping that Nicole would find us in time for lunch. But by two-thirty, when the café crowd was shifting from diners to drinkers and smokers, the sun disappeared behind dark gray clouds, making it too cold to linger at our sidewalk table. Reid, encouraged by his Senate research, agreed to spend the afternoon poking around the offices of the Chamber of Deputies. I decided to foray into Public Works. We'd meet back at the hotel around five.

That afternoon my visit to the Department of Public Works turned up two current employees named Morel. One, a 45-year-old named Georges, worked right there in administration, and we met for a quick introduction. Georges, a pleasant enough paper-pushing type with pasty skin and an unimpressive salt-and-pepper beard, said his family was from Bordeaux.

"My parents, grandparents, aunts, uncles, they're all in the wine business one way or another," the bureaucrat said. "I couldn't wait to get off the farm, away from those musty barrels, and out of the country. I'm the only one who escaped from Bordeaux." He had come to Paris when he was twenty-five, secured a job filing documents for the department, and here he was. "I've had a few promotions over the years," he explained. "Now I'm filling out paperwork for the new roads projects, and somebody else has my old job of filing it." He seemed quite proud of his progress.

"Have you come across anyone else named Morel, either at work or in your personal life here in Paris?"

"Oh, occasionally people ask me whether I'm related to Gilbert or Louise or somebody, but I don't think so," he answered. "Like I say, it would take a crow bar to pry my clan from the wine business."

"Thanks for your time," I said. "And congratulations on your promotions."

As I turned to leave, Morel added, "They say that Gilbert works at the Louvre. You know, when they ask if we're related."

"Outstanding."

31

Reid: February 28 — Paris

I AMBLED BACK TO THE HOTEL after an unproductive afternoon at the Chamber of Deputies, surprised that my feet ached from all the walking in Paris. It wasn't like me to tire from an easy exercise like walking, but the distances in Paris were deceptive. My energy spiked when I noticed Nicole huddled up to a small lamp in the corner of the hotel's cave-like sitting room, reading a tattered copy of *Pride and Prejudice*.

"Miss Nicole, what a pleasure!" I reached out to shake her hand, but she came at me with a hug.

"I was so pleased to get Witty's message," she said. "Have you fallen in love yet?" My ears prickled with heat. "With Paris, I mean," she added.

"It's an extraordinary city, isn't it? I expect I've just started to scratch the surface."

We caught up on the last few days, our respective research, and our plans for the week ahead. Nicole suggested that when Witty arrived, we all find a quick bite to eat and then make our way to a literary salon that her cousin planned to attend that evening.

"Forgive me, Nicole, but what's a salon?"

"My cousin says they're all the rage here in Paris." She put a hand on my arm. "Apparently there are a few intellectuals — some with money, some without — who adore the arts and want to promote young artists among their friends. They host gatherings in their homes, invite their friends, serve a little food and drink, and wax poetic about literature. Who knows. Let's find out. What d'ya say?"

"And this is an ongoing event?"

"I guess some people host a weekly salon, and others might be less regular. Tonight's shindig is on the Rue de l'Ancienne Comédie, just a few blocks from here," she said. "I hear there are others, more about visual arts. You know, painters and sculptors and such. One woman, Natalie Barney, who's an American heiress here in the city — I think over by the Luxembourg Gardens — her Friday afternoon literary salon draws two hundred people!"

"All the rage, as you say."

When Witty returned from his afternoon at the Department of Public Works, he joined us in the sitting room. He lit up at the idea of attending a literary salon, and insisted we dine first at the Café le Procope, not far away on the Rue de l'Ancienne Comédie. We gathered our heavy overcoats, hats, and gloves to brace against the chill of Paris by night.

A plaque outside Café Procope asserted it was the world's oldest café, dating back to 1686. It also professed to be the most famous center of literature and philosophy in the eighteenth and nineteenth centuries, a boast that I doubted would stand up in court, but who cared. The plaque listed some of the café's more famous and notorious patrons: La Fontaine, Voltaire, Benjamin Franklin, Napoleon Bonaparte, Balzac, Victor Hugo, and even Robespierre.

"I hope we're appropriately dressed for such distinguished company," Nicole said.

We peeked in through large windows and I thought that, if anything, we might be overdressed.

Inside, several gentlemen gathered at the bar, which nestled under an elegant marble stairway that climbed in a grand curve toward a dining room upstairs. Witty requested a table on the ground floor, where he could people-watch and keep an eye on the crowd collecting at the Comédie Française across the street. We sat at a small table opposite the café's enormous staircase and perused a limited but elegant menu. I cringed at the expense.

After a tasty meal, Nicole identified the salon address by its blue door, which opened to a small courtyard carved out of the four-story, seventeenth-century building. We climbed to the top floor and found people spilling out of an apartment that took up the building's northeast corner.

The flat's modest sitting room had wooden beamed ceilings and a fireplace of white marble bordered by an oversized carved oak mantle supporting an ornate mirror. Witty, who knew all about these things, pointed out that the honey-colored wooden floor was *point de Hongrie,* or flame stitch parquet. It took us a while to find Nicole's cousin Guillaume, who introduced us to the hostess, Florence Ashton. She appeared to be in her thirties, a lively woman dressed in colorful, flowing clothes that hung on her thin frame to create an exotic look, as if she belonged in India or Brazil. She pointed out a few guests, including an American poet and critic named Ezra Pound, who was developing quite a reputation as a supporter of starving artists.

"Not that he isn't starving, himself," Ashton offered, "but somehow he comes up with enough to keep his friends and himself in bread, cheese, and wine." She apologized that there wasn't enough seating for people to get comfortable. The crowd included an astonishing number of young Americans, along with a good number of French who seemed to cover a broader age range.

The young poet read a few pieces in English, and it occurred to me that the artist's passion far surpassed his talent. When the poet switched to French, I shifted my attention to the crowd, peeking to see whether they seemed genuinely enraptured or politely mute.

"He was enthusiastic," Nicole said with neutral diplomacy after the reading.

"Too bad his enthusiasm won't translate to the printed page," Witty said. "It's one thing to hear the lad in person, but how will those words carry in a book?"

Before relinquishing the crowd's attention, Miss Ashton encouraged her guests to drop in Friday at Shakespeare and Company, the English bookstore, for a sip of wine and another reading.

I wasn't surprised that Witty secured another drink and then sidled up to two young women who had found seats in a cozy corner. He never missed an opportunity to meet the ladies. After a little small talk with various guests, Nicole and I went to collect Witty, whose full attention was on the girls.

"These ladies came to Paris from Chicago six months ago," Witty told us by way of introduction. One was studying fashion and trying to get her foot in the door at *Soeurs Callot*, while her friend had signed up for cooking classes. With the weak franc, life was irresistibly affordable in Paris, and they planned to stay until their money ran out. They shared an apartment on Montmartre, for the equivalent of $25 a month, and food and wine were a mere pittance.

"It appears the Bohemian life is suiting you well," Nicole said to them.

"There's no end of things to do," the taller one said. "Every night there's a salon, book event, play, concert, or party. And the art! The galleries are endless!"

"And heaps of free concerts," the smaller one added. "Check out the churches — Sainte Chapelle, Notre Dame — they have free stuff all the time."

"Yeah, and they're not even religious," her friend offered.

"Delightful," Witty said. "Simply delightful." He gave them a long look from head to toe and back again, and waved us off. "Why don't you two head back without me." He had no intention of letting two lovely young things get away. "If I don't see you again tonight, let's plan to meet up at Shakespeare and Company tomorrow when it opens." He gave me the address and sent us off into the chill of the night.

I'D HEARD OF SHAKESPEARE AND COMPANY. It catered to the expat crowd, which had grown tremendously since the end of hostilities in the Great War. Packed to the rafters with books of all sizes, stacked this way and that, it felt more like a madwoman's hoard than a library or book store. Sylvia Beach, the owner, supported American writers who flocked to Paris to pursue the Bohemian life, writing in cafés, drinking too much, and smoking *Gauloises* well into the night. Some of them had enough money to live in decent houses or flats, while others relied on the mercy of friends or patrons of the arts to rent them a room or put them up for a while.

Witty, Nicole, and I strolled in just after opening to find the place empty but for the owner, Miss Beach.

"Make yourselves at home, compatriots," she shouted from the top of a ladder that disappeared into the rafters. "I can hear from your voices that you're American. I'm guessing one of you is from Boston, from the sounds of it."

"Excellent deduction, my dear," Witty replied. "My friends here think I speak oddly, too, but they're too polite to say anything."

"Can I help you find anything in particular? You're welcome to just browse." She leaned to reach for a book tucked at the very top of the store's highest shelf, prying it from a spot that almost touched the ceiling. "We have everything from the great philosophers to the latest literature. The fun is in finding it."

We elected to roam the store for a while. I went in search of writings by Francis Hutcheson, a Scottish philosopher who wrote of the relationship between man and nature. I thought I might find time on this journey finally to get around to reading Hutcheson, an author Father had recommended for years.

A young gentleman bounded through the door and shouted for Miss Beach, who scurried down the ladder to greet him. He threw his arms around her, lifted her off the ladder's bottom rung, and swung her around in a circle.

"Hemingway!" she screamed in delight. "What are we celebrating?"

"Money!" he shouted. "I finally got paid!"

"Who?"

"*The Saturday Evening Post*. It's not a lot, but enough to pay off a bit of my debt to you, my sweet."

"And to buy yourself a few drinks, from the smell of your breath, you scoundrel. Where have you been drinking this early in the morning?"

"Oh, I just had a few sips. Ran into Scott near the Dome and we decided to celebrate my newfound riches."

"I'm glad you saved some for your old friend Sylvia. I have mail for you, too."

Witty had told me that Beach loved her starving artists. She gave them a home base where they could receive mail and find a friendly face. She lent them money, and even took a chance on publishing some of their riskier work. She stirred up more than her share of controversy with the old establishment, and rumor had it that her sexual preference ran toward women.

I found my way up a small spiral staircase at the back of the store, which led to a tiny loft with a ceiling too low for my six-foot-three frame. Space was so limited in Shakespeare and Company that the underside of the staircase doubled as a bookshelf, with volumes crammed into every horizontal surface and stacked at odd angles to take full advantage of the available area. By some small miracle I found two books by Hutcheson, *Thoughts on Laughter* and *The Observations on the Fable of Bees*. I thumbed through the pages and decided they would make excellent reading on the next leg of our journey.

As I paid for the books, Miss Beach told me about several events that might be of interest. "We're having a book signing for James Joyce on Saturday evening. Friday afternoon is the literary salon chez Natalie Barney, of course. And I think there's a free concert in Sainte Chapelle this evening. It's worth going early to catch the setting sun on the stained glass windows. Doesn't matter what the music is, just go sit and admire the building."

"We'd like to swing by the Louvre, as well," Nicole said. "Is it open to visitors today?"

"Odd thing is, it's open to foreigners every day of the week, so you're in luck," Beach said. "It's just the poor French who have to wait until the weekend to get in. Go figure."

Witty bought a couple of books and offered to bring in some of the ones he'd finished on the Atlantic crossing. Beach said she welcomed used books, as long as they were in English, and would be happy to pay him a few francs, depending on their condition. His next stop, Notre Dame Cathedral, was not far away. He hoped to find someone there who could share records the church kept on births, deaths, and christenings, although such an enormous entity was likely to have either far too many records or not enough. It was worth a try in the hunt for Morels.

Nicole and I, meanwhile, headed to the Louvre. I would inquire about an employee named Morel, and she aimed to learn more about the Culbert/Colbert connection. We found the Rue de Rivoli and headed northwest toward the gigantic horseshoe of a building that had evolved from royal palace to one of the world's great museums. We entered the courtyard, heart of the horseshoe, and paused to take in the magnificent architecture, details of the massive building's archways and windows, and its dozens of statues perched high in the façade.

"There's your man," I said after a few minutes of taking in the sights.

"What are you talking about?" Nicole said, grabbing my arm.

"Jean-Baptiste Colbert, right there in stone, looking down on us from above."

"You can't be serious."

The statue depicted a trim man with angular features framed by a full head of long, kinked hair tumbling over square shoulders. Costumed in an elaborate waistcoat and tight pants to the knee, he sported high boots with large buckles. His gaze indicated a gentleman of strong intention.

Nicole let out a little laugh. "Looks like a man with the fortitude to battle reckless spending by spoiled monarchs, even if it was a hopeless endeavor."

"You think?"

"He looks nothing like any of my relatives."

"Oh, I don't know. You just can't tell much from a stone statue. Maybe that hair had your exquisite auburn hue. And those eyes your special shade of green."

We turned toward an enormous wooden door in the archway of the Richelieu wing. Inside, we asked a uniformed gentleman where we might find someone who could help Nicole with historical research into the era of Louis XIV, while I inquired about personnel records. Nicole was directed west to a section on the third floor, and I headed east and into the basement. We agreed to meet back at the same door in three hours.

I set off for the personnel office, determined to go straight there without lingering to enjoy the artwork along the way. *No time for that now,* I told myself. But when I arrived at the base of a magnificent double staircase, I just had to pause to admire its craftsmanship. A sign indicated that it was the Escalier Lefuel. Shaking my head, I moved on, unable to get my mind off the opulence that had surrounded the monarchs while the masses suffered. No wonder the French had revolted. Such a stark difference in class, brandished so shamelessly, was bound to have consequences. It just reinforced my deep belief, passed on through generations of my family, that wealth is not something to be flaunted. If anything, the fortunate ones should share with those less privileged. The way I was raised, the notion of showing one's wealth — even wearing jewelry or driving a fancy car — was simply inappropriate. These were values that Grace and I had agreed to pass on to our daughters and we hoped they would share them with the next generation.

I wound my way down endless corridors, pausing only to admire exquisite sketches by Louis de Boulogne, known as the *Premier Peinture de Roi*, from the early eighteenth century. I dropped into a dimly-lit stairway, and found my way through more hallways, their rough stone walls indicating that the east end of the Louvre, the bottom of the horseshoe, was the oldest section.

In the personnel office, the clerk did find a record of a gentleman named Morel, first name Gilbert. He worked as a night watchman whose shift went from seven to seven, four days a week. He would be on duty that night, the clerk said.

"Can I meet him then?"

"No, sir, nobody but staff is allowed in the building after six o'clock," the clerk said.

"If you don't mind, I'll leave a note for him. Maybe he can meet me when he gets off work tomorrow morning," I said. "Is there a café where you would suggest we meet?"

The clerk recommended a little coffee stand in the Jardin des Tuileries where many of the staff fueled up on their way to or from their shifts. He took my note and promised to see that it was delivered to the night watchman.

32

Witty: March 1 — Paris

I HAD NO LUCK AT NOTRE DAME CATHEDRAL, although I did enjoy listening to a young man rehearse on the enormous pipe organ that dominated the cathedral's west end. Its sound filled the vast chamber and reverberated through my chest, transporting me to a place beyond this world. My fears about church records were well-founded; I realized that Paris was far too immense, and its history way too deep, to find any family records that would be meaningful in our search for the rightful heirs to Marcel Morel's fortune.

"The proverbial needle in the haystack," I told the young priest who was eager to help but came up short.

Back at the Hotel des Marronniers later that afternoon, I found the charming young lady who had offered an aperitif when we first arrived. "I'll take you up on that offer now," I said. She gave me a look that indicated she had no idea what offer I had in mind, but then realized that I just wanted a drink. What a cutie pie. The sun streaked into the courtyard, so I took my sherry outside and settled in with my new book from Shakespeare and Company.

At the far end of the courtyard, two women reclined in lounge chairs under an iron gazebo, blankets fending off the cold. The bits and pieces of conversation that I overheard had something to do with *enfants* and *école*. A pigeon descended to eat a few flakes that remained from a buttery croissant on a small white metal table. A couple sitting near an ivy-covered wall, speaking in a Scottish brogue, chatted about their visit to the museum and mulled over their choices for dinner that evening.

At the next table, a young lady, just old enough to be at University, sat across from a white-haired gentleman. She spoke halting French to the man, who responded in a clear and deliberate way, with a deep, rich tone that made it clear he was a native speaker. I surmised from her dress and her difficulty pronouncing the French "r" that she was American. I understood enough French to construe that they were discussing the nuances of *Cyrano de Bergerac*. The older gentleman posed questions about grammar, setting, and plot, and then asked her to reflect on the vagaries of love, honesty, trickery, and deceit. She appeared to be an advanced student, with a passable accent, but evidently had not yet mastered the subjunctive — nor the vicissitudes of *l'amour*.

I had dozed off, my novel open to page five, when Reid and Nicole returned to the hotel.

"You've caught me napping, my friends," I snorted. "Pull up a chair and give me a full rundown on the day's discoveries." They shared stories of their day, reflecting on the overwhelming magnitude of the Louvre and the sheer beauty of Paris. Nicole was encouraged that her research on the Colbert line might lead to a more concrete connection to her wandering relatives, but she couldn't quite pin it down yet.

"I found out that my ancestor — if we're actually related — was single-handedly responsible for putting the kibosh on construction of the Louvre for darned near a century," Nicole said. "How's that for a family legacy?"

"What on earth...?"

"In the official history of the Louvre, it says that in 1674, Jean-Baptiste Colbert put a stop to work on the Louvre because of budget over-runs. Louis Quatorze left for Versailles, and the buildings of the *Cour Carrée* were left unroofed and exposed to the elements."

"Well, if I ever get kicked out of my house, I hope my fallback is Versailles," I offered.

"They left the buildings open for close to a century," Nicole said. "Can you believe that?"

"If I were you, I'd change my name. Culbert is still too close to this Colbert character," Reid said with a wink. "Somebody might be holding a grudge."

"And what have you learned, Witty?" Nicole said.

"Well, let me tell you about the conversation I overheard just before you arrived." I took a sip of sherry. "It was ostensibly a French lesson for a young American woman, but I would venture to say it turned into a more of a life lesson for the naïve little thing. They discussed *Cyrano de Bergerac*, and dove into the deeper questions — all the while in passable French."

"What deeper questions were those?" Nicole prodded.

"Oh, you know, the basics: how important are looks, brains, and beauty? What's more crucial?" I turned to Reid. "I mean, how do you feel about Gracie, my friend? There's no doubt that you love her. I've seen that for myself. But what if she were maimed in an accident, or wracked by disease? What if, on the other end of the spectrum, she kept her looks but lost her mind? What then?"

Reid uncrossed his legs and recrossed them in the other direction. He looked like he had just swallowed a handful of thumbtacks. It hadn't occurred to me that in his family, love was not something you talked about, even with each other. It was just there — of course it was there — and to mention it out loud would be to degrade its value. Reid stared at his shoes.

"Should Roxane love Cyrano?" I continued. "Does she have a choice? Do any of us have a choice when it comes to the one — or ones — we love?" My gaze alternated between my two companions. "Does his deceit indicate that he's unworthy? And where does humility fit into the equation?"

Reid glanced at his watch. "It's getting late, and I promised myself I'd write to Gracie this afternoon." He stood up and kept his gaze on his shoe-tops. "Before you know it, it'll be time to dress for the evening if we're going to make it to Sainte Chapelle by sunset, take in the concert, and then find supper."

THE THREE OF US DID MAKE IT TO THE Sainte Chapelle in time to witness the sun's last rays through fabulous stained-glass windows. The delicate, narrow cathedral was simply stunning. Intense blue light streamed in through an enormous array of windows lining the first floor. But the real awe didn't strike until we climbed to the second floor, where the ceiling soared and colorful glasswork stretched heavenward. Azure and scarlet hues of glass gained surreal intensity with the low sun firing through. An ornate rose window graced one end of the chapel, while an altar adorned the opposite end, framed by even more colorful glass. I looked up to admire the ceiling's ribbed vaults, lined in royal blue with gold *fleurs de lis* that glistened in the day's fading light.

"The Catholics didn't spare any expense in their cathedrals, did they, old boy," I said, nudging Reid from the side.

"You might say that," Reid replied. "No Presbyterian would ever dream up this ostentatious show of riches, beautiful as it is."

"These buildings are amazing. Houses of cards, really. The flying buttresses have to be placed just right, or the arches collapse outward."

"Remarkable how they came up with the proper engineering, not to mention construction."

Nicole secured three seats toward the front and craned her neck to admire the soaring windows. As the day's light faded, six altar boys entered the chamber and lit hundreds of candles whose soft radiance danced on the walls. A choir of twenty young men, on tour from Germany, took their place on risers at the base of the altar. Their rich voices filled the room, where the hard surfaces of stone arches, glass, and wood sent each sound bouncing toward keen ears. I could swear the deep voice of the bass made my chest rumble with every note. I stole a glance at Reid and, for just a moment, I thought I saw a tear in his eye.

33

Reid: March 2 — Paris

EARLY FRIDAY MORNING, WELL BEFORE THE SUN cleared the horizon, Nicole and I braced against a bitter cold wind as we made our way across the Jardin des Tuileries. Nicole scurried over a crushed granite pathway, her steps keeping double-time for each of my lanky strides. We rushed, not because we were late, but because the near-jog provided our only hope of keeping the dewy chill from penetrating right to our bones. When we finally reached the little café on the north side of the park, we knew it would warm us well, as steam completely obscured every window. The smell of buttery pastries and strong coffee filled the room. I approached the barman and inquired, in my rusty but returning French, about a Monsieur Gilbert Morel.

Yes, the barman knew a Gilbert, and he normally arrived by quarter past seven for a *café au lait* and a croissant. The barman promised to point out Gilbert, and noted he would be in uniform because he was a guard at the Louvre.

"Thank you for meeting me so early to tag along and help interpret." I pulled out a chair for Nicole. "Your French is so much better than mine."

"I hope I can help," she said. "But your French is coming back just fine. That's what happens when you learn it as a youngster. Anyhow, I'm so curious to see what this fellow's all about."

The uniformed Louvre guard strolled in, raised his chin to greet the barman, and bent his slight frame into a seat by the fogged window. He rubbed the glass with his sleeve to peek out at the garden's stark and steely morning light. I couldn't guess the man's age at first glance. He appeared drawn and tired, but I supposed that anyone would appear a bit ragged after a twelve-hour shift roaming the halls of the sprawling Louvre.

"Gilbert Morel?" I extended my hand.

"*Ouais,*" he said, standing up from his small table. He was not a tall man, falling about half way between my six-feet-three inches and Nicole's five feet and change. His dark, thick hair framed an angular face with a prominent nose and Van Dyke beard. Unruly eyebrows nearly hid his chestnut eyes, which peered out at the world with a slightly overwhelmed look. The long nose and close-set eyes were reminiscent of a collie, not unlike the photograph I had of Marcel Morel.

Our conversation proceeded in French, with occasional help from Nicole's interpretation and everyone's generous hand gestures. I introduced myself as a lawyer from Los Angeles, which caused the Frenchman to raise his eyebrows and lower the corners of his mouth, followed by a sideways glance and little chin thrust. I quickly explained that nobody was in trouble with the law, and in fact, I was trying to locate the relatives of a French gentleman who had recently passed away in California.

I was intrigued to learn that Gilbert was from Paris, was forty-three years old, had never lived anywhere else, and had never been to the *Département de Vaucluse*. Paris, Gilbert said, had so much to offer — even if it was gritty and harsh — and rather unforgiving for the aspiring musician.

"Aspiring musician, you say," I repeated.

"Yes. Viola. But there's no money in it."

"So you took a job at the museum," I surmised.

"It's a living." Gilbert took a sip of his coffee. "Not a bad one. Next to music, art is my second choice." He kept looking out the window where he had rubbed off the condensation, reluctant to make eye contact with Nicole or me. His answers were short, and it took some work to keep the conversation going. In response to specific questions, Gilbert said it took him seven hours to make his interior rounds, covering the entire building, if he didn't pause too long in any one area.

"Do you have a favorite section?" Nicole asked. I appreciated that she was trying to soften him up and keep the conversation going. It wasn't easy.

"What I don't like are the Old Dutch Masters. I call it the still-life-with-dead-rabbit section." In describing the style, he crooked his neck at a right angle and rolled his eyes up into his head, no translation needed. "Best paintings are by Corot, at the southeast corner, and Pissarro. He has a whole hallway, and I never rush through there." The old religious works left him cold, although the architecture of their rooms, he said, provided a welcome distraction.

"The best part for me is to be there alone with my favorite artwork," Gilbert added. "One-on-one, all alone, with no sound — nothing but me and the paintings and sculptures. They're all mine for the night."

"What type of music do you play?" I asked.

"Mostly Bach, some Stravinsky," Gilbert said. "But it's no way to make a living. I teach a few students, which helps pay the rent."

"Are you from a musical family?"

"They say my father played viola, but I never met him," Gilbert said. "He died before I was born. My mother raised me by herself. No musical talent there."

"Who taught you to play?" Nicole asked.

"I guess I was always musical," Gilbert said, holding eye contact for the first time. "I remember that, as a little kid, I would twang out songs on a rubber band. I'd hold one end of it in my teeth, stretch the other end with my left hand, and pluck it with my right." He demonstrated with an imaginary rubber band. "Somebody — I think she was a lady in the church choir — figured out that I had what they call perfect pitch, and the congregation rounded up a used viola for me to play." Gilbert said he was mostly self-taught, with a little guidance from members of the church who gave him pointers along the way.

"What about aunts and uncles, grandparents?" I was starting to wish that Witty were there with his sense for genealogy. I was just the lawyer.

"Musical? I guess. They say my grandmother loved music, but I never met her, either. Mother never talked about family."

"Not at all?"

"Some sort of scandal," he said, breaking off the end of his croissant, which sent a shower of flakes into his lap.

"Do you know where she was from, at least?"

"Goult."

"Your father, too?"

"Look, we're not a close family. Whenever I got curious, *Maman* shut me down, so I suppose I gave up asking questions. Why does it matter?"

"Oh, I'm just trying to uncover various family connections, on the off chance they lead back to our character in Los Angeles."

"But he's dead, right?"

"Yes, and there are some legal issues to clarify in the wake of his death." I didn't want to disclose the value of the fortune at stake, for fear of starting another gold rush of false claimants in France to mirror the one at home.

"Look, I don't really want to talk about this." Gilbert grabbed his coat. "Not right now. Excuse me."

After Gilbert left, Nicole shot me a sympathetic look. "We didn't even get his parents' names." At least we knew his mother was from Goult.

SUNLIGHT GRACED THE TOPS OF THE TUILERIES' bare trees when we left the steamy café. I took Nicole's elbow in my hand and guided her to the west when we walked out into the morning chill.

"*A gauche, monsieur,*" she said, pulling me the opposite way. "Our hotel is this way."

"*Je sais, ma cherie,*" I said. "I know. But I'm in no hurry to get back. Can you walk with me for a while?" I'd been dreading this moment, but also knew it would provide a break I had to take. Since meeting Grace I had never been drawn to another woman, another soul, until Nicole. The thought of doing anything that would harm my precious Gracie or, God forbid, our three girls, sent me into a spin. I hadn't slept a wink. Much as I tried, I just couldn't deny my growing connection to this effervescent, enthusiastic, exotic young woman. I tried to convince myself that I was just caught up in the excitement of foreign travel, clinging to a warm friend as we both navigated the mysteries of a strange culture.

There was no denying that my heart sped up a little each time I saw her, and that I thought about her too often when were apart. When an idea occurred to me — about the trip or anything else, for that matter — I imagined sharing it with Nicole. *No,* I told myself, *put those thoughts in your letters to Grace. She's your* intime, *as the French would say. Your mate for life, your partner, your love.*

Our shoes crunched over crushed granite past manicured hedges and empty fountains. We paused to admire statues of nymphs, minotaurs, and Pegasus along the way. The obelisk marking the center of Place de La Concorde loomed ahead.

"We'll be leaving Paris tomorrow, Nicole," I said after a long silence. "We'll take a train to Provence."

"But you said you were staying for a week," she said. "That would be Tuesday."

"We received some pretty disturbing telegrams last night at the hotel," I said. "The clock's ticking — more like a time-bomb — and we've got to wrap up our research in Provence and get back to Los Angeles before this case gets away from us."

"Can't you stay through the weekend, at least?"

"Busby, the reporter back home, said there are now almost two hundred claimants. A couple of them seem to be putting together reasonable stories, complete with evidence that we'll have to refute in front of the judge. Looks like it'll be a jury trial, which can be risky."

"How will you deal with that?"

"We don't know yet, and we'll have to hit the ground running when we get back. We won't have much time to build our case and figure out ways to disprove the others' stories. And, of course, we still have to follow our leads here in France and see if we can come up with solid proof that Morel was who we think he was, and that he had relatives who should inherit his fortune."

"I got a good feeling about Gilbert, didn't you?"

"Yes," I said. "He's an odd duck, but so, it appears, was old Marcel. We'll have to see if we can track down any solid evidence, but I have a hunch he's a blood relative of our mystery man. He's the right age to be a son or a nephew, and he bears some physical resemblance…"

"And the viola," she mused. "That was a remarkable story about the rubber band and his perfect pitch. I can just picture him running around in knee socks, twanging out the William Tell Overture." We chuckled at the image.

I stopped in my tracks and turned to her. She smelled like fresh rain. I ached to put my arms around her, pull her into my warm coat, hold her body against mine, put my lips on the nape of her neck. I wouldn't ever kiss her lips. No, that would cross a line. But just an embrace. Just to let her know how she delighted my senses, inspired my imagination.

She turned and reflected my steady gaze. I felt my ears flush as her eyes pierced my defenses. She could read my every thought.

"I expect you'll be anxious to see your wife and daughters," she said after what seemed like forever. *Thank God she's broken the spell*, I thought. *What was I thinking? Of course I'll be thrilled to be home with my wonderful family.*

"Thank you," I said, turning to walk up the stairs by l'Orangerie. "Thank you, thank you, thank you." I placed a light kiss on her temple and picked up the pace, turned to cross the Seine, and headed back toward the hotel.

WITTY WAS SITTING IN THE HOTEL COURTYARD when we returned, flushed and invigorated from our morning walk and our encounter with Gilbert Morel.

"How did the interview go, my young friends? Any luck?"

"Promising," I replied. "We might be on to something."

"With any luck, he's Marcel's nephew," Nicole said. "Maybe even his son."

"Good work. We'd better let May Wu and Busby know that we have a lead — anything — and be sure they convince Judge Murphy to give us some time. We'll need a bit of time in Provence, and then with any luck we'll have solved this thing and can get ourselves back to California."

Witty and I agreed to pack up and catch a train to Avignon as soon as possible. Nicole said she would stay with her cousins in the short term, and reckoned she might just stay in Paris through the spring. The city was growing on her, and she found the prospect of joining the burgeoning expat movement very tempting. We said our goodbyes and promised to stay in touch. We walked her out to Rue Jacob and watched her disappear around the corner.

"Lovely girl, that," Witty said with a little nudge to my ribcage.

"You're right about that."

When I stopped at the front desk to make arrangements, the clerk handed me a letter from Grace. I clutched it like a winning lottery ticket and found a quiet corner of the courtyard to savor its every word. The letter was newsy and affectionate, full of stories about the girls, and supportive and inquisitive about our progress. Maureen had a few new scrapes and bruises — nothing to worry about, she reassured me — because she'd been spending lots of time with the neighbor boys. They'd convinced her to climb trees, which she was fairly good at, and they gave her a go at a bicycle, which she wasn't. She'd fallen and scraped her knee, but barely shed a tear because she didn't want the boys to stop playing with her.

"She wants to know when she can have an older brother," Grace wrote. "Maybe we can work on that when you get home." I smiled, held the letter to my nose, and then placed it in the breast pocket of my overcoat. I would read it again on the train to Avignon.

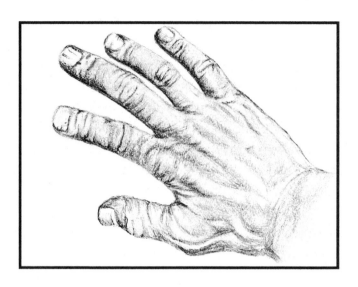

34

Busby: July 9 — Los Angeles

JUDGE MURPHY GAVE EVERYBODY A much-needed break for the Fourth of July, which fell on a Wednesday, plus we got the next two days off. The trial was already breaking records as the longest civil trial in U.S. history, and fatigue seemed inevitable. I know I felt it. When we came back the next Monday, Tresan put Randy Hardaway on the stand.

Despite a good scrubbing and grooming, Hardaway still smelled faintly of cigars and petroleum when he took the oath. I figured Tresan had made him go to a manicurist in a desperate attempt to remove the tar that stained his nails and lined every crack of his weathered right hand. No luck.

His testimony came across as stilted, like something he'd tried to memorize. I had to wonder whether jurors would buy it. Reid told me he never took these things for granted. Tresan prompted his witness through a brief tale of meeting Morel, and Hardaway did a credible job describing his physical appearance and reserved manner. After all, he had met the man. But Tresan was relying on Hardaway to convince the jury he'd witnessed the alleged affair between Morel and Colette — which led to baby Babette — and Hardaway stumbled.

"Look, I'm no expert on *ro*-mance." Hardaway put the emphasis on the first syllable. "But I could tell they was in love. He had it bad for her, and her likewise."

"Do you recall how they met?" Tresan prompted.

"He went to some play she was in, her being an actress and all, and it was love at first sight. He told me so."

"And that was in the summer of 1888?"

"Yeah, that's right. She came and went a few times, you know, when her job went here and there, but she kept coming back to L.A." Hardaway ran his scrubbed hand through his clean hair. The gloved hand remained limp in his lap. "She kept coming back because she had it bad."

"Thank you. Were you aware that she was with child?"

"Morel told me he was tore up about it. Bugged the shit out of him."

"I will remind the witness to refrain from profanity in my courtroom," Judge Murphy jumped in.

"Oh yeah, sorry." He scratched his crooked nose. "He wanted to do right by her, but she wouldn't stay in California. And he just would not go back to France, no matter what."

Hardaway's testimony continued for fifteen minutes with only minor profanity peppering his answers. I wondered if the man even knew the difference between swearing and proper speech.

"MISTER HARDAWAY, PLEASE STATE YOUR DATE OF BIRTH," Reid said during cross-examination.

"Objection. Relevance."

"I'll allow it," Murphy said.

"My birthday is February sixteenth," Hardaway said.

"What year?"

"Oh, I was born in 1868 in Pittsburgh, Pennsylvania." In response to questions, he confirmed that he grew up there, didn't finish school, and got a job working in a flour mill.

"What caused you to stop working at the mill?"

"Accident." He held up his left arm as best he could. "Caught my sleeve in the machine and it damn near ate me alive."

"I'm sorry. Do you remember how old you were when that happened?"

"Happened two days before my twentieth birthday. I was still nineteen."

"I assume you spent some time in a hospital after that," Reid said.

"Didn't get out of that hell hole until I was twenty-one. Even spent Christmas in the damned place." So much for cleaning up his language.

"That was in Pittsburgh?"

"That's right. When I got out I went straight to West Virginia, and I never went back. No way."

It was perfect. Reid had what he needed, and it took him no time to do the math for the jury. He showed that Hardaway had spent most of 1888 in a Pittsburgh hospital, so he could not possibly have witnessed the alleged liaison between Morel and Colette. He then planted doubt about whether Colette even existed, and he promised to justify those doubts with his next round of witnesses.

IV. PROGRESS & PREDICAMENT

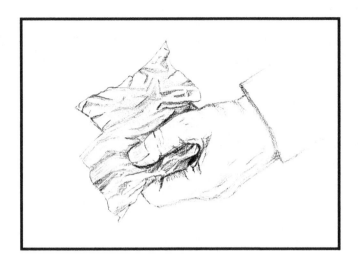

35

Busby: July 11 — Los Angeles

L.A. summer continued to roast the courtroom, and I dreaded another day of trying to sit still in the stifling heat. But the trial was getting pretty interesting. Plenty to write about for the *Times*.

During the last couple of weeks, I'd heard Reid apologize in advance to Witty for having to put him on the witness stand. He realized it would be painful and embarrassing for Witty to share the tale of meeting Babette, taking her with him to Goult and Roussillon, and then bringing her to Los Angeles. I imagine Witty knew his testimony was essential to discrediting Babette, who had put on quite a show for the jury.

"When did you first tell Miss Reville about Marcel Morel and your search for his heirs?" Reid asked Witty, who kept dabbing at sweat as he sat in the witness stand.

"That would have been in Avignon, the first evening I met her, in early March of this year."

"Do you recall the exact date?"

"March third." Witty had done his homework.

"And was she present while you conducted research relating to this case?"

"Very much so. She accompanied me from Avignon to the Luberon Valley — Goult and Roussillon and so on — where we discovered the existence of Marcel's living sister, unearthed documents, visited graveyards, interviewed villagers, and whatnot."

Reid no doubt had coached Witty against using vague terms like "whatnot" and "so on," but there was no changing his speech patterns at this point. Old dog, new tricks. "What sorts of things did you discuss during your time with Miss Reville in Goult?"

"Each evening, after conducting my research, I would dine with Babette — Miss Reville — and sort of debrief on the day's findings. She seemed very interested in my work and, I thought, in me." Witty glanced at her with the look of a wounded puppy. "She asked a lot of questions about the case, the workings of American inheritance law, genealogy, evidence, and whatnot."

"Did you share with her the details of Monsieur Morel's family lineage, his brother's tragic death, his father's suicide, and his departure to America?"

"Oh yes, we discussed it at length."

"And did you disclose the circumstances of Marcel Morel's death in Los Angeles?"

"Yes, I was very forthright about all the details, including the enormous sum of money at stake. We also discussed the rush of fortune seekers, and how their efforts might be discredited. I even told her that the only one who could prevent Gilbert and Marie — the rightful heirs, I might add —"

"Objection!" Tresan's objection was sustained.

"Okay, I explained that the only competition for the fortune would be a living child of Marcel." Witty took a deep breath. "I'm afraid I revealed far too much, in hindsight, regarding strategy."

"But you were in love," Reid said.

"Yes, I'll say it under oath." Witty again turned his gaze toward Babette. "I fell in love with the beguiling Miss Reville."

"Did you indicate that you might seek her hand in marriage?"

"Well, no." Witty's cheeks took on a new flush. "In fact, I indicated that I was not the marrying type — at least not at this stage in my life — and I'm afraid it led to the end of our romance." He described bringing his paramour back to Los Angeles, staying at the Biltmore, and then making a quick trip to San Francisco. It was obvious that he really was shocked when Babette refused to accompany him on the trip north.

"When I returned to Los Angeles," he testified, "she'd packed up all her things and disappeared. She left no indication of where she was going, or why."

"She disappeared without a trace?"

"She did leave a note." Witty took a crumpled note from his pocket and handed it to Reid. I thought I heard Babette gasp, but Witty kept his focus on Reid.

The note, she realized, would be used as evidence.

36

Witty: March 6 — Roussillon

MARIE'S HOUSE LOOKED LIKE MANY OF THE OTHERS in town, with its natural red walls and contrasting blue shutters. The whole village took on a rosy glow that mirrored the canyon and cliffs all around.

Reid and I, with the photographer LaRusse in tow, followed Marie through an arched doorway into a small vestibule lined with hooks, a bench on each side, and an array of jackets, shoes and boots lining the walls. Marie took our coats and removed her shoes, stepping into clogs that looked like they dated back to the revolution.

"Please come in," Marie said. "No need to remove your shoes."

The house opened into two main sections on the ground floor: living room and kitchen. The modest kitchen featured a small fireplace and heavy farm table at its center. The living room resembled a music studio. Marie's baby grand piano dominated the room, and sheet music occupied most horizontal spaces. Two music

256

stands and a metronome graced one corner, and a small bust of Beethoven rested on a bookshelf.

She offered us a cup of tea, which we declined, having spent the last two hours drinking coffee in the village. When she threw back the shutters along the southern side of the house, the March sun, strong and low in the sky, streamed in through modest windows. And then she opened double doors to reveal a spectacular garden perched on a precipice that overlooked the Luberon Valley. This may not have been the largest or fanciest house in town, but it had an incredible view and perfect southern exposure.

"May I take your photograph in the garden?" LaRusse suggested. "The light here is beautiful. Strong enough to avoid using a flash." While photos got underway, Reid and I took a few minutes to stroll through rose bushes, lavender, and irises, all the while enjoying the panoramic view. I inhaled air fragrant with rosemary and meandered into a small vegetable and herb section where everything from leafy greens to onions and sweet peas flourished. I recognized oregano, thyme, mint, and parsley among the herbs. My mother would have loved it.

"What an extraordinary place you have here, Madame," I said. "Simply delightful."

"I'm happy to call it home," Marie said.

"It suits you." Reid picked a piece of rosemary and rubbed it between his fingers.

"It's a good place for my two loves: music and gardening." She seemed unaffected by the camera. "And the children. Kids come here to learn music, but I put them to work in the garden when we're done with their lessons."

After a few photographs in the yard, we all climbed upstairs to a small room that served as Marie's office. It had been her late son Marc's bedroom, but now functioned as a very comfortable study. Four small photographs sat on her desk, including one of her mother Estelle, two of her late husband, and one of Marc in uniform.

"Would it be possible for us to take these to California for the trial?" I asked.

"Really, they're all I have," she said. "I'd rather not let them out of my house."

"Excuse me, sir," LaRusse offered, "I think we can capture them with a few photographs, especially if we move them into the light of the garden."

"Would that be acceptable evidence, Reid?" I asked. "A photograph of a photograph?"

"I don't see why not," Reid said. "We might even set up a sort of display, with labels in Madame's handwriting, to show who these people are."

"An elegant solution." I patted Reid's shoulder. "We're agreed, then." I asked whether Marie had more photographs, especially of herself as a child, preferably with her parents and brothers.

"I've kept all of that in a box," she said. "I'll have to find it. It's not something I dare to open often. The memories, you know."

I followed her as she searched for the box in question while Reid and LaRusse descended to the garden and began setting up photographs that would prove useful in court.

MARIE HAD NO DIFFICULTY FINDING THE BOX she had marked "Paul," but hesitated to open it.

"Sorry," she said. "It's a bit painful to reminisce. Forgive me if I get emotional."

I took a step back. She kept the box on a top shelf in the far left corner of her closet, up high where it stayed out of sight and out of mind. "The last time I opened this was on what would have been Paul's fiftieth birthday, nearly thirteen years ago now. It's not easy. Even after all these years, I still think of him every day."

"When was that birthday?"

"Well, it was 1910 when I spent the day going through these treasures. I have to admit, I spent most of the day in a daze, switching between crying and laughing, and then weeping some more.

It was so strange to realize he would have been fifty, because the image I always have of him is the strong, lively 18-year-old boy he was on the Friday morning before his death." The whole family had eaten breakfast together, as usual, and Marie had gone off to school while Paul and Marcel headed to the pear orchard. The boys said they'd be away for the weekend, camping with friends. Nobody could foresee, nor would they have wanted to know, that it was the last time they would sit together as a complete family. That weekend, their world changed forever.

She sat on the floor and slowly removed the box lid. She handed me a touching photograph of Paul sitting on a cliff overlooking the Luberon Valley. He was barefoot in the photograph, as had been his preference as long as she could remember. "Our mother was always asking him where he'd left his shoes, and half the time he had no idea. I thought it was funny, but Mother reminded him that shoes didn't grow on trees, and that he would not be getting another pair if he lost the perfectly good ones he owned. Of course, her threat meant nothing to the boy who preferred to go without."

In the photograph, Paul sat on the edge of the precipice, hugging knees to chest, gazing out over the valley. "Look how the veins in his feet repeat the pattern of veins in the cliff's rocks."

"It gives the illusion that he was one with the earth," I said.

"More than an illusion. He truly seemed connected to the natural world."

Looking back, the thing she admired most about Paul was his indifference to the judgment of those around him. She said he skated through school with mediocre grades, not because he wasn't bright — he may have been one of the smartest in his class — but because he couldn't be bothered getting things right for the sake of a grade, or for a teacher's approval. Their mother had always said he was nearly impossible to discipline, not because he was mischievous — he decidedly was not — but due to his lack of need for approval, hers or anyone else's.

"As a boy," Marie said, "He pursued his own interests, exploring the natural world around him, playing his viola, and drawing marvelous landscapes and fine botanical images. But he never wanted to share his artwork or perform his music, in case people might criticize or praise him. Either sign of judgment would ruin everything." Marie kept a few of his doodles in the memory box, including a quick sketch of oak leaves and a broad view of the family's pear orchard. I could see that the boy had talent.

She picked her way through the collection, setting aside a few family photographs that might be useful. She showed me birthday cards that Paul had made for each member of the family over the years. His artistic skill was irrepressible, and he made cards out of whatever material was available at the time. One birthday card for Marcel featured a clever collage using a broken violin string glued to the page, with frayed ends poking out of a violin he'd drawn in pencil and ink. Inside, the card said, "Marcel — Have a plucky birthday, brother — Paul."

Another card, this one for their mother, used pine needles as the quills of a porcupine he drew. Its cartoon-like face had expressive eyes and a huge smile, with a balloon extending from its mouth to say, *Bonne anniversaire, Maman!*" Marie's favorite card was one that Paul had created for her thirteenth birthday, featuring a pressed flower that he embellished with his own doodles and a few bees and butterflies.

"It's no Monet, but I cherish it more than all the artwork in the Louvre."

She set aside a couple of letters that Paul had kept. They were private, from his girlfriend, Annette. In the first years following his death, Marie read the letters once or twice, but always felt she was invading his privacy, so for decades she left them folded and tucked into the end of the carton. She had barely known Annette, since Paul kept his relationship with her separate.

"Looking back with the advantage of forty years, I have to admit I didn't like the idea of any girl taking my dear brother from me. In my heart, I wanted him to stay home and be my brother forever, even though my mind knew better."

The next layers in the box were report cards and health records, which her mother had divided into separate envelopes for each child. Marie gasped when she lifted the last envelope and found a small willow whistle underneath. Tears spilled out of her eyes and down her cheeks. Paul had whittled the whistle for her out of a willow branch he'd harvested from beside the creek at the far end of the pear ranch, she said.

"Paul played it with perfect pitch, a gift I don't share. People think I have musical talent, which I suppose is true enough, but I don't have perfect pitch." She gathered herself, wiped her cheeks, and suggested we descend to the garden.

The boys were just finishing their photo session, and they asked her to pose with some of the photographs. It would connect her to them, leaving no doubt she was the person who provided this evidence. She showed Reid her treasures — the cards, notes, report cards, medical records, and more photographs — and he knew we'd hit the jackpot. It was thrilling to discover concrete evidence, including birth certificates and health records for each Morel sibling.

"I can take photographs of Paul's birthday and holiday cards for you, so you'll at least have those while the hand-made pieces are away for trial," LaRusse offered. It seemed to provide some consolation. I shot her a sympathetic look. What an ordeal she'd had, and we were making her relive it.

"It's okay," she said. "I haven't been through that box in a decade. The memories are mine, regardless."

"Thank you so much for sharing," I said.

"Is anyone getting hungry?" she asked. "I have a pot of vegetable soup and a baguette, if you're interested."

"How delightful." My stomach had been grumbling for the last forty-five minutes.

"It's not much, but it will tide us over," she offered.

After lunch, LaRusse spent another hour taking photographs. Reid formalized his notes and had Marie sign them. I drew up a family tree, with Estelle and Jean-Louis Morel at the top, then the three offspring — Marcel (1859-1923), Paul (1860-1879), and Marie (b. 1862) — on the next line. It showed Marie married to Fernande Mathieu (1862-1918), and dropped down to their son, Marc Mathieu (1889-1914). I wondered whether to add Annette, Paul's girlfriend, and their illegitimate child, Gilbert (b. 1880), but decided against it for now. I could add it later, once we'd verified the information and broken the news to Marie. She signed the chart, verifying it for the record.

"What's your next step?" Marie asked as we gathered our coats and offered sincere thanks.

"We thought we'd explore the cemeteries of Roussillon and Goult," Reid said. "We'll have Monsieur LaRusse photograph the relevant tombstones."

"You won't find Mother in either one," Marie said from the doorway. "She couldn't decide whether she wanted her remains returned to Goult to be with Father, or to stay here in Roussillon. I like to think her heart remained here with the Mathieu family and the community that opened its arms to us. Anyhow, she chose cremation, so I have her ashes here. Some day they'll be buried with me."

THAT NIGHT AT DINNER IN GOULT'S TINY RESTAURANT, Le Renard, we allowed ourselves a bit of a celebration. I ordered a bottle of champagne for starters, and Reid took a tiny sip from his glass as Babette and I guzzled ours.

"Good God, man, you're drinking champagne!" I said. "Welcome to my world!"

"You seem to like the stuff." Reid raised the glass back to his lips, which crinkled in a way that indicated he didn't care for the taste.

"Babsie, my little dumpling, you are witnessing a monumental day," I said. "Not only is this man sipping alcohol, but I believe he had his first taste of coffee this morning at the Café de la Paix."

"Didn't care for that, either." Reid put down his glass.

"Well, *santé*," Babette toasted. "To progress on your case,"

For the first time, we truly believed that we were getting the full picture, and we had evidence to back it up. Of course we still faced the challenge of documenting Gilbert's connection to Marcel, but we were hopeful about gathering enough evidence, even if circumstantial, to convince the court that he was a rightful heir.

"Lord knows, Gilbert could use the money," I said. "He needs it far more than Marie." My favorite part of this job, apart from the sleuthing and adventure, was bringing wealth to people who had no idea they had it coming. I remembered back to the O'Dea cousins in Ireland, who lived in a small shack with no electricity, minimal heat, and no indoor plumbing. They'd seemed so unimpressed with the news of inheriting a fortune — so unable to fathom how money might improve their lives — that I wondered whether they might have burned the paper money in the fireplace, just to generate a little more heat for their tiny hovel.

Babette excused herself to powder her nose. I watched her walk across the crowded little restaurant, and realized that most of the establishment's other male patrons also trained their eyes on my voluptuous sweetheart. I felt a mixture of jealousy and pride. Reid and I discussed wrapping up our time in Provence, spending a few days in Paris to follow up with Gilbert, and then making our way back to Los Angeles. LaRusse had said he'd need a day or two to develop the film and make prints, and we agreed to spend one more day to visit the Sorgue River where the boating accident had occurred. We figured that, by the weekend, we could return to Avignon and catch a train to Paris.

"Babette will be joining us," I told Reid.

"To Avignon?"

"Yes, and Paris, at the very least."

263

"At the very least? Do you mean to tell me you're thinking of taking her back to the States? Have you lost your mind?" You'd think I had suggested robbing a bank.

"Yes, yes, and yes — or maybe," I responded. "Yes to Avignon, Paris, and possibly America, and the 'maybe' applies as to whether or not I've lost my mind. Do you really think it's so crazy? I've grown quite fond of her."

"But Lyle," Reid began, using my given name in that judgmental tone again, "may I be so bold as to point out that you seem to have a propensity to grow fond of any woman who catches your eye? And there have been quite a few, from what I've observed."

"Look who's talking, my young friend," I said. "And you, a married man — which I remind you that I am not — you cannot deny that you are besotted with Nicole. And heaven only knows what your relationship with May Wu is all about. I just can't see what gives you the moral standing to judge my feelings for Babette."

Reid took long drink of water, perhaps hoping to avoid saying something he would regret. "Nicole is a charming woman, and I had nothing but a gentleman's relationship with her. It was always proper."

"Proper yes, but you have to admit you had feelings for her," I said. "And May Wu…"

"As I told you before, that subject is off the table," Reid cut me off. "Look, I just worry about Babette's motives."

"Oh, so you think the only reason she's latched on to me is for my money. Couldn't possibly be that I'm an attractive fellow. No, sir."

"I didn't mean…" Reid seemed to grasp for words that would repair the damage, but the click of Babette's heels across the floor interrupted him before he had a chance to finish.

"*Mon dieu*, what did I miss?" She couldn't believe the anger in our faces.

"Oh, horsefeathers!" Reid said as he stormed out.

37

Reid: March 7 — Goult

THE RAIN IN GOULT WAS RELENTLESS ALL NIGHT LONG. I heard wind and rain pounding against the roof of my attic hideaway, and I could see lightning fill my little loft, even through closed eyelids. Between the storm and my own mental torment, rerunning the argument with Witty in my over-active mind, I got very little sleep. Did Witty really think of me as a philanderer? Was he so convinced that my relationship with May Wu was illicit? Was the man right about the strength of my connection to Nicole? What about Grace?

In the past, I had never put myself in a position requiring me to withhold anything from Gracie. Not once. In fact, in most ethical dilemmas, I relied on Grace to be my moral compass. She was my north star. That was one of the best things about our relationship — we shared values based on our faith and a clear sense of right and wrong that stemmed from a solid upbringing. May Wu was my other confidant, of course, having shared so much.

But now, a continent away from my comfortable California existence, I struggled with my conscience. I realized, there in the attic, safe from the storm, that Witty's remarks cut me to the bone because they were rooted in truth. Even though I'd been careful to keep my feelings for Nicole in check, I had let the friendship go beyond the acid test: *Did I do anything with Nicole that I would not have done in the presence of Grace?* The answer, as I thought back on our last stroll through the Tuileries, was probably yes.

Rain tapered off in the morning, and by nine o'clock Witty, LaRusse, and I were ready to cram ourselves and the photography gear into the Citroën one more time and make our way to the site of Paul Morel's watery death. I rode quietly in the back seat, groggy from a poor night's sleep, a tiny bit nauseated from the curves of the road, and a tad embarrassed by the previous night's conversation with Witty.

LaRusse knew the route to Fontaine de Vaucluse quite well, as he often came to this river for landscape photography. He shared a little history while Witty maneuvered the Citroën on a narrow road that wound through steep hills. Scraggly oaks on either side looked barely strong enough to suck water and nutrients from the alkaline soil.

"You'll see in a little while why it's called Vaucluse, which means 'closed valley.' And you know, Vaucluse is the name of the whole *Département.*"

"And we're going to Fontaine de Vaucluse, right?" Witty said.

"Yes, the source of the Sorgue River. We can park here and walk up to the pool at the top," LaRusse said. "It's about one kilometer, and this morning the trail is likely to be pretty muddy."

The path started out wide enough for a good-sized car. Through a canopy of trees we could see the river, perhaps fifteen meters wide, with its swift current carrying an unfathomable volume of deep green water past rocky banks. As the river gorge narrowed above us, the trail steepened to a tricky climb over slick rocks and muddy chutes. I wished I had my hiking boots, but of course Witty and I had only our slick leather-soled business shoes. LaRusse, in proper hiking attire, found it much easier to navigate the trail, despite his limp and the untold weight of cameras, tripod, and paraphernalia on his back.

To our right, the river turned from its swift dark green flow to impressive white water, surging over enormous boulders with a roar that drowned out any attempt at conversation. We stopped to observe the sheer power of the flow, and I mimed to LaRusse the snapping of a photograph, fingers clicking imaginary shutter releases. He nodded and found a spot to set up his gear.

"Do you know how far the boys made it in their boat?" Witty shouted over the roar of the rapids.

"Not really," LaRusse said. "I hate to think they made it this far. The sheer terror of being in that water would kill me long before I hit this drop."

"How on earth did Marcel survive this?"

When LaRusse was satisfied that he'd captured enough pictures from that vantage point, we continued up the ever-steeper path into the deepening gorge. Witty and I had done a fair amount of traveling in our lives, but neither of us had ever seen a river gorge with this kind of power. The narrowness of the canyon, the angle of its drop — not quite a waterfall, but steep enough to create almost 500 meters of non-stop rapids — inspired awe and humility in both of us.

"We're almost to the top," LaRusse shouted with a jut of his chin toward the trail.

We scrambled over rocks and navigated through mud until the trail suddenly opened to a flat basin. The roar of the river dropped away, and we gazed out over an enormous pool, its depth far beyond anything we could see. The pool, such a deep green that it seemed almost black, appeared to be ten or twelve meters across. Three sides of it were defined by cliffs that soared straight up at least 200 meters.

I craned my neck, letting my jaw fall open, and took in the height of the cliffs above. "Where does the water come from?" No waterfalls dropped over the cliffs into the pool. No river rushed in. Water from the deep pool simply poured over a single outlet and charged relentlessly into the canyon we had just hiked up.

"That's the miracle of this place," LaRusse mused.

"The pool reminds me of the one that separates Yosemite's upper falls from its lower, but in this case there's no 'upper' about it," I said. "The pool looks so calm, and then — boom — unbelievable turmoil below."

"That still-looking pool is actually a full-fledged river gushing up out of the depths," Larusse explained. "It's called a karst spring, and this is one of the biggest in the world. The flow has been measured at twenty cubic meters a second."

"Do you think the boys put the boat in here?" Witty said.

"Maybe the dare was to paddle around the pool and get close to the outlet," I speculated. "Maybe they never intended to go over the falls."

"You know, I wonder if Marcel was even in the boat," LaRusse said. "I just don't see how you could survive a beating like that."

"They said he suffered some injuries," Witty said.

"Yes, but that could have been from running down the trail, trying to rescue his poor brother," LaRusse said. "They did retrieve Paul's body, didn't they?"

"They did, indeed," Witty said, removing his hat from his head. I took a moment to reflect on the tragedy that had unfolded here more than forty years ago. If Paul were the only one in the boat, and Marcel watched helplessly from shore, the survivor's guilt may have been even greater than if he'd been in the boat with Paul. He may have spent the rest of his life thinking he — not his little brother — should have taken the risk.

"I've tried over the years to capture a photograph that conveys the power of this place," LaRusse shook his head. "But it's just about impossible. The trick is to get up high enough to show the cliffs, the stillness and depth of the pool, and the power of the rapids below." He excused himself to scramble up to a vantage point that he thought might work. We watched him set up his gear, perching on a narrow ledge well above the level of the pool.

"I hope we don't end up with another tragedy on our hands." Witty gestured toward the precariously perched photographer.

"You can say that again," I said.

"Do you want us in the photograph, or should we head back down the trail?" Witty shouted up to the intrepid young man.

"Stay there," LaRusse said. "I think you give it a certain scale that I've been missing."

By the time we made it back to the trailhead, the sun's rays were just hitting the tops of medieval castle walls that perched on a rocky outcropping on the opposite side of the river. The remains of the ancient castle of the Bishop of Cavaillon teetered high atop the ridge.

"Can you imagine trying to launch an attack on that place, back in the day?" Witty pointed to the castle walls anchored to sheer cliffs.

We piled back into the Citroën and followed the road down the canyon. Within a kilometer or two, the Sorgue widened into a gentle river that descended into a vast valley. The terrain quickly shifted from rocky cliffs with a heavy canopy of trees, to rolling hills and then to a bucolic valley floor, marked by a grid of agricultural production that extended as far as the eye could see.

The town of Isle-sur-la-Sorgue, known as the Venice of Provence because of its canals, lived up to its billing as a picturesque hamlet. About a kilometer east of town, at the *partage des eaux*, the river split several times to create various channels. A central island, the heart of town, was large enough to support substantial civic buildings, parks, and houses. Even as the river divided into channels, its flow remained strong and swift, and village inhabitants had harnessed its energy for centuries to power their paper, silk, and wool businesses. Moss-covered mills still turned along the river's edges throughout the town.

A row of houses lined the south side of the main channel. Each home had windows opening out over the river, and a competition seemed to be underway for the most spectacular window boxes. Many of the houses featured a door that opened to a small dock, and several kept a little wooden boat tied against the current.

"It'd be easy for a couple of teenagers, lubricated by a little alcohol and on a dare from their pals, to steal a boat and try something crazy," Witty said. "The Morel tragedy was years ago, but can't you just imagine it happening with today's kids?"

"Unfortunately, I can," I agreed.

We crossed the main channel on a footbridge that led to a small park. We strolled west, crossing two more channels into the historic village center. Streets narrowed between multicolored buildings rising three and four stories on each side, with pale blue shutters providing a common thread.

"You'd think the whole town would flood every spring," I said as we entered the Café Belle Vue, undoubtedly named for its perch where the river split three ways.

"Apparently the water has enough places to go that it doesn't back up here," LaRusse said. "Many of these buildings have been here since the fifteenth century."

We grabbed a quick lunch overlooking the river, but didn't linger. LaRusse was anxious to get to work developing his film. "If all goes well, we may have prints ready tomorrow afternoon."

WITTY AND I AGREED TO SPEND THE NEXT DAY APART. We had to wait for LaRusse to develop his prints, and Witty said he could use a day off. He and Babette planned a trip to Gordes, a stunning hilltop town built right into the cliffs. He'd heard about an excellent restaurant where they could go for lunch and then have a leisurely afternoon in the heart of the village. I welcomed a break from the lovebirds. Needless to say, Witty was getting on my nerves.

I decided to return to Roussillon to tie up a few loose ends. For one thing, I wanted a written statement from Marie about her mother's remains. And I hoped to go over her principal statement again and see whether she could offer any further detail. The evidence we'd collected so far seemed rock-solid, but my mind never rested until a case concluded.

I also wanted to make sure that Marie knew about the possibility of a living nephew who would be entitled to part of the inheritance. While I doubted she would have any qualms about splitting the money — since she evidently was not lacking for funds and didn't seem like a person prone to greed — I did worry about the emotional strain of coming to grips with the possibility of an illegitimate son of Paul becoming part of the equation.

When I knocked on her door, Marie seemed pleased to see me and invited me for a cup of tea on the terrace.

"I thought of another item that might interest you," she said.

"What's that?"

"Last night I remembered that I've carried this in my prayer book all these years." She opened a tattered treasure, her prayer book since childhood, and took out a mourning card in her brother's honor. "I've used it as a book mark. Not that I would ever need a reminder of Paul. I think of him every day."

"Still, it's a lovely thing to carry with you."

The gentle spring sun warmed our faces as we sat and chatted over black tea and biscuits. I quietly introduced the possibility — the likelihood — that we had come across a second legitimate heir. "If the evidence supports this theory, of course, you and that heir would each be entitled to one half of the inheritance," I explained.

"Who is this other heir? It has to be a blood relative of Marcel, right? Did he have a child?"

"Not that we know of, no." I shook my head and took a long pause. "We believe that your brother Paul, well, that his girlfriend Annette was with child at the time of the tragedy. You mentioned yesterday that there was some speculation to that effect."

"Yes, but I assumed it was just talk." She put down her tea cup. "Not that it's impossible. I mean, Mother and I left Goult and never looked back."

I waited for the news to sink in.

"But don't you think we would have known, eventually?" She gazed past the garden. "The Luberon Valley is not so big that we'd have been completely in the dark all these years."

"It appears that Annette left Goult about the same time that you and your mother moved to Roussillon. But she went all the way to Paris. It seems that she never looked back, either."

"In those days, she would not have been welcome back. A girl with child and — you know, unmarried — would have been wise to disappear into the city." Another long pause. "What do you know about this child?"

"We believe his name is Gilbert, and he's forty-three years old," I said. "If we're right, Annette gave him the family name of his father, Morel, but apparently she never told him anything about Paul or the rest of the family."

"I wonder why not." She had a distant look in her eyes.

"It may have been too painful for her, or she didn't want him seeking out his roots in Goult," I speculated. "Who knows why people make the decisions they do, especially after the trauma you all endured."

"And this boy Gilbert — this man — what can you tell me about him?"

I described the night watchman at the Louvre as a humble man who seemed very quiet and a bit odd. With few friends in evidence, he seemed absorbed in art and music. Having seen Marie's family photographs, I thought I recognized a resemblance, although I was anxious to reacquaint myself with Gilbert now that we had more to go on.

"Your description of his personality sounds a bit like Marcel," Marie said. "No social skills, lots of musical talent." She got up to pull a few weeds from around the lavender bushes. "Is Annette still alive?"

"You know, that's an excellent question. We'll know more next week when we return to Paris. But tell me, Marie, how do you feel about us sharing your information with Gilbert? I'll honor your wish, whether you choose to reveal yourself to this man or remain at a distance."

"If he is who you believe he is, though, he'll have to know that he's splitting the inheritance with someone," she said.

"True, but I respect your privacy and will do my best to keep your identity discreet if that's your wish. Your identity eventually will be part of the record, but I can keep it quiet as long as possible, and — who knows — he may never inquire."

She walked to the edge of the garden overlooking the Luberon. How would it feel to meet the son of her dear brother Paul? Surely he could not fill the void created when her precious soul mate was ripped from her life. But that wouldn't be her expectation. "Even if Gilbert had one ounce of Paul's gentle, sweet demeanor..." she started. It might be a salve on that old wound. "Of course, I have to remember he's forty-three. You know, I still think of Paul at age eighteen." What if he were disappointing, or even unkind? After all, without his father to raise him, who could say that he would have acquired any of Paul's sensibilities? How much was in his genes, and how strong were the influences of Paris? She had no way of knowing.

"May I give you an answer later, Mister Foster?"

"Of course, Madame." I went to stand by her side. "It's an important decision, and you can let me know your wishes when you're ready. Until then, I'll use my utmost discretion in my deal-ings with Gilbert. You have my word."

She met my gaze with genuine appreciation.

Before I left, I asked to see her mother's ashes. She retreated to the music room, where she opened a large cedar chest filled with sheet music, books, and a couple of blankets. She rummaged to the bottom, where she retrieved a metal box with a hook-style latch to secure its hinged lid.

"I don't believe in having this on display, like some people do," she said. "No elaborate urn on the mantle or bottle by the bedside. Mother would not have wanted it that way."

"I understand," I said.

She opened the box and gently untied a cloth bag filled with ashes.

"If I may paraphrase Jeremiah, *I wish you beauty for ashes, the oil of joy for mourning, and the garment of praise for the spirit of heaviness,*" I offered.

Marie signed a statement that I had prepared about her mother's remains, in case it might prove useful in court. Upon taking my leave, I realized I had developed a great deal of empathy for this woman who'd been a stranger until twenty-four hours ago. I promised to do everything in my power to ensure that her brother's estate would be settled properly, and that she would receive her full entitlement — whatever it may be.

38

Busby: July 12 — Los Angeles

THE NEXT WITNESS REID PUT ON THE STAND was a linguistics professor from the University of Southern California by the name of Victor Marlin. He looked the part of a linguistics professor, if ever there were such a stereotype. Tall and lean, with graying hair combed to one side, he wore a tweed jacket. His round tortoise-shell glasses gave him a professorial air, and his demeanor came across as calm, confident, and avuncular. I figured the jury would have no problem trusting him.

After establishing the professor's credentials, which were as long as the Nile, Reid directed the jury's attention to two poster-sized exhibits. One was an enlarged photograph of Babette's note to Witty, and beside it, on an adjacent easel, sat an enlargement of the anonymous letter to the judge claiming that Babette was Marcel's daughter. I still couldn't believe the *Times* had reprinted the letter, flimsy as it was, allegedly from some guy who said he was dying (how convenient) and had failed to fulfill Marcel's wish to find his daughter, Babette. Oh brother.

"Would you compare these two exhibits and share with us your observations?" Reid began.

"Let's start with the homophones, dear and deer."

"And a homophone is..." Reid prompted.

"Sorry, a homophone is a word that is pronounced the same as another word but has a different meaning. Spelling may be the same or different, but they sound the same."

"Continue, Doctor Marlin."

"In Miss Reville's hand-written note to Mister Whitman, she starts with 'my deer,' — d-e-e-r, like the animal — instead of 'my dear' d-e-a-r, meaning darling or beloved. We see the same usage in the anonymous letter: 'I was his very deer American friend,' right here." Doctor Marlin, with Judge Murphy's permission, descended from the stand and approached the exhibits. He used a pointer to call the jury's attention to the words in question.

"Let's move on to the misuse of the word 'which' in place of 'who' or 'whom.' This occurs in the first sentence of the anonymous letter, 'I am writing you in regard to Marcel Morel which died this year.' Of course, it should say '*who* died this year.' And in the note to Mister Whitman, Miss Reville wrote, 'You are a fine man which I like very much.' That should say '*whom.*' These are understandable errors for a person who's not a native English speaker." I noticed a few heads nod in the jury box.

"You can also see that the use of contractions is consistently incorrect in both missives," Marlin said. "In the letter we have the apostrophe at the end of hadnt', couldnt', and dont', but of course it should be placed between the n and the t, marking the elision of the vowel o."

"And in Miss Reville's note to Mister Whitman..." Reid led.

"She makes the same error in the sentence..."

"Objection!" Tresan interrupted. "Witness is only assuming that she wrote the other letter."

"Excuse me," Marlin said before the judge had a chance to respond. "The letter, whoever wrote it, shows the same error. 'But I know you wouldnt' marrie me.' And that brings us to the next consistent error, the use of 'ie' at the end of the words marry, sorry, body, and worry." You see it three times in the anonymous letter and once in Miss Reville's note." He emphasized the word "anonymous" in a tone just short of mocking.

"Yes. Does anything else stand out here?"

"The use of the term 'deprimed,' which you see in the anonymous letter, is quite interesting. The French word for 'depressed' is *deprimé*, but we don't use 'deprimed' in English. Language can be very confusing. It's an understandable mistake for a native French speaker."

Reid kept an eye on the jury, as he always did, and saw that some members were fascinated while others may have been losing the thread. He thought it best to return to specifics. I, personally, ate this stuff up. "So you're saying that the anonymous letter may well have been written by a French person, based on the use of the word 'deprimed.' "

"That's right. In addition, I see a couple of what we linguists call 'false cognates,' or *faux amis* — false friends. They can be very challenging in learning a new language. The word 'chance' exists in both French and English, but they have different meanings. In French, it means 'luck,' as in *bonne chance* — good luck. In English it means opportunity, as in I did not have the chance to do something. You see in the anonymous letter that the author says, 'I looked for her for months but had no chance so I stopped looking.' I suspect that a native English speaker would have said he had no luck or no success."

"That's a subtle difference, Doctor Marlin," Reid said, "but I see your point. Are there others?"

"Well, this may sound obscure, but to me it's significant. The word 'actually' in English means 'in truth or in reality.' In French it means 'right now,' or 'at this moment.' Where we would say 'actually, I'm very depressed,' a French person might say, *'en realité.'* You see the phrasing 'in reality I am severely deprimed' in the anonymous letter. This supports my opinion that it is written by a French person."

"Yet the letter claims to be from Monsieur Morel's American friend. Are you confident the anonymous letter in question was written by a French person?"

I thought Reid was picking up steam, but I'm a writer. Language is my thing. The jury seemed to follow it well enough.

"One more thing," Marlin said. "The letter uses the expression 'the carrots are cooked.' It's strictly a French idiom, *les carrottes sont cuites.* We'd say it's a done deal, or the writing's on the wall, but an American would never say the carrots are cooked."

"So it means something is done and there's no turning back," Reid clarified. "I'll ask again, Doctor Marlin, are you confident the anonymous letter was written by a French person?"

"I'd go further than that. Considering all of the linguistic characteristics of the anonymous letter in comparison to Miss Reville's note, it is my professional opinion that both were composed by the same person," he said. "And that person happens to be French, yes." He nodded toward Babette. Tresan started to get up from his chair, but thought better of it.

The questioning continued, with additional exhibits of the letters that Tresan had entered into evidence. One of the letters that was supposed to be from Marcel to Colette, using an odd mix of English and French, contained the word 'marrie' instead of marry. Doctor Marlin pointed out that Colette's alleged response, all in French, claimed that she was *deprimée.* By the time Doctor Marlin finished, Babette had pulled her hat down over her eyes and slouched down in her seat. She didn't even know about the next witness Reid had lined up to discredit her.

39

Witty: March 12 — Paris

BEING BACK IN THE HOTEL DES MARRONNIERS after our foray in Provence, things remained a tad icy between Reid and me. Maybe I'd been a little hard on him about his obvious attraction to Nicole, so I resisted the temptation to look her up while we were in Paris. Chances were, she was still having fun with her cousin Guillaume. While Babette and I lived it up over the weekend, Reid did his own thing. I think he mostly stayed in the hotel poring over LaRusse's photographs from Provence and noodling strategies for the Los Angeles court case. The poor fellow might worry himself to death.

We got a telegram from Marie saying it was okay to share her information with Gilbert Morel. I was looking forward to meeting the fellow. From Reid's description of their brief meeting near the Louvre a couple of weeks before, he sounded quite odd, but how lucky could one man be? If we were right about him, the night watchman was about to become a millionaire.

On Sunday evening, I met Reid back at the hotel. He'd checked with the personnel office at the Louvre, and they confirmed Gilbert had the night shift that night.

"We'll have to get up before dawn tomorrow in order to find Gilbert at the café in the Jardin des Tuileries," Reid said.

"Up before dawn? Good God, man, you're going to make a Puritan of me yet," I said with an eye roll.

"We'd better turn in early, then," Reid said. The ice hadn't thawed.

GILBERT DIDN'T RECOGNIZE REID at the café in the Tuileries. After a brief re-introduction, he remembered their conversation and asked after Nicole. Reid introduced me and ordered coffee and tea from the barman. Things started clicking when Reid finally had the chance to ask Gilbert his mother's name. It was Annette. Another piece of the puzzle fit.

"Does she live in Paris?"

"No, she died several years ago," Gilbert said. "Consumption."

"So sorry."

We spent the next two hours filling Gilbert in on what we'd learned in Provence, drawing up a family tree to illustrate the connections as we understood them, and sharing family photos. Now that we could compare the images to Gilbert, we were certain we had the right man. Gilbert and Paul shared a certain look that was hard to pinpoint. They both appeared slight and angular, with thick brows over eyes that conveyed a look of wonder verging on anxiety. The long nose and close-set eyes seemed part of the gene pool, passed down from Estelle to both her sons and her grandson.

"I want to show you some photographs from my school days," Gilbert said. "I think you'll be surprised by how much I looked like Paul at that age." He seemed overwhelmed by the revelations about his new-found family — stories that his mother took to her grave — and by the knowledge that an aunt was alive and well in Roussillon. What struck him most, though, was the artistic side of his father, which he could see in the birthday cards and doodles that Reid showed him. "I was always drawing pictures and carving little things out of wood," Gilbert said. "I loved to dabble in art. My mother wasn't particularly encouraging, though."

"She wasn't?" I asked. "Why in the world not, if you don't mind me asking."

"I can't say that I blame her. You see, my doodles and carvings were often on the walls of my bedroom, or right into a table, or on some school assignment. She thought I was destructive, you know."

"But she encouraged your music?"

"Yeah. When I was old enough — maybe twelve or thirteen — she gave me a viola." He positioned his hands as if playing the instrument. "Huge step up from the miserable little piece the church ladies found for me when I was younger. It's my favorite thing. Always has been."

"You still have it?"

"Sure. I play it almost every day." He took another swig of coffee. "Now I wonder if it was my father's instrument."

"She didn't tell you?" Reid sorted through the photographs that Marie had provided, and found one that showed the three siblings — Marcel, Paul, and Marie — posing with their musical instruments. Marcel may have been sixteen years old, pinching his violin between chin and shoulder, right arm poised to bring the bow across its strings. Marie sat at a small upright piano, her adolescent face beaming over her right shoulder toward the camera. And Paul stood beside the piano holding the viola across his chest with his left hand, bow in his right.

"My God," Gilbert said. "That's it. That's my viola." He pointed out a detail in its carving on the scroll and a scratch in the body. "That's the very same instrument." He wiped a tear off his cheek with the back of his hand.

Reid asked whether we might impose on him within the next day or two to visit again, this time with a photographer who could create some images for evidence. We would want pictures of the viola, and of course of Gilbert, and anything else that might be relevant. We agreed to visit him the next afternoon at his home, a room he rented on the Rue de Fleurus, not far from the Jardin de Luxembourg.

GILBERT MOREL RENTED A ROOM AT 49 RUE DE FLEURUS from a woman named Isabelle Brieune, a widow in her late sixties who'd been a friend of his mother, Annette. She had taken him in when Annette died, five years earlier, of congestion of the lungs. Gilbert had always lived with his mother, never able to make enough money with his art or music to strike out on his own. Madame Brieune received him gladly, renting him a small room on the third floor for just thirty francs a month, well below going rate for Rue de Fleurus. The street had become quite well known because of the popular salon hosted not far away at the home of Gertrude Stein and Alice B. Toklas.

At three o'clock, Reid and I, photographer in tow, walked up the steps and knocked on a large wooden front door nestled into an arched portico. Gilbert invited us into an elegant sitting room with high ceilings and intricately carved moldings. Double-casement windows let in a good deal of light from the tree-lined street. A fire warmed the sitting room, and an eclectic collection of artwork crowded the walls.

"Aunt Isabelle — Madame Brieune — wanted to meet you," Gilbert said, "so she'll join us for tea. But first, come up to my room so I can show you a few things." We walked up a wide wooden staircase with treads worn in the middle from years of footfalls. On the second floor, I peeked past an open door to catch a glimpse of the master bedroom. An intricately carved ceiling caught my eye, and light streamed in through an open window to create striking shadows in the woodwork.

Moving along, we climbed a narrow stairway to a small room on the third floor, which had its own tiny bathroom. It appeared that Gilbert packed everything he owned into this cramped space, including music, artwork, books, clothes, and who knew what else. There was nothing neat about the place, but I guessed the price was right.

The photographer followed us up the stairs, but there was no way four men could fit into the tiny room, so he suggested that he set up downstairs where the light was better, and that we bring key items to him when we were ready.

"Here's the viola." Gilbert gingerly handed the instrument to Reid. "You can see the carving here on the scroll, and this scratch that's been there forever."

"Just like the photograph shows," Reid said.

"And my school photos." Gilbert offered them to me. "I think you'll notice a resemblance, you know, between the teenage versions."

"Without a doubt." I handed the photographs to Reid. Discoveries like these — the viola, photos, family traits and stories — were my idea of heaven. And to think I could make a living tracing roots and whatnot.

Gilbert also showed us some of his sketches. Although Reid didn't expect they would be particularly useful as evidence, they left no question about his artistic leanings. It shed light on his passion for the job at the Louvre.

We descended to the sitting room and set up the photo shoot.

Madame Brieune glided into the room with a silver tea service, her falsetto voice asking who would like a little drink and a pastry. She directed Gilbert to bring in some plates and small forks, along with the tart she had bought from the *boulangerie* on the corner. She wore a long house coat, which may have been her definition of casual, but it appeared elegant on her statuesque frame. She wore her graying hair in a loose bun at the top of her head, not worried about the few strands that fell down her long neck to her shoulders.

"It's so rare that Gilbert has visitors," she said, "and never from the United States. Such a treat!"

I took her hand and gave it a little kiss, introducing myself and my sidekick. "Enchanted, my dear lady."

"This could be habit-forming," she said. "I could start my own salon for handsome young American men, just like my neighbors down the street." Charming.

"You're too kind, Madame," I demurred.

"But that's not why you've come," she blushed. "Tell me about your little project." She poured tea and we settled into chairs that might have suited Napoleon and Josephine.

Reid gave her the short version of our quest and touched briefly on our encounter with Marie in Roussillon. I shared the family tree we'd sketched, showing Paul and Annette as the parents of Gilbert. Madame Brieune looked a little uncomfortable that we were discussing the family in front of Gilbert, who was now serving up a beautiful apricot tart. Reid picked up on her discomfort and assured her that Marie had been pleased to learn that she had a relative in Paris, and that she would look forward to the chance to meet him some day.

That said, Madame Brieune relaxed a bit and told us that she'd known Annette since childhood.

"So you are from Goult," I said. I'd noticed the family name of Brieune in the cemetery there, but didn't want to make any assumptions.

"Yes, I went to school there and married Simon Brieune when I was twenty." A half smile came over her face. "Don't do the math, but I'll tell you that was in 1874. We moved to Paris two years later so Simon could study medicine." She said they never looked back, although they did stay in touch with relatives and friends in Goult. Simon became a doctor and they enjoyed a lovely life in Paris. She looked around the beautiful drawing room, implicitly expressing her appreciation for their life together.

"So you left Goult while Annette was still in school." I had done the math and figured that Annette would have been six or seven years younger than Isabelle.

"That's right," she said. "When things got difficult for Annette, a couple of years later, she sought me out in Paris." Madame Brieune seemed to tiptoe around the details of those years, not wanting to upset Gilbert. Or maybe unplanned pregnancy and an illegitimate child weren't subjects a lady of her stature cared to discuss in polite company.

"Such a tragedy about the boating accident, and the toll it took on the family," I said to move past the awkwardness.

"Yes, it was so tragic." She reminded us that she had already left Goult before all this unfolded. "I didn't really know the Morel family all that well. Marcel was a couple of years behind me in school, and he really kept to himself. Paul seemed like a nice boy, but we didn't know each other well. Marie was quite a bit younger." She recalled seeing them at church and at community events — how could you not, in a town the size of Goult — but said they had no close ties. "They were always doing something musical, though, just like Gilbert."

"How did you get to know my mother so well, if she was so much younger?" Gilbert asked.

"I was her babysitter," Isabelle said. "Annette was an easy child. I quite enjoyed those times." She went on to describe how Annette found her in Paris, through the medical school where her husband studied. They'd helped her settle into a small apartment in Paris, find work as a secretary, and take care of little Gilbert. With a fresh start in the big city, she operated on the premise that she was a widow, since nobody needed to know that her husband perished before they had a chance to marry.

"And she never fell in love again?" Gilbert asked.

"Oh, honey, I don't think her heart ever had a chance to mend." Isabelle topped off her tea. "From what I could tell, we were her closest friends, but I never felt that she really opened up to me. She kept everything to herself."

"She sure didn't share it with me," Gilbert said. "I knew nothing about my father. She just wouldn't talk about him."

"She kept a wall around her emotions the size of the Louvre, Gilbert. It wasn't your fault."

The conversation continued until darkness fell. The photographer took his leave to begin developing the film, and Gilbert excused himself to get ready for work. His shift began at seven o'clock, and he needed to have a proper supper before it began. Madame Brieune offered to answer more questions, but we thought we had enough to go on. We just confirmed, once Gilbert left, that Annette did not have any other children.

"No, she was a bit of a wounded soul, poor thing," Isabelle said. "She did love Paul, and never seemed to recover from losing him. Of course, she loved her son, but she seemed almost afraid to love him too much for fear that she would lose him, too, if she allowed herself to get too close."

Isabelle confessed that she worried about Gilbert. "He's such a talented boy. I know, he's a man now, but I'll always think of him as a boy, I suppose. Anyhow, he has his music and he loves art, but he's a bit odd. I don't think working the night shift helps anyone's social life, but it's particularly limiting for him. He just doesn't seem to have any friends."

"A bit like his uncle Marcel, then," I ventured.

"That's right — quite a bit like Marcel, now that you mention it. From what little I knew of Marcel, he lacked social skills, as well."

Madame Brieune clearly was very articulate and no doubt would be able to write a good narrative of the facts surrounding Gilbert's history. Reid asked whether she might be willing to write a statement, just a few pages, that he could use as evidence.

"If it will help Gilbert, I'd be more than happy to write something for you," she said. "I sort of promised Annette that I would look after him." She expressed a little concern about format, and Reid advised her to think of it as a letter to him. He suggested she begin with her childhood in Goult, her acquaintance with the Morel family, her relationship with Annette, and then of course the arrival of the young woman in Paris to begin a new life with her infant son. "Keep in mind that we're working to establish that Gilbert is the nephew of Marcel Morel," Reid suggested. "You might want to mention the musical thread running through the family, and any other family traits that reinforce the connection."

"Excellent." Madame Brieune swept toward the door. "Why don't you come back tomorrow evening, and I'll be sure to have it ready for you. And then you can join me for the salon at the home of my neighbors, William and Edna Thomas. There will be lots of young Americans there, along with the French literary crowd. Bring your friends."

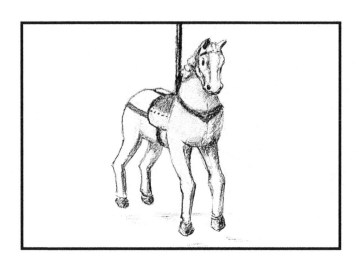

40

Reid: March 14 — Paris

WITTY AND I SPENT WEDNESDAY MORNING at the Hotel des Marronniers discussing the evidence, making arrangements for our return journey to California, and communicating with contacts back home.

"Babette will be joining us," Witty said in a matter-of-fact tone. "She will travel at my expense, Reid, so you needn't worry." I simply nodded.

We were able to secure passage for three on the *Berengaria*, scheduled to depart from Cherbourg on March 16, just two days away. We booked train passage to Cherbourg for the following morning.

Now that we had reservations to return home, I allowed myself to feel the homesickness that I'd kept at bay during almost two months away. This trip had the flow of a river, starting slowly and meandering around blind corners. We'd navigated a few rapids, picked up speed, survived some twists and turns, and now it felt like we were on a slow, wide patch that would take us home. Who knew whether a waterfall might surprise us downriver, in the form of the trial ahead. We'd left home on January 26, and I estimated I'd be back by mid-April at the latest. My thoughts raced: reuniting with Grace and the girls, sleeping in my own bed, making love to my gorgeous wife, returning to my practice in my cozy little office, catching up with May Wu, making sure she was safe from that awful oilman. These thoughts had crossed my mind many times during the journey, but I'd always forced myself to focus on the task at hand, and not dwell on the past or future. Now I allowed just a few moments to anticipate homecoming, and it felt good. It felt wonderful. I loved seeing new places, adored the charms of Paris and Provence, thrilled to the adventure of tracing families' histories, and thrived on the challenge of gathering solid evidence. And the greatest thrill of all would be to return to my family.

Witty and I noticed Babette sitting in the hotel garden. She was paging through a fashion magazine or some such thing.

"It's our last day in Paris, puddin'." Witty bent to kiss her. "Let's make it our best."

"Oh, Witty, I'm so excited about going to America," she gushed. "But I do love Paris."

"I've booked lunch for two at the Tour d'Argent. And then we'll take you shopping. You'll need clothes and whatnot for the journey. Bring your magazine, and show me what suits your fancy."

"I'm not sure you can afford me," she said. "Are we not living too high in the pork?"

"What? Oh, high on the hog." He stroked her cheek. "I've got a good feeling about this case. Let's just say that today I'm feeling flush. You'd better take advantage of it while it lasts."

"How much time do we have before our lunch date?" No doubt she found this extravagant man irresistible.

"For you, my love, there's always time." I looked away as he kissed her long and hard. "For you, there's nothing but time."

I SPENT MY LAST AFTERNOON IN PARIS TAKING IN SOME of the sights. From the hotel, I walked west on Rue Jacob, which soon became Rue de l'Université, running roughly parallel to the Seine toward the Eiffel Tower. I was curious to see the enormous structure, which had been controversial since its erection for the 1889 World's Fair. I'd read that a group of prominent artists, poets, and architects of the time, including Charles Garnier of Paris Opera fame, protested that the "useless and monstrous" 300-meter tower would dominate Paris like a gigantic black smokestack, crushing under its barbaric bulk Notre Dame, les Invalides, and even the Louvre. The tower held the record as the tallest structure built by man, dwarfing the great pyramids of Egypt and surpassing the Washington monument. The stated intention was for the tower to come down after the World's Fair, but three decades had passed and there was no sign that the enormous steel structure was going anywhere. I wanted to see it for myself.

Standing directly under the base of the tower and looking up, I could only admire the tremendous engineering that it represented. Not one to embrace ostentation, I expected to dislike the colossal beast. But I couldn't help but appreciate the sweeping design that melded the pure strength of its steel with intricate delicacy of elegant style. Just as the Bradbury building, which housed my office in Los Angeles, blended wrought iron with marble staircases to create an ingenious mix of industry and art, the Eiffel Tower brought together the marvels of modern technology with undeniable grace and panache.

I hiked up the stairs to the first viewing platform, and then decided to pay a franc to take the elevator to the second level. The views, of course, were stunning. High above Paris, I gained a new appreciation for the enormous city's design, radiating from the original Ile de la Cité and Notre Dame in the heart of the Seine. I gazed northeast to the white domes of Montmartre's cathedral, and then found the Louvre and Opera Garnier in the city's maze.

My eyes panned from the Arc de Triomphe down the Champs Elysée to the Place de la Concorde, its obelisk looming over the square's elaborate fountains. Beyond them, I could see the entrance to the Jardin des Tuileries, right down to the Arc du Carousel and the courtyard of the Louvre. In my mind, I retraced the steps I'd taken on that morning with Nicole, when we braved frigid air to venture out and meet Gilbert. I smiled at the memory of our syncopated rhythm, her short steps against my long strides. I remembered how we shared the thrill of making those first connections to the man I now knew was Marcel's nephew. But the stronger memory was the pleasure of strolling through this remarkable city with Nicole on my arm. I wondered whether I would ever see her again. *The answer,* I thought, *should be no.* I had to admit that Witty was right, that my connection with Nicole went beyond friendship, well into dangerous territory. I promised myself again and again that I would not contact her at her cousin's place in Paris.

I walked to the other side of the tower's immense platform and gazed south, as if walking away and redirecting my focus could remove the longing I felt for Nicole's companionship. *No, it can never be,* I thought. *Some day, I'll come back here to enjoy this view with Grace and the girls.*

I made my way back toward the hotel by meandering through streets leading roughly east from the tower. Having gained the perspective of Paris from the second platform, I found new confidence in navigating its crooked streets. I knew that I could work my way east and a little south, and I would soon come to the glistening gold dome of les Invalides.

AT THE SOIRÉE ON RUE DE FLEURUS, Babette swished into the salon with a new, more elegant look. Witty, dressed in his tuxedo, seemed proud to have the sophisticated-looking young lady at his side. As a rule, I paid little attention to fashion, but even I noticed a difference in her appearance.

"Allow me to elaborate on today's shopping success," Witty offered. He seemed fascinated by fashion. "The elegant miss Babette sports a slip-over with a triple-tiered skirt ending just above the ankle, creating a refined and simple line. Note the beaded embroidery and metallic thread, providing a subtle sheen to the contemporary look."

It was the least I'd seen of her legs since she'd barged into our lives in Avignon. There was nothing subtle about the color, a cranberry red. Her copious lipstick matched the color of the dress, and I looked away as she brazenly reapplied it in public several times during the evening. The dress's long sleeves and square neckline provided far more coverage than she normally wore, a refreshing change from Babette's usual emphasis on her ample bust. To say she looked sophisticated may have been an overstatement, but she came far closer than she ever had.

That said, she wore a ridiculously large hat, probably a meter in diameter. She wore it tilted to one side to expose black satin gills that I thought resembled the underside of a portabello mushroom. I worried that she would knock over someone's drink with the gigantic headpiece, and I gave it a wide berth.

Madame Brieune made sure that Witty and I received the proper introductions, not only to our hosts, but to some of the more interesting American guests, including Sylvia Beach, whom we'd met at Shakespeare and Company, and Ezra Pound, Pauline Pfeiffer, and Janet Flanner.

"Miss Flanner has just arrived in Paris and is writing a weekly column for a magazine back in the states," Madame Brieune said.

"Do tell," Witty said with his usual charm.

"It's a weekly letter from Paris for *The New Yorker*," she said. "My pen name is Genet."

"We'll be sure to look for it. I have no doubt it will be delightful. What a thrill to meet you."

"What are you writing about now?" Babette asked.

"Fashion," she said, with a long look at the portabello hat. "I think I'll do an article about millinery." She excused herself to chat with friends who were just arriving.

I worked my way across the crowded room to follow up with Sylvia Beach. I reminded her that we'd met a couple of weeks earlier in her marvelous bookstore.

"I thought you looked familiar," she said graciously. "When were you in?"

"It must have been almost two weeks ago, although for me it feels much longer," I said. "We've been to Avignon and points beyond on what looked for all the world like a wild goose chase."

"Did you catch your goose?"

"Actually, I'm fairly confident that we found two of them, as luck would have it."

"Congratulations." She lifted her drink in salute. "Will you be staying in Paris long?"

I explained that it was our last night in the city; we would sail from Cherbourg in two days. I thanked her for finding the books by Hutcheson, which no doubt would provide fascinating reading for the passage home.

"Well, *bon voyage*, as we're so fond of saying in these parts. Perhaps someday you'll write a novel about this wild goose chase."

"Highly unlikely. My mind is too prone to the straight and narrow — too lawyerly, if you will — to weave a good tale. Maybe one of my daughters will tackle it one day. My eldest is already making little story books, complete with illustrations."

"How old is she?"

"Maureen just turned five." It tore me apart that I'd missed her birthday.

"My heavens," Miss Beach said. "Sounds irrepressible. I expect she may show up at my doorstep one of these days looking for a publisher."

"One can always hope," I said.

"*Bon voyage*, and *bon courage*."

As the evening wore on, the room filled and people began spilling out in all directions — into the kitchen, dining room, and even into the courtyard, though frigid night air kept them coming back inside to vie for space by the living room's massive hearth.

The crowd grew quiet when our host, William Thomas, made a few introductions and then invited two poets up for short readings. Among the introductions, much to our surprise, were Witty, Babette, and me. Thomas explained that we gentlemen were just in from America to conduct important research, although he did not specify what type, and that Babette had graciously joined us to improve the visual impact of our presence.

"But don't get too attached to them," Thomas said. "I understand they're heading back to America tomorrow."

During the first reading, I felt someone place a hand on my shoulder. I turned and saw a woman's hat, a modest black piece with feathers adorning its little brim. Auburn hair poked out around its edges. The woman lifted her chin to look up at me, and I let out a small gasp. Nicole smiled up at me, with her lively eyes and exquisite cheekbones. She slipped her arm through mine and tugged at me to come outside so we wouldn't interrupt the reading.

In the garden, I gave her a long hug and realized how much I'd missed the human embrace. In my chest I longed to hold her and not let go, but I made myself release her.

"How long have you been here?" I asked.

"Just a little while," she said. "It was so crowded by the time we arrived, we almost didn't come in. It's a good thing Mister Thomas introduced you, or I might have missed you altogether."

"Let me look at you." I held her at arm's length. "How have you been?"

She looked radiant. Paris seemed to suit her.

"New outfit?"

"I've been shopping. The fashions here are delicious. You can't tell in the dark, but this dress is crepe satin in crow black — just a subtle luster and a hint of shine." Its waist, sitting just below her natural waist, flattered her figure — not like some of the drop-waist dresses of the evening that gave the women a boxy, androgynous look. Her modest hat added the perfect touch. "I never thought I'd care about fashion, but how can you not, when you're in Paris."

We strolled through the little garden and marveled at the night sky.

"*Canst thou bind the sweet influence of Pleiades, or loose the bands of Orion?*" I quoted, nodding toward the constellations. We caught up on each other's latest adventures, sharing tales until the chilly night air drove us inside. We dodged the crowd by finding an alcove off the kitchen where we could continue our conversation. Nicole had made good progress on her research about family ties and had already met several cousins that she'd not known about before coming to Paris.

"It's amazing how much these cousins and I have in common," she said. "There really is something about family connection that's unlike anything else. I mean, it runs deep, beyond physical traits. Aptitudes, personalities."

I agreed, sharing my experience of finding the remarkable musical ties that ran through the Morel family. And, I reflected, Marcel may have been an odd duck much like Gilbert. "Come to think of it, Gilbert gives me a better understanding of Marcel. Now I can imagine his isolation in Los Angeles, and how his death could have so little impact on the people around him."

"I like to think somebody would miss us if we popped off," Nicole said.

"You'd be missed." I gently drew her into my arms. Again, I wanted to hold her there forever, but reminded myself of my vow not to do anything I would not do if Grace were right there at my side. I took Nicole by the shoulders and looked into her sparkling eyes. "But don't go popping off any time soon, alright?"

"I hadn't planned on it."

The noise of the party picked up, indicating that the poetry readings were over, although we were too far away to see what was going on in the drawing room. We found it difficult to talk over the din, yet we had so much catching up to do. I suggested we go find a cup of tea and have a proper chat.

"Did you come with anyone?" I asked.

"Just my cousins. I'll let them know we're leaving."

I found Witty and Babette deeply involved in conversation, both a bit lubricated by the free flow of champagne.

"How are you two holding up?" I asked.

"No more champagne for me, or I'll fall in the apples," Babette oozed. I tilted my head and raised an eyebrow.

"French idiom, meaning she'll pass out." Witty explained. "What are you up to?"

I said Nicole and I were stepping out for a cup of tea, and I agreed to meet them in the hotel lobby by eight o'clock the next morning to catch the train.

"Don't do anything I wouldn't do," Witty joked, jabbing his elbow into my side.

As Nicole and I emerged into the brisk night, we realized it really wasn't a cup of tea we wanted, but a good walk and the chance to truly catch up. We headed toward the Luxembourg Garden, just down the street, and entered the park.

"Let's go to the carousel," she said. "It's my favorite thing."

We walked down the crushed-granite path, barely visible under a sliver of moon that sat low in the sky. Ducks scooted across the inky water of a pond to our right, and an owl called in the distance.

"Listen," I said. *"The clamorous owl, that nightly hoots, and wonders at our quaint spirits."*

"A Midsummer-Night's Dream. One of my favorites," Nicole said. "I think the carousel is down this path to our left. I've never been here at night."

The carousel, like the rest of the park, was dark, but Nicole led me around the edge until she spotted her favorite merry-go-round animal, a lion with enormous teeth and wild eyes, forever in pouncing position. "Help me up." She placed her hands on my shoulders.

Nicole was feather-light in my arms. My stomach felt like a pit writhing with snakes. If I opened my mouth, vipers' heads might slither right up my throat.

She sat sidesaddle on the lion and kept a hand on my shoulder for balance.

"It's a shame you're leaving tomorrow," she said.

"I know, but our work here is done." I tried to look away. "There's tremendous pressure to get back to Los Angeles and start legal proceedings."

"And your family's waiting," she whispered.

"Yes, my family is anxious to see me," I said. "And I them."

Nicole tried to hide her tears in the dark, but she found herself losing control. "Forgive me, Reid. I know I shouldn't tell you what I'm about to tell you." She wiped a tear from her cheek. "It's not at all like me, but I think the prospect of losing you forever…"

"It's not that…"

"No, let me finish," she said. "I've fallen in love with you, Reid. It started on the *Berengaria*, deepened in Paris, and tonight I just have to let you know the truth. I'm utterly and hopelessly in love."

"But…"

"I know you're a married man, and my feelings for you are completely inappropriate, but I can't help myself."

"Maybe you're caught up in the romance of Paris, and the fact that I'm leaving in the morning."

"No, I mean…yes, of course. I'm silly and naïve and romantic. But you have to admit that we share a deep connection."

"Of course we do." I worked up the courage to look into her misty eyes. "I've tried to deny it, myself. In fact, I *have* to deny it because there's nothing I can do but return to my family."

"But you do have a choice," Nicole pleaded. "I know it's crazy, but I have to tell you that I think we could make a life here in Paris.

It's a place to reinvent yourself, choose a new life, make a fresh start. We could do that together."

"Nicole, you don't understand." My brain was on high boil.

"All I need to understand is that I love you." She sobbed quietly. "And I think you love me."

"That's not the point. The truth is that I love God, and I love my family, and I made a commitment to all of them. Whether or not I love you is not the question. The fact is, my life is back in California, and that's where I must go."

She lowered herself off the lion's back and into my arms. Her lips found mine, and I tasted her warm, salty tears on my tongue. I felt dizzy, floating away in her embrace, letting myself feel for just an instant what my life could be.

"I can't do this," I said. "I just can't. Let me get you back to your cousins."

She straightened her hat and smoothed her coat. "I'm so embarrassed, Reid," she said as they walked back through the park. "Can you ever forgive me?"

"Nicole, you will always be dear to me, but you will never be mine."

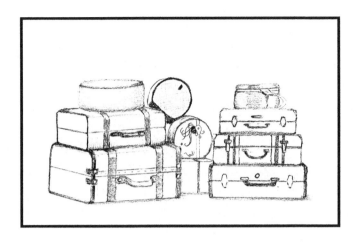

41

Witty: March 15 — Paris

Leaving the Hotel des Marronniers, it was not at all certain that we three travelers and our luggage would fit into one cab. Babette's shopping spree had generated a trunk full of clothing and accessories, plus a slew of hat boxes and whatnot. Just the enormous hat she'd worn to the salon the previous night needed a box that dwarfed most normal luggage. She corralled a second trunk of "necessities" and three sizable bags of "personal items." The concierge suggested we get a second cab, just in case.

"Looks like you had a successful shopping spree yesterday," Reid said with just a hint of judgment in his voice.

"Just can't get enough of the Paris fashions!" Babette pulled on her gloves.

The train to Cherbourg was not crowded. Reid, mister precise, made a point of sitting on the right side of the car. Said he wanted to take in his last views of the beautiful French countryside and let the morning sun warm his face. Of course he'd thought through

299

which side would have the morning sun as we headed north, and where the best views might be.

"What do you think of our beautiful country by now?" Babette asked him.

"I've grown quite fond of France in our short time here," he said. "I really like the strong sense of community in little villages like Goult and Roussillon. Los Angeles could learn a thing or two." He was right; rural France knew the value of a small village with a single church, a central gathering place such as Café de la Poste, and a few key providers like the town baker, grocer, and the occasional art gallery. "Soon L.A. will be one massive metropolis, especially if cities like Eagle Rock are annexed to provide water to the dense downtown population," he went on. "Of course France has its enormous cities with their own charms, like Avignon and Paris. But the other thing I notice is that houses don't encroach onto fertile farmland. They build on higher, rockier ground. Sure, back in medieval times, the high ground provided defense against intruders, but now it means protection of precious agricultural land below." He'd obviously given it a lot of thought.

"Come have a drink with us, my friend," I said.

"We're celebrating," Babette added with a giggle in anticipation of yet more drinks. I hadn't told her about Prohibition in America yet. She'd find out soon enough.

"No thanks, you go ahead," Reid said.

We swayed down the aisle toward the lounge car, which was nearly empty at ten o'clock in the morning. Nonetheless, we ordered two martinis from the young man tending bar and serving coffee, and we found another couple willing to join us for a pop. They had two young children in tow, a boy and a girl who were glued to the window.

"Is this their first time on a train?" Babette asked the parents.

"Yes. They were a little frightened at first, so we told them to keep track of the number of cows we passed," the mother said. "They haven't left the window since we emerged from Paris."

But cow-counting ended when they heard my bassoon playing Alouette, a song I'd picked up during the Great War. Soon the kids were mesmerized, and I remembered the trick of blowing smoke through the instrument.

"Anybody have a cigarette?" I asked. The father offered one, so I lit it, took a deep puff, and blew into the instrument. Smoke billowed out the end while I picked up Alouette where I'd left off. The children screamed with delight.

Before long, I put down the bassoon and pulled out a couple of coins and my handkerchief. The children were completely baffled and fascinated by my sleight of hand, despite my limited repertoire.

"So much for their fear of train travel," the father said.

"But we'll never know how many cows we passed," Babette noted.

Arrival in Cherbourg seemed to send Reid into a funk. I took him aside.

"What's on your mind, old boy? You worry too much."

"It's nothing."

"No, really. I know I've been a little hard on you, but let's move on. Tell me what's on your mind. Are you fussing about the case?"

"Well, that, and…"

"And what?" I wondered whether anything had happened with Nicole on our last night in Paris, but didn't dare ask. I could see they shared a spark, and it must have been tough to say goodbye. No telling what happened after they left the salon.

"It's personal."

"You know, I've got eyes. Just say it. Are you thinking about Nicole? How long it might be until you see her again?"

"I can't ever see her again," he said. "Never."

"Never say never, my friend."

"No, last night she ruined it for me, the fantasy that we could be friends and maintain an innocent connection. That's gone." I wanted to hear more, but he turned away. He wasn't the sharing type.

When we checked into the hotel — the same one we'd used on our way to Paris — Reid retired to his room to write one more letter to Grace that might make it home before he did. He also took a few minutes to send a telegram to May Wu and another to Busby, just checking in from Cherbourg before sailing. He figured that the crossing would take eleven days, and then he would take the train from New York to Los Angeles, leaving Babette and me to bring the car out in a more leisurely fashion. It would be more expedient for him to take the train, and we could use a break from each other. With any luck, Reid would be home in just over two weeks.

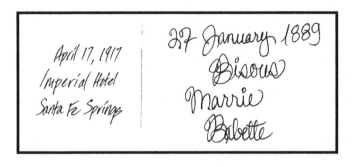

April 17, 1917
Imperial Hotel
Santa Fe Springs

27 January 1889
Bisous
Marrie
Babette

42

Busby: July 13 — Los Angeles

I'M NOT ONE FOR SUPERSTITION, but when the trial convened on the morning of Friday the thirteenth, I had to wonder if Reid felt a little extra pressure. He was in the middle of destroying Babette's claim to the fortune, and it seemed to me today would be make-or-break for him.

The next expert witness Reid called to the stand was Walter Butz, a forensic document examiner, more commonly known as a handwriting expert. Reid established the man's professional credentials and made sure to differentiate between the science of document analysis, which Butz did, and the art of graphology. Graphology was more like palm-reading, where one claimed to be able to determine personality based solely on handwriting.

"The primary basis of handwriting analysis as a science is that every person in the world has a unique way of writing," Butz testified. "In primary school, we all learned to write based on a particular copybook — a style of writing — which, by the way, differs between America and France. At first, most of us wrote in a similar style, but as we grew up, we developed individual characteristics that are unique to each of us."

"But don't people write differently depending on their mood, or how tired they are?" Reid asked his witness, this time knowing the answer in advance. "Surely we don't write exactly the same way all the time."

"That's true," Butz offered. "But we can compare individual characteristics, and the chance of two or more people sharing twenty or thirty individual characteristics is virtually impossible. One or two, yes, but tens, no."

Butz explained how he worked, starting with an exemplar, or a writing sample known to be written by an individual in question. In this case he used Marcel Morel's handwritten ledgers and business records, which Morel had kept over many years, as the exemplar. He then compared the exemplars to Jake Tresan's exhibits, the two letters that Morel allegedly wrote to Colette Reville back in 1889.

"What, specifically, did you consider when comparing the exemplars to the questioned documents?" Reid inquired.

"The good news was that we had so many good, untainted exemplars spanning a number of years," Butz began. "While each person's handwriting is unique, no person writes exactly the same way twice, as you said. Using a magnifying glass, I considered a variety of traits. Letter form includes slants, curves, the proportional size of letters — and by that I mean height difference between tall and short letters — and the links between letters. I also look at the initial stroke, and factors like I-dots, horizontal crosses, loops and circles, and whether there's a crosshatch through the z or the number seven. And I look for proportion within a letter, such as whether a capital B has a larger base than top enclosure."

"What else?" Reid asked. The jury seemed totally engaged, and I sure was.

"Line form," Butz continued. "Here I look at how smooth and dark the lines are, which indicates how much pressure the writer applies, as well as the speed of writing. For this I use a microscope."

"Any other factors?"

"Yes, the third consideration is formatting. This includes spacing — between letters and between words — placement of words on a line, margins at the edges of a page, and spacing between lines."

In his next step, Butz displayed side-by-side enlargements of one exemplar and a letter allegedly written by Marcel to Colette. As an exemplar, he used one of Morel's financial ledgers with plenty of written words, such as the names and descriptions of properties, lenders, tenants, and dates. The questioned document was the first letter, dated 27 January 1889. The differences flew off the page. In his financial records, Marcel's handwriting appeared stark and compact, with a forward slant. Each downstroke fell at about ten degrees right of vertical, well defined, and quite pronounced. Loops were so tight they were barely visible. The dot over each i seemed more of an accent, also at about ten degrees right of vertical, indicating a high speed of writing. Tall letters generally rose about twice as high as short letters, and letter and word spacing were compact. Furthermore, Marcel's ledgers put the month first, then the day, then the year.

In contrast, the alleged 1889 letter looked airy and loopy, with a backward slant. Loops were very round and fully formed. Even the downstrokes appeared rounded, and leaned slightly left of vertical. Tall letters topped out just above short ones, and the i-dots looked very round and deliberate. The pace of writing, Butz said, was very slow and careful, which he verified under a microscope by looking at how much ink was on the paper.

"You will notice, in the date at the upper right of the letter, that the number 'seven' has a crosshatch and the 'one' in '1889' has a long leading stroke. These characteristics are typical of the style books used in French schools," Butz said, using his pointer for emphasis. "In contrast, Monsieur Morel, in his ledger, has dropped the leading stroke from his 'ones,' and there are no crosshatches on his 'sevens.' Not to psychoanalyze the decedent, but I would venture that he made a conscious choice to adopt the American style when he left his native France forever."

"Objection!" Jake Tresan leapt up from the table. "Speculation!" He was getting desperate to find any way of slowing down this testimony.

"Sustained," Judge Murphy ruled. "The jury is to disregard the last remark."

We all knew that the jury would not forget the point, and Reid calmly urged Walter Butz to continue.

"Well, I can state with complete confidence, and it is my professional opinion, that the documents in question — the letters — were not written by the same person as the exemplars, the ledgers of Monsieur Morel," Butz declared. "In addition, it is my professional opinion, if we're ready to move on," he looked to Reid for a nod of approval, "that the letters submitted into evidence — all four of them — were written by the same hand."

Butz unveiled a third exhibit, an enlargement of the letter allegedly written by Colette Reville on 3 January 1889. He detailed the numerous ways in which the lettering was similar to the correspondence allegedly from Marcel. The Colette letter appeared slightly more loopy and slanted even farther to the left, and the i-dots were actual circles. But with the three exhibits side by side — Marcel's ledger on the left and the two letters clearly displayed — the differences and similarities became obvious, even to me.

"Mister Butz, if you are certain that this letter was not penned by Monsieur Morel, do you have any idea who wrote it?" Reid asked.

"If I may, I have one more exhibit," Butz said, nodding to a fourth easel while Reid unveiled another enlargement. Jake Tresan let out an audible sigh. "Here we have the note that Miss Babette Reville penned to Mister Lyle Whitman on or about May 15 of this year."

I glanced at Witty, who looked a little green around the gills. This couldn't have been easy for him.

Butz explained that, since this was a known sample of Babette's writing, it would be considered an exemplar. From this note, Butz was able to point out one similarity after another. Most of the comparison repeated the patterns that he detailed before in the alleged exchange of letters between Marcel and Colette. He added that the proportion, slant, and circle formation in the capital B were the same in Babette's signature and "Bisous" of the alleged Colette letter.

"Normally, in my profession, we like to have several exemplars," Butz said. "But in this case we have just the one for Miss Reville. It is an excellent sample, and it is my professional opinion that it shows that Miss Reville penned the exchange of letters alleged to be between Monsieur Morel and Colette Reville. But I wanted more certainty. So I did a chemical analysis of the paper and ink."

I watched the jury as Reid led Butz through a description of his scientific method. Reid had Butz detail the chemistry and then asked for his conclusions. Despite the technical subject matter, the jury was glued. So was I.

"It is my opinion that Babette Reville wrote these letters, and that she did so within the last month. We can tell through examination in the laboratory, with a high degree of certainty, how long ink has been on paper," Butz said. "If these letters were written thirty-four years ago, as their dates indicate, the ink would be much more integrated with the paper. The paper, in fact, would have aged significantly, and almost certainly would be drier and far more yellow. Modern paper manufacturers use chemicals now that minimize yellowing, but before the turn of the century the chemistry was different."

"So you can say without a doubt that these letters were written within the last year," Reid said.

"That is correct. I have no doubt whatsoever," Butz said. "Further, they were likely written with the very same pen. At least the ink is the same across the letters and the note."

I had no idea this type of science existed. Butz had laid it out, clear as a bell.

In cross-examination, Jake Tresan did his best to discredit the witness. His approach was to attack the whole field of handwriting analysis, saying it was in the same category as tarot cards, Ouija boards, and crystal balls. It was a good thing Reid had established early on the difference between document examination and graphology, and Butz handled the cross like a champ.

43

Reid: April 4 — Los Angeles

I HAD FORGOTTEN HOW MILD the Southern California weather could be, especially compared to Boston and Paris. I arrived home on a Wednesday night and promised Grace that the rest of the week would be all about family. Work could begin the following Monday. We spent the first precious days taking advantage of glorious spring weather. We planted summer vegetables in our kitchen garden. Inspired by the courtyards I'd seen in France, I also put in lavender, rosemary, roses, and rows of herbs — thyme, oregano, sage, basil, and mint. We packed a picnic for the whole family and took the trolley up to Mount Lowe, where we had always loved the stunning views of the entire Los Angeles basin. The girls were delighted when the trolley car made an unscheduled stop to let passengers ramble out into bright fields of golden poppies, an orange carpet at the base of the San Gabriel Mountains. The extraordinary bloom happened only once every few years, and it became as much a tourist destination as Mount Lowe itself.

I couldn't get enough of the girls, who'd grown unbelievably quickly in the two and a half months I'd been away. Normally, when I was home with them, they seemed to change overnight, or even when my back was turned. But the transformation of their young lives during my absence was beyond comprehension. Dorothy had begun walking in late March, and she was starting to string together words. Margaret was shy with me at first, hiding behind her mother's skirt and keeping her distance. She'd always been quiet, but now her reluctance toward me made my chest ache. I didn't push it, though, knowing that she would do things on her own schedule. She always did. Within a couple of days, she took to crawling into my lap when I read the evening paper.

If Margaret was like a cat, scooting in when I paid her the least notice, Maureen took after an irrepressible puppy bouncing around me in search of attention. She was more talkative than ever, weaving stories that seemed to mix reality with a very imaginative narrative voice living in her head. Grace encouraged her to illustrate her stories, and they'd put together little picture books that Maureen just couldn't wait to show me. They were little more than stick figures and a few words, but with her help I managed to decipher them.

My reunion with Grace felt like Heaven. I had no intention of ever letting her know about my feelings for Nicole, of course. No need to hurt her. I would mention Nicole as a friend and as a pleasant addition to the journey. In truth, my close call with Nicole served to remind me how precious my wife and children were to me. They were my home base, my touchstone, my moral support, my soulful connection, and my reason for living. In fact, I returned home with a renewed sense of gratitude, knowing that what I needed was right here in front of me. Father once told me love was a visceral feeling that took over when a person's priority switched from one's own wellbeing to that of his beloved. Now I understood.

"I thought we could have May Wu join us for dinner this weekend, if you're not too tired," Grace said. "She's been so good with the girls while you've been away. She helped me set up a little Easter-egg hunt, and then we all went to church services."

"I'm so sorry I missed it. Did you get photographs of the girls in their Easter dresses?"

"Yes, and your mother was there in fine form. Father stayed in the desert. Anyhow, I expect May Wu will want to catch you up on business, but when she's here we try to talk about anything but work. For her sake and mine."

"That's a wonderful idea." I put aside the newspaper. "Can't wait to see her. I'm sure she'll have things in good order at the office, though I can't imagine I'll be able to see over the top of my in-box on Monday morning. The mere thought of it is beyond overwhelming."

"Work'll come soon enough." She leaned over my chair and put her hands on my chest, placing her cheek on the top of my head. "Let's just enjoy the weekend, first."

"Grace, what would I do without you?" I pulled her into my lap and looked into her eyes with genuine appreciation. Slowly, I brought my lips to hers. I had never felt anything so soft and delicious.

Grace roasted a chicken for Saturday's dinner. I could smell rosemary blending with the chicken's crispy skin all the way from the sitting room. Grace asked me to come in and help with mashed potatoes and green beans, my favorite side dishes. I plodded into the kitchen and inhaled the luscious aroma of apple pie baking, with extra cinnamon, just the way I liked it. It wasn't quite the full Easter dinner I'd missed the previous Sunday, but it came close.

I put my hands on Grace's cheeks and planted a long, deep kiss on her open mouth. "Delicious," I said.

"The potatoes." She handed me the masher.

May Wu brought two folders from the office, with profuse apologies to Grace. "There's much more on his desk, but I thought he should see at least these," she said.

"It's inevitable," Grace sighed.

The first folder contained newspaper clippings regarding the Morel case, including the ones Busby had written for the *Los Angeles Times*. Some described a few of the fortune hunters who had surfaced during the last two months, and May Wu said stacks of information on that front awaited me at the office. "Busby's come by a few times, just to toss ideas around and see if I had any inside information from you in France," May Wu said. "We compared notes about that awful guy, Randy Hardaway, too."

"He seems like a real creep. Did he ever threaten you again?"

"No, but I kept the door locked the whole time you were gone. Anyhow, it seems like you hit the jackpot in Goult."

"Goult and Roussillon both," I said. "It was amazing to see these little villages, so close that one looked across the valley to the other, yet they were worlds apart in terms of families and communities. I mean, when Estelle Morel fled Goult to begin a new life, all she had to do was move to Roussillon, and she and Marie pretty well started fresh from there."

"How far is it?"

"Less than from here to downtown, I'd say. I commute farther every morning on the Red Car."

The second folder contained communication with Judge Murphy, including a few letters and documents that May Wu had provided in my absence. I would read them later. But today all that mattered were family and friends and reconnecting.

After dinner, we gathered in the living room.

"Tell us a story, Auntie May," Maureen pleaded.

"Maybe your father has some stories for us," she said.

"Or maybe you have a story for us, Maureen," I said. The thought of Sylvia Beach and her authors brought a smile to my face.

"Okay. When Maureen and Margaret and Dorothy were little," Maureen began, with her third-person narrator in fine form, "a man drove to their house in a big yellow car. It was a very fancy car, with big shiny metal on the front and fancy tires that had white sides. The man came into the house and opened a long black box. The box had a long tube in three parts, which he put together to make a baboon." We chuckled.

"Go on," I said, not wanting to correct her.

"Next, the funny man lit a cigar. He took a deep puff and then he blew smoke through the baboon and made a song."

"A torch song, you might say," May Wu said.

"Do you remember Witty?" Maureen asked me. "He gave us silly nicknames."

"Of course I do. He and I have been on a big adventure across the Atlantic all the way to France and back."

"Will he ever find us again?"

"Yes, dear, I expect we'll see him again very soon," I said. "I'm not sure exactly when, but he's on his way." I took a minute to wonder where Witty might be, and what sort of diversion Babette had created during their road trip across the country. The case work could progress to a certain extent without him, but we'd need him back soon.

44

Busby: April 11 — Los Angeles

I TOOK THE STAIRS OF THE BRADBURY BUILDING two at time, bounding up to Reid's law office for my eleven o'clock appointment just in the nick of time. I slicked down my hair, straightened my tie, and put on the suit coat that I'd carried over my shoulder. I hoped it would cover the ink stain in my shirt pocket. My lucky/ leaky pen had done it again. I entered the office and found May Wu at her desk.

"Th-the boss is back, eh," I said, looking out the fifth-floor window to the busy street below.

"Yes, in body, anyhow. I think his mind's still on the journey."

"It must have… don't you… I'm guessing it was quite an adventure. Chasing here and there, tracking down clues about this Morel character," I said.

"Mister Foster will be just a minute. Can I get you a cup of coffee, tea, water?"

"Water, if it's not too much trouble." I was overheated from my jog here from the *Times* building, so I took my jacket back off. *Ink stains be damned*, I thought. Summer had already pushed its way into Southern California, sending daytime temperatures into the high seventies.

May Wu peeked her head into Reid's office. He was ready to see me.

"Mister Busby, it's a pleasure to see you again." I'd forgotten how tall Reid was, and he didn't look any the worse for wear after his long journey. The man looked ready for a screen test. "Have a seat."

I pulled a stark wooden chair up to his desk. It was piled so high with paper that Reid had to push stacks to either side and form a channel for us to communicate

"Pardon the mess," Reid said. "As you know, I've been away for nearly three months."

"Yes, sir. Thank you for the telegrams. It sounds like you had a productive trip."

"We sure did. Very productive."

"What would you...um...do you mind if I interview you and work it into an article for the *Times*?"

"I'd be happy to bring you up to date, Brick," Reid said. "But first I wonder if you could do the same for me. May Wu provided a few of your clippings, and I'd like to go through the facts as you understand them. You've been here with your ear to the ground while we've been off chasing clues around Paris and Provence."

"Of course." I loosened my tie. "How can... What do you want to know?"

"First off, how many claimants do we have by now?"

"Well over four hundred, I'm told."

"How in the world..." Reid started, but his voice tapered off while he collected his thoughts. He said he'd spent Sunday afternoon reading my articles, which shed some light on the developments since Morel's death. The first article, dated January 22, carried the headline, "Rich, He Lived Like Poor Man." A sub-head said "Makes $5,000,000 in L.A.," and just below it, in smaller type, "Heirs of Wealthy Marcel Morel Still Unknown." The triple-header definitely was overkill, but the editors insisted. No doubt their desire to sell papers also ramped up the fortune-hunting frenzy. My article described Morel as a reclusive millionaire whom passersby might have thought a hobo because of his shabby dress and unkempt appearance. Not only did he dress in tattered, mismatched clothing, but he'd been seen hitchhiking around the area in an old straw hat. Little did people know, the article said, he was seeking a ride to visit property that he owned in Santa Fe Springs — land that he leased to oil companies "at a figure that is said to have rolled fortune into Morel's bank account." My article portrayed him as a modest man who had come to Los Angeles in the early 1880s with a small amount of money in his pocket.

"After looking over the virtual pueblo with its horse-drawn streetcars, Morel decided he would build a house and rent it out. And he did," I'd written. "When that panned out, he built more, and then more again. Through hard work and shrewd planning, he achieved his ambition of building thirty rental houses. Next he invested in land, and soon oil was discovered on that land. From these humble beginnings grew the Los Angeles fortune which few, if any, persons knew Morel had." Reid didn't seem terribly impressed with my writing, but, hey, I was just getting started.

I made a point of embellishing Morel's oddities, his eccentric ways, his good luck, and the "magic rise of land values in Los Angeles and the discovery of oil on the acreage once considered far out in the sticks." I wrote that the man had few friends, few clothes, no automobile or other luxuries. And he left no will.

"This article must have generated quite a bit of interest," Reid said, holding it up behind the packed desk.

"Ah yes, that's when the court started getting flooded with inquiries." I sat up a little straighter. "You know, the *Times* is

316

distributed around the country, and even into Canada, so the court heard from people as far as Virginia and Quebec."

"In your articles, I didn't see any mention of that awful man — Hathaway, was it?"

"Hardaway. My editor nixed that, but I still think he had something to do with Morel's death. Just can't prove it."

The next article that Reid picked out of the folder, which was written by a woman named Deborah Malone for the Inland Express, made me look like a contender for the Pulitzer Prize. She described the flood of inquiries and claims that had inundated the Superior Court, highlighting one from Mary (a.k.a. Minnie) Moreau, inmate of a Hartford, Connecticut almshouse, crippled and very much in need of even the smallest portion of the $5,000,000. The claimant had learned of the Morel death in the *Times*, and alleged — through an attorney — that her father and the millionaire shared roots in Toronto, although she offered no details about the specific relationship between her parent and the decedent.

"I'm a bit confused about this one," Reid said, reading a passage to me. *"Minnie's attorney discovered that her father was 'something-or-other' to the millionaire's father."* He shook his head. "How can a newspaper print this drivel?"

"You know, that paper is basically a compilation of the social pages." I fidgeted in my uncomfortable chair. "They don't do much editing there. I suppose it's a little vague, eh."

"A tad."

Miss Malone's article went on to describe a thrilling adventure across the high seas, "a journey during which genealogist Lyle Whitman and his sidekick, Los Angeles attorney Reid Foster, scoured the countryside for the rightful heirs." It read a bit like a cheap novel, with flimsy allusions to French cheese, Impressionist art, and dancing girls. Reid wondered out loud whether Judge Murphy took time to read these articles, and whether they might tarnish his own standing before the court.

"I'd like to write a serious article about your French adventure," I said. "You can see from my last piece that I dropped a few hints about the clues you picked up in Paris and Roussillon, which you mentioned in your telegrams. Can we go deeper?"

"Let me discuss it with my colleague and let you know." I could see that Reid, by nature, was reluctant to share details of their trip, or their evidence, with the press. But he might find it useful to convey that they had serious evidence, in hopes of discouraging frivolous claimants like Miss Minnie what's-her-name.

"What are your next steps?" I asked.

"I'm just preparing a statement of heirship on behalf of two relatives we found in France, and we'll include what's called a 'Partial Genealogical Chart.' It's a sort of place-holder until the trial gets underway." Reid had to cut our meeting short, but suggested we meet Thursday at Cole's Diner for lunch and conduct the interview there. I assured him we could get the corner booth where we wouldn't be interrupted.

"D-do you remember Violet, the cute little waitress there?" I asked. "You know, she was the one who always served Monsieur Morel. Anyway, she and I are dating now."

"Congratulations. I'm pleased to know that something good has come of this case already."

"Yes, and she holds the corner booth for me at lunch when she can. I've taken to writing my drafts there, which I consider a real step up from the coroner's office."

"Well done," Reid chuckled. "See you there at noon."

THE INTERVIEW WENT QUICKLY, and lunch hit the spot. Reid said he missed the elegant food of France, but also appreciated the simplicity of a place like Cole's Diner. He enjoyed a scrumptious bowl of tomato soup and a hot roll, and I went with my new favorite, the French dip and fries. I have to admit, I was nervous. My crazy long legs kept jiggling against a post that supported the table, causing bottles of condiments to rattle incessantly. The only time I stopped shaking was when Violet came by to check on us.

My article appeared on the front page, taking up about seven column-inches. "Attorney Travels 15,000 Miles to Find Estate Heirs," the headline declared. "Bearing a trunk full of evidence collected in connection with the fight for the $5,000,000 estate of the late Marcel Morel of Los Angeles, Attorney Reid Foster last week returned from a trip to France. He and forensic genealogist Lyle "Witty" Whitman collected solid evidence and took statements that will be used to determine the rightful heir or heirs of the Morel estate in proceedings before Judge Fergus Murphy."

The article provided specifics about Reid's discovery of a nephew in Paris and a sister in Provence. "Foster took statements of witnesses in the remote villages of Goult and Roussillon, and documented family history in the Luberon Valley of Provence. Morel, who died in January, left no will. He was unmarried and no living brothers or sisters, nieces or nephews, parents, aunts or uncles were known — until now."

Judge Murphy issued an order that all petitions to claim heirship must be filed by May 1. He made it clear the court would not consider any petitions received after the deadline, and that a proceeding to determine heirship would begin on May 3. The first steps would be to hear preliminary statements, which were expected to number in the hundreds, and begin to eliminate claims unsupported by evidence. "Our aim is to separate the wheat from the chaff so that when these depositions are finally read to a jury, weeks or months hence, the proceedings will meet with no delay," the judge said.

V. RESOLUTION & REFLECTION

45

Witty: June 25 — Los Angeles

THE TRIAL DRAGGED ON AND ON as the long line of fortune hunters streamed through the process. I thought they seemed like kids at a carnival, lining up for their shot to toss a ring or throw a dart in hopes of winning a big prize. But this time the trophy would be more than five million dollars. We had arranged for Gilbert Morel to come to Los Angeles, in case Reid needed him to appear in court. I could only imagine the shock he was in for, going from night watchman at the Louvre — never having left Paris — to America where he most likely would become a multi-millionaire.

I'd made it a point to be at Union Station on the afternoon of June 25 when Gilbert stumbled off the train, so exhausted that he looked like his feet had stopped communicating with his head somewhere back in Chicago. The relief he felt when he saw me waiting on the platform nearly buckled his knees.

"Do we need a porter to get your trunk?" I asked in my rusty French.

"Trunk? I just have this bag." Gilbert patted the duffle that rested on his weary shoulder. "And my viola, of course."

"That's it? Where are all your clothes, books, toiletries?"

"This is it. I don't have many clothes," he said. "For work I wear a uniform, and otherwise I just have this one suit." He wore a brown wool suit rumpled with travel, and I noticed the distinct odor of lanolin and sweat. Even if a cleaner could restore the over-worn suit, it would be far too heavy for the Southern California summer. It was clear we had some shopping to do.

I took the duffle off Gilbert's shoulder and whisked him off to my Packard. The poor man tried to keep his eyes open to take in the sights of Los Angeles, but within three blocks he slumped against the window with eyes closed and mouth slack. I took him straight to the hotel. We could shop for clothes later.

It was five o'clock in the afternoon when I checked Gilbert into the Biltmore. All the Frenchman wanted was a hot shower and sleep, so he declined my offer of tea in the Rendezvous Lounge. He had slept fourteen hours when I met him for breakfast the next morning and then embarked on a mission to dress and groom the poor fellow. By noon, he had a new haircut, a close shave, two summer suits, and an appropriate selection of shoes, shirts, and shorts.

We dropped the shopping bags at the hotel and strolled over to Cole's Diner, where we had agreed to meet Reid and May Wu for lunch.

"How go things at the trial, my friends?" I asked while we waited for a table.

"More of same, so far," Reid said. "Weak pleas and wishful thinking, for the most part."

"But they're getting toward the end of the list of claimants," May Wu said. "I think I glimpsed the proverbial light at the end of the tunnel this morning."

"I just hope the light isn't a train barreling toward us." Reid rubbed his forehead.

The four of us slid into in a booth by the window, and Reid switched to French to try to explain the menu to Gilbert. He found himself using American terms like "sandwich" to describe other American terms such as "hamburger," and finally asked Gilbert what he was in the mood for. They settled on a steak and fries, with a side salad.

When Violet approached to take our order, she stopped dead in her tracks and stared at Gilbert. The sight of him knocked the wind out of her.

"Pardon me," she said after a pause. "Don't tell me who this is, because I can tell you without a doubt that he's a dead ringer for Marcel Morel. It's my pleasure to meet you, sir, and I'm sorry for your loss." She held out her hand to shake his, and then turned to Reid. "His son?"

"Nephew, in fact. Gilbert, meet Violet."

"*Enchanté*," Gilbert rose slightly off the brown leather bench seat.

"I knew your uncle," she said. "He ate here most days. Fine man."

Gilbert nodded, although he understood nothing beyond "uncle" and "man." He could tell by her tone and gestures that she was saying nice things about the gentleman he'd never met, and never knew existed until six weeks ago.

After Violet took their order and moved on to another table, May Wu said, "There's your ace in the hole."

"I completely agree." Reid smiled, looking more encouraged than he had for a while.

"Did you see her reaction to Gilbert?" May Wu shifted in her seat. "You couldn't have a better testimonial about family resemblance. We didn't introduce them, but she knew immediately that he was related to Marcel. He hadn't spoken a word. Think about it."

"You're so right," I said. "Violet would be dynamite on the stand."

46

Reid: July 12 — Los Angeles

Since Gilbert's arrival in late June, I'd had him sit in on the trial a couple of times. Witty sat in the back with him and explained what was going on. I didn't want the poor guy to be a deer in the headlights if we did end up putting him on the stand. Still, I hoped it wouldn't be necessary. I think his favorite aspect of the trial was noon recess, when we often went to the Broiler or Cole's Diner. The Frenchman had discovered the joy of an American hamburger and did not hesitate to return to it again and again.

On July 12, the day after Witty's testimony, we all headed to the diner for lunch. May Wu and I each ordered a bowl of soup, and Witty feasted on his usual steak and fries. Gilbert had a burger. We discussed the morning's proceedings. I don't know what made him nervous — maybe seeing Witty on the stand — but he seemed pretty upset.

"Will people know who I am?" he asked. "If I testify."

"We'll have to explain to the jury who you are and how we found you in Paris," Witty said.

"You seem concerned," I said.

"I am embarrassed," he said.

"Why? You've done nothing wrong."

"I was born wrong." He put down his burger. "The word we use for a child whose father isn't married to the mother is 'bastard,' and it's also used as an insult."

I caught May Wu's eye for just a moment, and then she reached for a bread roll in the center of the table. Her French was good enough, having studied it in school, to get the gist of the conversation. Body language filled in the nuances.

"Ah, that," Witty said. "Yes, the terminology is the same here."

"Will I have to testify?"

"As I've said, it's possible that we'll put you on the witness stand," I said. "But at this point it's unlikely. I doubt it'll be necessary."

"Won't people be angry that this bastard is going to get so much money?" Gilbert asked.

I heard Witty chuckle to himself. He might have been just a tiny bit delighted that Babette would be furious if the jury granted the money to this lucky bastard. But he answered Gilbert in sincere tones, reassuring him that we were only finding the rightful heirs, and that he needn't worry.

"Will I be in the newspaper?"

Witty and I immediately glanced at the corner booth, where Busby sat, feverishly writing up notes from the morning's proceedings. "Oh yes," I said. "This story is big news. But please don't worry, Gilbert. You are just the victim of circumstance, and soon — if this trial goes the way it should — you will be its beneficiary, as well."

"Good God, man, you stand to inherit millions of dollars." Witty couldn't keep his thoughts to himself any longer. "Who cares if somebody calls you a bastard?"

"It's not that simple," May Wu said.

I looked at my watch and signaled for the check. It was time to head back to the courtroom.

THE NEXT TWO DAYS OF TRIAL WENT VERY WELL, and I thought the jury understood the proof Marlin and Butz provided regarding linguistics and handwriting. By the time we broke for the weekend, I felt confident we could spare Gilbert the agony of testifying. I did have one more witness, just to put a bow on it.

My final move was to bring Violet to the stand, where she described her first encounter with Gilbert Morel. She was a little nervous, but I guided her through a series of very simple questions. We established her familiarity with Marcel Morel, whom she had served for several years at the diner. She probably knew him better than anyone, which was a sad commentary on the man's life.

"When did you first meet Gilbert Morel?"

"It was just last Wednesday, July eleventh."

"Did anyone tell you who he was?"

"It was the strangest thing," she said. "I saw him across the room, and at first I thought Marcel was back."

"But you knew Marcel had passed away."

"That's right. So then I thought he must be Marcel's son. There was no question they were family."

I displayed a photograph of Marcel and then had Violet identify Gilbert, who had moved to the front row for her testimony. The resemblance was unmistakable.

After that, Gilbert shied away from the courtroom and steered clear of reporters. He found the entire process embarrassing and overwhelming.

47

Busby: August 1 — Los Angeles

ELECTRIC FANS IN THE COURTROOM PROVED no match for the sweltering Los Angeles heat on the afternoon of August first when the case finally went to the jury. It looked to me like a pretty clear-cut case, by the time the various claims made it through the process. Most were dismissed because, well, they were downright weak. No evidence to speak of, just wishful thinking. Reid did a bang-up job of destroying the credibility of the remaining claimants. At least, that's what I thought. But I wasn't on the jury.

Reid looked pretty confident. Rational people, it seemed, would have no doubt that Gilbert Morel and Marie Morel Mathieu were the only rightful heirs to the fortune. But he told me once that his faith in juries ranked just above his belief in fairies and goblins.

I had a chance to ask Reid why we never saw the second heir, Marie, at the trial. Reid said he'd sent weekly telegrams to her in Provence that "struck a tone of optimism without instilling undue confidence." He respected her decision to remain in Roussillon.

Her testimony would have been helpful, but he felt confident that their case put them head and shoulders above the rest.

"Why interrupt her placid life in Provence?" he said. I got it.

I spent that evening putting together a comprehensive story for the *Times*. My suggested headline, subject to the whim of my editor, was "L.A. Jurists to Debate Morel Distribution." I wrote that more than 700 documents had been introduced, nearly 500 depositions presented. The enormous court fees hadn't been tabulated, and it wasn't clear who would absorb the costs, but they would be astronomical. The case initially attracted roughly 450 claimants and more than 150 lawyers, but by the end, the number of serious claims had been whittled down to just a few. I wrote that the jury would need a long time to sort through the evidence, and I encouraged readers to check back for a verdict in the coming days or weeks.

Reid would try to convince the judge to have the losing claimants cover court fees, since they'd made it such a complex case, but he told me, off the record, he wasn't particularly worried about it either way. While costs were going to be sky high, he also knew the Morel fortune had been growing at a healthy rate of almost 10 percent annually since Marcel's death. That meant that, in eight months, it had added well over $300,000, plus regular income from all the rental houses and oil fields.

48

Witty: August 1 — Los Angeles

R EID AND GRACE HOSTED A DINNER at their home in Eagle Rock that night for Gilbert, May Wu, and me. Absent a verdict, it fell well short of a celebration. It was more like an enormous exhale of relief that the case finally had gone to the jury. I, of course, entertained the girls, to their unmitigated delight — and mine. Gilbert seemed exceptionally withdrawn. Grace tried to engage him in conversation, but her French was very limited. It seemed that, even if they spoke the same language, the man would have little to say. Maybe we were getting a glimpse of the personality that had made his uncle, Marcel, such an eccentric. These things ran in families.

After dinner, the girls begged to stay up with the grown-ups. They insisted that they were not sleepy, although Maureen could not resist the temptation to rub her eyes.

"Play us some music, Witty," she said. "Please."

"What a brilliant idea, my young friend," I said. "In fact, when I brought Monsieur Morel from the hotel, I insisted that he bring his viola, as well."

The two of us took turns playing short pieces, I on bassoon and Gilbert on his father's viola. Soon we developed a sort of call and response, and then played tunes in the round, starting with *Frère Jacques.* It's always so delightful to realize that relative strangers who speak different languages can communicate through music. Such fun! Maureen got up and danced around the living room floor, and Margaret waved her arms as if she were a world-renowned conductor. Little Dorothy, despite all the commotion, fell sound asleep on May Wu's lap. Gilbert's demeanor changed completely with his beloved viola tucked under his chin. He made eye contact with the girls and his entire body became more animated than I'd ever seen him, even at home in Paris. The only other time he'd shown a glimpse of passion was when he'd discussed the Impressionist painters in the Louvre, but there could be no doubt that music made his spirit soar.

We visited well into the night, mixing music and stories. After a while, Reid waxed philosophic about family.

"You know, this trip taught me a lot. Father always said that travel is essential, not just for the light it sheds on foreign lands and cultures, but for its fresh perspective on home," Reid said. He hadn't even had any alcohol. "In talking with various people about their lives — their family complications, village scandals, births, deaths, lost connections, tragedies of war — I realize that family is at the core of our existence. And here I don't just mean family as defined by blood lines, but maybe the better word is community, or even tribe, or kin, meaning how people connect to one another."

"Amen," May Wu said.

Grace suggested that they get to bed, in case the jury came in the next day, but my response was something along the lines of, "Fat chance."

"Maybe I'll actually be able to sleep tonight," Reid said, putting an arm around Grace's waist. "At least I won't be awake in my office until two or three, for a change."

"Thank goodness for that. It'll be so nice to have you back," she said.

49

Busby: August 2 — Los Angeles

MY GUESS ABOUT THE JURY'S TIMING WAS WAY OFF. In fact, they needed just six hours of deliberation to reach a verdict. They named only two legal heirs — Gilbert Morel and Marie Morel Mathieu — to the $5,000,000 estate. State and federal inheritance taxes were to be deducted first, and expenses would be paid, leaving just over $4,000,000 to be split evenly between the two heirs. The best part of the outcome, according to Reid, was that the jury issued a separate verdict specifically denying inheritance to Babette Reville. Jurors left no doubt regarding their opinion of her claim to be Marcel's illegitimate daughter. Several self-asserted first cousins, nieces, and nephews were also denied, along with Audrey Fife and Mildred Dodge.

Reid and Witty split their fee down the middle, each getting 5 percent of the fortune, or about $250,000. Witty had experienced this kind of success twice before, to a lesser degree, but for Reid it truly defied comprehension. On the courtroom steps, he gave a few quick statements to the press and then said he had to get back to the office. Really? He told me later that, in truth, he couldn't wait to tell Grace.

EPILOGUE

1/15/1923
Morel dies

5/3/1923
Trial Begins

8/2/1923
Verdict

Reid: August 2 — Los Angeles

AFTER A QUICK PHONE CALL HOME TO GRACE with the good news, I prepared a telegram to let Marie know of our success. Her success. I also helped Gilbert write a message for Madame Brieune. Then May Wu and I sat in the office in stunned silence, enormous grins refusing to leave our faces.

"What will you do with the money?" she asked.

"Invest it wisely." I thought for a minute. "My family should never have to worry about money again. The girls can have the best education. Grace and I can travel. And you and I, partner, we're set. We can stop worrying about money, about our future. No more sweating about whether this little law practice is going to make it."

"Are you going to break down and get an automobile?" she asked. "Your client would be so impressed."

"The Auto Club can keep its autos. I'm quite satisfied with our public transit." I shook my head. "What about you, May Wu? What would you like to do now?"

"I don't know. I've been thinking about Gilbert. He seems so conflicted about his lack of a normal family. I think he's a good man, just terribly shy."

"With a good dose of self-loathing. I wonder how this will change him."

"What would you think of taking him out to Coachella?"

"That's an interesting idea. I've been wanting to talk to Father about something, come to think of it. Haven't seen him since we were headed to France."

"Let's do it. I'm sure he'd love to see us."

Feeling flush for the first time in my life, I rented a convertible Model T Ford to load up the family and drive to Coachella to see Father. Even my mother agreed to come along, although Priscilla warned that she might simply melt in the desert heat at this time of year.

"Why that man stays in the winter house all summer is beyond me. I've ordered him to return to Eagle Rock a million times, and told him what a fool he is to stay in the desert," she declared without a hint of irony.

Witty drove May Wu and Gilbert in his Packard. Both cars were loaded with bedding, toys, clothing, musical instruments, and enough food to get the troupe through four or five days. Father's quiet, simple life was about to be turned upside down with the onslaught of visitors.

"Let's keep it low key," Grace suggested. "His malaria's been acting up since you last saw him. You might be a little shocked by his condition, but don't let it show." It pained me to see his health declining.

When we arrived late Saturday morning, Father was dozing in his favorite garden chair. A phonograph played Beethoven's sixth symphony, and *The Age of Innocence* balanced precariously in his lap. Maureen gently woke him and wiggled in for a hug. He marveled at how the children had grown, and then slowly rose to greet his gaggle of guests. Priscilla announced that she would retire to the bedroom for a while, hoping to adjust to the heat by hiding in the darkened room until lunch was ready.

"How are you feeling?" I asked in a moment alone with Father.

"I've been better," he said. "I think this is just a bad patch. Malaria's such a fickle disease. And you, son, you look wonderful."

"Thank you," I said. "We're just so pleased to have this case behind us."

THE GROUP SETTLED INTO A COMFORTABLE, slow rhythm in the desert. May Wu and the children slept on the porch at night, listening to crickets while they drifted off to sleep under brilliant stars. The Coachella nights were so warm that the girls used their blankets for extra padding under them and used only sheets for covers. Witty reacquainted himself with the less-than-optimal sofa. He had taken a strong liking to Father on our first visit, and their conversations about botany, travel, and diverse cultures picked up where they'd left off.

Gilbert might as well have been plopped down on Mars. He'd never seen anything like the desert, having lived his whole life in Paris. He could not believe the open spaces, the dry, hot air, and the enormous mountains that soared up from the valley floor. He spent hours just exploring the garden and walking through date palms. In the late afternoons, he sat at the edge of the porch and played his viola, its sound vanishing quickly into the thin desert air.

Father spoke French well enough to make basic small talk with Gilbert, so he asked him about the Louvre, its history, its current status as a museum, and the works he most enjoyed. Between the language challenges and Gilbert's shy nature, the conversations were limited, but the Frenchman took an instant liking to the old missionary.

On Tuesday morning Grace, Priscilla, and the girls packed a picnic and headed up to Idyllwild, a small community in the pines located a mile high in the San Jacinto Mountains. Grace had driven only a few times, but she'd practiced a bit with Witty over the weekend and built up confidence to navigate the lightly traveled Palms-to-Pines road. Idyllwild's lofty setting would provide relief from the desert heat, and they planned a short hike through enormous pine trees and boulders.

Father felt good enough that morning to cook breakfast for those who stayed behind, so we enjoyed a small feast on the porch around mid-morning.

"You know," he said, "nobody has really filled me in on details of the case. I'm aware of its basic outcome, but does anybody feel like talking about it? I'd like to know more."

"Reid was spectacular," Witty said. "You know that the jury took only six hours to return its verdict."

"And they not only recognized Gilbert and his aunt Marie as the rightful heirs," May Wu added, "but they specifically denied any inheritance to Babette Reville."

"How are you feeling about all of this, Gilbert?" Father asked.

"Overwhelmed. Ashamed."

"Why ashamed?" my dad probed.

"Maybe you don't know the full story," I said when Gilbert struggled for words. I gave Father a quick run-down on the Morel family history, including Paul's tragic death before the intended marriage to Gilbert's mother, Annette. "Annette moved away — or was sent away — to Paris, where she gave birth to Gilbert in 1880."

"Is your mother still living?" Father asked Gilbert.

"No, she died several years ago." Gilbert looked down and rubbed his knuckles.

"Gilbert is very fortunate to have a strong connection with a wonderful lady, Isabelle Brieune, with whom he lives in Paris in a lovely home near the Jardin de Luxembourg," I said.

"She's a bit like an aunt, wouldn't you say, Gilbert?" Witty offered. He nodded without looking up.

"So let me get this straight," Father said. "You feel shame about something over which you had no control. Your father died when he was just a teenager, never having had a chance to marry your mother. And you feel guilty."

"Well, yes. I suppose," Gilbert said. "In France, to be a bastard child is a very negative thing."

"I understand," Father said. "There's some of that stigma here, too. But of course the child has no control of how, when, or where he was born. We don't get to choose, do we, May Wu."

"No, we don't," she said.

"What…" Witty picked up on furtive glances between May Wu and me, just as he had in the diner a week ago.

After a brief silence, May Wu said, "If it helps you in any way, Gilbert, I should let you know that I am the product of a love affair between two unmarried people."

340

"Did you know your father, May Wu?" Witty asked.

"Yes. I still do. He's sitting right here." She reached out and put her hand on Father's arm.

"Good Lord," Witty said. "Oh my goodness. I'm beginning to get the picture."

"Yes, Witty, Reid is my brother." Her quicksilver eyes penetrated his disbelief. "We've always been close, something not lost on you."

"I'm gobsmacked," Witty said.

"I'm so lucky to have him, and this entire family," May Wu said. "You see, when my mother died, David was brave enough to tell Priscilla about his love for my mother." She looked at Father. "And for me. Priscilla could have rejected us both, but she saw it in her heart to take him back and to welcome me into their family. They brought me to Los Angeles, gave me a home, provided an excellent education, and — most important of all — the love of family."

A light breeze moved the palm fronds in the distance.

"You see, Gilbert, family is what you make it," Father said. "It can be messy, difficult, out of control. And it can be supportive, loving, fun, unruly, unplanned — all at the same time. Let me just say, in front of God and all of you, that May Wu's mother was a wonderful, remarkable, kind, thoughtful woman and I loved her deeply."

Witty couldn't wipe the look of amazement off his face.

"Gilbert," Father continued, "if you're lucky enough to have a place you call home — and I don't mean just a physical home, but a home for your soul and your spirit — then you have family. It sounds to me as if Madame Brieune is your family now, and I expect you'll build a new tie with your aunt Marie. But remember, family doesn't always fit neatly into a genealogical chart."

NONE OF US WANTED THE DESERT STAY TO END. It was a relief to have May Wu's secret out in the open. I'd never told anyone but Grace. Of course, she'd always been discreet and had happily treated May Wu as the children's cherished auntie. Priscilla, in her matter-of-fact way, had raised May Wu as her own, although a certain reserve exceeded even her usual level of detachment.

Gilbert seemed to relax a bit, knowing that these people accepted him as he was. He also told me he had a new appreciation for Madame Brieune, who truly was like an aunt. She had supported Annette when her own family sent her away to Paris. She provided a sanctuary for soul and spirit. After Annette's death, Isabelle stepped in as the only family Gilbert knew.

Too soon, the time came to head back to so-called normal life. Gilbert would make his way back to Paris, where his new riches would create a whole new definition of normal. Witty planned to return to Boston to be near his mother. He would always be on the lookout for the next adventure, and he let me know that he'd be honored to work with me again if the opportunity arose. My family would return to the usual routine in Los Angeles, although I was already thinking about a way to take Grace to Paris and Provence to enjoy the fabulous culture, art, food, and architecture that I'd come to love.

"Reid, my good man," Witty said when we found a little time alone during our last evening in the desert. "Reid, I owe you an apology."

"What on earth for?"

"I misjudged you. Didn't understand your relationship to May Wu. I assumed you were in love. The two of you are so close."

"Understandable. I do love her. She's family."

"Now I see that, of course. And it's heart-warming, really. Your parents are to be commended."

"As Father said, we don't get to choose our parents. May Wu and I are both lucky."

"I also apologize for coming down so hard on you about Nicole," Witty said. "It was an ugly, defensive reaction during the whole Babette debacle."

"That one cut close to the bone, I must admit," I said. "And the reason it did, well, it was true. I was falling in love. To this day, she floats upon the river of my thoughts."

"It happens to the best of us."

"Yes, and I apologize for being hard on you regarding Babette. I didn't realize you felt so strongly about her, and of course I didn't like the way she was taking advantage of you."

"You're a wise man." Witty reached his fleshy hand up to my shoulder. "Young, but wise."

"I thank the good Lord that I was wise enough to end things with Nicole before they got out of hand," I said. "Now that I'm home, with my true family, I appreciate them more than ever. I guess this adventure was a lesson in gratitude. Gratitude for family, whatever form it takes."

"Indeed, my friend. As your erudite father said, family doesn't always fit neatly into the genealogical chart."

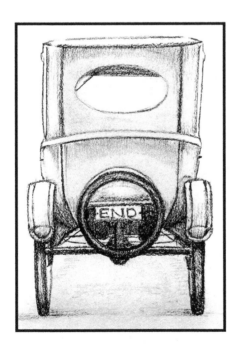

Acknowledgments

My mother, Dorothy Chadwick, and her sister, Anne Leeper, sparked my curiosity early on about the O'Dea case in which their father — a prominent L.A. lawyer — teamed up with a genealogist to track the heirs of a great fortune left by a mysterious millionaire. The case took my grandfather and his sidekick to Ireland and culminated in one of the longest civil trials in U.S. history, rife with fanciful fortune hunters, myriad attorneys, and witnesses of every stripe. Although my grandfather died long before I was born, his story came to life through my mother and aunt's telling, along with their treasure trove of newspaper clippings and law journal articles that became fodder for my highly fictionalized rendition.

My cousins Betty Clifton and Andrea Simpson enriched my understanding of genealogy through their own sleuthing of our family ties, which include the Colberts of France and a missionary doctor in China. I admire their curiosity, knowledge, and enthusiasm. Julie Ward brought a lawyerly perspective to an early draft, as did my brother Glenn Chadwick. Any errors are mine.

I appreciate the encouragement and thoughtful editing by Kim Bateman, Richard Pattie, and Jean Snuggs. Additional literary support came from various coaches at the Whistler Writers Festival and Squaw Valley Community of Writers. I am particularly grateful to writers Olga and Henry Carlisle, who welcomed me to their 400-year-old farmhouse in the heart of the Luberon Valley. The cover illustration is drawn from a photograph I took near their home in 2003.

Deep gratitude to John Muir Laws, whose generosity of knowledge, time, humor, and spirit gave me the courage to pursue my interest in drawing. The Nature Journaling community, especially Yvea Moore and the kindred spirits of "Pencil Miles & Chill," provided a nurturing environment to develop the book's illustrations. Mike Hoover fostered my creativity in all its forms, even a nascent desire to put pencil to sketch pad.

Thanks to Waights Taylor Jr. of McCaa Books for patiently bringing the book to publication, and to Susan Hewlett for urging me to contact him.

With apologies to anyone I've neglected to mention, let me extend gratitude to all friends and family who feed my soul and cultivate my creativity.

About the Author

Anne Chadwick is the author of *Pacific in My Soul*, a book combining her passions for photography, conservation, and creative writing. She is a leader in several organizations devoted to protecting the environment, advancing the arts, and providing outdoor education. Anne has traveled in Africa, Asia, Europe, South America, New Zealand, Australia, Canada, Mexico, and Alaska. Retired from a career in agricultural trade policy and communications, she splits her time between Sebastopol, California, and Vancouver, British Columbia.

www.annechadwick.com

Made in the USA
Las Vegas, NV
13 July 2021